LULU M. SYLVIAN

WOLVES OF WET WATERFALLS

THE COMPLETE TRILOGY

INCLUDES

STEALING JOY

FINDING HOME

ENDING TORMENT

WOLVES OF WET WATERFALLS: THE COMPLETE TRILOGY

WOLVES OF WET WATERFALLS

LULU M. SYLVIAN

GRIFFYN INK

Editing by Full Bloom Editorial

Cover by Laura Medeiros

❀ Created with Vellum

For all the nurses, CMTs , and caregivers who put up with cranky patients.

PART I

STEALING JOY

1

The car wound its way up the side of the mountain. I had no idea where he was taking us. We headed west, and that's all I knew. Everything had changed on me. At this point, I was more concerned with how soon before he would finally kill me over his intended destination.

I pulled the coat around me the best I could. It was awkward trying to put it on backward over the seat belt. But my butt and back were content against the seat. It was my arms, legs, and feet that were cold.

The heater spat out more dust and engine exhaust than it did warmth, and Gordon wouldn't let me have shoes. So, I did my best by tucking my feet under me and using his coat. At least he let me have that.

It was safe to say this was *not* what he promised me.

Flashback not quite a week ago—my mom smirked her knowing little grin as Gordon flashed a charming smile and winked at her. He put my bag in the trunk of his car, and I skipped my way to the passenger seat, waiting for our vacation to begin. My first vacation with a boyfriend, okay more like an extended weekend, but still.

Mom had been dropping hints all week that this was like a faux pre-honeymoon for the two of us. She was dying to ask if I had condoms, and was I ready to be changed for life. I think she thought I was a virgin. Gordon and I had already been doing the horizontal mambo for at least a few months.

Six months? No, I needed to think about this. I had known him for six months, so sex for maybe five months. And he wasn't my first. But the big deal was the out of state vacation, only the two of us. That's not something I had ever done before—at least, not without family.

Her eyes looked misty as she kissed me on the cheek and said, "Have a joyous time, Bailey." I know Mom somehow felt she was losing her little girl.

It turns out she was not wrong.

"I gotta take a dump," the asshole kidnapper named Gordon announced.

He admitted that actually *was* his name. Nothing else about him was honest or true.

"The sign back there said there's a rest stop in ten miles." As soon as the words were out of my mouth, I felt sick. I pulled as close to the passenger side door as I could. I had no idea what would set him off. My commentary was instinctual. Announcing what the road signs say. Remembering signs that indicate restrooms.

He took to hitting me whenever I said anything that contradicted him. Hell, he hit me for speaking, end of story. I had a lovely bruise on the side of my mouth since that was where his reach naturally put his hand every time he lashed out. My lips were tender, and if he kept it up, they would be cracked soon. The black eye was from a completely different hit, at a different time.

"You'd like that, wouldn't you? A rest stop? You think

anyone is going to believe you? You aren't getting away from me."

So far, Gordon had been right. I wasn't getting away. That's why he had my shoes. That's why he was pulling off on the side of the road to relieve himself, not waiting to use a facility with toilets and toilet paper, and running water.

This time, Gordon was wrong.

There was barely any shoulder where he pulled over and even less wooded area away from the road for him to do his business. It was more like a crack in the side of the mountain. I watched him for a little bit, tripping over logs and shit on the ground, as he made a path away from the road.

Whenever I had to pee, I wasn't allowed away from the car. I had to do it right there on the shoulder just outside of the door, which was the only thing blocking me from anyone's view. Basically, I was peeing in full view of everyone and their uncle.

I hadn't had a bowel movement for at least three days now. I didn't feel very good and knew it was a combination of fear and lack of facilities.

Gordon disappeared from my view, so I switched to looking in the review mirror. I wanted to make sure if the car was hit, I at least saw it coming. He picked a stupid ass place to leave the car, on the blind side of a long curve, on the side of a mountain.

If I couldn't see Gordon, could he see me?

I'm pretty sure that was the last cohesive thought I had. My seat belt was off, and I slid across to the other seat, throwing open the driver side door. A semi truck's horn blared as it passed by close enough for the air pressure to rock the car.

I was out the door and running across the freeway. More

horns blared, but I was deaf and blind to any danger. I rolled over the concrete divider, pressing myself back against it as I mentally adjusted for traffic from a different direction.

I didn't even wait to catch my breath before I was running again—across two lanes of freeway and over the metal guard rail, and then down in a sort of running-falling trajectory down the side of the mountain. It was steep but not sheer. The horns continued behind me, but I didn't stop running.

Rocks and branches bit into my feet. I had to have gone at least a mile before I felt anything. There was no way Gordon could have caught up. No way he'd be able to see me. He took care of that. There was nothing bright on my body. I blended.

Spinning his nasty camo coat around so it was on properly, and not backward, I crouched down and scuttled over next to a tree and huffed in the air. Between the camo, the gray sweats, and my now brown hair, I was effectively hidden in the sparse forest on the side of whatever mountain, in whatever state this was.

The only person out there who might even be looking for me *was* Gordon, and he wasn't going to find me. No one else knew I was kidnapped. As far as work, friends, or my parents knew, I was on a fuck-fest vacation, screwing my way from state-to-state as part of our fun mini road trip. If I counted the days right, I wouldn't be missing for another two. That was two days I didn't plan on spending in his company.

I let my breathing ease up, and my heart finally stopped pounding in my ears so I could hear something other than my own noise.

Nothing.

Gordon wasn't a hunter, or any type of outdoorsman,

that I was aware of, so if he were looking for me, I'd hear him.

Damn, it was colder than I realized. I needed to get moving. The sun would set soon. Even though fall had really just started, the days were getting shorter, and I needed to find some form of shelter.

My hands slid in-and-out of all the freaking pockets on this coat as I searched for anything that might be useful—a second pair of socks, a lighter, a cell phone, a pair of hiking boots. It was a big fat *no* to any of those. I did find a half-eaten Kit Kat and a tin of mints.

I should have known Gordon was a psychopath. What kind of freak bites directly into a Kit Kat without snapping the individual pieces off? Well, this kind of freak finishes it. I hadn't eaten much at breakfast and didn't realize how hungry I was until I saw that chocolate covered piece of cookie goodness. I made sure to actually chew, and not swallow it down like the starving woman I was.

I shoved my hands into the pockets and continued down. I had no clue where I was headed other than away from Gordon.

Stumbling through the cold, I let my mind wander back to the beginning of what I thought was going to be a romantic, sexy-time adventure. It started off well enough. Gordon wouldn't tell me where he was taking me, didn't want to ruin the surprise. And of course, I had been too excited to call Mom and tell her all about the sweet little B and B once we arrived.

The car rumbled to a stop in front of a picture-perfect gingerbread laden Victorian. The colors were crazy—wild purples and greens.

"What the hell, Gordon? This place is gorgeous. Like a fairy princess lives here," I gushed.

"That's the plan, sweets."

The trunk closed with a thunk, and he followed me up the front stairs. I held the door as he carried our bags inside.

"Hello?" I called into the empty living room. Even with the sign out front, I felt like we had walked into someone's home and not a business. I turned to Gordon. "Are you sure we're in the right place?"

"Yeah, it's fine. We have reservations." He fished a folded up printout from his back pocket and shoved it at me.

Okay, we *were* in the right place. There was no denying the photo on the printout as the front of this house.

"Sorry, I was in the kitchen and didn't hear the bell." A movie-perfect older lady with snow-white hair piled up on her head, and a dusting of flour across her apron scurried toward us from somewhere in the back of the house. "You must be the Dryers. Gordon, right?"

He gave her that charming smile of his that melted my toes. "That's right, Mrs. Fey. We aren't too early, are we?"

"No, no, not at all. My bell has been on the fritz, and I didn't realize you were already here until I heard voices." She moved to an old fashioned, roll top desk in the corner and fished something out.

I didn't notice it was the key until she held it out to me. "You're in the Cupcake room. Gordon said this place was perfect for you." She eyed my bright magenta and orange hair.

Not everyone appreciated my personal aesthetic, but clearly, this lady did. Heck, her house was purple and green, and the living room looked like a fairy princess' dream, with bright rainbow colors and little fairy creature figurines tucked in almost hidden places. I noticed a fairy door along the floorboards, and a sprite peaking out of the curtain treatments. If the toys could move, I would've sworn I was in a real fairy's house. I wanted to live here when I grew up.

I took the key with a smile and followed her ample backside up the stairs. I was not kidding when I said she was movie-quality perfect, with enough extra padding to know she made cookies and put out milk for stray cats.

"Will you be joining us for dinner? I was getting ready to start preparing the pie crusts, and wanted to make sure I made enough."

I turned to Gordon, a silly grin on my face, nodding furiously. Pie!

"What's on the menu?" Gordon asked.

"Homemade chicken pot pie for the main dish, my special stuffed mashed potatoes with plenty of cheese, sour cream, and bacon; and roasted Brussels sprouts, if you need a vegetable. For dessert, I have banana cream pie and cookies."

I may have made a sound deep in the back of my throat. I was in a fairy house and ready to eat pie! "Yes, we are *definitely* staying for dinner." I didn't give Gordon a chance to say anything.

That was my first mistake of the week. No, I take that back. Leaving with him was the first mistake.

Once inside the room, I spun on my heel like some star of a musical—my arms wide with a smile on my face as I took in all of the magic of this perfect place. "This place is amaze—"

That was the first time he hit me.

I stumbled back and held my hand over my cheek.

"That hurt." I really didn't understand what was happening.

"*Never* make a decision again without consulting me."

I'd never seen that expression on his face before. He looked completely different.

"What? Because I said yes to dinner? Gordon, pie. You know I love me some pie." Damn my face really stung. I stared at him with wide open eyes.

"Hey, hey." He bundled me into his arms and pressed my head into his chest. "I'm sorry. I don't know what got into me."

I snaked my hands around his waist and sank into his warmth. Whatever that was, it was a fluke and over with. We were in fairyland, and dinner wasn't for another couple of hours. "Do we want to go explore her garden or have wild monkey sex?"

Wild monkey sex it was. I vaguely felt guilty about banging the headboard around in the middle of the afternoon, but not too badly. At least the house wasn't full of everyone else who would be banging away all night. Just the main fairy and I'm pretty sure she knew she ran a high-class fuck palace. I mean why else would anyone come out to spend a few nights in a fairy house in the middle of nowhere?

2

———————

I'm not exactly sure how it happened, if it was a mistake or if Gordon engineered it. At the time, I convinced myself it was a complete fluke. I knew better now.

A bottle of liquid cold medicine exploded in my bag. All my clothes were coated in a pink, sticky mess. Neither of us had colds, so I wasn't exactly sure why the bottle was packed. And if my brain hadn't been rattled by his devil penis magic, I would have clued in a bit earlier.

Gordon groused at me, and it seemed so unlike him. I didn't pack cold medicine in my clothes, and wouldn't have. If I'd packed it, it would've been in a zippered plastic baggie, inside my bathroom case. But he spoke with such authority as if he saw me do it. For a hot second, I thought... maybe I had.

Between the sweats Gordon gave me, and Mrs. Fey letting us use her washer and dryer, all was good. I didn't mind. The plan for tonight was more monkey sex anyway, so I didn't need clothes until the next day, and my laundry would be done by then.

I hated having to attend dinner, that Mrs. Fey served

family style with everyone at one big table, wearing boring ass gray sweats. I wanted my fluff and colors. I belonged in this house, and I packed the perfect outfit. Well, it would've been the perfect thing to wear tonight, except it was in the wash, and going to need to hang dry for the rest of the trip.

The top was a unicorn, front and center, on the bodice, and I planned to wear it with a rainbow skirt, layered with tulle. I liked color. I might dress like a three-year-old, but hey, I embraced my inner fairy child and let her shine. Hell, my hair was orange with fuchsia and purple highlights. The orange was natural, the other colors enhanced.

Instead, I was dressed boring and drab, like everyone else. But I wasn't going to let that stop me from enjoying the pie.

"Mrs. Fey, this is divine," I may have mumbled around a mouth full of food, but it was true.

"Thank you, dear." Everyone was 'dear', 'sweetie', or 'kind, sir' when she spoke to them. She didn't have to remember names that way. It made sense to me.

"You made the whole thing from scratch? Even the crust?"

She nodded to all my stupid questions.

"You need to go on one of those baking shows. You would totally win."

Everyone else at the table mumbled some form of agreement. There really wasn't much conversation. It was very much unlike any rom-com movie, when they end up at a quaint B and B. There was no lively banter with the other guests. So disappointing.

The lady across from me stared at my hair and then whispered into her chest at her partner. I was trying to be PC, and not assume he was her husband. And truth, I don't think he was. I think he was her lover, and her husband and that guy's wife were still back at their respective homes.

The other couple was cute and made me feel old. They were on their honeymoon, at the ripe old ages of nineteen and twenty-one. Kari, the girl, was the one to declare herself to be old. After all, she had already been out of high school for *two* years.

I thought she was crazy young. But who am I to judge? At her age, I was still a virgin juggling college classes. Hell, at twenty-four I felt young. Maybe it was all in the mind. Perhaps, if I were dealing with rent, bills, and a husband at nineteen, I would've felt old too.

Gordon behaved as he normally did. So, I knew the smack earlier had been a total mistake. I probably danced into his hand as he was stretching at high speed, toward my face.

After dinner, I held Gordon's hand and we strolled in the garden under the almost full moon. He pulled me against his chest and I giggled.

"Do you love me?" he asked.

My stomach did a flip. I knew it! I knew he loved me. I knew this trip was going to be awesome.

"Yes, I love you." My cheeks felt like they were going to burst off my face I smiled so hard. It's hard to kiss when you're smiling like a rank idiot.

And I was a total rank idiot. It was getting colder. The sun had set, and I continued downhill. The full moon illuminated the forest so I took advantage and kept walking. I needed to find some shelter, a cave, some rocks, maybe a tree with low branches.

Why were there no fucking trees with low branches in the woods? How stupid was that? There was a flash of silver-white fur. I headed toward it, maybe if there was a dog, there would be campers, or a house, or something. My climb evened out and I stepped into a small clearing. The moon reflected off the back of a white dog.

"Hey Doggo, is your master around here?" I called out after the creature, but it took off in the opposite direction.

I guess that meant no.

A few moments later, it came crashing back into the clearing with a stick in its mouth. Oh, it wanted to play. Its tail wagged, and it ran about half the distance to me before turning and trotting away. It did that a few times until I clued in and followed.

It never got close enough, but it was clearly leading me on a chase.

"Doggo, your people are soon right?"

It yipped and wagged at me. So, I kept following.

I kicked something. Pain shot up my leg and exploded in my head. My feet were numb with cold. I never knew numb toes could hurt so badly. I cried out and sat with a heavy thud. I think that's when I started crying. I don't know.

Doggo left me behind. Maybe it wasn't really leading me anywhere. The moon was still up, so I scanned around looking for anything. About thirty yards away was a fallen tree. The log was pretty big, so I figured it would provide a little protection. There were enough leaves and forest floor litter against it; maybe I could get some additional protection from the cold if I buried myself.

I found a sturdy stick and hobbled over to the log. It was cold enough I wasn't worried about bugs. Hell, I was worried about my toes. I'd sleep with a bunch of cockroaches if I thought they would keep me from getting frostbite. And that was a very real worry at the moment.

I began digging dirt and leaves away from the log, giving myself a hole to crawl into. I sat and dug deeper, creating a space for my feet. I poked at my toe, the one I stubbed earlier. I don't understand how it hurt so badly. I couldn't feel it at all now. I wondered how long my socks had been wet. That wasn't good.

The dog came back. Only this time, it approached me all the way. Close enough I could tell he was a *he*, and monstrously large. He whined and head-butted me. I should have clued in that he wasn't someone's dog. He was too freaking big, and no collar. He was friendly, and I was tired, so I didn't think about it.

It was clear he wanted me to keep moving.

I buried my hands into his fur, oh gods he was warm. "I can't, Doggo. I can't. I can't walk any farther; I can't feel my stupid feet."

I wiped my snot against his neck, and he didn't seem to mind. He sat there, big and warm, and panting at me. I guess he figured out I wasn't going anywhere. After a bit, he took off. One second, he's sitting there keeping me warm, the next he was running away through the woods.

"Fine, leave me to die on my own. I was going to die anyway," I yelled after him. "At least this way, it's on my terms." I always heard freezing to death was easy—you're cold, then you fall asleep.

It hadn't started snowing, but it sure as hell felt cold enough for it. My breath made smoke. I wasn't in a good mental place to enjoy that fun little bit of science as my warmer breath caused condensation in the air.

I pulled the stupid camo coat around me. I hated camo, no color. Maybe that was the point. But I loved color. I loved my own color. I yanked a section of hair so I could look at it. *Brown.*

~

We were at least a hundred miles away from the delightful fairy B and B when we remembered all of my clothes were left in the dryer. Neither of us remembered, we were told.

We were singing along to the radio, I mean who doesn't sing along when it's Bohemian Rhapsody, right?

Gordon's phone rang.

"Answer that for me." Not an unreasonable request since he was driving.

"Gordon Dryer's phone."

"Mrs. Dryer, this is Mrs. Fey." She sounded worried.

"Is everything okay? There wasn't a problem with my credit card was there?" I knew there wasn't. I made sure I had a zero balance and a nice fat available credit limit for this trip. And she knew we weren't married, my card didn't say Dryer on it.

"Oh no, dear, it isn't that. You left your clothes."

I groaned. She was right. I had totally forgotten I had tossed my clothes into the dryer after dinner and planned on pulling them out this morning.

"What's up?" Gordon shot me a glance before turning back to keep his eyes on the road.

"We left my clothes."

"Oh shit. If we go back, that throws off our entire schedule. Look." He thought for a moment. "Have her bundle them up, and we'll swing through on our way home next week.

I conveyed the information to Mrs. Fey. She agreed and

hoped our trip continued to be a success, even if I had to buy new outfits along the way.

We were up and out so early, I hadn't even thought about putting anything cute on. I slid back into the comfy sweats Gordon handed me and climbed out of bed and into the car. Gordon had a schedule. We had places to be.

"I'm sorry about your clothes. When we stop for lunch, let's find a place and go shopping. I need to pick up a few things for tonight's surprise."

Each night was a planned surprise. I was happy and excited, even more so when he tossed the makings for s'mores in our shopping cart when we finally stopped at a store.

I was a little confused when he pulled into a campground for our second night. But Gordon made it all better. Apparently, he arranged ahead of time for our cabin to be all set up with a fire pit, ready and waiting. Dozens of roses in vases festooned our cabin.

Okay, Gordon was doing really well on this trip. A fairy-tale B and B, and now a secluded, deluxe cabin full of roses. The bed was covered in petals. It was beautiful and so romantic. My heart hurt thinking about how lucky I was.

I pulled his camo coat around me and tucked in next to him by the fire.

"Gordon, this is all so perfect," I purred.

He stroked my hair. "I never want you to regret coming with me."

"Never." I hugged his arm as he roasted marshmallows.

Those were probably the best s'mores I ever had. They certainly were the last ones.

Gordon kissed me on my temple, handed me the stick with the marshmallow, and stood up. "I'll be a minute."

I sighed and looked into the fire. This trip was magical.

The fairy B and B, Gordon telling me he loved me, and now a campfire under the stars, and when I was ready, a thick comfy mattress and cozy blankets.

I watched the fire move and dance, rotating the marshmallow and watching as flames turned the treat from a toasty brown to blue with its own fire. I blew it out, waited a few seconds, and peeled that sticky burned sugar off with my teeth. S'mores were good—fire burned marshmallows were better.

I wondered what Gordon was up to tonight. I loved each little surprise along the way. To be honest, if we ended up in Vegas in a little wedding chapel, I would say I do.

The cabin door slammed open; the hinge was broken. I turned to see Gordon with a huge grin on his face as he bounced out of the cabin and back to my side.

"Are you almost done out here?" His hands massaged my shoulders.

I was torn, stay and get rubbed, or go inside and get rubbed even more? "I don't want to move, but it's warmer inside isn't it?" I moaned, possibly a little whine in my voice.

He nuzzled my ear and I felt little zaps of excitement down to my toes.

Toes I might not be able to keep if I couldn't get warm. Wet socks, half buried under dirt and leaves, lost in the freaking woods and now snow. The coat had a hood that zipped into the collar. I unrolled it and pulled it up around my face. It was that thin plastic fabric, really meant to keep water off your knit beanie, not meant to provide warmth. But I pulled it up anyway.

I slept in bursts and fits, only to wake up shivering. At

one point, I dreamed I was warm under heavy blankets. But by then, the cold was too deep in my bones and I couldn't stop shaking. I remembered being thirsty, but too exhausted to move. At another point, Doggo was back and curled around me. I wasn't sure how he managed to be at my back and in front of me so I could wrap my arms around him, and be curled up over my feet, but he did.

I watched as Gordon kicked the fire under the ash build up. We didn't want to leave it burning, even if it was in a fire pit. He gently led me up the stairs and into the cabin.

Once we were inside, he took his coat, kissed the side of my neck, and led me back to the bathroom.

It was warm and steamy.

I gasped, "You set up a bath for us?"

"For you. Your very own personal spa and masseur for the night." Gordon bowed with a sexy quirked grin on his face.

I grabbed him and kissed that face. I loved his lips. And tonight he tasted a bit like campfires and fall.

"May I?" He was ever so polite as he began removing my clothes. It was sexy as hell as he tended me for a bath. Once he removed everything, he guided me to the tub and helped me in.

The tub was one of those huge bubble jet things, but apparently, that function had been turned off. Either way, it was big and deep, and Gordon had scattered rose petals in the water.

I closed my eyes and sank down. Gordon got behind me and pulled my hair back into a clip. "What kind of fizzy bath bomb would you like?"

I turned to see what he was showing me and got a snoot full of baking soda and Epsom salts. I couldn't smell a thing. I sneezed like crazy. "I don't know, what smells good?"

Gordon held a small selection up to my nose. I went with the rose one mostly because it matched the theme, and not because I could smell it.

"Okay, now I'm going to give you a shoulder and neck massage, and then a hot oil treatment."

"You're spoiling me." I felt so relaxed. I wasn't going to have any functional limbs for monkey sex by the time he was done with me. All I'd be good for was to lay there and maybe grunt. This felt wonderful. I was going boneless.

"That's the point, sweets. Take care of my girl. My apartment doesn't have the panache to pull something like this off."

"Yeah, this tub is something else." I closed my eyes and let the warmth of his hands lull me into a half sleep. When he began playing with my hair, I may have fallen all the way asleep.

I woke up wrapped in towels, blankets, and Gordon. He curled around me and snored lightly. I don't remember climbing out of the tub, and I didn't think he was brawny enough to have picked me up. It didn't matter. I was in love, and so happy.

The next morning, I felt muzzy headed and things were off kilter. I thought we had paid for the cabin the night before, but Gordon insisted that I needed to go to the checkout and pay. He was going to finish cleaning things up while I took care of the bill. The checkout clerk said it was paid for and looked at me like I had four heads.

I shrugged and chalked it up to Gordon getting me out of the way to be sneaky. I didn't mind, so far a cabin full of roses is what I got when he surprised me. I was good with it.

I had been right; he wanted to make breakfast without me trying to fuss over him.

The man was brilliant; he managed to make buttery grits, bacon, and eggs over an open fire. Everything was wonderful until the hot buttery grits somehow ended up all over me. Some freak of misbalance flipped the pot over like a catapult, and the contents splattered all over my new clothes. Yeah, so it was maybe twenty-five bucks worth of big box clothes, but they were still my new clothes.

"Sweetheart, are you okay?" Gordon was by my side and wiping the hot corn mush from me.

"Yeah, I'm fine," I huffed. "Will you grab me some clothes from the car? I need to go change." This vacation was being extremely hard on my wardrobe.

I made it to the bathroom and looked at myself in the mirror. I screamed. I screamed like the first murder victim in a slasher flick.

Gordon crashed through the bathroom door. "Bailey, what's the matter?"

I had my hands in my hair trying to pull it away from my scalp. "My hair! What's happened to my hair?"

"Did you get grits in your hair? Do you want me to help wash it?"

"No, I don't have grits in my hair. Why haven't you said something about my hair before now?" Why hadn't I noticed it in the mirror? Shower foggy mirror, not wearing makeup today. Somehow, I managed to brush my teeth and get dressed without looking in a mirror. I guess no one could really call me vain.

"Your hair is fine. It looked fine before. Why? What should I have noticed?" He genuinely looked confused.

"I don't know? How about the fact that it's brown?" I shook my hair at him.

"You feeling okay, sweets? Your hair has always been brown. What color should it be?"

"Red. I mean orange. I'm a fucking redhead, a ginger. I don't have brown hair." Was he color blind? Holy crap, all this time I thought he loved my colors, and I was different shades of gray to him.

"What color is my T-shirt?" I held out the fabric to him.

"Bright blue?" His answer was spot on. Right, red-green color blindness was a thing, maybe that's why he thought I had brown hair.

I pointed at a leftover rose petal.

"Red. What's going on, Bailey?"

"My hair was orange, pink, and bright last night, and now it's dull and brown," I sobbed. What had happened that I had brown hair? Could the hot oil treatment have gone wrong? I began digging through the garbage.

Gordon caught my frantic hands and pulled me against his chest. He stroked my brown hair and made shushing noises. "You've never been a redhead, Bailey. Redheads are crazy, you know that's not my type. That must have been some wild dream you had. You know how sometimes dreams can seem so realistic, but they aren't? Like that time you were mad at me for hours before you realized the argument we'd been having was in your dream and wasn't real. It's okay. You were pretty sacked out last night after the tub. You might not be fully awake yet."

At first, I had my eyes closed and I leaned into him. But as he talked, I opened my eyes and stared into the distance. There was proof here somewhere that I was *not* insane. Got it. My nails were still blue. *See, Bailey, you do like color.*

I pushed out of his embrace. "Yeah, that sounds reasonable. Did you bring me in some clothes?"

He handed me a shopping bag with some of the things I

bought the day before. He left me to get changed. I sat on the tub and thought about his lies. I was too a redhead, and hell, even his pick up line, which I confess, worked really well on me, was, *"I've always been fascinated by redheads."*

I looked in the bag. More lies. It was a bag of lies. I dumped the clothes on the floor. Everything was gray or brown. The only color seemed to be the denim and the bright blue I was currently wearing.

These were *not* my clothes. These were *not* the clothes I put into the shopping cart.

I pulled off the food smeared T-shirt and jeans. I was a natural redhead, and that meant the carpet matched the drapes. I confirmed with a quick look in my panties.

"Fuck!" I stood in the middle of the bathroom in my drawers looking down my own panties like I've never seen pubes before.

"You okay in there?"

No, I was *not* okay. "Yeah, I kicked the tub." What the hell was happening to me?

Whatever had been done to the hair on my head was also done to the hair on my hoo-ha.

I cried. I stood there and cried. I was losing my mind.

And then I sat on the potty and cried some more. Eventually, I needed to pee, so I did. And then I noticed something important. The hair dye that had been used on my pubes didn't have very good staying power. The inside front of my panties had brown transferring onto the fabric—not I don't know how to wipe myself brown, but hair dye.

The person who did this to me must not have realized dye didn't always take to my hair. It's one of the reasons my pinks, purples, and fire engine reds were always being redone. My hair hated chemical dyes. And that went for the pubes also.

I took in a big shaky breath. Okay. Gordon was playing whacked out mind games on me. I was in a cabin, in the middle of the woods. So much horror movie fodder right there. I had no way of getting away from him if I made a break for it right now. Or did I?

I splashed cold water on my face and got dressed. I picked up all of my things and carried them out to the car. Gordon was sitting by the fire pit waiting on me.

"Hey, I think I left my credit card at the check-in desk. Why don't I go see if they have it, and you pull the car around?"

"Sure thing, sweets."

He was too agreeable; maybe this wasn't going to work.

The door chimed as I entered the campground offices. "Hello? Hello?" Why the hell was nobody around? I poked behind the desk, thinking I'd make a quick phone call. Of course, there was no phone. I mean, there was a cradle for a cordless phone, but no phone.

I riffled through some papers, careful to not mess anything up. I didn't find a thing.

Two beeps on the car horn and I jumped out of my skin. I put my hand on my chest, willing my heart to slow down. I didn't want to go. I wasn't going to.

I pushed my way into the "employees only" part of the office, and still, there wasn't anyone around. There also wasn't a back door.

I was curled up in a tight ball behind a filing cabinet when he found me. I put up a pretty good fight, but he hit my head pretty hard with something, a glass ashtray, I think. That's when I got the black eye. After that, everything was really hard. I couldn't focus. I had no strength.

≈

I had no fight when I was lifted in a pair of strong arms. My face rested against warm skin. A deep voice rumbled through my pillow. Chest. My face leaned against an extremely strong male chest. Crisp hairs tickled at my nose. I tried to wipe at them but I couldn't move my arms. I tried to blow at them, but I don't think I was particularly effective.

There were other male voices. They said *she, she, she, she.* I heard *fever* and growling. Oh good, Doggo was here and he was trying to protect me.

"Let me carry her, you're going too slow."

"Shut up and get out of my way."

"I get it, Max, we're moving as fast as we can."

"Dude, cut it out. I want to see you hauling an unconscious girl, while naked, through the forest the morning after a full moon. Let's see how well you do. You don't have opposable thumbs right now."

Nothing they said made any sense but their voices all had a nice rumble to them. I dozed, feeling safe for the first time in days. At least my dreams, while I was dying, were nice.

I came to for a bit and had the oddest sensation of being carried thru the forest. It was like I floated, but it was a rough, jerking floating. Sunlight filtered in through the trees. Birds sang. I was lulled by the movement back to sleep.

The next time I came to, I couldn't focus. I could tell I was inside. It looked like a party with a bunch of guys milling about. Maybe Doggo had gotten his people.

I tried to talk but I couldn't make much noise.

An angel appeared in my vision. He was heavenly—cheekbones, blue eyes, and wavy blonde hair. I must have been watching a movie; no one in real life was that pretty.

"Hey there, let's sit you up and get you some water."

A glass was pressed to my mouth and I swallowed the liquid down. I had no focus and could feel my eyes rolling back up into my head. I was back against pillows and my hand reached out for the pleasant weight on my legs. Yes, Doggo found his people, and he was still with me.

I don't remember being moved, but I do remember waking up in a moving car.

I screamed.

3

Absolute panic washed over me when I was finally able to come to properly. Gordon had me buckled in the front seat, and he hummed along with the radio as if nothing had happened.

"Good morning, sweets. You crashed right out once we got moving." He reached over and ruffled my hair.

I grabbed a thick strand and stared at it. It was brown. I dabbed lightly at my eye and flinched. I could only imagine the color it was. It felt swollen.

I looked down—I wore a brown T-shirt and gray sweats. The blue nail polish was gone from my fingernails, and my beautiful stiletto nails had been cut.

"Gordon, what is going on?" I needed a straight answer.

"Nothing, sweetheart. You mean the road? It looks like they have some potholes that didn't get fixed after last winter." He chattered as if nothing was amiss.

"Why aren't we on the freeway?" I had gotten distracted by the pothole talk.

"We always take this highway to cross over from seventy when we head this way."

I nodded my head. "Okay. Which way are we going?"

"North, and then west. Like we always do after visiting the family." He returned to humming.

I didn't say anything for a long time. I watched trees, and rocks, and ranches pass by outside my window. Eventually, we merged with a freeway, our speed increased, and the occasional road sign let me know we were in Wyoming. I know Gordon had been pretty secretive about our little trip, but Wyoming was never mentioned as being a destination.

"Hey, there's a rest stop coming up, can we pull over? I have to pee."

Gordon swerved the car and slammed on the brakes. "You will go pee when I tell you and not before." He reached across the seat and smacked me in the mouth.

The cars behind us blared their horns as they sped past. A knot of terror formed in my gut. Some truck was going to come by and eat us for dinner if he didn't start the car back up. I also really needed to go even more now. Another fright like that and I'd pee all over myself and the car.

"Okay Gordon, can you move the car?"

"I'm going to drive the way I want to drive. Don't tell me what to do." His face was pretty frightening at that moment. I nodded and closed my eyes, and prayed to any nearby gods that might be listening to get me through this moment, and if they could, to provide a toilet soon.

He finally got the car moving again. About twenty minutes later, he took pity on me and pulled over. Without any shoes, I had no idea when he took them, I didn't want to wander too far, so I was content for the moment with being able to squat and pee by the roadside.

∾

Doggo's nose was in my face, and he was licking my tears.

"Are you all right?" the handsome man I was leaning against asked. "Bad dream?"

"Bad memory," I slurred. "Car? Go where?" I couldn't focus, words were so hard.

"We're taking you to the hospital. You were in pretty bad shape when we found you. And then it took a couple of days to get you down the mountain and out to our lodge."

I liked his voice. His words sort of made sense. I understood hospital, and that I was safe. Oh, and there was a group of them. Doggo had done well, he got multiple people.

"Good." The hospital would be good.

It could've been better.

Strong arms carried me into the ER. I didn't open my eyes, and I didn't want to talk. Fortunately, the rumbly bass voices did most of the talking for me. They got me a bed, and Doggo was there.

"Can you tell me your name?"

"Bailey Icecreams," I think I said.

"So, your name is Bailey?"

"Hmm, yes. Bailey. Don't believe Gordon it's not Hanson, and I'm only twenty-four."

"You're twenty-four? And your name is Bailey Hasteen?"

"With an -ing. Hastings." I knew I was whispering, but talking was hard. I don't know if they gave me anything or not, but I felt pretty dopey.

At some point, there was an argument around me regarding Doggo.

"Get that animal out of here!" A low menacing growl answered.

"We can't treat her if he won't let anyone near her. And I'm not taking that dirty mutt back into my clean ER."

"He won't leave her side."

"Get him groomed and he can come back once we have her in a room."

"He's dirty, and she's got an infection."

I finally managed to join the conversation. "Get clean, Doggo, they'll bring you back."

"Come on, Max, you heard the lady."

Doggo licked my fingers before he jumped off the bed.

There was a sharp poke in my arm. I blacked out.

The third night of my romantic epic road trip didn't follow in the footsteps of nights one or two. Night three sucked. We slept in the back of the car in one of those truck pullouts—not a rest stop, just an off-again, on-again pull over for truckers.

Gordon slept wrapped around me. I didn't sleep. Between the abuse and the discomfort, I didn't feel safe. I was tempted, more than once, to get out of the car and wave another down. Problem was, there really weren't any other cars out on this stretch of road in the middle of the night. And there weren't any semis pulled in with us.

In the morning, the car shook with the rumble of a diesel engine. I slid out from under Gordon and high stepped it over broken up asphalt. I managed to knock on the driver's side door of the truck when Gordon caught me.

He swept me up like lovers playing. He laughed—I kicked and was loud.

The trucker ignored us completely.

Gordon tied me up after I tried that a second time.

I tried to sleep, or pretend to, most of the time. But there were times I was wide awake, and couldn't fake it. Those were Gordon's teaching moments. He tried really hard to convince me that my name was Bailey Hanson, and he was my husband Gordon Hanson.

"Who is Gordon Dryer?" I asked.

"I don't know, who?" He threw the question back at me.

"Gordon. You told me your name was Dryer, Gordon Dryer."

"Are you still going on about that weird dream you had. You were a stupid redhead, and my name was Dryer? Bailey, you have a very active imagination. Maybe you need to cut back on your sleeping pills."

"I don't take sleeping pills."

"Sure you do, sweets. Ever since, you know." He hemmed and hawed a bit.

"Ever since what, Gordon?"

"The miscarriage business, Bailey. You've taken sleeping pills ever since then." He glanced over at me with those big brown puppy eyes of his. And that's when I realized he was a fucking good actor. If he had been playing that scene in front of me, and not with me, I would've been convinced he was a man who loved his wife deeply and hurt that she had pain.

Oh, and he told me we were married. Had been for eight years. When I laughed and said that meant we got married when I was sixteen because I was only twenty-four, he smacked me and then continued on as if he hadn't. No, I wasn't twenty-four. We had gotten married when I was twenty-four. I was thirty-two, and when I was twenty-eight we started trying to get pregnant.

The rest of his convoluted, mixed-up fantasy had me unable to carry to term. There were years of treatments and miscarriages, after about thirteen of them I tried to kill myself. That apparently happened last year. I was better now, and we were returning home after a visit to my family.

But he wouldn't tell me where home was. I should know this. Well, asshole had another think coming because I grew up in a theater family, and I knew my fucking Shakespeare.

Sorry not sorry, I was no damned shrew to be tamed. No lord or husband was going to tell me what was what when he was straight up wrong. He couldn't gaslight me into thinking I was wacky. Sure, I would play along, because he hit me and it hurt. So, humoring the guy to avoid another bruise seemed reasonable.

Night number four wasn't nearly as pleasant as night number three. He got a little rapey. And yes, we had mad monkey sex a few days ago. I was all in at that point. I was not all in after that second morning. I wasn't all in at all. It was *not* good, and I did *not* play along for my own safety. The beating he gave me hurt.

That's when I realized he wasn't merely crazy, he was psychotic. This little act of his was only going to get worse. I was going to end up dead. Better dead by my choice than by his. Of course, that's not what I thought when I jumped out of the car and ran across four lanes of freeway traffic.

"Hey Bailey, are you awake yet? Can you open your eyes?"

I opened my eyes and glared at some guy in surgical scrubs.

"Good job, Bailey. Can you tell me what day it is?"

"No. It's hospital day. I don't know what day it is." It really hurt to talk.

"Can you tell me your name and birth date?"

"Bailey Hastings. September, I'm twenty-four." I passed out.

"She should be able to hear you, but she's not going to be very responsive." Someone gently rubbed on my arm. "Hey Bailey, your boyfriend is here."

I was wide awake, eyes open, and pushing up and out of the hospital bed. "Not Gordon, get him away from me. He's not my boyfriend. Keep him away."

I had a scrubs uniformed nurse on one side of me, and one gorgeous underwear model on the other side. Both were trying to keep me from flying off the back of the bed. I pushed with my legs, oh damn that hurt. There was a menacing growl outside of my door.

They couldn't let Gordon near me.

"Who is Gordon?" the model asked.

"I thought her dog's name was Doggo?" asked the nurse.

I settled. I looked frantically between them. "Doggo is here? I can see him?"

There was a woof, and then a missile of white fur came toward me.

He landed on the bed with a heavy thud, on top of my legs, on top of my... "Ow, what the hell did you people do to me? Get off, get off, get off." I shoved hard on the dog until he dropped down to the floor with a whimper.

His nose was back in my hand, and he was whimpering and almost crying along with me.

"You were in bad shape when they brought you in."

"Who brought me in?" I had a hard time remembering anything clearly after Doggo curled up with me in the woods, and I waited to die.

"We did. My pa—pals and I. We found you out in the deep woods. Or I should say Max here found you. He's pretty much claimed you as his own," the gorgeous man in low slung jeans with a fabulous ass said. Hey, I was sick and injured, not blind.

"You had a transmetatarsal amputation of your left outermost toe," the nurse answered.

"You did what? In English." I was confused. I really didn't know why I was here, other than basic exposure issues.

"They had to cut off your left pinky toe." I recognized that voice from my floating dream. Holy Hecate, the man that voice belonged to was stunning. He made the underwear model look like some average Joe.

The nurse fussed around my foot, getting it propped back up on a stack of pillows.

"Who are you?" I asked.

The nurse nodded at him, patted me on the arm, and said, "Buzz if you need anything," and then left me with two hot guys and one freaking huge Doggo.

"You heard that Max? Stay off her left foot. I'm the person to blame for your missing toe. When we found you, we didn't realize you had frostbite. I had the guys bring you into the lodge and try to get some broth into you instead of coming straight here."

"But with the frostbite, your toe was already gone. I don't think getting food into everyone would have changed that, Gage."

The uber hot one named Gage shot a glare at Pretty Boy. Pretty Boy dropped his gaze to the floor. I suddenly recognized him as the one who gave me water.

I patted the right side of the bed. "Hey Doggo, you can come up here." He took up as much, if not more, of the bed than I did. But I felt better with him there. I knew he was the reason I was alive.

Gage picked up one of the room chairs and brought it

next to the bed. Pretty Boy posed artfully on the window sill. "I'm Gage Masterson," he said as he sat. "And to the best of our ability to figure you out, you're Bailey Hastings, you had a birthday in September, and you're twenty-four. And you are terrified of someone named Gordon."

I dug my fingers into Doggo's fur. I couldn't quite figure out how to call him Max. Tears streamed down my face, and I felt the snot start to run too. I didn't care anymore. I nodded. "Can I call my mother?"

"Travis, phone." Gage held his hand out. The other man placed a phone in his palm. He handed me the phone and a tissue.

I stared at it. Mom's number was "call mom." I never had to remember her number before. I stared at the stupid phone and cried some more.

Gage slowly took the phone from me. "Do your parents still have a house phone?"

I nodded.

"Can you tell me?"

"Keith and Donna Hastings. Thirteen-thirteen, Sweet Briar Road."

"I need a phone number, not an address," he said quietly.

I could tell he was a little aggravated, but I had to go through the entire routine from kindergarten if I was going to get it. Name, address, telephone. I ran the rest of the routine silently until I got to the phone number. He dialed as I recited.

He handed me the phone.

"Mommy?" And then I couldn't talk I was sobbing so hard.

Gage took over. He seemed good at that. Doggo nuzzled, he was good at that.

Gage told her everything he knew, which meant he included that I was terrified of someone named Gordon, but not why. He told her what little country hospital I was in, and, "Yes ma'am, the police are on this."

"How are the police on this?" I asked a few minutes after he hung up and I settled down.

"Gage is a local county sheriff," Travis said.

"Are you really?" I sniffed. "That explains why you had authority to lop my toe off?"

Gage smiled. If I still had that toe, it would have melted right off. Damn.

"No, the doctors are the ones who made that call. But yeah, I'm with the local sheriff's department."

"Then I should probably report that Gordon raped me before I got away from him, and I should be examined to make sure all my parts are okay. I seriously doubt anyone took a look at those while they were lopping off my toe."

Gage cussed.

Travis dashed from the room.

Doggo growled.

Travis returned with the nurse. The look on her face was full of concern. "You need a rape kit?"

I nodded my head. "I don't know how long it's been, but I haven't had a shower or anything, and I know it's been a few days. And I don't know if it's gonna do me any good."

Gage rested a hand on my shoulder. "The sooner you report it, and anything that can be done, the better. It will help."

"Do I need any kind of official order, or a police report to go with it?" I asked the nurse.

"Not at all. I'll put in the request. I should have one up here in a matter of minutes. And I can do the examination if you're okay with that. My CRN will be in here with me." She sighed. "He's male, but I need a second. He'll stand by your head and—"

"It'll be fine," I said.

Doggo didn't want to leave. But after Gage growled right back, he hopped down and went with the two men.

I don't know if fine was the right description. Awkward, definitely.

"You know you shouldn't use drug store hair dye on your pubic region," she said mid-exam.

"I do. That was done to me while I was unconscious. Can you include that in your notes?" The relief I felt with that one little bit of acknowledgment sent me back to tears.

Before she left, the nurse injected something into my saline and antibiotic drip. "Rest."

"You can go back in, but let her rest. I gave her something, she should be asleep soon," she said to the two men who had become my self-appointed bodyguards. Doggo sailed from the door to my bed with the grace of a flying squirrel.

We were going to have to have a talk about flying wolves. I thought those only existed in video games.

4

Everyone left me alone to rest, except for Doggo, and my nurse put in a shower request. Not a sponge bath, but a legit shower.

Doggo snuggled against me. I don't know how he could stand it. I reeked. I itched. I was waiting for the doctor's orders to come through so I could take a shower. Honestly, I thought all I needed was an orderly willing to help get me over to the shower. I knew there was one in my bathroom. There was a seat, and we could prop my foot up on the toilet. I didn't want to wash my foot, just the rest of me. The hair dye wasn't helping matters either. My scalp and my privates wanted a serious rinsing.

Nurse Tracey, who conducted my exam, understood my need to rinse the dye off. When I told her it needed to be included on her report, she acted all cool, but her jaw dropped.

Travis came back with another man, equally as pretty.

"Gage is on duty tonight. So, he sent Zeke here with me." Travis slid into my room as the food was being delivered. Unfortunately, I was more excited about the food than I was over a horde of really good looking men visiting.

Travis and Zeke were like opposites twins. Travis was pale. Zeke was dark. Travis was messy and rugged. Zeke had a clean cut and dapper look going on. Both were built, and knew how to wear tight jeans. Zeke wore his with a button down and a bow tie, while Travis had some worn T-shirt with a rock climber on the front.

I made Doggo get down so I could eat. Travis took him outside for dog business.

I raised my eyes eagerly to the orderly pushing my tray over. "What's for dinner?"

The domes were lifted and I was presented with soup, Jell-O, and apple sauce. "You're kidding me right?"

My new nurse came in then. "Is there a problem?"

The orderly shrugged and left me with my liquids.

"I'm not getting any food," I complained.

"Let's see what the doctor ordered. I'll be right back." She left the room for a minute.

"Okay, it looks like no one knows how long it's been since you have had solid food. Including you. So this is a precaution. If you do well, then tomorrow you can have soft solids. Look, honey, you came in here dehydrated and banged up pretty bad. We want to take care of you."

I nodded in acquiescence and she left.

"She's right, we just want to take care of you." Zeke's voice was unexpected.

"How do you know me?"

"I was with the team that found you. Gage and Max want someone guarding you at all times. They want to know who did this to you, and why."

"Who is easy, my ex-boyfriend Gordon. Why? He's a psychopath."

"According to your mother, his name was Gordon Dryer." Gage strode in with Doggo at his hip. Damn that man was fine. Let's put it this way, if I had panties on, they'd be gone.

I honestly don't know why I reacted to him on such a cellular level, but I did. Let's get real. I should be completely repelled by men at the moment. I should be terrified of anyone coming near me. I should be skittish and weary. I was bone tired, well with what bones I had left—currently down three—sick, and injured. I shouldn't be looking at any man and thinking about how soon before I can climb him.

He wore that khaki uniform as if it were a tuxedo. Meaning, holy crap, he was gorgeous. Who knew khaki could look so damned good on a person. Not me.

A woman in a similar uniform followed him in. It didn't do the same for her at all. She carried some note pads. Gage pulled his chair back up and sat down. The woman stood at the end of my bed. Doggo whined and went to sit with my guardians. I still had the food tray across my lap, so there was no room for him.

At some point, I was going to have to ask Gage about him. I wasn't dumb, okay maybe I was cuddling up to a wolf, but at the time when I first did it, I was so far gone I didn't have a frame of reference to realize he was a wolf. Maybe I didn't care? And now? He proved himself to be cuddly and safe.

Gage sat, smiled, and hit me with a little wink. Damn.

"Officer Kelley and I are here on official business. We're here to take your statement and make a report. We'll collect the rape kit into evidence." Hecate help me, his voice.

Focus Bails, focus. "What if I don't want to file a police report?" Why was I sassing off to this man? All I wanted to do was climb up into his lap and have him kiss it better.

"You requested a rape kit in my presence. You are reporting this. I found you." Doggo barked. "Fine. Max found you. You have too many witnesses to the shape you were in not to file a report."

I swear Travis and Zeke were growling right along with Doggo.

Officer Kelley looked bored. How was she not a quivery pile of female goo around these men? I swear I felt like I was being washed in testosterone. Sexy, sexy, testosterone. Maybe that's why I needed a shower so badly.

"Look, Bailey, we want to find the person who hurt you and bring him in."

Doggo growled, again. I swear Travis or Zeke said, "Kill him."

"Pull up a chair, Officer Kelley. It's a long story, and you look like you're gonna be taking notes." I focused on the other woman in the room. I could think if I looked at her. Gage stole my reasoning.

I sipped on my soup as if we were having a pleasant afternoon's conversation, and not me telling them about my kidnapping and subsequent rape and abuse. It was all so very surreal.

Initially, I only went back a week and told them about the trip.

I kept my focus on Officer Kelley, it was easier. She was all business, and she didn't growl when I describe the nastier events. Funny, I felt very detached from past events. More like I had been an observer to the activities, not on the receiving end of certain actions. I told them about everything from Mrs. Fey up until I came to without a toe.

I'd been raped... *twice*. The one that caused the most damage, the one that robbed me of part of my identity, the one I couldn't push away and start forgetting about, was the violation of my hair. Fortunately, I wasn't looking in mirrors these days, and I kept my hair pulled back. My hair was long enough I'd catch glimpses of it, and it was wrong. I'd see a flash of brown too close to my eyes, and then there were Gordon's fists.

"Wait, go back to when you met this guy."

So I did.

～

I met Gordon at Yuki's birthday party, shortly after Easter. There was a small group of us acting like total idiots. I had on blue fuzzy bunny ears and a tiara. And no, I wasn't even dressed up the most. That would have been Yuki. She was in high Lolita mode. The skirts of her pink plaid dress were practically horizontal; the bow on the back, huge to the point of looking like big black butterfly wings.

I love that dress, but I'm too big boned for it to not look exceptionally stupid on. Trust me, I tried one on. I didn't do the Lolita look well. Yuki, on the other hand, owned it. Being half Japanese didn't hurt her there.

The wig she wore that night would've made a drag queen shiver with envy. It was big and pink. And while the rest of us all wore tiaras, I mean who doesn't want to wear a tiara? Yuki had on a Russian beauty queen's crown. I swear that thing was a foot tall. She looked like one of the Munchkins stole Glenda the Good Witch's crown.

We be-bopped our way into a honky-tonk, of all places. You could almost smell the pretend manure on all those new cowboy boots and Stetsons that came out of their hat boxes once a week to be shown off at the bar. The lights weren't as bright as a disco, and the music was loud but not throbbing. An old-time, classic country song was playing when we walked in.

"Yee-haw, if the party didn't walk in the door." He was skinny and already drunk. But we were here to party, so I had no problem letting him drape across my shoulders for a few minutes. "Ladies, you are in the wrong bar," the cowboy of the evening slurred.

Charlene scoffed, "Free beer, dance floor, and sexy men, how is this the wrong place?"

My drunken shoulder wrap transferred himself to her. "Well darlin', maybe I'm mistaken."

She giggled as the two of them went off to drink more beer. The rest of us found a table and ordered an obnoxious quantity of chicken wings. Before the order was even delivered, Yuki had been dragged to the dance floor. Sandy, Jade, and I continued to eat wings and laugh.

Yuki was quite the sight with her flared out dress, pink wig, and crown in the middle of a wall of cowboy plaid and denim. Actually, she looked like a square dancer who got stuck in Wonderland.

Gordon slid into one of our empty chairs, smiled, and began talking as if he knew all of us.

"She's taking over out there, isn't she?" He leaned close to Sandy, but his attention directed us all to look at Yuki.

"She is the star tonight," Jade answered.

"Clearly this is her night. Birthday or bridal party?"

"Birthday."

"Finally twenty-one? I mean I can't believe any of you are old enough to be in here." Gordon was smooth. A woman, no matter how old, loved to hear she looked young.

"Yuki is twenty-five. She's old enough to know what she's doing."

"But young enough not to care," I finished Jade's thought.

Gordon turned his gaze on me at that point. He had dark eyes and sculpted dark scruff. His hair was trimmed neat, with extra length around the front. Slurp. I may have drooled.

"My name's Gordon. What's yours?" I was the first one of us he asked.

I smirked a little flirty half smile. "Bailey."

"Baileys and cream. Come with me." He held out his hand, and I followed his nice ass out onto the dance floor.

Okay, at the time I thought it was the best ass ever. But it really wasn't. It was flat—practically no gluteus muscles what-so-ever.

Maybe it really wasn't when Gordon claimed to be fascinated with redheads that I succumbed to his charms. Maybe it's when he said, "Spank my ass and call me daddy," after I drained a beer in one gulp.

In college, I learned a valuable skill for impressing stupid boys, open your throat and let gravity drain a can of beer. It took a little coordination because you had to spike the can on the bottom to let air in. If you didn't do that, the beer chugged itself out of the can instead of fell. The second half of this skill was not to belch and go puke as soon as humanly possible. I didn't need a can's worth of beer in my gut, speeding up the drunken process.

It impressed and scared. Qualities I found helpful for guiding others to properly form opinions about me.

～

At some point, my tray table was pushed aside, and Doggo was back with me.

"You aren't underage. But..." Officer Kelly stopped to think. "Did you willingly travel across state lines with this man?"

"Yes and no. Look, I willingly left on a road trip with him, but after that second night, I was no longer willingly doing anything. At that point I wanted to go home."

"Do we need to call in the FBI?" Kelley looked at Gage. I mean she looked at him like she just worked with the man and wasn't even vaguely interested in peeling his clothes off.

Yes, even having to review all that I went through, I wanted Gage. Maybe I wanted the security he represented. Maybe I was projecting my fantasies of a rescue hero onto him. Maybe I like the idea of replacing a bad memory with a new memory that was beautiful and wonderful and love, not anger and hate.

I don't know what was wrong with me. I seemed to be getting worse the longer I was around him. He had to have some kind of magic pheromone juju. Typically, a freakishly good looking man would have me unsettled for a few minutes until I gathered my cool about me, or accepted that I was just going to dork my way through our interaction. But Gage had me wanting to start humping things, mostly him.

He needed to go or I was going to seriously embarrass myself. As if he could read my mind, he stood up. I followed his motions and gulped. He approached the bed. Doggo shifted and positioned himself less like a pillow to the side and more like a blanket across me. I couldn't hear him, but I could feel the low growl in his chest. My protector.

Gage looked down at me. I couldn't read his expression, but damn if those green eyes didn't melt me. Doggo kept me in place.

"So, you're coppery orange under that? Huh. I've always

liked redheads." His eyes cut to Doggo who was audibly growling. "Get over it, Max."

I hated him. I hated him for walking in here for the past two days as if I mattered. I hated him for having someone watch out for me when he had to work. I hated him for saying that as if he knew a man who liked red hair was my kryptonite. I hated him for being so damned hot I couldn't think straight.

I grinned like the idiot I was. I ruffled Doggo's ears and whispered, "I think I'm in love."

5

Mom swept in the next morning like a frazzled crazed person. Mostly because she was. Dad strolled in like he was casually meandering through a mall. I swear that man had been stoned for the past twelve years of my life. I'm not complaining, mellow dad was just fine. But he clearly needed to share with mom.

"Bailey, baby." She plastered herself across me for a hug.

Fortunately, I had been given a shower that morning, and Doggo had made space for her.

"What did that man do to you? Why did you dye your hair for him?" The barrage of questions began.

My dad was going around the room introducing himself.

"Guys, this is my dad Keith and my mom Donna."

Today, I had Travis, Zeke, and a new cutie named Mark. Gage had swung through long enough to turn my spine to jelly and say he'd be back later. I missed his presence the way three-year-olds missed dinosaurs, with everything in their little bodies. But unlike a three-year-old, I wasn't going to be satisfied with some plastic toy.

"Who are these men, Bails?" Instead of smiling at the

crew of handsome men I seemed to have gathered, she scowled at me.

"They rescued me."

Doggo yawned at me. By now, I had figured some of his communications out. Not everything was a growl, and he didn't yip unless he was away from me and needed to make a point. The yawn meant he was tired of everyone getting credit before he did.

"Doggo made sure they rescued me. Didn't you?"

He answered me with another yawn and by pushing his nose under my hand. I complied and scratched behind his ears.

"That's a very large therapy dog. I'm not sure I approve of them letting him in your bed while you have an open wound," Mom huffed.

"Hey guys, will one of you get my mom a chair?"

Zeke zipped out of the room.

"The thing with Doggo here is, no one lets him do anything. He just does it. Except they did make him take a bath or they wouldn't let him in here."

"And he sleeps up there with you? Does he follow you to the bathroom too?"

Zeke reappeared with a chair for mom. She glanced at him, barely offering a thank you, and then sat down.

"Look, Doggo found me. He tried to lead me to where his people were. And when I couldn't walk any further, he brought them to me. As far as I'm concerned, he can stay. And since he is very protective, I'm actually not very freaked out that Gordon could show up at any moment."

Doggo let out a low growl at the name.

I smiled, ruffled his neck, and kissed him on the nose. "See, he knows to not like Gordon. And Gordon is stupid enough to think he could take Doggo on."

"Why would that man be afraid of your new dog?" Mom asked.

"Donna, you know that's not a dog right?" my dad asked.

"Get down, show off." I pushed Doggo off the bed.

His head was even with my mom's. Okay, so she was sitting in a chair, but that's still a few feet up. Typical dogs aren't that tall.

"Bailey." She spoke my name quietly.

"Don't intimidate my mom," I told the wolf.

He sat, and gave her a big doggy grin, and slapped his tail against the floor.

"Guys, I think you should take Max out for a walk."

Gage leaned against the doorjamb. Tall and built, but not in uniform, he was a presence to be reckoned with. I wanted out of this hospital so I could do a bit more than reckon with him.

"You heard the man." Travis stretched as he stood up. It was so hard to not stare at his abs as the T-shirt lifted and exposed him.

"After you, Max." Zeke stood with his arm extended, inviting the animal to go with them.

"How come everyone else calls him Max? Hmm?" Mom looked at me over the tops of her glasses. Now that I was back in arm's reach, I guess it was safe to nag at me.

"His name is Max, but Bailey didn't know that when she first found him. I guess Doggo has stuck. And he doesn't seem to mind. Actually, he seems to like it. A special nickname from the beautiful lady." Gage didn't go to my parents to shake hands. He came to my bedside and smoothed my hair back from my face.

I flinched and then every muscle melted and all nerves in my body started to thrum. That wasn't the protective instinct of a sheriff. That was a man making a move. Yeah, baby!

"And who are you?"

He gave my arm a squeeze. The type of action someone does when they aren't into kissing in public, but if they were, it would be a kiss, not an arm squeeze. Demeter and Isis, what was going on? Gage walked around the bed and approached my mother first.

"Sheriff Gage Masterson." He shook mom's hand and then dad's. "My guys were out on a team building expedition when Max alerted us to someone needing help in the area."

"So, you follow some big dog around? What is he, Lassie?" Mom was sharp as cut glass today.

"Ma'am, Max is a wolf. He was raised to be a tracking animal, so when he alerts me to a possible situation, I pay attention. Canines are remarkable creatures. Don't underestimate Lassie."

"So why did it take so long for anyone to call me?"

"No one knew who I was. Apparently, I was out of it. I don't know if it was cause I got sick, or if Gordon drugged me."

"Don't say that man's name," she snapped. "I don't want to talk about him."

"Mrs. Hastings, don't give him that power over your lives. Say his name and curse him. But don't allow him to set up fear in your hearts."

Damn, Gage was good.

"So the rest of those young men who were in here, they're sheriffs too?"

"Oh, no. They're part of a search and rescue team. We provide services when there is a big man-hunt for missing hikers. We like to get out for a casual hike without any expectations occasionally. If all we ever do is go out for search and rescue, the joy of camping gets lost. It becomes a chore."

"We're really glad you were out there," my dad said.

"When do you get to come home?" Mom asked.

I shrugged. I hadn't even asked that yet. "Not a clue. I got upgraded to soft solids today."

"For an amputation like hers, probably a week. But she had an infection when we brought her in, so maybe longer. You folks have a place to stay? We have plenty of room up at the lodge. You won't have to worry about a hotel that way."

Mom started to say something but Dad jumped in. "That's very kind. Are you sure we won't be putting you out?"

"Not at all. It's an old hunting lodge. Right now, between seasons, only five of us are living there. We have more rooms than you can shake a stick at."

"That's very kind, but we don't want to be a bother. And I like to have my own space." Mom turned Gage down.

Okay, not that I want my mother to be making googly eyes at the guy I really wanted to bone, but I know she appreciates the finer examples of human males. They didn't come much finer than Gage, and she hadn't even blinked at him. Not once. Typically, she would be a little extra giggly, or her eyelashes would start wagging around a good looking guy. But with Gage, nothing.

Maybe I was delusional and he wasn't good looking at all, and I was suffering from hero worship or something. What was the Stockholm Syndrome equivalent of falling in love with your rescuer?

"I understand." Gage's voice rumbled through me. "We do have some suites, so it wouldn't be like a guest bedroom in someone's house. You can have your own TV, mini fridge, and bathroom. If you plan on staying more than a few nights, hotel rates can get expensive fast. But if you insist—"

Dad gave Mom a look. I guess he wasn't too mellowed out today. "We appreciate your offer. I think we'll be here until we can take Bailey back with us. So yes, we would be delighted to stay at your lodge."

The guys came back and Gage directed Travis to take Max back out for a bit, and for Zeke and Mark to show my parents how to get to the lodge. And to get them settled into one of the premium suites. Dang, it sounded like Gage also ran some kind of resort.

Doggo was not happy about being told to go back out with Travis. He looked at me and then at Gage. It's like he knew something was up. With a sneeze, a huff, and snarl, he left. That wolf was expressive for a beastie who couldn't talk.

As soon as my door was closed, Gage was by my side. His expression earnest. His eyes searched my face. It was all very intense and I was about to close my eyes and lick my lips in a "take me I'm yours" move.

"We may have narrowed down your Gordon. When I come back later, I should have photos for you to identify. If he is one of these men, Bailey. Shit, woman." He ran his hand through his hair and began pacing. "There is no easy way to say this—"

"He was going to kill me. I already know that. I also already know what little fairy tale he was weaving for himself. I was to be his meek distraught wife. Depressed to the point of suicide because I couldn't bear his children. He laid it all out in a very obvious fashion. But I don't know why he thought it would work?"

"Because it's worked for him in the past. The FBI is coming in. They should be here in a few hours and that makes things tricky." He sat on the edge of my bed and picked up my hand.

I let my fingers twist into his. "How tricky?" Mighty Bast he touched me. I'm pregnant. I have to be. "Why the FBI?" I was so proud how cool I played that one off. Gage was impregnating me by magic touch alone and I pretended that I gave a rat's ass that I'd been lured in by a serial killer.

"Fucking-A, a serial killer." I dropped his hand.

"Yeah. Fucking-A is right."

6

I didn't know what was going on between Gage and me, but it seemed pretty damned clear that all of a sudden there was a "we." I mean the guys always deferred to him anyway, but now they did it in a way that felt weird. Before I could ask for one of them to get me some junk food, and as soon as I was on solid food, I could count on Travis to smuggle in some chicken nuggets. Now, he would hem and haw and say he'd have to run it by Gage.

Look, dude, Gage wasn't my boss, and other than some serious toe tingling hand holding, nothing had transpired between us.

If my mom wasn't around, the doctor would ask Gage about my treatment.

Hello, I'm right here, stuck in bed with no undies and a back opening hospital gown as my only clothing. Doggo at least listened to me. And I swear it felt like he really was. I could read his noises and yawns better each day. It was almost as if he could talk straight into my head.

Mom brought me some color stripping shampoo, and I was allowed to attack my hair with my next shower. The pubes responded, and the dye was washing out faster on my hoo-ha than on my head. But then again, that also has something to do with the nature of body hair versus head hair. I'm not sure why, but courser hair likes dye even less than my red hair does.

I wasn't going to be a redhead again anytime soon. I needed serious time in a stylist's chair. Maybe if the brown stuck around, I could parlay it into one of those ombre fade hair color treatments.

He took my dignity, my identity, my fucking toe. I was going to need some serious time in a therapist's chair too.

I scratched Doggo's ears. "If you find that bastard, kill him for me okay?" I whispered to my fluffy savior.

He licked my face. *He's a dead man walking.* I heard in my head.

I liked the words I put into this wolf's mouth.

We would all kill him for you, but Gage and I will do this.

I cut my eyes to glare over at Zeke who sat quietly, reading by the window. It didn't sound like him.

"You say something?" I asked.

He looked up, his dark eyes full of concern. "Did you need something, Bailey?"

"Nope, thought I heard someone. Must have been out in the hall."

You heard me. There is no one in the hall. You'll be able to hear me better and better as our bond continues to develop and become strong.

I looked at Doggo. "Stop freaking me out."

He whined and put his head down.

I was getting bored, which was a good sign. I was healing. My toe itched like a son-of-a-bitch, also a good sign. I was ready to leave this place. My doctor wasn't. He wanted me to stay in the area. Mom had announced the second I was sprung she was packing me in the car and taking me back to St. Louis.

Gage also wanted to keep me in the area for their investigation. Apparently, he and the doc pulled some strings to keep me. So, instead of expecting to be hospitalized for the rest of the week, it was more like another ten days.

My toe throbbed. I hit the call buzzer for Tracey.

"I need ibuprofen," I answered when she asked what I needed. "And a trashy romance." I doubt she heard me regarding the book.

She came in, scruffed Doggo behind the ears, and handed me my pills. "Are you sure I can't get you something else?"

I shrugged. In the past three days, we had tried Percocet, the codeine sort of helped but it didn't last long enough. Instead of playing pain killer roulette, I knew that a big Motrin would take the sharp edges off, and that was the best I was going to get. When it really hurt, I held on to Doggo tightly and watched the one action movie they had available on the hospital's television. The middle of the night was the hardest.

There were times I'd hurt so bad I couldn't move, just hold on. And somehow my guards knew I needed an extra boost. I never noticed them slipping into bed with me, but I would wake up surrounded by a hot guy holding tight on one side and me holding tight to Doggo on the other. Their comfort was better than any drug.

As much as their comfort helped, I couldn't help but notice Gage was never one of the men in my bed.

Speaking of, he strolled through my door as if it were his house.

"Thought you might be bored." He handed me a bag.

"Oh, pressies," I declared as I began pulling a selection of smutty and Amish romance books out of the bag.

I held up one particularly titillating Amish title, *A Suitor of Hope.* "You're kidding me right?"

"Zeke texted me, said you wanted trashy romances. I don't read that shit. Give me Jack Reacher or Clive Cussler any day."

At least he read. "I should make you read one, so we can talk about it," I teased.

He smoldered at me. My limbs went weak.

"I'll read one of yours if you read one of mine."

That's it, I was done. My throat went dry, my mouth filled with drool. Other places in my body got damp.

I tried to pull myself back together. I wanted to run away from his flirting, but the best I could do was a painfully slow hobble. And that was with help. "Okay, but I don't think it's going to be one of these. Bring on your spy thrillers. I'll find a good tawdry romance for you. I think it will need to involve kilts and time travel."

"That doesn't sound like romance. Time travel?" He laughed and pulled up a chair.

His hand found mine, and my heart rate skipped as our fingers twisted together.

You're mine first.

I blinked and looked around. Now I know that wasn't Zeke, and Gage hadn't said anything.

I looked at Doggo. It felt like his eyes bore into me. I shivered.

He can have you, but you are mine first.

I stared at the wolf. I started to pull back, he was creeping me out. The voice in my head was the same one I used when I pretended Doggo was talking, but there was no way I would make up something like that. No way. My brain didn't think I needed to belong to some animal. It wanted Gage.

"Max, stop scaring her. Get out of her head."

I flinched and pulled back from Gage.

"Hey, Zeke, why don't you take a break. I'll sit this shift." Gage turned to face the other man.

"Sure thing, boss." Zeke packed up his few things, phone and book. He smiled at me on his way out the door. "Let me know if any of us needs to pick anything up."

Gage nodded. He watched the other man leave before he stood up, crossed the room, and closed my door.

"You read romances with time travel, so maybe you can deal with a little real-world science fiction." Gage started. "Max there is a bit more than some highly trained, intelligent wolf. And me and the guys are a bit more than really protective and possessive."

He stopped and looked at Doggo. It was very much as if they were communicating but not using words. Every now and then, one of them would glance over at me. It was weird, surreal. I didn't have the right kind of pain meds for this shit.

"You won't believe me if I tell you everything because I have no way to prove anything today. Can you accept there are monsters and magic, and things science cannot explain in this world?"

I nodded. Of course, I could believe that. There were too many strange and unexplained happenings.

"Max has decided to speak to you, so you can understand him. He can get into my head as well. It's possible that someday, you and I will be able to share thoughts without words."

I laughed, "A lot of couples can do that after being together. They get on the same wavelength."

As soon as the words were out of my mouth, I blushed. Gage, me, a couple. Oh, gods.

"Exactly." He smiled and picked up my hand again.

Holy Hecate. Oh, God. Yes, please. I needed to calm down.

"But this is a little different than an old couple who have been together forever. This is more I'll be able to send you pictures and concepts."

"So you're telling me Doggo, Max, can talk to you? And that the crazy murder voices in my head are really him?"

Gage leaned over and rubbed his chin on my fingers. Damn if I wasn't pregnant again. He sighed. "I'm sure some of those murder voices are your own. If he's telling you we will hunt down this Gordon and slaughter him, that might actually be him."

He looked into my eyes. His gaze shifted and he picked up a strand of my hair and rubbed it between his fingers. "I might do it just for what he did to your hair. I've always been partial to redheads."

I was a quivering collection of human-shaped cells waiting to dissolve into a puddle of ooze.

That's when he kissed me.

His breath was warm and his lips were soft. I closed my eyes and let Gage fill all of my senses. He skimmed his hand behind my head and grabbed a fist of my hair, holding me to him. I started to reach for his neck and Doggo growled low in his chest. I smacked his nose. No dog was going to tell me to stop kissing this hunk of a man. I refused to listen to any of the words Max was trying to put into my head.

All I could think was lips, warm, kiss, yes. Colors and lights danced behind my eyelids. Gage's low moan was all I heard.

He licked his lips and sighed when he pulled back. "I've wanted to do that for days."

"What took you so long?" I wanted to cry with the sheer amazement of his mouth on mine.

"You haven't been well, Bailey. I wasn't going to take advantage of you. And I certainly wasn't going to push something you might not want."

"Why wouldn't I want you to kiss me?"

When he answered, I felt stupid. "Honey, you're the victim of abuse and rape. I wasn't about to come near you until I thought for certain…"

Yeah, that made sense.

"You kiss really, really well. I know exactly why I'd like you to kiss me some more. But other than the promise that under this brown hair dye there is a redhead, why did you want to kiss me?"

Gage stepped back. He took a few pacing steps and ran his hand over the back of his neck. "That might be best left to monsters, and magic, and mental wavelengths?"

I laughed. I liked that one better than love at first sight. But I wasn't much to fall in love with based on the condition I was in. When I ran out of the car, the side of my mouth was purple and green and my lips were swollen. I had a vivid green, yellow, and black bruise around my eye. I was cold and sick, and my hair was a greasy mess, having not been washed since Gordon dyed it several days earlier. I wasn't pretty and feisty. There was no sparkling personality to dazzle him.

"Unless you have a thing for bruised up, half dead, sick women you find in the woods, I might have to get you to expand on that. But for now, okay, I'll accept that as a reason." I sighed.

"Okay, then chalk this up to monsters and magic. You're

about to get your period, I'll send one of the guys out to get you—"

"Nope." I cut him off. "I would die of embarrassment."

"Fine, then I'll do it. What do you want? Tampons or pads?"

I covered my face. Help me Hecate, hot guy and grown-up talk. "Tampons, regular."

I lowered my hands. "Hey, how the hell can you tell?"

"Your scent is changing. More metallic, copper and iron. Blood."

"My scent? You can smell me? Right, monsters and magic, and just go with it. What? Do I have to wait until a full moon?"

Gage stopped moving and stared at me. He didn't move. He might not have been breathing.

I started shaking my head. Oh, hell no. "That's not real. No. No way. No."

"Can we leave it for now?"

"I'm on drugs, and no. No." I held up a single finger. Wait, just wait a minute while I wrap my brain around that. "No."

I held my hands up.

"I'm gonna leave. I'll be back later."

I pointed at the door. "Yeah, you go."

The door clicked behind him, and for the first time since I came to after surgery, I was alone. There was no one to guard me. Panic burned the back of my throat with bile. What if Gordon found me?

Doggo nosed under my arm, so it dropped onto his back. *You are safe with me.*

7

Tracey came in with a clatter, and her hands full of something she was unwrapping.

"Are you ready to start walking?" she asked.

"Walking? I don't have a toe."

"All the more reason to get you up and about, you need to find your balance. And we don't want you developing clots." She looked around my empty room. "Where are all your keepers?"

I shrugged.

"I was counting on one of them helping you."

"I've got Doggo." I pointed out.

She shook her head. "Not until you're a little more stable. I need someone who can catch you." She said putting the package she had, what I could now see as some type of boots, on the working counter with all the medical stuff. "Have one of those fine young men come and get me when they get back, and we'll get you all set."

She left.

I picked up one of the books Gage brought. "Hmm, Amish romance." Why not, love is love right?

I settled in and started reading.

I made it a good three or four chapters into Ruth's angst over Jerimiah, who spent part of his Rumspringa living with the English. Now he exhibited the occasional hint of not holding with tradition. Dude was an Amish bad-boy. I guess the bad-boy appeal was universal. I kept reading even though I knew she was going to tame his wild ways.

There was a knock on my door and the two FBI agents I met earlier came in. Last time they had arrived with Gage, and a stack of photos for me to look at and identify.

If I had my phone, it would be easier. I had pictures of Gordon.

Today, neither of them carried that tell-tale folder of photos or note pads.

I didn't like that they were here and I had no one as back up. I guess I'd gotten used to constantly having someone around.

"Special Agents Smith. Or is that Smiths, since there are two of you? You know, one of you really should consider changing your name to something more remarkable. Someone might mistake you for CIA or something."

Smith-one laughed, Smith-two glowered at me.

"What do you know about the CIA?" he asked.

"Seriously? I read. I watch movies. They always use some name like Smith or Jones, and everyone knows it's a fake name, but they do it anyway."

"Trust me, our higher ups got a good giggle and did this to us on purpose." Smith-one was younger, slighter build. He wasn't unattractive in his hyper clean-cut ways, but after being surrounded by model quality beauty and the raw sexual appeal of Gage, this guy was blander than bland.

Smith-two had zero sense of humor. I guessed him to be middle-aged, divorced, and bled dry of any joy.

"We wanted to get some clarification on parts of your story." Smith-two pulled over a chair.

I shrugged. "Sure."

Wait. Don't talk to them before Gage gets back.

I stared at Doggo. I don't know if this mind talk went both ways but I projected back at him— *Gage left, walked out, isn't coming back any time soon.*

All I got was, *Wait for Gage.*

Fine. Maybe this whole monsters and magic thing was real, and Doggo had some insight and communications with Gage. Whatever. I could stall these guys for twenty minutes. If Gage didn't make an appearance, I'd get chatty.

"Don't get too comfortable. I was about to call the nurse for a bathroom break."

"We can wait," Smith-one said.

I buzzed in my request, and Tracey said she would be with me in a minute.

I didn't exactly know how to tell them to leave. I didn't want them around when I got out of bed, flashing my goodies, hobbling across the room, and then peeing with the door wide open. I had no humility when it came to using the toilet this week. I wasn't afraid to ask for and accept the help I required.

Most of the time, one of the guys would scoop me up and carry me the ten feet across my room. That could get a little humiliating, especially if I really had to pee. But the bottoms of my feet had been shredded on my trek down the side of a mountain.

Tracey swept in and began unhooking me from assorted monitors. "Fellas, I think now would be a good time to wait in the hallway."

Thank you, Tracey!

"Bedpan?"

I shook my head. I really hated that thing.

Getting out of bed wasn't pretty. I thought I was doing well with general complaints instead of actual cussing. I must have upset Doggo because he'd growl every time I said ouch. Which was every time I put a foot down.

"Seriously, Doggo, this hurts, and you aren't helping."

"We'll get those walking boots on you later, and that will make all of this easier." Tracey stepped out of the small bathroom to let me do my business.

I wiped. Well, fuck a duck.

"Hey, Gage isn't out there yet is he?"

"He hasn't come back in. You want me to check?" she asked.

"Would you, please?" Damn that man and his monsters and magic nose. I certainly hoped he was coming back and with supplies.

I only had to hang out in the bathroom for something like five minutes before Gage showed up and rescued me again.

Tracey handed me a small paper bag. "When I told Gage you were asking about him, he said you were waiting for this. He then crossed his arms and set in to wait with the FBI guys."

I tried not to be too enthusiastic, but yay for feminine hygiene products.

I wasn't as circumspect upon leaving the bathroom, and this time I cussed. Gage was in the room in a hot second and sweeping me into his arms. I didn't want to complain. I mean hot guy lifting me with ease, all kinds of wowza.

"Really Gage? I won't take sass from Doggo, same goes for you. I say ow and you rush in to save the day?"

The glare he gave me was the best one yet. It was some

sexy combination of a smolder and glare mixed with concern.

"Thanks for rescuing me," I whispered before he eased his arms out from under me. He straightened my hospital gown as Tracey got me plugged back in.

I adjusted my foot, and its pillows, as Gage opened the door for the Smiths to come back in.

I had no extra details. I had left nothing out. Okay, maybe I didn't elaborate on 'we made love' at the fairy house. They didn't need to know those details. Doggo and Gage stiffened when I went back over that first night.

Could Gordon have dyed his hair? Of course, but if he did, he had it professionally done. It never smelled like dye, and he never left any residue on pillows or towels.

"But you also said you didn't smell any chemical dyes on your own hair, could maybe he have used the same product?"

I nodded. "Yes, that's a possibility. But his scruff was dark, so were the other hairs on his body, so I didn't think anything was off with him having dark hair."

"What do you mean 'hairs on his body?'" Smith-two asked.

"Really? What do I mean by body hair? Specifics? Okay, pit hair, chest hair, pubes, the little hairs on his ass. Hair on his body. Maybe he bleached his hair for the other incidences."

I wished I had my phone. I had pictures of him on my phone. He didn't like me sharing pictures of him online, so anytime I wanted to, he always covered his face with hands or behind his jacket. So while I had pictures proving I had a boyfriend, no one would be able to identify him from any of them. Unless...

"Hey, do you have a laptop I can borrow? I want to get online. I had a thought."

Yuki documented her life incessantly. There was a good chance I might be able to find something from her birthday.

Smith-one went back out to their car to get a laptop. I logged on and began searching. Damn, Yuki takes a lot of pictures, and scanning back over six months looking for a chance glimpse of someone was taking time.

My first choice of social media outlet provided nothing. I did find his eyebrow in a picture, but a shoulder blocked the rest of his face. Nothing.

I sighed, dejected. I know I didn't have pictures because when I tried to take a selfie with him, he told me no. It had to do with his job, and he found it easier to have a limited online presence. Color me surprised, someone who didn't spend half of their social life online.

Okay, until all of this happened, I wouldn't have thought it possible. I was attached by the retinas to my screens. Now, not so much. I had my mom post that everything was fine and due to technological reasons, I was phone free for a bit.

The FBI wouldn't let me get a new phone. They were trying to use their not so secret spying tricks to track my phone, hoping it was still in Gordon's car. Even I thought that it was a pretty good shot that Gordon switched cars by now. It was possible he was that dumb. But he had masterfully manipulated me and my affections.

I closed the lid to the computer. "Nope, sorry. I thought maybe my friends might have gotten a pic of him at Yuki's birthday party. The best I got was his out of focus eyebrow."

"It's okay. Thank you for trying." Gage caressed my hand as he picked up the computer.

I didn't know how I felt anymore. He claimed to be

something not normal. He definitely had a connection to a full moon. And there was a large wolf in my bed, putting words in my head.

I directed my focus to FBI-dee and FBI-dum. "I'm sorry. I didn't recognize him. But let's get real; I probably wouldn't recognize myself right now. I'm covered in bruises from everything—from the beatings, to running down the side of a mountain, to the heparin shots they are giving me. I'm not the same color I'm used to being. Would I even know myself? So I don't know if I would recognize my ex in different clothes, with a different hairstyle."

"What do you mean you don't think you would recognize yourself?" Smith-two asked.

"Have you seen what I normally look like?"

They looked at each other, and then to Gage. He gave them a shrug. "Apparently, we do not."

"What, you didn't look me up online? I thought that's what you did. You know profile the victims in order to track patterns and shit like that."

Gage snickered. The FBI guys looked sort of blank.

"Am I the only one who reads books and watches movies or TV? Come on."

"I thought you read romance."

I pointed at Mr. Sassy-pants Masterson. "Romance novels include a lot of cool stuff like suspense, and intrigue and mystery, and—"

"Schmaltzy love stories," Gage interjected.

"I thought they were all, you know Mommy-Porn," Smith-one did the air quote thing around Mommy-Porn.

"Damn skippy, there is some grade-A melt your toenails sex in some of those books. You might want to pick one up and get a few pointers." I sneered back at Smith-one and Gage.

Smith-two had opened some image files on the laptop. He twisted it to face me. There was a patchwork of photos too small for me to see clearly from the bed. "Look, Miss Hastings, all of the victims matched the same profile. All about the same height, weight, and coloring."

"How many of them had dyed hair?"

He flipped the computer back around and tapped on the keyboard. "Looks like two of these first three dyed their hair."

"And I match the description, but that's not me. Go to my friend Yuki's social media photogram."

Smith-two grunted as he typed in the location I gave him.

"Now search on my name, Bailey, or Bails."

He flipped the laptop around and there I was. Bright as daylight. My hair was down and I had a purple undercut of color. I had obviously curled it that morning since it lay in half exhausted coils. I wore a kitty-ear headband. The image was a selfie with Yuki, so only the neck of my shirt was visible.

Gage chuckled and kept smirking at me. I don't think he had bothered to look me up either.

"Look, I'm a fucking majestic unicorn of color. I embrace the shit out of it too. The only black I wear is jeans. I like things cutsie and sparkly. The only dull grey sweats I own are the ones Gordon bought after he sabotaged my clothes. And trust me, I didn't pick them out. I picked out the pink ones."

"Fellows, this isn't your case is it?" Gage asked.

"No, we aren't working the case, we are here to gather as much information from Miss Hastings and pass it along."

Smith-two gave Smith-one a death glare. He shot one right back and continued. "We don't have any back information on these victims beyond a basic description. I'm sure there is another connection, but we don't have it. We were in the area and sent to collect enough to determine if the agents who are working this case need to be sent."

I raised my eyebrows at him. "Well, they need to be sent."

"I agree." Smith-one stood and stepped up to the bed. Doggo growled.

"He's a good guy. Hush."

Smith-one nodded to the wolf. "You keep this one around. He'll keep you safe." He extended his hand for a shake. I took it. "Miss Hastings, I'm sure you'll get a visit from another set of FBI agents in the next day or two. I'm definitely letting them know this is a related case." He turned to Gage and shook his hand.

Smith-two packed up the laptop and nodded at us.

Their exit didn't go smoothly as they sort of crashed as my mother came in. "How are you today, baby?"

Smith-one nodded and said, "Mrs. Hastings, Mr. Hastings." Smith-two wormed his way out the door.

"Bailey has already told you everything, you gentlemen need to leave her alone," Mom chastised the man.

"Unfortunately, I can't say that's going to happen. More agents are going to be in within the next day or so. There will be more questions. Are you staying in the area?" he asked her.

"Why would they need to question me again? I told you everything I knew about that man. I thought he was one of the good ones. If I hadn't, do you think I would've sent my baby off with him? I waved goodbye to my little girl, and instead of coming home a woman, I had to drive over two states to come rescue her from God-knows-what atrocities."

I blushed and tried really hard not to laugh. It was the perfect combination of embarrassing as fuck and hysterical. So, Mom did think I was a virgin. Yeah, I wasn't planning on telling her otherwise.

"No, Mr. Smith, I don't think I will make myself available for your colleagues," she continued.

"I'll be sure to make a note of that, Mrs. Hastings." He stepped past her and out the door.

"Bailey, sweetie, I brought you some makeup. I thought it might make you feel better."

I liked makeup. So I sat up a little and squirmed with excitement. Okay, Mom and I had to have a little discussion on what makeup meant. It meant fun and colors; it didn't mean foundation and contouring nudes. I let out a bit of a dejected sigh.

"I thought you might want to cover up those bruises so no one can see them. And then give your face a little shape." She loved me and was well meaning. "You don't want to have to face those FBI agents all exposed? Or what about all those young men that seem to be in and out of here?"

"Thanks, Mom, but I think its best that the hospital staff sees how the bruising is healing day-to-day. And the police and FBI need to be completely aware of my damage. I'll hold on to this for when I get released."

"Did they say anything about letting you go yet?"

"Bailey isn't getting out for a while. Ten days at the earliest. The doctor wants her here for continued treatment," Gage answered.

"She can get care at home," Mom huffed.

"Mother." She was on a tear; I doubt I could derail her.

"I'm sure she can, but this hospital is one of the best for treating this kind of injury."

"Ha! This little county hospital in the wilds of Wyoming?" Mom laughed, it wasn't a happy laugh.

Doggo growled, I felt it more than heard anything. I doubt anyone else heard it.

Tension rolled off Gage. Somehow, he seemed taller as he took on an authoritative role. Maybe Mom wouldn't have laughed at him if he had been in uniform.

"This little hospital treats more frostbite on stupid city hikers, or skiers who go off course for a little adventure in a month than your fancy state-of-the-art city hospital back home does in a year. They don't specialize in it because they want to, but because they need to. Let them do their job and get your daughter healthy."

"I just..." she started.

"I understand. You want her home, you want her safe. Why do you think me and my guys are here? Is your hospital back home going to let Max stay with her?"

"This isn't home, how can she be comfortable and rest?"

"Mom, it's a hospital. I'm more comfortable here than I will be on a long car ride. You're staying at Gage's lodge, right? Is it not working out?"

"The suite we have is fine," she said with a bit of a huff.

Dad stepped in, to clarify the 'fine.' "Mr. Masterson has provided us with a very nice suite. It's large, it is comfortable. But it's not home, so your mom worries. We're going to have to go back for work before you're released it looks like. She doesn't want you to be kicked out of the hospital and stranded."

"That would never happen. Bailey has a place to stay at the lodge if it comes to that. Or if she needs to stay in the area for a follow up with the surgeons here. If you do need to go home for a few days for responsibilities, next time you come back, you're more than welcome at the lodge."

Mom patted under her eyes—she never wiped away tears. I think she shocked Gage when she pulled him in for a mom squeezing hug.

He patted her on the back. "We all want what's best for Bailey. She's special."

8

I really couldn't tell how many days I'd been in the hospital. Nurse Tracey was replaced by someone else for the day and someone different at night. I felt like I used to be able to remember things better, like names. I feel sort of bad not remembering their names.

I blamed my lack of ability to remember things on the antibiotics. And to be honest, there were times I felt fuzzy, that Gage said could be from the anesthesia.

So day X in the hospital, okay under a full week, but more than four days, I managed to finish that Amish romance, and the movie selection the hospital offered changed.

Two people I expected the least to see here peeked in and crept through my door.

"Jade! Yuki!"

Yuki did her adorable little step-walk to me and gave me the biggest hug, and then without hesitation grabbed Doggo by the fur at his neck, sort of ruffled-slash-shook him, and got her face right up next to his and talked baby talk.

Doggo clearly had no problems with this and his tail beat my healthy ankle.

"We came as soon as your mom mentioned you were here," Jade said.

"Did you call her?"

Yuki popped up from canoodling with the wolf. "She put it on her social media wall."

I sighed. I wasn't exactly thrilled that she'd done that. "Please tell me she didn't post a picture."

"Oh no, she only checked in here. Yuki and I knew she wouldn't be someplace like here if you weren't in trouble. So here we are," Jade explained.

I still hadn't gotten a chance to hug her because Yuki was half laying over me adoring on Doggo. I got that she never met a dog she didn't like, but what was I, chopped liver? Must be, completely ignored.

Jade and I exchanged looks.

"I guess she has a new devotee," Jade said and flopped in the chair Gage had vacated a few moments earlier.

He was my "guard" for this shift. At least that's how I thought of it. In a few hours, Travis, Zeke, or Mark, or some combination of the three, would come strolling in, and it'd be their turn to guard me. He had abandoned post because I was thirsty, and instead of letting me ring for the nurse or a CRN, he volunteered to get me a soda.

I went to shrug, but Doggo decided he needed his belly rubbed, and rotated, shoving me out of his way as he moved and squirmed.

"Dude, what the freak? This is my bed, not yours."

He looked up at me with his upside down doggy smile, tongue rolling out of his mouth as Yuki scratched his belly.

She continued to coo at him. "Who is such a big fluffy puppers? Who is? You is."

"So, I take it the wolf is friendly and not going to eat her?" Jade asked. She was a sharp one, and always keeping an eye out for Yuki and me.

I understood why she felt the need to watch out for Yuki. I did too. She was always so happy, and a little too pure sometimes. Like she never saw the bad in the world. Jade, more than any of our group, made sure she never did. With me, Jade was the first one to check in. Jade was the one to show up. She paid attention.

I was tired of being squished between Doggo and Yuki, so I pushed on him. "Go make out with your new girlfriend somewhere else. Get off my bed."

Doggo hopped off the bed, waited impatiently as Yuki pulled over a chair, and slid his face onto her lap the second she sat down. It took some awkward positioning on his behalf to sit that way because Yuki was so petite and he was a big wolf.

"Traitor," I commented.

"What did I do?" Gage asked. He walked in the door with a pop and hiss as he opened a soda for me.

I turned at the sound of his voice.

He stopped in the doorway, eyes narrowed at Jade. Taking in the new person, his entire demeanor shifted when he looked at Yuki and Doggo. His shoulders relaxed, his eyes widened, and a soft smile crossed his face. I lost him to her too.

Don't get me wrong, but I was tired of losing to Yuki. I could never be mad at her. It wasn't something she did on purpose. Does light know why it attracts bugs? No, it shines and that's what happens. Same with Yuki, she just was, and people were drawn to her.

Maybe that's why Jade felt the need to be her defactoguard. Who knows. All I knew, was my stomach bottomed out for a split second, and I honestly wanted to cry.

"Max finally gave up his spot for me," Gage announced as he sat on the bed with me. He sat sideways so his left knee rested on the bed. His leg brushed against mine, and I squelched my pity party. I hadn't lost Gage.

He leaned forward and handed me the drink. "You okay?"

"I'm fine, but as you can see, Doggo has abandoned me for my friend Yuki."

"I see that. He hasn't been out of this bed willingly for days." Gage nodded at Yuki.

She gave him a dazzling smile in between her 'conversation' with Doggo.

"And this is Jade. She said they knew I was in trouble when mom kept checking in at the hospital online. So they came." I loved that they knew me enough to come. I loved that neither of them mentioned my bruises or my hair. Then again, so far the conversation from Yuki was a constant "Who's a good boy? You're a good boy."

"Yuki, Max hasn't been out for a bit. Would you be interested in taking him outside for a little walk?"

Yuki perked up and rejoined the humans in the room. "Sure thing, where's his leash."

"He doesn't need one. He won't leave your side," Gage explained.

Yuki stood, and Jade made a strangled noise in the back of her throat. She didn't even hesitate with the whole Doggo/Max name thing. Puppers needed walkies. She was on it.

"She will never be safer than when she is with him or his," Gage said coolly to Jade.

She nodded.

They were silent until Yuki was out of the room, and down the hall.

"Why are you here, witch?" Gage grumbled at Jade.

"Gage!" Holy Hecate how rude.

"Wolf?" She cocked her head to the side and stared at him.

I gave myself whiplash turning from him to her. I was about to point out that the wolf left the room with Yuki. But something stopped me.

I mean, I didn't want to admit it. I had already taken the small bit of information from Gage and shoved it down the crack in the pillows of the couch in the living room of my brain palace. But there it was, out in the open, and somehow Jade knew.

Jade knew something I didn't want to admit.

"What? No. How?" I looked from Jade to Gage. "More monsters and magic?"

"Gage? Jade, what's happening?"

Gage stood up and walked around the bed to face Jade.

She sat cool and poised.

"The other one? She is Light and Happiness?" He pointed back at me. "What is she? Who is she?"

Jade smiled at me. "You okay there, Bailey?"

"I'm a little confused," I admitted.

"How much has this one told you?" she asked, completely ignoring Gage.

"Just a bit. Monsters and magic exist. And I think he wants me to believe he is one of the monsters." I laughed. Gage wasn't a monster. "If monsters and magic do exist, then so do heroes. He is definitely one of the heroes."

"Don't say that, Bailey," he growled, more of a grumble.

"I'm one of the monsters. You don't have a reason to believe me yet."

I wanted to tell him I loved him, so there was no way he could be a monster. No way.

"Yuki is—"

Jade was cut off as two men in black suits, followed by a nurse, Travis, Zeke, and Officer Kelley rushed into my room.

"What's going on?" Gage switched from quiet threat mode to full on Officer Masterson. Everything from his posture to the tone of his voice changed.

Suit number one stopped and looked at me. "You Bailey Hastings?" He flipped open his ID. Suit-two did the same. "We're agents Smith and Jones."

The nurse was fussing with my IV. Travis and Zeke looked tense. Something very serious was going on but, I lost it.

Laughing I said, "Really? The FBI has to either come up with some better fake names or you should change your real ones. The last guys they sent were Smith and Smith."

Suit-one looked at me and then at Gage. His eyes were wild and he clearly thought I was out of my mind.

"Sorry, but come on. It's funny."

Jade was the only one to acknowledge me. "Smith and Smith? Really? That's so fake."

"I know, right?"

"Miss, we need to move you now," Jones spoke with authority.

"Sheriff Gage Masterson, What's going on here?" Gage introduced himself and stepped into an in-charge attitude.

"We came directly here instead of trying to call," Officer Kelley began.

"Agents Smith escalated your case once it was established that this was indeed related to a case Smith and I are lead investigators on. We have been tracking your phone to no avail, but last night we caught a ping on your credit card. We were able to follow the original trip as you described to Smith, and we were headed out to Boise following the spending activity on that card. Apparently, no one thought to have called into your bank?"

"I guess I had other things going on." I don't think that ever crossed my mind.

"It may have saved your life."

At that moment, a wheelchair arrived and the nurse pushed Jones out of her way. "If you're taking her, do you have a set up for her to travel with the IVs?"

"No. she'll need to be fully disconnected. We can make arrangements when we get to the new location," Suit-one answered.

"Where are you taking her?" Gage asked.

"For now, a hotel. That credit card, it's back in this county. Miss Bailey needs to be somewhere safe while we lay in wait. As far as the hospital is concerned, she is still a patient, and still in this room." Jones leveled a glare at the nurse. "Understood?"

"Of course."

"Not a hotel," Gage barked. "She'll be safest at the lodge. Travis get my SUV, pull it around to the back ambulance entrance. We don't want to go out the front door in case he's sitting in the parking lot. Zeke, Max is outside with a woman named Yuki. Get them into your car and head up to the lodge. We'll meet you there."

Both men left in a rush.

I was lifted out of my bed and placed in the wheelchair. It was cold on my butt, but honestly, I didn't care. Shit seemed to have gotten really real, really fast.

"I should be with Yuki," Jade announced.

Gage shook his head. "She's as safe as she can be with Max. Zeke will get them to the lodge, and we'll figure all the details out from there."

"This lodge of yours, more of you?" she asked.

Gage gave Jade a half smirk. "A whole pack of us."

I heard that and knew what he meant. I wanted to suck in my breath in shock, but instead, I hissed in with pain. Lifting the footrest was apparently not an easy process, and it whacked into my injured foot. I wanted to cry. I probably did.

Someone tucked a blanket over my lap and off we went with a *woosh*. The interior of the hospital passed me in a blur. I was a little more confused than I should've been. I was leaving the hospital because my credit card was being used.

Did that mean they thought Gordon was in the area? It had to.

Big glass doors swept open—a large, gray, dirt splattered SUV waited, engine running.

Gage swept me up into his arms, blankets and all. Which was a good thing because the chill hit me, and I wasn't wearing much.

"Take shotgun," he directed Jade.

And with his arms full of me, he climbed into the back seat.

Travis had the car moving before the back door was even closed.

Gage smoothed my brow and held me tight. "Shh, it's okay. I've got you. There is no way I will let that man come near enough to hurt you ever again."

Apparently, I had begun shaking. I don't know if it was from the cold or from fear.

I tried to climb inside of his jacket, and nestle against his chest. I found comfort surrounded by his warmth and strength.

"Where are your parents?" Gage asked. I guess he figured my sudden disappearance from the hospital might cause them some concern.

"Hmm?" He was nice to snuggle into. "Mom said she was going to go shopping and then take a nap."

Gage shifted rather awkwardly and pulled a phone out from somewhere.

"Are the Hastings there?" He waited in silence for a moment. "Good, keep them there. We're headed back. Get a room set up for Bailey. She'll need enough room for medical equipment if we need to bring it in." Another pause in his conversation. "Yes, a bathroom."

He ended that call, looked at his phone, and was talking into it again. "Can you get Tracey out to the lodge? She'll know what's needed." He grunted and hung up.

Travis let out a long sigh. "That was exciting. So, what the hell is going on?"

"Not fully apprised of the situation. Kelley and the FBI will have to fill us in. What do you have to do with this witch?" Gage grumbled at Jade.

Travis swerved the car. Everything rocked side to side as he corrected back onto the road. He glared at Jade before turning his eyes back to the road.

"Stop calling my friend 'witch,'" I said.

Jade turned in her seat to look back at us. She glared at Gage and then gave me a smirk. "It's okay, Bails, I am a witch. A guardian to be exact."

"Some guardian you are. You let Bailey out of your sight and into a lot of danger. She could have been killed."

"Yeah, about that," Jade hemmed and hawed a little. "I'm not Bailey's guardian. I'm Yuki's. Bailey isn't fully infused, but since she and Yuki are frequently together, I keep an eye on her."

"How did you know where she was if you aren't her guardian?"

"The internet, wolfman. Probably the same way—you said Gordon was behind all this? I didn't think he was manipulative enough—the same way Gordon knows and that's why he's headed back this way. Her mom likes to "check-in" and basically tells everyone where she is all the time. She's gotten better about checking in at people's homes, but if she is staying at this lodge of yours, she may have already told Gordon where we're all headed." Jade swallowed. "Accidentally."

Delight is safe.

I felt Doggo's words with a stab of pain. I flinched. It was gone in a second.

"Bailey?" Gage ran his warm hand up and down my arm. "You, okay?"

I pressed my fingers to my temples. "Yeah, Doggo got in my head and it hurt. It never hurt before."

"Did you say that other wolf can talk straight into your head?" Jade asked.

"Doggo is the only wolf around here,"—Travis snorted, but I continued—"Yeah, he can put words in my head."

Jade's glare became more intense as it looked like she tried to bore a hole through Gage.

"Why glare at me? He's the one who claimed her." Gage sounded almost like a whiney teenager.

"I would have thought you were the one to have claimed her." Jade nodded at how Gage was holding me.

"He claimed her first. But I can't seem to accept that. I'm human and he isn't challenging my actions."

"Hey, wait a sec. No one gets to claim me," I complained.

"Max did. He staked his claim first. That's why he can talk directly to you. He beat me to it."

"Oh, hell no, you guys don't get to call dibs on me. What the hell? Why didn't you claim me first then? Huh?"

"He did it as soon as he found you in the woods," Gage explained.

I was mad. "So he just goes around and says 'this is mine' to everything he sees, just in case?"

Gage made a little side tilt head motion with a shrug. "Pretty much. I wanted to claim you the first time you smiled at me. You were pretty delirious, so I thought I'd wait. Make sure I wasn't making a rash decision. By then, it was already too late. I couldn't stop myself."

"Let me guess," Jade said with a sigh. "You claimed her anyway."

I rolled my eyes. I couldn't believe this conversation. I barely noticed as the road got rough and the SUV jostled me about.

"I'm not a fan of this whole being claimed thing. What am I, lost luggage? That stupid wolf didn't try to pee on me to mark his territory did he?"

"You are precious to us, Bailey. I couldn't figure it out before, but now I know that's because you're more than just a survivor. You are something that plays into my world." Oh, the sound of that man's voice when he spoke to me in lowered hushed tones. Okay, he could claim me, but only if I could claim him right back. Hell, in a few days, I'd be good to claim him all night long.

"Are you saying I'm monsters?"

"No, darling. You are magic."

The SUV continued to drive over excessively rough terrain. I didn't have a good view out of the window, wrapped up in Gage the way I was, but it looked as if there wasn't a road.

"Um, Travis? Where did the road go?" I asked.

"Taking a short cut," he answered.

"What? Through the backyard?" I muttered.

"Basically," Gage said with a laugh. "We'll get you to the lodge, and make sure everything is secure. I'm going to need to see your mom's online use, make sure she hasn't tagged the lodge as one of her check-in points."

The SUV finally leveled out as Travis guided the vehicle back onto the pavement. He stopped and Gage was hauling me out of the back.

"Whoa," Jade said with amazement as she stared up at our new location.

"Oh good, you guys made it." Yuki ran out of a large door and onto the front decking, surrounded by wolves.

I looked past Yuki and up at the building. Whoa was right. Of course, right then I wasn't sure if Jade was whoa-ing the wolves or the lodge.

"This is home? It's a freaking resort."

"It's an old hunting and ski lodge. And it's home," Gage said, not even winded as he carried me up the front steps.

"It's not ADA compliant so it's no longer a commercially viable property unless we make the upgrades," Travis started explaining. "We still run some rescue training and executive team building excursions."

"You said you were a trail guide, is this what you meant?" I asked

Travis held the big front door open. I probably should've been impressed with the craftsmanship of it, rough-hewn and hand polished. The lodge was a log cabin work of art. But I was distracted, a cold breeze licked up my exposed backside.

I must have squirmed because Gage complained. "Do you want me to drop your ass? Hold still."

"My ass is exposed to the elements. I just got an overly friendly breeze up my butt. I didn't want to flash everyone."

Gage nodded at someone past my head. I heard a ruffle of fabric and then I was being lowered onto a warm blanket on a large leather couch. Gage didn't even kiss my forehead or anything; he put me down and began making some kinds of plans with Zeke, Travis, and Mark.

Yuki, surrounded by her own private pack of wolves and Jade, sat in some chairs opposite of me.

"Can we stay here, Jade? This is so much nicer than that hotel we saw as we drove in," Yuki asked. She finally stopped talking baby talk to the wolves.

"I don't think it's up to us. I mean, he did say it's a private lodge. That means exclusive. Expensive," Jade said.

I adjusted the blanket around my lower body and pulled another one around me. Hospital gowns weren't very thick, and I was cold now that I didn't have Gage's body heat keeping me warm.

"Gage is letting my parents stay here. I'm sure he'll let you two as well."

"Bailey!" my mom called out as she appeared at the top of a broad set of stairs. In any other location, those would be the elaborate formal stairs that a hundred brides would pay the big bucks to descend. But this wasn't a wedding destination and those stairs were heavy and solid. A masculine presence in this very robust wood lined lobby. It was a lobby, but it also was comfortable like a homey living room. Maybe that's what Gage meant when he said it was home. It felt like one.

Mom rushed down the stairs and came straight to me. She wrapped me in a mom quality comforting hug. "Why didn't you say they were going to release you? I would've brought you something to wear, so you didn't need to leave in a hospital gown."

She lay a hand on my arm and I winced as she touched my IV port. I still had tubes and everything taped to my arm.

"Why do you still have all of this? What's going on?" she asked a lot of questions.

"I wasn't exactly released. There's been a situation."

9

Mom stood up and faced Gage as he approached us. Mom wasn't a tiny woman. She's five foot seven, packing some middle-aged weight, and can be a domineering mama bear when it needs to happen. She rounded on him like a luchador heading in for the final round. Gage made her look tiny. I mean, I thought he had a presence in my hospital room, but that's one not so big room. Here, he still dominated the space, and this time, the space was cavernous. Mom still didn't back down, no matter how big Gage was in comparison.

"Sheriff Masterson, I think you need to tell me exactly what is going on here. Why has my daughter been taken from the hospital? Why wouldn't that young man, Mark, let us leave?" Without letting him answer, she turned and finally noticed my friends. "Girls, what are you doing here?" She pulled Yuki out of her chair for a hug. Everyone hugged Yuki.

Gage cleared his throat. "The FBI will explain matters when they get here."

"The FBI? Those men asked very personal questions,

and I don't think they really knew what they were doing," Mom complained.

"Different FBI, Mom. The Smiths were the scouts checking out my story. They sent in the guys who are in charge of the case." Holy flaming crap. I clued in that there was a case against Gordon.

"Mom, you didn't check-in when you got here did you?" I asked.

"What do you mean check-in? No, they gave us a room. There was no check-in. Are they going to charge us now after insisting we stay here?"

"Not that kind of check-in, Mrs. Hastings. But internet check-in, you know like how you did at the hospital?" Jade asked.

"Now that you mentioned it, I don't think I did." Mom reached to pull her phone out of her pocket.

I think everyone in the room reached out for her and shouted "No!" at the same time.

She fumbled and dropped her phone. "What the hell was that all about?"

Gage scooped Mom's phone up and handed it back to her. "Please don't. We don't want anyone knowing you're here. More importantly, we don't want Gordon to find out Bailey might be here."

"How would he know that?"

"It's how we knew Bailey was in trouble. You checked in at the Wet Waterfalls Hospital and Bailey hadn't come back or called. So we came out to see her," Yuki explained.

"And if they figured it out, there is a good chance Gordon, who lost Bailey a day's hike from here, might also figure it out," Gage said.

Mom stood there looking grim. She wasn't shocked

holding her mouth in a big O or covering her mouth with her fingertips in shock. She nodded.

"I should have thought. But at that point, I really hadn't made those connections. Oh shit, Bailey. I'm so sorry. I'd never put you in danger on purpose."

She sat at the end of the couch, careful not to touch my feet. She reached for them, and then pulled her hand away, knowing that touch would hurt.

The door swung open and we all directed our attention to the newcomers. Nurse Tracey with a cart and a big bag of supplies clattered through followed by Officer Kelley.

The darker of the wolves around Yuki got up and pressed against Tracey, blocking her movement. She hip bumped the wolf. "Hi babe, get out of my way, I have a job to do. Bailey, you're getting more and more exciting as a patient," Tracey laughed.

"I'm sorry," I said. I really didn't want to cause trouble, but it certainly was following me around this week.

"Don't be. None of this is your doing. We need to adjust a little in our care routine. Zeke, why don't you show me where I need to set up?" She headed toward the stairs. Zeke jumped ahead of her and they went upstairs.

Officer Kelley stopped in front of Gage. "The FBI wanted to do a little recon on the hospital first. See if maybe this guy might have been staking out the parking lot or something. I gave them your number. They'll call when they're ready." She continued up the stairs after Tracey.

I yawned. All of this excitement was the most activity I had since before the surgery. The adrenaline eased off and I became acutely aware of all the pain in my body, from my missing toe to the IV in my arm.

I wanted to talk to Yuki and Jade, but I also wanted to

sleep. I must have whimpered or something because Gage was by my side in an instant.

"I need some pain meds, and I'm cold. Can I get more blankets?"

He did better than that, he wrapped me in his arms again and lifted me. If I hadn't mentioned it before, I love that he can carry me. I'm a little bit on the tall side at five-foot-eight. I come with some curves, and I'm densely packed with muscles. I'm about average on a size scale, but I weigh more than I look because of the weight training I do. I know, right, me a weight lifter. Don't judge, it's fun.

Gage carried me up those stairs as if I were a small child.

I imagined the blankets trailing behind us were a long wedding dress train, and that this was a romantic carrying off of the bride, instead of what it really was, carrying the invalid with her ass hanging out upstairs into a make-shift hospital room.

However, the room he carried me into wasn't being set up with IVs. The large bed in the middle was unmade. The top of the dresser was messy with personal stuff—a watch, something that looked like a gun holster without a gun, change scattered everywhere.

Gage lowered me into the bed and grabbed a few pillows to tuck under my left leg. He disappeared into another room and returned with a few pills and a glass of water. He sat on the side of the bed as I tossed the pills down and gulped the water.

"Rest here while they are getting your room set up. It's too busy downstairs. You need to sleep."

He got up to leave.

"Gage."

He turned those emerald green eyes on me and I melted.

"This claiming thing, do I get a say in it? Cause I'd like to call dibs on you."

I was in a different room with different smells, in a different bed, when I woke up. Travis was snuggled against my side. He now occupied the side where Doggo had been during my hospital stay. He was pretty to look at and comfy to cuddle with, but I had made a declaration for Gage.

I didn't think it was very copacetic to be snuggled up to a different hot guy.

I tried to move my arm and felt the familiar restraining tug of a hooked up IV. I heard and then felt the familiar hum and soft squeeze of the leg compressors. Since I couldn't get up and move around much, I had to have them in the hospital along with heparin shots to help make sure I didn't develop clots.

I may not have been in the hospital, but I was restricted to bed as if I were, with all the bells and whistles and gadgets.

"You woke up." Travis had a great groggy morning voice.

I needed to focus and not swoon. Long messy blonde hair, square chin, infectious grin, oh yeah, he was one hell of a cutie.

"Hey dude, you're cozy and all, but why are you in my bed?"

He reached up and brushed back a strand of hair. "You were having some pain issues and were clearly uncomfortable. Since Max wasn't around, as usual, I crawled in with you. It helped last week, so I figured it would help again."

"Ah..." I started.

"You sleep better when someone is in bed with you."

I closed my mouth. He was right. And it hadn't been the first time I woke up with him, without Doggo around, it seemed scarily intimate in a way it hadn't before.

"What if Gage finds you in here?"

He shrugged. "We are pack. You are ours."

"Excuse you? I'm not yours."

"He means, we are pack. We are yours." Gage stood in the door. He had a soft smile on his face. I expected him to get mad, or at least mildly put out that Travis was in bed with me.

I have to admit, I was a little disappointed that Gage wasn't getting territorial.

He gave his head a sharp nod to the side, and Travis was up and out of bed. So much for the feeling of intimacy, I didn't even get a hug upon his departure. Okay, so there were no sparks between us, but he was still hot.

Gage, on the other hand, walked into the room and sparks were flying off him like ferrous metals on a grinding wheel. He wore his uniform. Sigh.

"You do sleep better when someone is curled up with you. You do best with Max, Travis, or myself."

"I haven't slept with you." I would know if I had slept with him.

"You were hurting pretty bad on those nights. I doubt you remember much of it right around your surgery. But yes, I have been in bed with you. There is more room in this one, it will make nights much more comfortable. Especially since Max isn't crowding you out."

"So, where is that traitor?"

"Your friend Yuki has bespelled the wolves. Even Brooks isn't paying as much attention to Tracey as usual."

"I have lots and lots and lots of questions, and you are looking all sexy and official." I tried to sit up; it wasn't as easy in a regular bed. I already missed the ability to push a button and change my position.

Gage was by my side and helping me up. Pillows magically appeared behind me. Turned out there was a stash of them on the floor for that purpose.

He rumbled against my neck. "You really shouldn't call me sexy. That makes things difficult to focus, and yes"—he cleared his throat and stood up—"official. FBI is downstairs waiting for you to wake up. Your friends are eager to spend some time with you. At least the witch is. Yuki seems content to be surrounded by our furries."

I snorted. It wasn't a ladylike noise.

Gage laughed at me and winked.

"Did you really call those wolves furries?" I shook my head.

"It's a bit more than a lifestyle around here. But keep that on the down-low when you're talking to Jones and Smith."

Gage moved as if he were going to leave me. I didn't want him to go. I said so.

"You chased my cuddle buddy off; can I get a few minutes alone with you?" I asked.

"What was this?"

Okay, so we had just spent some time alone together, but that's not what I meant and he knew it. I didn't consider myself to be bold, but maybe I was because I had no qualms telling Gage I wanted to curl up against him for a few minutes before I had to face the FBI.

"Not a good idea, Bailey."

"Why? Because you're on duty?"

"Because I won't want to get out of that bed. Because Max claimed you first and it's a new moon in a few days. I'll send Travis back so you don't have to be alone."

He left. My room was silent except for the whir of the leg compressors inflating.

He came back in with a smile and a wink, and two men dressed in black suits and skinny black ties. Did they actually try to perpetuate the stereotype, or were they really that boring?

10

Curled up next to me with his back against my hip, Travis's presence was a comfort I hadn't realized I needed until he was back in the bed. Gage sat at the end of the bed but on the opposite side. He rested a hand on my knee.

Travis, I could reach, so I pet his back. He really had replaced Doggo for me right now. Gage, I couldn't reach or touch. At least he touched me.

The FBI sat in chairs Travis had brought in for them.

"Miss Hastings, we know you already told our colleagues everything," the one I think was Jones began. "But we need to hear your story again, in your own words. Can you do that for us?"

I sighed.

"Before I do, can you maybe tell me a little bit more about what happened this afternoon? I was distracted by my friends when you came barreling in."

Smith shifted in his seat and nodded. "You didn't cancel your credit card."

"The one I thought I lost?"

"We don't know about that, but the one you paid for a night at The Sugar Plum Bed and Breakfast, and then you made a sizable purchase at a Target in Nebraska," Jones pointed out details I already knew.

"Was that Nebraska? I thought we were still in Missouri." I shrugged. "And I paid for the cabin too."

The two FBI agents nodded.

"We have been working on getting a trace on your phone, and watching your credit card. It was last used in Nebraska, which fits your story. And then a few days ago, activity was recorded in the Boise area. We tracked it and the suspect was staying in the area, but slowly moving west. At some point in the past forty-eight hours, he backed tracked and we received notification that he was back on the western edge of this county. Used the card at a truck stop," Jones continued telling me what they knew.

Smith cut in. "We think he was buying gas. Thing is, we don't know if that is a coincidence or not. We camped out at the hospital with the help of the sheriff's office and kept an eye out on anyone who met your description, or the description of who we think we're looking for."

"So far, nothing. And no one came to the hospital to visit you after your two young lady friends." Jones looked at me with a steady even gaze.

Okay, they didn't know anything for sure. That meant I didn't need to panic. Gage was sitting on my bed, there were three fucking wolves in this house and one of them could talk into my head, and he had already threatened to kill Gordon. I had nothing to worry about.

I swallowed. "Okay, so how far back do you want me to go? When I met Gordon or just the trip?" I asked. I really wasn't ready to go over all of this again. I wanted it to go away. The more I talked about it, the less it actually went away.

Smith looked around the room. "Miss Hastings, would you be more comfortable with another woman in the room while you told us your experience? Should one of us go get your mother?"

I froze, that was not a good idea. Mom was already having a hard time with what she did know of my ordeal. I didn't want her to have to know the details.

"Not Mom, I don't want her to know some of that. It will break her."

"You want me to get Yuki?" Travis sounded chipper. I guess he liked Yuki too.

"Not Yuki," Gage cut him off.

I had to agree, not Yuki, she was too sweet to have the gritty reality of the world put on her shoulders.

"Tracey or Jade would be nice. Tracey already knows the sordid details, and Jade is strong and reassuring."

Gage nodded. "Get the wi—" He stopped himself from saying witch, I could tell. "One with the dark rainbow colors in her hair."

Jade's hair looked like a black opal. It was colorful like a rainbow on an oil-slick. She did my hair, so I half expected her to have said something about the brown right away. But if she was a witch, then maybe she had some other senses and knew how sensitive I was about the whole thing.

We waited in awkward silence while Travis went and got Jade.

"You wanted me?" she asked as she came into the room.

Travis didn't come back.

Jones explained why they asked her to be there for me, and asked if it was okay with her. No one wanted to force my story on anyone who didn't want that burden.

Jade agreed and excused herself for a moment to prepare.

Travis returned with a nice chair for her. He also brought me a couple of pain pills and a bottle of water. I'd be talking a lot.

When Jade returned, she handed me a small bag filled with rocks—three of them from the feel of it. She sat in the chair. Travis had positioned it close enough that she could reach up and touch my shoulder, or I could put my hand on her knee. Smart boy, he knew I'd need to draw on the strength of those around me to get through this one again.

I rotated the stones in the bag as I spoke. When I got to the hair, I swear Jade growled. When I got to the rest of it, Travis and Gage growled. I fisted my hand into the shirt at Travis's back, and Gage had my blankets clenched in a tight fist. And when I described my foggy rescue, I swear they were both purring, happy to be my rescuers, happy I was safe.

It was easier to tell the story this time. I was able to relax, and remember little details that had no meaning, like the truck that whooshed passed me as I made my escape was red; and how I couldn't find a trace of even my shimmery hair extensions that were ubiquitous like glitter after I pulled them from my hair.

It sucked, it sucked hard. By the end of it, Jade sat in the bed behind me. She stroked my back. Her touch grounded me, kept me from getting sick to my stomach.

"How many more times am I going to have to tell this in my own words?" I was exhausted. It wasn't fair how much energy telling all of that stole from me.

"If we catch him, we'll need you as a witness. At least once for a deposition, and again when it goes to trial."

I let out a shaky sigh. "I want to be done with this, so I can start forgetting it sooner than later. You know?"

"We're sorry to have to put you through that again, Miss Hastings. Bailey, he fits the MO perfectly, but you're the only victim to have gotten away from him. We need you to be willing to tell your story as many times as it takes."

Gage growled and surged to his feet.

"I get it, and I will. I want that bastard to pay."

"And if, say an accident were to happen to Gordon where he got dead, how many more times would she have to endure this?" Jade asked.

"Are you threatening the life of this Gordon in front of FBI agents and law officers?"

She scoffed. "I'm not that stupid, Agent Smith. Did you hear me actually threaten him? I mean it's totally logical; he hurt my friend, and as far as everyone can tell, planned on murdering her. So sure, why wouldn't I want him dead? But I didn't threaten him. You didn't hear a threat on his life, as much as I would be interested in making one. Now, when he is dead, how many more times are you going to make Bailey go over this?"

Jones cleared his throat. "If the man we expect is Gordon Harrow also known as Gordon Jamal, you called him Gordon Dryer, were to end up dead before we were able to identify him as this serial killer, Miss Hastings would be questioned every time another case came up."

"And if you had a confession before his untimely demise?" Gage's voice was low and menacing. "Hypothetically speaking."

"We could close the case, and Bailey could forget that part of her life to the best of her ability," Jones said.

"Good to know," Gage replied.

"Yes, good to know," Jade agreed.

I got a chill from both of them. I could tell they were both plotting convenient accidents to happen if he ever got near me again. I approved.

"There's more isn't there?" I asked the FBI guys.

"There is," Jones confirmed.

"Can we take a break? I'm really tired, and sort of hungry," I whined.

Jade kissed me on top of my head. "I'll go find you some noodles okay?"

She knew my comfort food. "Extra cheesy." I nodded.

"You like mac and cheese?" Gage asked.

"It's probably my most favorite food. I'm not a fan of the boxed stuff, but doctor it up with some real cheese and it will work."

"Mac and cheese," he repeated.

"Yeah, so?" I felt really self-conscious of the way he grinned at me.

"I'll go shopping tomorrow and make you some of the best-damned mac and cheese you've ever had. You good with onions and jalapenos and bacon?"

I stared at him. "In my noodles and cheese? Hell yeah. You cook?"

"Does he cook?" Travis scoffed.

"We'll leave you to rest, and we can pick this up after your dinner," Jones announced.

I watched as he and Smith left the room, but I kept cutting my gaze back to Gage.

"I cook. We all cook."

"Yeah, but you can make more than I can. I can only make a few basics plus chili."

"Nothing wrong with the basics. You can feed yourself, and you can feed a group out on the trail."

The conversation between the two men was wildly interesting. I don't think I had ever met a man who admitted he could cook; which was a shame, because I knew far too many guys my age who were clueless about how to take care of themselves.

Eventually, they stopped talking about cooking, and Gage stood up like he was going to leave.

"Travis, do you mind?" I tried to waggle my eyebrows at him to get him to step out of the room. I wanted Gage for myself for a second before he had to go anywhere.

Travis gave me a dejected sigh and headed toward the door. "You know you could make out with me here. I'd be okay with it. We are pack." He sort of sneered those last words, telling Gage he belonged here too. I think.

I glanced up at Gage. "Pack?"

"You're tired, rest, eat. Let's finish with the FBI before we delve too far into the other areas you have questions about. It's best you don't know just yet while the FBI is around. That way nothing slips out accidentally."

"Are you saying I can't be trusted with your secrets?" I asked.

"I'm saying you can't share secrets you don't know." He leaned down and inhaled the air by my neck.

I wrapped my arms around him.

He pulled back and looked into my eyes. "I can't believe you are even willing to touch me after all of that."

"You're safe, you're my hero. You make the bad memories go away like a puff of smoke. Tell me about the pack later."

He kissed me on the tip of my nose.

Travis came back in and crawled into bed next to me when Gage left. He snuggled into my side all warm and comforting. "We are pack. We are yours," he whispered.

~

My stomach lurched. I wanted to puke. Maybe having two bowls of cheesy-noodle-goodness wasn't the best idea. At least the photos were in black and white. Well, the "after" images were.

All the women were like me. And those pictures were in color. If I had met anyone of them, we would've been besties. Crazy hair colors, frills, and tutus. Cupcake purses. Kawaii and cute to the max. And Gordon had taken all of them and killed their shine. Took their clothes and put them in dull drab colors. Removed all color and fun from their hair.

There were a few pictures from surveillance cameras, and the two women were bowed and stooped, and hunched up into themselves, barefoot and scared for their lives. Their short lives.

Gage sat on one side of the bed, Jade the other, and the pictures spread over my good leg on top of the blankets. Six of me, dead. I would've been the seventh in five years.

"He built up trust. He fooled all of them and their families," I whispered.

"They're all like Bailey," Gage said. He wasn't looking at the pictures, but at Jade. He wasn't talking about the shared sense of style. He had asked what I was when he first met her. That's what he meant.

"What were their names?" Jade asked softly. "It's important."

"The first victim was Bliss Haverty. Joy Cummings, Joy Reynolds. Uh, I can never pronounce this one right, Aye-oye-efee. It's spelled A O I F E."

"Ayfa," Jade corrected. "It's Celtic and guess what it means." She lifted her eyes to Agent Jones.

He nodded. "Joy. We noticed that. But there was also an Allison, a Toni, and you, Bailey."

"Bailey is Joy," Gage said so quietly it was practically under his breath.

Smith cleared his throat. "Bailey doesn't mean Joy." He was looking at his phone. "It means... it means capable."

"I didn't say her name meant joy. I said she is Joy. That explains everything."

It explained nothing. "My middle name is Jovie, so yeah, I fit right in," I said dryly.

"Did Gordon know?" Gage asked.

"About my name?" I shook my head. "I don't think so."

"He wouldn't need a name to confirm what she was," Jade sighed. "Let me guess, all of these women were described by their friends as vivacious, life of the party, lit up the room, would show up and make everything better. Those kinds of things?"

Jones agreed.

"He is killing joy."

All I could do was stare at Jade. That was me, never met a person I couldn't make smile. I think that's why I loved being around Yuki so much, when the two of us were together, everyone was happy, everything was good. Even if it wasn't to begin with, we fixed it.

"Sorry, but Bailey doesn't seem very joyful at the moment," Jones said.

Gage tightened up.

Mom whisked into the room. "My daughter is a source of constant happiness and sunshine." She brushed past Jade and kissed my cheek. "Aren't you, baby? She's allowed a little downtime after everything she's been through. Don't you think?"

She gave the FBI man a squinty glare, daring him to say otherwise.

"Zeke said he is going to head out and grab some DVDs, did you want anything?" she asked me.

"You know what I like, why don't you go with and grab something."

"No," Gage's voice was very loud, very big, very annoying. It was enhanced because both Jones and Smith also said 'no' at the same time.

"What do you mean, no?" Mom beat me to it.

We are pack. You are ours. Telling me and my mom what to do, who did Mr. Hot Sheriff Pants think he was?

"If Gordon is out there, he'd recognize your mom. Yuki and me too. We need to stay put, so that if—big if—he is poking around town, he only sees the people who are normally here," Jade explained with a cool even tone.

"Okay, that makes sense," I agreed. "Mom?"

She nodded. "She's right. That makes perfect sense. But you boys have got to stop being so jumpy. Scare me half out of my skin, because I mention going to pick out some movies. Geez. Rom-com and buttery popcorn, girls?"

I nodded.

"Mrs. H, can you ask him to get some ice cream too. And tissues if it's a good movie, you know how Yuki gets before the happy ending," Jade added.

"Mint chocolate chip for you. Yuki still likes strawberry?" Mom headed for the door.

"You had better ask her. She's been on a peach-mango kick lately," Jade said.

"Will do." Mom waved and left to give Zeke a shopping list. Man, I hoped he picked out a decent movie.

Everyone watched as Mom left the room.

Jones turned back to Jade. "What do you mean he's killing joy?"

"You mean like a killjoy?" Smith asked.

"A killjoy is a party pooper."

I looked at Gage, he confused me. Hot, commanding, in charge, and says things like 'party pooper'.

"She means he is killing women who... bring joy, let the sun in, point out how beautiful lightning is in the middle of a threatening storm."

When he met my eyes while describing a thunderstorm, a shiver zigzagged down my spine and straight into my core. My nipples pearled. I wanted to kick everyone out of my room right then.

Gage closed his eyes and inhaled. When he opened them again, he wasn't smiling. His gaze was intense and sexually charged.

"Lordy, you two need a room," Jade muttered.

I pushed on her with my shoulder. "I have one. Everyone is in here."

"New moon is in a couple of days," Gage said as if I would know what he meant. I mean, I think for some reason he had to wait, but, I don't know... it wasn't a full moon, so who the hell knew.

"Let me see if I get this straight. If he is killing women who exhibit or embody, joy like you say, why Bailey? Why not Yuki?" Smith held up his hand, palm out toward me. "Please don't take offense, but while it's pleasant to be in your company, Yuki Jasper radiates..." He rolled his eye up to the ceiling looking for a word.

"Delight," Jade offered.

"Yeah. So why didn't our killer pick up her instead?" he asked.

Gage slid his hand into mine. I looked down at our fingers wrapped around each other and felt a strange belonging. He was telling me he'd always pick me over Yuki. Always. I sort of knew the answer, but it was a valid question. More than once, I wondered how I ended up with a cute guy, and Yuki ended up with stuffed animals. But more than that, I lost the boy of the hour to fawn at Yuki's feet. Like how I lost Max.

"That's easy. Yuki doesn't do sex. She's asexual. Bailey is—"

"Don't you dare call me a slut."

"I would never." Jade glared at me. "And if you are, so am I. Geez girl, I was going to say Bailey is sexual and certain men can tell the difference right away. Some men don't care and bask in whatever glow Yuki emits, while others prefer a much more visceral connection and lean toward the energy you radiate."

The FBI guys got their paradigm shift and understood what Gage and Jade were saying regarding joy. It finally came after a very surreal side conversation where Yuki's lack of sexuality was explained in detail. Yet, everyone, and I do mean everyone, loved to be around her.

Eventually, they cleared off for the night. Jade left to put on some pajamas and make sure our popcorn was properly buttered and to dig Yuki out from underneath a pile of wolves.

Gage nuzzled into my neck. I giggled.

"You smell like sex." His voice was low and seductive.

I shoved him off. "You're on duty, sheriff man." I reminded him. "I can't help it, you heard Jade. I'm visceral." How was I supposed to tell him one sideways glance and he made me wet?

He laughed. Not exactly the reaction I was going for. A nice growl and a lunge pushing me back against the mattress was what I really had in mind.

Not until you are mine first.

I rubbed at my temple. Seriously, Doggo in my head right now?

New moon in two days. Two days.

"Max again?" Gage asked.

"Yeah, he said the new moon is in two days? What's the deal with the new moon? If you're what you keep hinting at, it's a full moon you need."

Gage stood up and pulled my fingers to his lips. Holy Hecate they were soft. Then he began nibbling and my body could not take it.

"I'll explain everything with Max in two days. Timing couldn't be better." He grinned.

"What's that supposed to mean?" I asked.

"Your period. Should end tonight or tomorrow."

I glared at him, which was hard because I was blushing like a stop sign. I knew what he was hinting at.

"Counting days?"

He tapped the side of his nose. "I don't have to."

I was left mouth hanging open as he left.

I wasn't alone long before Yuki in a furry unicorn jammie onesie scurried in carrying a large bowl of popcorn and a DVD.

"No puppers, you wait outside," she admonished the wolves as they crowded around her trying to all get through the door at once.

I had to laugh. It was ridiculous to watch these huge beasts—each one outweighed her by at least eighty pounds —press up against her as if she were their source of air.

Jade's jammies were just as thick and warm looking, and equally fun. She wore a blue fuzzy monster onesie.

"They can come in. But they are staying on the floor. The bed will be too crowded with the three of us."

Doggo jumped up next to me as if he had never abandoned me.

"Yes, that goes for you, Doggo. Get out of Jade's spot." I pushed on the beast until he moved.

The movie started. Jade plopped a new box of tissues onto Yuki's lap and then scooted in next to me.

Yuki put her unicorn head on my shoulder. I leaned my head onto hers. Jade leaned on my opposite shoulder. Collectively, we all sighed. Friends, ice cream, popcorn, rom-com; now, this was good medicine.

"Bails?" Jade asked.

"Yeah?"

"So now I know you didn't change your hair on purpose, can I please strip that color out? It's so not you."

"Would you please? I hate it. He dyed my pubes too, can we strip those?" I wanted to cry, she was going to help me get me back.

"What you need is to wax those off. Rip! And bam no hair, no worries." Yuki's sweet little voice sounded evil the way she described waxing.

"She's got a good point. Shaving might actually do less harm to your skin than the chemicals would. And you don't want that shit near your lady bits, you really don't."

I nodded. Yuki handed me a tissue and I blew my nose. I guess I was crying.

11

I bit my lip and tried not to cry, or cry out. Tracey was as gentle as she could be, but my feet were a mess, and they hated me. The tiny bit of walking I did wasn't doing my recovery any good.

"I've got to call Doc MacGee about getting you another round of antibiotics," Tracey announced as she held up one of the bandages from my right foot, the one with five toes. The seepage from the damage was turning a funky color.

At first, it was bloody and red, and then as I started to heal it was gold with some blood in it. We were at the stage I should start having no blood and the gold colored weeping ooze should start to clarify until it disappeared without any color. I wasn't a medical professional, but even I knew brownish red of old blood and a gray-green tinge was bad. Really bad.

When I transferred from the hospital to the lodge I was on the last round of antibiotic. I still needed the saline because of reasons, remember I'm not a professional. But I had gone more than twenty-four hours without any antibiotics. It was a bummer that I was going back on them.

It was extremely difficult to not walk, especially when that was the only way to get to and from the toilet. I didn't want the bedpan, that thing was so gross. And pee didn't behave properly. Introduce a bedpan and suddenly pee defies gravity, and I'm stuck in a damp hospital gown, in a damp bed waiting for an orderly to come change everything. So undignified. And there is no pooping in a bedpan. Uh uh, the body won't do it.

Of course, having someone carry me to the potty, and then stand over me while I take care of business, or wait outside the door makes it near impossible to take care of business. It's like my bladder knows there are ears listening.

Having a walking boot on for a few hours a day had really made the bathroom more convenient. I hated it, but I could hobble there and back on my own. Nice thick cushy sock on the right, walking boot on the left.

That nasty colored bandage meant my walking days were gonna get set back.

"Could that be why I'm super tired all of a sudden," I asked.

"You aren't running a fever. Maybe..." Tracey paused and pulled her phone out her pocket. A few clicks later and, "I sent a few pics to MacGee. There is a possibility it's a surface issue and not something we need to treat systemically."

She proceeded to squirt a cold liquid, which had the horrible effect of tickling and hurting all at once. She finished washing off my foot.

"I want to let that have some air time before I wrap you back up."

She began working on my left foot. I couldn't watch. I was curious, but also scared and freaked out. I was missing a toe and a portion of the side of my foot. I caught a glimpse a few days before, and as soon as I saw spikes of black stitches I looked away. I wasn't ready to look again.

"This foot is doing much better. The suture is also looking good." She moved my foot around getting a good view. "The bottom is healing nicely. No discharge at all. You're doing well, Bailey."

I had my eyes clenched tight and my head turned into the pillow.

The cleaning process didn't hurt as much or take as long.

She was re-bandaging my foot when she screamed out a *whoop*, and my foot fell onto the pillows.

I opened my eyes. The darker of the wolves that typically swarmed around Yuki was nosing into Tracey's butt.

"For pity's sake, Brooks, I'm working here. I know tomorrow starts the new moon."

She bent over and placed her forehead against the wolf's brow. She held her clean hands up and away from him. She hummed and the wolf began to make a singing noise in his throat.

He yipped and bounced away from her. She laughed and returned to my foot.

"Something tells me that's why you had no problems with Doggo in the hospital bed with me."

She laughed. I liked her.

"Yeah. One, I'm not afraid of the hairy brutes, and two, I'm a private nurse."

I cocked my head and scrunched up my eyebrows.

"You didn't know that? Yeah, Gage has me work with people in custody. I mean, I'm a hospital employee, but I have an in with the Sheriff's office. He knows I'm good with difficult situations."

"Are you saying I'm difficult?" I squeaked as she did something to my foot.

"Hardly. The guys, however, they're being difficult. Max was not letting anyone near you. Gage was as snarly but in human form. I finally had to put my foot down and insist on no more than two of them at any given point in time. And only Max, no other animals."

Before I could ask her to elaborate, Jade knocked and then pushed open the door. "Hey, gimpy! You ready to become a redhead again?"

Was I ready? Two weeks and I was beginning to forget what I had looked like before.

"Hells yeah, I'm ready. Bring it on."

Tracey laughed at us, and I forgot to ask her more about why the guys were all weird around me.

Jade bounced on the foot of the bed.

I winced.

Tracey must've seen it because, in no time, she was handing me my favorite dose of Motrin and a cup of water.

Jade dumped her arm full of goodies on my lap—dandruff shampoo, vitamin C pills, a small mixing bowl, and slightly bigger mixing bowl, a spoon, cling wrap.

"How is this going to help?" I asked picking up the dandruff shampoo.

"I'm not a licensed hairdresser for nothing. There are no beauty supply stores in town and even if there were since we're all on house arrest, I can't go. So we make do with what we cobbled together." Jade rubbed her hands together like a mad scientist.

"Are you going to need the shower chair?" Tracey asked.

"Yeah, probably." Jade nodded.

Tracey disappeared into the bathroom for a moment.

"All set up. I'll be back to check on you. Will you be a ginge when I get back?"

"Hey now, don't go throwing words like ginge around. I believe the proper PC version is ginger-American."

"Shut up," I picked up and tossed the spoon at Jade.

"Have fun ladies," Tracey said as she left. Brooks was plastered to her hip. I had forgotten him since he lay down after goosing Tracey.

Jade opened the vitamin C and poured five or six tablets into the small mixing bowl. She handed it to me with the spoon. "Crush these up as small as you can make them. While you're doing that, I'm going to get us some ice cream." She jumped up and left me to my grinding. Mark slid into the room. I wasn't used to seeing him alone.

"Is Jade around?"

"She's getting ice cream. If you wait a minute I'm sure she'll be back."

He shuddered. "Naw, I'll leave this here for her." He looked at me funny and made sure I saw where he placed a razor on the counter near the medical stuff Tracey had set up. "Fresh blades, just as she asked. She can toss the blades; I will need the handle back at some point."

"Okay, thanks." I didn't really think about it until he was on the other side of the door. Why had he shuddered? Why had he given me the stink eye? Why a razor? Did I need to shave my legs that badly?

I looked down. Nope, my legs seemed fine to me. I tucked my hand into my armpit. Oh yeah, those were getting fuzzy.

My jaw dropped open and I could feel the flush spread across my face. Right, shaving would be healthier than trying to strip the color. I wasn't sure how I felt about that. I mean I know most chicks my age go bald, and a lot of the guys I dated seemed to really like it that way. But bodies came with hair for a reason. I'd have to think on that—brown pubes or none at all. How could I ask Gage on the sly what he preferred? He had some nice chest hair going on. I bet he didn't mind a little body fuzz.

Jade came back with a huge bowl of pure vanilla ice cream. I know, right? Everything in my life was a riot of color and sensation. But I swear, nothing beats a bowl of unadulterated perfect vanilla ice cream. No chocolate sauce, no cherries, nothing, just sweet, sweet creamy vanilla.

"Yum." I put the grinding of the vitamin C tablets down and got a whiff of orange flavored dust up my nose. I snorted trying to clear my nose of the offending powder.

Jade picked up the pulverized vitamins and began blending in the shampoo.

"Is that really going to work?" I asked between bites.

"I'm a witch, what do you think?"

I gave her a level glare.

She said nothing for a full thirty seconds. "Okay, so I saw this on Youtube. If it doesn't work, it won't hurt your hair. The only other option we have until I can get you to a salon is to bleach it. And you won't be any happier with that than you are right now."

The goo she pasted in my hair smelled like chemical oranges. It wasn't bad, and it smelled a million times better than any bleach I've ever had on my hair. I loved the feeling of Jade massaging the concoction into my hair. Hell, I loved the feel of hands in my hair and getting my head scratched.

That's probably why I kept getting my hair highlighted and dyed wacky colors all the time, just to have my hair played with.

"I'm so sorry, Bails."

"What?" Part of me wanted to sit up and face Jade. I

was afraid my hair was falling out or something. I really shouldn't move. It had taken some serious pillow jockeying to get me situated where I could relax back, Jade could get to my head, and I could keep the four toe wonder elevated.

"That you got hurt. The bastard even did your eyebrows."

"Yeah, it sucks." I shrugged. "But you are fixing me. It, you are fixing it."

"The skin around your eyebrows is pissed off. Burned. I don't want to put this mix on there and burn you more. You're going to have to live with brown for a while. How did he do this to you?" I know she wasn't seriously asking the physical how, after all, she had heard me tell the FBI that I had have been drugged to have slept through it. And I couldn't smell anything because I had a bath bomb up my nose.

"I didn't notice the eyebrows right away. And by then, I was more concerned with the black eye."

Jade lightly touched my brow and cheekbone. "It's fading, but it's not pretty. God Bails, you got away. I'm so glad you got away." She let out a ragged sigh.

"Hey shut up, no crying. Let's talk about all the freaking hot men who saved me instead." I didn't want to wallow, I didn't want to live there.

"You certainly did land yourself one hell of a harem. And I bet Max is a god."

"Max is a wolf and I don't have, ew, not going there." I shivered all over. Ew.

"Bailey."

I don't think I ever heard Jade use her serious "mom voice" before. I know she would frequently give Yuki her "mom look" which came before the voice because Yuki would say something about it. But damn. I felt the need to sit up straight and say yes ma'am.

"You know what he is." Her voice was flat.

"Actually, I don't. Gage won't tell me. He is saving it for tomorrow. So I'm going to pretend I don't have any ideas about it because if I start thinking about it, I'm gonna freak out."

"How about you don't freak out over that and start freaking out over the fact you're so getting laid tomorrow night."

"Okay, so it's not just me?" I squeaked.

"Gage couldn't be more obvious unless he had a neon sign embedded in his forehead. He's not even chill around your parents, and it is cracking me up."

I groaned. Mom was weird about sex. "You know she thinks Gordon was my first. And don't you dare tell her otherwise."

"She won't hear it from me. So you probably don't want me to tell you..." She stopped for a dramatic pause.

I stuck my fingers in my ears. "La la la la la la la."

She wrapped my head in the cling wrap and wrapped a towel around that.

"I'm gonna go see if Zeke has any more movies, or do you want to watch the one we saw last night again?"

The one from last night was an auto-tuned musical nightmare. "Uh no, find something else. How long do I need to keep this in?"

"About as long as it takes me to find something for us to watch, and for us to watch it."

A few movies later Yuki bounced into my room. She was only surrounded by two wolves, instead of the normal three. Doggo and Oz.

"You look so much more like you," Yuki said as she tried

to get past the wolves and climb up onto the bed with me. She touched and played with my hair. "And it feels so soft. That brown did *not* suit you at all. Are you feeling better?"

My hair was almost all the way back to normal. It wasn't quite as bright, there was still a layer of brown darkening the color, but I was back to orange. The purple and pinks were also seriously faded. Stripped out with the rest of the dye.

Yuki sat and bounced the whole bed. I smiled. Yeah, I felt a whole lot better. The shower and rinsing of hair had been a bit of a circus, but Jade and I giggled and cackled the entire time. Travis was my hero for the afternoon and he happily lifted me to and from the shower and even fetched an arm full of dry towels when it was all over.

"Hi, Nurse Brooks," Yuki called out when Tracey came in. She had the third wolf pasted to her side.

Brooks was the wolf.

I looked from Tracey to Yuki to Brooks. I think I made a connection in my head, but not being certain, I didn't want to say anything too foolish out loud.

"Are you excited for the new moon? Everyone seems to be all amped up," Yuki said.

"Yeah, the new moon is a big time around here," Tracey answered. "It's the only time all of the men can get together. So they have a big meal to celebrate. This month, with all of you here, it's going to be a big party."

"Sounds like fun. Do you think I'll be able to get out of this bed for it?" I groused a little. My feet were hurting. I was keenly aware that my renewed orange coloring made my facial bruises even more vivid. I was cranky.

"Of course you will be. You'll have to be carried down, cause I got word from the doc that you are off your feet for at least three days. And you are back on the antibiotics."

Tracey held up and wagged a bag of liquid drugs at me. As she attached the medication to the IV she continued, "You'll be attached, but the IV pole is mobile. Besides I don't think Max will let you out of his sight."

She finished hooking me up, checked my line and patted my arm. "All set. And I love the ginger-American look. I can see why you were having a hard time with the other."

She lifted her brows and wiggled her finger in a circle at my girlie parts. "Did you do down there?"

Jade sucked in a hiss. "Nope, the lady parts didn't need to be harassed any further. Bailey is contemplating leaving it and letting it fade and grow out or shaving it."

Yeah, this was my life, discussing my dyed short and curlies with my best friends and my nurse. "Ok, so I'm waffling. I'm not a fan of either the color or the ingrown hairs."

"Damned if you do. Damned if you don't. I still vote waxing. R-r-r-rip!" Yuki had a cruel streak in her. She giggled.

Tracey leaned in, she was trying, and failing at suppressing a smile. "Mind if I'm slightly unprofessional for a moment?"

I shifted in my spot. Yuki leaned in. Out of nowhere, Jade was by my side with her hands clasped in her lap. I think we all had eager expressions on our faces. Nurse Tracey was going to be inappropriately unprofessional. We live for moments like this.

She took a big breath in and looked out the door, and then shifted her glance to the wolves carpeting the floor. "Hairy guys don't mind a little body fur. Gage is clearly not big on the man-scaping." She made a gesture indicating the visible chest hair at the base of his throat when he was out of uniform and those top three buttons of his shirt were undone.

She tilted her head to the side with a little shrug.

The three of us on the bed collapsed in laughter.

"What's all the noise going on in here?" Gage stopped in the door frame.

Oh, he looked nice. His uniform was fresh and pressed. And he did that little curl over his forehead.

I laughed even harder.

He stepped into the room.

"Wow, Bailey." He came toward me like I had him in a tractor-beam and he couldn't stop or control his movements.

Of course, I couldn't breathe I was laughing so hard. There was the hairy guy of the hour, and all I could think was some random furry comment he made the other day and Tracey motioning about his chest hair.

"You look nice today, Officer Masterson," Yuki said sweetly as pie.

"Thanks Yuki, but it's just a uniform. I was heading out for the evening and wanted to say bye." He made it to the side of the bed and reached up before dropping his hand back down.

I managed to stop laughing, but the smile I had hurt my face. I loved the look on his face as he took me in as a redhead for the first time.

His jaw was a little slack, and his eyes wide. He closed his mouth with a little grin. He sighed.

I was a goner, and he was looking at me like he really liked the renewed ginger coloring.

"God, Bailey." His eyes moved over my hair and then my face, and back to my hair. "I don't know what to say."

"You like? This is what it's supposed to look like." I bit

the side of my lip. I think he liked it, but I still needed some confirmation.

"I like it very much." He reached up again, and this time he picked up a section of my hair. I died and I went straight to heaven when he pressed his face to my hair and sighed. He kissed it as if he was kissing the back of my hand. "I'll check in on you when I get home."

"Won't it be late?" I asked. I mean, he was leaving now and it was already afternoon.

"Is that a don't bother?" He sounded hurt.

"Not at all. I'll be asleep and will miss it, that's all."

"But I won't, and that's the point." He winked at me and I melted.

"Hey Gage, it wouldn't bother you if carpet and drapes don't exactly match would it?" Jade asked with a perfectly straight face.

I think I stopped breathing.

Tracey snorted.

Gage looked up at the window. His brows crinkled, and then rose as he got what Jade was saying. His whole face relaxed into a smile, he nodded and then shook his head. He leveled his gaze on Jade and ran his tongue along the inside of his cheek, pushing it out. He adjusted his posture. "When the drapes are stunning who cares what color the carpeting is, as long as there's something to keep the toes warm."

He turned on his heel and was out the door.

I was dead, completely dead. Tracey turned her back to us and quaked with laughter.

Yuki and Jade cackled.

The furry beasts on the floor actually had the nerve to make complaining woofy sounds.

12

I'm not the kind of person who feels energy or can read an aura, but I swear, the air in the lodge vibrated.

Yuki burst into my room, buzzing with the same energy. "So exciting. Are you excited?"

"What?" I asked.

"It's the first night of the new moon."

"The new moon is only one night," I said. I looked at her like she had an extra head growing between her eyebrows.

"I know that. Nurse Brooks was telling me they have three nights at the new moon, and three at the full moon. The night before, the night of, and the night after. After that, the pull of the moon is too strong or too weak for the changes to occur."

"So what's supposed to happen?" I asked.

"I don't know," she squeaked. But she sure was happy about it.

It wasn't until then I noticed there were no animals with her.

"Where is your flock?"

She shrugged. "Brooks has been with his Tracey for a

couple of days already. Max and Oz went out running or something."

Gage stopped at my door. I swear it's the only way I got to see him anymore.

He was in uniform.

"Hey, I thought you were on duty really late last night?" I asked. I hated that he had to work so much. But most people had regular jobs. We didn't all get to stay in bed for days at a time. I know Zeke and Mark also had jobs. I have no idea what they did. I felt a twinge of guilt realizing I had never asked them. Travis was between seasons, so he wasn't too worried about working. He told me if he needed any extra cash, he'd pick up handyman work around the local businesses. But, he typically made enough as a guide and instructor in the summer, and once ski season started.

"I'm headed in early so I can be home tonight. Is that okay with you?" He sounded tense.

Right, new moon, and—my insides did a certain acrobatic flip—the culmination of a whole lot of freaking flirting. Jade was certain Gage was saving closing the deal until tonight.

I opened my mouth and closed it again. I couldn't think of anything snarky to say.

"I miss seeing you. So if that means I get to hang out with you then I think that's okay with me."

Gage came into the room then. He looked worried. "I can't promise that's going to work out, but I'll do my best."

He leaned in and kissed me on the cheek. I didn't want a kiss on the cheek.

"I thought you... I thought we would, you know?" I whispered. I thought I was thinking it, and that I hadn't actually said anything out loud.

His face didn't leave mine. He rubbed his cheek against

mine like some big cat. "I do. Let's see how tonight goes with Max okay?"

I nodded, and he was gone before my brain caught up with what he said after 'I do.' What the hell does a big wolf have to do with whether or not Gage wants me?

Eventually, Jade joined Yuki and me and we watched a movie.

Nurse Tracey and Brooks came in. She changed my bandages, declared my right foot wasn't showing signs of getting worse, but it wasn't looking any better. It would take a few days. I had a lot of damage to heal, and then this slight infection wasn't helping any. She gave me another bag of antibiotics.

Brooks did his best imitation of a rug. He left when she did.

Mom brought me a sandwich for lunch and made Yuki and Jade leave me alone so I could take a nap. By then, Doggo was back and had set up camp in my room.

After my nap, Mom let the FBI agents come in. Apparently, she made them wait while I slept. Of everyone in the place, from the big men to the wolves, I honestly think they were more afraid of my mother than anyone else.

There hadn't been any more activity on the credit card. But they didn't have confirmation that he wasn't in the area.

"Is there any way he knows I'm alive? I mean, if Doggo and Gage hadn't have found me, I would be dead out there somewhere. He can't know if I survived can he?"

Jones sighed. "If he started calling the hospitals, they may have released information. We have no way of knowing."

I threw my hands up in the air. "Holy Hecate, how many hospitals can there be out here?"

All I really knew was I was in the small town of Wet

Waterfalls, a place I'd never heard of before that happened to have a county hospital. I didn't know how far away the next county with a hospital was.

"If he started calling around, who knows. He could call around a bigger town to see if anyone was brought in."

"In other words, you have no idea if he is in this town, or cruising down the highway back to where ever he was headed when he backtracked."

"Boise. He was going home to Boise," Smith said flatly.

"How do you know Boise is home?" I asked. Doggo had jumped into the bed at some point. I dug my fingers into the fur at his neck.

My stomach hurt. I really didn't want to hear what they were about to tell me.

"All of the victims were discovered in Boise. Four of them were Boise natives. We think he was taking you back there."

I nodded. I didn't want to know this.

By the time our conversation was over, I wasn't feeling well. The energy of the place vibrated through me and I had this odd sense of foreboding creeping up the backs of my arms. The FBI left me with a cold sense of dread. I couldn't shake the heebie-jeebies.

I was curled around Doggo when Gage came in carrying my dinner. I guess I'd spend a good part of the day distracted and dozing because he was home and out of uniform. I shifted to get a good look at him. He was so gorgeous. His dark hair was clean-cut short, but he had a curl right over his forehead. If he let his hair grow, it would be messy and curly. I wonder if he was the type who would grow his hair out a little if I asked. Then again, he probably had to have a certain look for the job.

Bummer.

Tight jeans hugged his butt, and he had a great butt. Not me just liking his body parts because I liked him, and making excuses for thinking a little flat ass was cute, but an actual the-man-worked-out-and-did-squats kind of an ass. I let out a little laugh. The top three buttons of his chambray shirt were undone, and chest hair was visible. He also had the sleeves rolled up showing off his forearms. Was he dressing sexy on purpose?

He placed the tray he carried down and rushed to my side to help me into a sitting position. Extra pillows and warm arms made me feel better. I tried to smile at him, but he wouldn't look me in the face. Was he shy and as nervous as I was?

"Gage?"

He brought over the bed tray and placed it on my lap. Tonight there was a single rose lying across the tray. I picked it up and smelled it. It was lovely. I felt a sizzle of nervous energy in my middle. I didn't know if I'd be able to eat.

"Sunset is early. I wanted to let you know how I feel."

I turned my head to look at him and his lips were on mine. I melted into him. Our lips moved over each other. He pulled my lower lip in between his teeth. I moaned, and it might have been out loud. I reached up to wrap my arm around his neck and I hit the tray.

The clatter of dishes pulled him out of the kiss. "Careful, you don't want to spill."

I didn't care about spilling. I wanted to kiss him more. But he was gone from my side. He was across the room and by the door.

"Remember how I feel about you, no matter what happens tonight." He left, closing the door behind him. He looked hurt. I was so confused.

What did sunset have to do with anything? Why was I

getting my dinner so early? And why had he left me? I thought he was planning on seducing me tonight. I thought that's what the rose was all about, and that kiss.

Doggo made a loud whiney yawn from the floor. I looked over at him, concerned. He sounded like he was in pain. He stretched out with paws extended in front of him. I had two thoughts at the same time—the first was holy crap, he really was a big animal and the second being, that's why that position in yoga is called the downward dog.

He made another almost pained sound, his fur shimmered. I rubbed my eyes because he was glitching, in and out of focus. Sometimes crying messed with my clarity of vision, and that's what was happening. I thought.

I didn't gasp. There wasn't enough time for me to make a sound.

Energy crackled and sparked like a Tesla coil. Lightning extended from Doggo's fingers. Whoa, what? Fingers, hands, arms. The change rolled over him, up his arms, over his head, down his back.

He groaned with discomfort as the sparks ran over his skin.

Gage had been worried about spilling from a little kiss. Clearly, he overestimated my ability to keep calm in the wake of this. The tray went sideways and my dinner went in two directions. I was barely aware of it. Lying fully extended on my floor was a huge man. A huge naked man. Okay, he was face down, but those buns were cloth free. Waves of dark hair, sun bleached at the ends covered his shoulders. His skin was warm and golden. No tan lines, I mean the buns were as dark as his shoulders.

His skin rippled like silk over hard muscles.

He made more noises that weren't quite pain. He stretched out to his full length and then spasmed into a curled up ball. He growled and stood up, shaking his hair out.

His golden gaze pierced me in place. I wanted to scramble away from him. I wanted to scream. I wanted to roll over and wake up from this freak show of a dream. But I couldn't move. It didn't matter that my leg was getting uncomfortably wet from my spilled water, or that a glob of Jell-O wobbled next to my knee, or that mayo and mustard from my sandwich were smeared over the blankets. Nothing matter beyond those eyes.

He shook his head at me. There was so much to take in, his smile, the mischievous twitch to his lips, those lips, and so much hair. Glorious hair. Wide shoulders roped with thick muscles. At first, I thought the faded old tattoo on his pec and shoulder was a bruise, but then I realized it was a random pattern of some ethnic origin. It looked Aztec, Mayan maybe?

His face was beautiful, exotic. Native something. I don't know. I didn't really care.

My mouth went dry. "Doggo?"

This creature tossed back his head and let out a howling laugh.

I laughed nervously with him. Holy Hecate in a hellish hand-basket, he was a god.

Of course—Max. Now I got it. I think.

I squeaked. I couldn't make words.

He closed the space between us and wrapped a hand around my neck.

He whispered my name and then he was kissing me. All ten of my toes curled—even the missing one. His lips moved over mine like a starving man getting mana for life. I wrapped my arms around him and pulled his head closer.

His tongue didn't bother to lick, it plunged and I sucked him in.

The blankets I was mildly worried about earlier were ripped from the bed, and Max was over me. His legs straddled mine, and he continued to kiss me as if I were air. I knew he was everything I could ever need or want at that moment.

I had no idea how long he kissed me like that, but at some point, I thought my lips should be sore from this workout, but they weren't and I wanted more.

He broke the kiss and shifted positions so that I was sitting in his lap.

I stroked his face and gazed at his beauty. "Max?"

He sucked a finger into his mouth and I felt the pull lower in my body.

"I thought I lost Doggo to Yuki. Why are you here?" Apparently, even though I wanted to ignore what Gage had been hinting at, I accepted that Max became a man on the new moon. "How long do I have you for?"

"I've got three days, and then we have to wait another month."

"That kind of sucks. But why aren't you with Yuki?"

He laughed at me. "Yuki is delight. She has the innocent joy of a child. You know that. I don't have sex with children."

"I know, but you have been by her side since she arrived. And she's not a child, she's twenty-five. I was at her birthday party."

"The same magic that infuses you with love and joy, is in her tenfold. Even if I misinterpreted her magic, she wouldn't." He shook his head. "Besides, we are pack, we are yours. She is not pack."

"Oh, is this that whole 'I'm gonna pee on that and make it mine' thing?" I asked.

He looked at me like I was crazy. "Bailey, I admit I have to live with a strange furry situation, but that doesn't mean I'm into kink. I'm not going to pee on you, and I don't want you to pee on me. No golden showers, please."

"Ew, no." I laughed, and he kissed me.

Kissing him from this new angle was magic since he had to lift his face to mine. I felt like I had the power.

His hands ran over the skin on my back and ass. I still wore a hospital gown; so essentially, I was almost as naked as he was.

I held his face to mine, playing with the heavy scruff that grew along his jawline.

I know I made noises as his lips devoured down my neck and onto my shoulder. He grunted as he ripped the snaps apart along my left shoulder. The gown dropped exposing one breast. He made another guttural sound and his lips trailed scorching hot kisses down until he sucked in my nipple.

He had to hold me in place, I tried to levitate out of bed as he teased and licked, and activated every freaking nerve ending in my body.

I cried out and instantly realized what I was doing. I should've been doing this with Gage. No wonder he had been so sad. Had he known? I pushed Max away.

He looked up at me and saw the tears of guilt stain my face. He was gentle as he wiped them away with his thumbs. His fingers were rough.

"Do you want this?"

I nodded, I did, but... "I want Gage."

"Call him," Max directed.

I started to open my mouth the shout out Gage's name. He would never hear me from my room. The lodge was huge, and who knew where he would be.

Max stopped my shout with a finger across my lips. "Here." He tapped my temple. "The way I can talk into your head, call him. Tell him *we* need him."

I sniffed, and closed my eyes, focusing on the words in my head. *Gage, I need you. We need you. Please, Gage. I love you.*

I can't imagine what he had to think when he burst through my door. I was half naked, a breast hanging out and sitting with my legs wrapped around a very naked Max.

My stomach clenched as if I had been punched. I bit back more tears.

"I'm so—"

Gage slowly shook his head and I stopped talking. His eyes glowed with an intensity I hadn't seen before. He closed the door behind him and in the thick silence in the room; I heard the snick of the lock.

I was terrified. Gage was going to start yelling, or worse he was going to charge and attack.

Max reached out to him.

Gage stepped forward and took the other man's hand, letting Max pull him into our embrace.

I died. This was a death dream, this couldn't be real. Reality wasn't ever this sexy.

I couldn't breathe as Max kept pulling Gage in and they kissed. And they didn't simply kiss. They kissed each other with ferocity and passion. I knew because they each had kissed me like that. Fuck.

If I hadn't been turned on and in need of man's skin on me before, I certainly was now. I buried my hand into Max's hair and held on as he attacked Gage's mouth. I ran my other hand over Gage, touching his neck, shoulders, back, arms. I held them and they worked each other's mouths in a way that made my lips jealous.

Max reached up and ripped the snaps from my other shoulder. My hospital gown dropped between us. Their kiss broke. I made some low guttural sound as if I was the one who was no longer being kissed.

"Bailey, you have to say yes, or this stops right here, right now." Gage looked at me with those eyes and I was definitely dead. Was he giving me permission to be with Max?

"I get both of you?" I couldn't believe what was happening.

"We are pack. We are yours." It sounded like a chant when they both said it.

"Fuck yeah." I wanted them to be perfectly clear, I was all in.

Max grabbed my hips adjusted me. Holy Hecate! I have never felt anything as magical as that man entering my body.

His mouth sucked in my breast. Gage wrapped an arm around me and grabbed on to my other breast and then before I could scream out in ecstasy his mouth descended on mine, and I was kissing him with as much need and want as I witnessed in their kiss seconds before.

Finally enough mouths, enough hands were on me. I had never had a three-way before, and I swear, I don't think I could ever go back to one-on-one sex again. All of my nerve endings had the attention they needed to be worked into a frenzy. My position lent to an awkward lack of leverage, but Max's hands on my hips took care of that. He growled and shook his head. I had to clasp a hand to his head to hold him still and not pull my breast off.

Gage pulled away from our kiss and smiled at me. He licked his lower lip and stepped back. He began taking off his clothes. Max pulled my arm over so that I faced him fully and he increased his speed. I thought I was going to explode when he pulled me off him.

"Knees," he directed. He was a man of very few words.

I shifted and got my knees under me. Gage ran a warm hand across my ass and back as I scooted my knees to the edge of the bed. I melted. Max pulled me in for a kiss. I swear calling what he did to my mouth a kiss seemed like calling New York City a little town.

Max lifted his mouth away from me and I continued kissing down his neck to his chest. I licked the sweat from between his pecs. He tasted like salt and sweat and heaven.

Gage pressed his hips to my ass and I lifted my hips back.

He hissed and muttered. He stepped back. I focused on Max until I felt fingers spread wide rake down my hips in a nastily familiar sensation.

I froze. I had a hard time finding my breath.

"Oh God, Bailey. I'm sorry. We can stop." Gage sounded hurt.

"No!" The sound ripped from my throat.

"I shouldn't have traced the bruises."

"Touch me," I ordered. "Touch me in any other way. I need you to erase him. Erase the memories, erase the sensations. Replace the memory with something I want, Gage. Replace them with you. Please." I didn't want to cry. I didn't want to give Gordon the power to ruin this.

"I'll give you new memories." Gage's voice was low and so damned hot.

I gasped as he ran his manhood across my delicate flesh.

"Yes." I backed my hips up as far as I could.

I returned to kissing Max's abs. Man, I could file my nails on this man, but his skin was soft to the touch and it covered the most amazing physique of rock hard everything. I'd say muscles, but the erection I sucked into my mouth felt more like it came complete with a baculum and was not only engorged with blood.

I cried out around the skin I sucked on as Gage did the unexpected. Instead of sinking into me and ramming me against Max, he sucked me into his mouth and used his tongue to toy with my clit. I couldn't breathe. It was all too much. And I wanted all of it and more.

I spit out Max and all his glorious length so I could suck in air. I whimpered, "In me, in me, let me come around you."

I cried as Gage slid into me and began pounding. I lowered my head onto Max's lap and held on to his erection for dear life. I guess I squeezed and moved just right. I felt him thicken and pulse. He let out a gasp as I felt warmth spill over my hand. I couldn't enjoy it as much, as making a man come typically delights me, because I seized up and couldn't move as my own orgasm exploded through my body. I guess we all came at the same time in some miracle of sexual prowess and magic. Gage roared and thrust hard against me.

We froze, pressed into each other until our muscles could work again. I let go of Max and tried to roll. My IV line got caught on something, and I felt trapped. Gage extricated himself and managed to get me free. He lifted me into his arms. We gazed into each other's eyes and I felt all my nerves begin to twist and twitch again. He lowered me to the bed, and Max demanded my attention. He rolled over me and kneed my legs apart.

I didn't expect him to be able to penetrate, after all, he had released all over my arm. Typically, that meant the guy had to recharge. Clearly, Max was not typical. He slid into me for a second time and I closed my eyes. This was all so weird. I held Gage's hand as Max took his pleasure with me under him. I took my pleasure as well, because damn that man could fuck, make love. I don't know. I wanted him. My body needed him, but until an hour ago, he was a wolf. Did I have an emotional attachment? Physical? Hell, yes. And maybe I'd fall in love after all of this, after all, no one had ever worked my body so beautifully as these two men were.

The kiss I got was beautiful. Gage. I could tell from the angle the lips were at. How could I not love the man loving my body? Could I be in love with more than one man at once?

Hell, these two didn't seem to have a problem sharing me. They tagged teamed pretty damned well. I didn't want to think about how many times they had done this before. These talents had to have been refined somewhere.

I cried out another orgasm into Gage's mouth while Max continued to thrust. Max yelled out and I swear I felt him fire hose into me. Damn, if I could get pregnant just holding hands with Gage, there was no way I was walking away from this without every ovary in my body fertilized.

Max sighed and lowered to my side. He shoved Gage's face away from mine and pulled me to his lips. I barely had time to catch my breath before Max took it away again.

He tasted like so much sex and love. Yeah, I was in love with him too. Damn this really called for the "it's complicated" button for my relationship status.

Max broke the kiss and rolled off the bed. He padded off to the bathroom. Gage slid into the bed next to me. He didn't say anything, just stared at me.

Max returned and handed me a glass of water. I passed the drink to Gage, and then he kissed me with his cool wet lips. I rolled away and reached out, handing the glass to Max.

I sucked in a breath as Gage placed his still cool lips to my breast. "Oh, gods." It was heavenly.

Max climbed into the bed behind me and adjusted me so that I leaned against him. Gage did not detach the entire time. He shifted so that he was now the one between my legs.

I lifted a leg and wrapped it around his hips, urging him to slide in. It was perfect. Max was also perfect, so Gage was a different perfect. He moved with a slower coaxing action. I was done the second he started. I twitched and clenched. My body felt on fire.

Max leaned forward, lifting me toward Gage. Instead of lifting his head to kiss me, Gage pushed up higher. I loved how taut his arms were. I ran my hands over the bunched up muscles. The two men closed over me, and I watched from underneath as they kissed and sucked on each other's tongues. Damn their necks and jaws were super sexy as they moved into each other's mouths.

Max held Gage's head to his as Gage thrust into me. I counter thrust as best I could without pushing my feet into the bed. I enjoyed my view and the sensation of being trapped between their sweat-sheened chests. They loved each other, Gage made love to me, and I caressed both of them.

Max held tight as Gage growled and shoved his hips hard against mine. I laughed in triumph as another orgasm took over my body.

I woke to the most obnoxious beeping noise I hadn't heard since the hospital. I was wrapped around a warm naked Max, and Gage was wrapped around me.

Nurse Tracey shushed me back to sleep. "You've gotten all tangled. No wonder the IV alarm is going off."

I'd worry about how she got into my locked room later.

The next time I woke, Max was teasing a nipple, my four-toed foot was flung over Gage, and he was twirling fingers in my hair.

I looked down at Max. He was enjoying himself, I could tell by the noises and the pulsing erection against my thigh.

I sighed and looked over at Gage. I was wholeheartedly in love with this man. I was in love with Max too. It was all so strange. I closed my eyes as his face came closer and he claimed my lips.

Damn.

One of Max's hands found my free breast and rolled the nipple between his fingers. Tightening the muscles in my back, I pressed my breasts into Max. Apparently, that was the signal for game on.

Gage's free hand began toying with my sensitive feminine flesh. I should've been sore, but I throbbed for more. Max's hand abandoned my breast, and I felt the two of them have a hand slapping fight for position as they both felt the need to manhandle my bits. I wrapped one arm around Max's head and held him close as he made love to my breast with his mouth. He teased and tugged, and sucked and bit.

My other arm was wrapped around Gage as he kissed me senseless. I had both of their hands on me in a seriously intimate team effort. One hand ran circles around my clit, the other plunged my depths.

It took both of them to keep me in the world, and on the bed. I felt like exploding and lifting into the sky.

Their hands shifted jobs and I melted. I think I could tell whose touch was whose. Then again, maybe I was wrong. It didn't matter, they were both magicians of sex, and they worked my body with the right amount of rough pressure and delicate touch. They coaxed my body to heights of pure pleasure I had no idea were even possible.

By the time I was tapping out because they drove me hard, and for longer than I thought was even possible, Gage was the one sucking on my nipples and Max was sucking on my tongue.

It was a glorious way to start my day.

I guess it was a good thing I was on bed rest and had to stay off my feet, cause there was no way my legs were going to work.

Max took the first shower, and Gage helped me with mine and showered at the same time. It was sexy simply because of the man, but there was no hanky-panky under the water. We had to be careful and juggle everything to keep my feet dry. I can't even describe the amazing feeling of sitting in the shower, knowing what a naked Gage looked like with his firm body and the wavy patterns his chest hair made when it was wet, standing behind me, washing my hair, and gently soaping and rinsing me off.

He did kiss me, and I loved the feel of the water running over us as our mouths pressed together. No wonder they always include a kissing in the rain scene in movies. It's all kinds of wow.

I wasn't sure how I was going to face anyone and everyone today after Gage and Max rocked my existence. But no one reacted as if they hadn't heard screams and banging coming from my room all night long.

Tracey didn't say a thing when she came back in the morning. A tall movie star good looking man followed behind her.

"Bailey, this is my husband Ben." I swear she blushed.

Maybe she had been making some noise of her own the night before.

"Hi, Brooks," Yuki said as she skipped in and jumped into my bed. Had she called Ben the wolf's name?

Tracey finished swapping out my antibiotics and left. Ben was by her side just like that wolf had been.

Oh, I got it. Tracey knew because... Oh right, Brooks. I was going to have to find out what happened. I can't imagine how hard it was to only have someone you loved with you three days a month. My heart seized. Everything hurt and my eyes started watering hard. I was only going to have Max for two more nights. That was it. I missed him already.

I fought to breathe again. I needed to not worry about that until it happened.

"Two for one special, huh?" Jade asked as she flopped down.

"Oh gods, does everyone know?" I groaned.

Jade lifted an eyebrow. "Maybe?"

I wanted to hide under the covers. I was suddenly so embarrassed.

"So what?" Yuki said. "You get lots of love, that's good. You need two men willing to die for you after what you had to endure. It's all good."

"But my mom is going to freak," I whined.

"Look, your mom barely seems to notice that Gage has been pining after you at all. I doubt she'll notice a thing. She hasn't even noticed that there isn't a swarm of wolves circling around like there typically is." Jade shrugged.

"Did you do that?" I asked.

"I'm not that kind of witch."

Gage stepped in and leaned against the doorjamb. He grinned at me, and I felt all full of butterflies. "Your parents won't notice anything out of sorts."

I drank in every second of him as he walked over to the bed and leaned in for a kiss. I hummed with pleasure.

"Ah, you're in love, that's so great." Yuki gushed.

"You have magic?" Jade asked.

Gage shook his head and lifted his shoulders. "Monsters and magic. It's a new moon. Those three have different magic surrounding them than the rest of us." He looked back at me. "Your parents and the FBI won't even question why there are three extra guys around, and why they have the same names as the wolves. I don't know how it happens. We are all learning this as we go and faking it at best. This certainly didn't come with a user's manual."

"You mean you?" I didn't finish, because I wasn't sure what to say.

"I'll explain, promise. You be good today. I'm headed out to the grocery store for the big feast. More ice cream, ladies?"

"Of course," answered Yuki.

13

————

Travis may have claimed to not be able to cook much beyond the basics, but the man was a grill master. There was snow on the ground and he still knew how to grill steaks and salmon to perfection. All of the guys apparently pitched in and made a feast once a month. I understood this was a big family celebration for them. Tracey and Ben joined as a very happy couple. I and mine were welcomed with open, loving arms.

I ate until I thought I was going to pop. Of course, I kept eating. It was better than Thanksgiving. They played music via satellite radio and at some point, people were up and dancing. Oz caught Jade's attention, and he was the middle of a Yuki and Jade dance sandwich. My parents danced in an old fashioned style, even though they really weren't that old. It's not like they grew up doing that type of social dancing, I've seen what dancing in the seventies and eighties looked like. Tracey and Ben were also up. Occasionally, Mark or Zeke would jokingly twirl Travis across the floor.

It was wonderful and happy. Next time, I'd be able to

dance, and I wouldn't have to worry about my backside hanging out cause at some point, I'd be able to put something other than a hospital gown on.

I needed to get off antibiotics before I could start wearing regular shirts because of the IV line. Of course, I'd have to send someone out for them, or I bet I could order some. Gordon had my credit card, I guess not. I just wanted to be able to put my kind of clothes on once I was set free from this snapped together drape. I didn't want another drab colored t-shirt, and never again did I want to wear gray sweats.

I'd be able to wear panties as soon as I was allowed on my feet. Without the ability to balance to pull my drawers down, it didn't make any sense to wear them. The hospital gown and blankets made sure my bits were covered.

And even though I had easy access under my clothes, both Gage and Max behaved like perfect gentlemen. It was awesome. They made my heart soar like it had wings. Gage had carried me down and I swear he looked as smitten as the day he carried me up the stairs and I felt like a bride, even if I was an invalid.

Max gave me a proprietary smack on the lips and made sure I was comfortable. Gage sat with his arm around me. It was those annoying sweethearts being sticky sweet on each other kinds of actions that made me want to shiver and brush my teeth when I see other couples acting like that.

Okay, I get it now. It's really hard not to be sappy as fuck when you are really in love this way. No one said boo that it was three of us behaving like that. Hell, the guys didn't even growl or anything when Travis snuck in and kissed me. I was a little surprised, especially when he winked and told me, "We are pack. We are yours."

"Come sit next to me, Oz." Yuki hung off his arm, excited for the movie, or life in general.

Oz shoved away from Yuki. "I'm going out," he growled.

I don't know what happened between them, but clearly, something had. A few minutes ago he was in a good mood, now he was cranky as fuck.

"I thought you would want to stay and watch a movie with us." Yuki sounded hurt.

She didn't understand his anger, and he didn't understand her lack of interest.

"I'm not interested in your stupid movie. It's a waste of my time. I'm going to go find some friends to hang out with."

"I thought I was your friend?"

"Oz, wait, I should tell you about Yuki." Jade stood up and approached him, reaching out to touch his arm.

He batted her hand away. "I don't need to be friend zoned by some virgin. I don't have time for that shit. I've already spent too much time with her."

"Then you should've been aware of what she was." Max sat back down next to me.

"You can go to hell. You claimed a mate the second you saw her. Hell, you were also all over Yuki as soon as she got here. You don't get to have all the women." Oz's neck tightened and the tendons stood out.

"Chill out, man. All I was trying to say was you can't get mad about Yuki, and you aren't being friend zoned by some shy virgin. I don't think you can call someone who isn't sexual a virgin. It's not a measure that applies."

"Fuck off. You're only not interested in Yuki because you have Bailey. Brooks has his wife, what am I supposed to do?" Frustration rolled off him in waves. Everyone in the room could feel it.

Thank the gods my parents had volunteered to do the dishes. This was awkward as hell to witness.

Oz was clueless. Jade was interested and willing to jump his bones, perfectly happy for no strings attached rumpus time with some pretty abs and strong arms. But he was too butthurt that Yuki wasn't going to flip up her skirts and let him at her.

Max gave him a knowing look and looked at Jade. Even he knew Jade was interested.

Oz shook his head, threw his arms up and stomped out of the area.

I watched him go. I think we all watched him go.

He paused and looked at Travis. "How do you put up with it? I'm so sick of their shit." He kept going until I couldn't turn my head anymore.

Travis caught my eye and winked before leaving in the opposite direction.

I huffed and turned my attention back to Jade.

She stood perfectly still in the middle of the seating arrangements. Her hand rested across her abdomen. A sneer grew on her face as she looked in the direction Oz left. "Asshole."

She was pissed, she was so pissed. And she was hurt. I knew her. I could feel her sucking in energy like an ocean pulling the tide back out. I had experienced that sensation before. I never knew or recognized it for what it was.

Yuki was up and wrapped around Jade. "Don't be sad, friend. Boys are stupid. Men are smart. Oz is clearly a boy in a man's body. You know what, I think Mark is a man and he likes you."

Everything about Jade softened, and she wrapped her arms around Yuki. They hugged for at least a minute, and the tension in our little area dissipated.

"Mark? Huh? I think he's scared of me." Jade laughed.

"There is nothing wrong with having a man be a little afraid of you," Zeke said.

Mom and Dad approached carrying two huge bowls of popcorn. Travis had an armful of drinks, cans of sodas and beer bottles.

"That nice Mark said he would finish up so we could come watch the movie with everyone," Mom announced. She handed one of the big bowls to me.

Travis pulled a handful of brown paper lunch bags from his back pocket and started handing them around. "For the popcorn."

He sat on the floor in front of me, so I had him and Max surrounding me.

This was nice. Almost everyone was here.

"Did you leave Gage in the kitchen with Mark?" I asked my folks.

"I'll go swap with him," Jade announced. I guess she decided having Mark a little afraid of her wasn't such a bad idea, especially if Oz was being a super douche and ignoring what she was offering. Besides, Mark was hotter, in my opinion. But I knew Jade preferred the stockier build and blonder look of Oz.

I expected Gage to come join us at some point. I forgot about it as I was sucked into the movie.

About halfway through, I really had to pee.

"I'm sorry." I couldn't apologize enough for disrupting the movie.

Someone put it on hold while Travis and Max had to get up in order to lift me from my nest on the couch.

Max carried me effortlessly to the bathroom. I awkwardly dragged my IV pole along. The bathroom had a stall and a sink. The stall was left over from when this had been a commercial property, kept because they still ran it as an exclusive training facility. Max didn't seem to mind, and I was embarrassed.

"Bailey, it's my privilege to take care of you." He knew the right things to say.

When we headed back to the lounge area, everyone was up and running about. Okay, maybe not running, but something was going on.

Zeke jumped down the stairs two at a time. "No Gage. Jade and Mark are occupied."

Oh good for her.

"What do you mean no Gage?" I asked.

"I guess he wasn't in the kitchen. He's probably taking the garbage out."

Travis shook his head. "He's not out back. It's snowing, so if he left footprints they're covered, no tracks. No way of knowing if he went out that way."

Max lowered me back onto the couch into my nest of blankets. "Stay here. I'll be right back."

Where was I going to go, and more importantly how was I going to get there? "He wouldn't have left because of you?" I asked. Max seemed to know what I meant because tonight Max claimed me solo. Of course, I would think after last night Gage wouldn't mind, because he would get me solo as soon as Max shifted back. I shivered. I didn't want to think about that.

"No, that wouldn't send him off."

I didn't have a chance to ask him more questions. He kissed me, and my brain melted. All I could do was watch him stride like some kind of superhero out the front door. He didn't even grab a coat, and it was snowing.

Yuki climbed onto the couch with me.

I know Mom saw me kiss Max, but she didn't say

anything about that. Maybe she had missed out on all the sparks between Gage and me earlier too.

"He'll be fine. He's a police officer after all. Why don't we finish the movie?" She started the movie.

It was a good attempt at distracting me.

It didn't work.

The movie ended. I don't remember what happened. I mean, it was billed as a rom-com so I assume they ended up together. I don't know why they would; they really didn't like each other. I was getting tired of that whole enemies-to-lovers trope. Especially when I was blindsided with attraction, why the hell would I even want to pay attention to someone who antagonized me so much?

Mom and Dad announced they were going to bed. "You should get to bed too, and soon. This has been more activity than you're used to."

They said their goodnights and left Yuki and me cuddled together on the couch.

Yuki and I watched them climb the stairs, and then we looked at each other. We were alone. No wolves, no guards.

"I'm gonna go get Jade." She was off the couch and then I was alone.

The living room was creepy and too big now that everyone had left. The entire other side of the room was in the dark since we were all gathered around the big screen TV for the movie. I hoped Yuki and Jade would come back soon. Hell, I wished anyone would come back soon. I didn't like the thought that Gage had left without saying something.

I heard shouts from outside. I turned and nervously watched the front door. I wanted to get up and go look out the window. Suddenly, there was a loud thunk and something heavy hit the wall from the outside. That was it; I had to go see what was going on.

I wish I could say I ran across the room and looked out the front door, but that's not what happened. I started trying to limp my way across the floor. I walked on the heel of my left foot and a slow step with the entire right foot so that I didn't put weird pressure on the areas trying to become infected.

I stopped in every seat I encountered. All two of them. I just couldn't walk.

There were shouts and yells and I couldn't get to the door.

Jade ran in front of me. Her hair was a mess, and she was wearing Mark's shirt. Go, Jade!

"What the fuck do you think you're doing?" she yelled at me.

I pointed, and Mark was already ahead of us and throwing open the door.

"I don't know what's going on, I was left all alone, and Gage and Max are out there."

Mark dragged someone in by the armpits. He lay Gage down on the floor. His face was covered in blood.

"No!" I cried out. I couldn't tell if he was breathing.

Mark was up and out the door.

I wanted to throw myself across Gage's chest and sob. But I was stuck, I hurt, I didn't have it in me for one heroic adrenaline push of energy to get to him.

Fortunately, Jade was mobile.

She knelt by his side and put her hand on his neck.

"He's alive."

I sat back and sucked in air.

Jade continued to do something to Gage's head but I closed my eyes, he was okay.

I heard the rest of everyone run back inside one at a time. Heavy footfalls accompanied by heavy breathing.

"That was fucked up," Travis announced as he came in last.

I got up on my knees and turned so I could see over the back of the chair I was in.

Mark kneeled by Jade. Travis was next to the closed front door, hands on knees. Zeke was holding his nose; a stream of blood ran down the lower half of his face and onto his shirt.

Max glowered over Gage.

"What happened?" I asked. I hated that I was helpless in the face of something that looked really really bad.

"The official story is going to be a bear," Max grumbled.

"That wasn't a bear," Travis said standing up.

Mark helped Jade roll Gage on to his side.

I hissed.

The back of his shirt had been torn like party streamers and the skin underneath shredded.

Jade leaned in and sniffed his back. She flinched.

"Witchcraft." Jade's voice went funny. "It tried to move into him, but he already has his own monsters." She sat back and coughed.

Her eyes locked with mine and my blood ran cold.

"Whatever is trying to get to you through Gordon, tried to get into Gage. But he's protected." Her gaze landed on each of the men in the room. "You're all protected."

"What are you saying?" I felt hopeless and dumb.

"You aren't only dealing with a serial killer, you have a demon on your hands, kiddo. I always thought Gordon's aftershave smelled funky. But I can smell its scent on Gage. Torment. Torment kills joy."

Max lowered himself and picked up Gage as if he were light as a feather.

He directed Travis to take care of Zeke, and Mark to get Tracey. He turned to me. "You don't go anywhere until I come back for you. Stay off your feet. Jade call the FBI. Can you suss them out? Make sure they're clean somehow?"

"Only if I can be in the same room with them."

Max grunted. "Do what you need to, this asshole went and made everything about twenty times more complicated."

"What about Oz?" Yuki asked.

"He's probably found a nice warm bed to occupy himself in. I'm not worried about him, so neither should you be."

Everyone went to their assigned tasks, and yet again, I was left on my own. I refused to be helpless in the face of this new information. I stood up. It lasted about two seconds and then I was in Max's arms.

"What did I tell you?"

"I hate being like this. I can't even walk across a fucking room," I cried.

Max picked up my IV pole with the hand of the arm under my knees. He carried me upstairs like it was no big deal.

Gage was already in my bed when we got there.

"He'll heal better with your comfort. And this room is already set up with all the medical toys."

"Toys? Seriously, Max," Tracey chastised him. "If you guys keep bringing injured people in at this rate, I might finally convince you to set a proper medical ward, with hospital beds and everything."

Gage's shirt lay around him, clearly, it had been cut off.

Tracey used swabs to clean the cuts along his back. I

couldn't see because I lay in bed next to him, staring at his face.

He hurt, and some of the cleaning caused him to wince.

I stroked his face. I was rewarded with him opening his eyes and giving me a weak smile.

He grabbed my fingers, hard, and kissed them. "I feel better already."

"Jade said a demon did this?"

He nodded. "I fucking hate demons. Bailey, I think it was Gordon."

PART II

FINDING HOME

1

I woke up after a night of the second best sex of my life with a large fluffy white wolf in my bed. When I had fallen asleep, he had been a very sexy, very muscular man. If that didn't illustrate how bizarre and fucked up the past two and a half weeks of my life have been, I don't know what would. My very ex-boyfriend took me on a romantic getaway which turned into a kidnapping that I managed to save myself from. During my escape I caused severe damage to my feet, resulting in losing a toe to frostbite, falling into the company of a group of the world's sexiest men, and discovering that one of my best friends is a witch. Oh, and it turned out the ex might be a demon, and he was definitely a serial killer.

I snuggled my face into the wolf's fluffy ruff and took a ragged breath. I didn't want to cry.

"I love you, Max."

In return, I got a whiney growl. Nice.

"Good morning, Doggo?"

He thumped his tail on the bed and squirmed until I lifted my face away from him.

I got a face full of doggy breath, and a drooly lick. I shoved on his vast body. "Get out of my bed you big phony."

He rolled off the bed, and with the agility of a cat, landed on his feet. Had he merely been a big dog, there would've been a definite thud, but he was wolf plus extra, and that extra gave him some additional skills. His paws were back up on the bed, and he gave me a big doggy grin before trotting out of my room.

I laughed. The gloom chased away by the big silly fluff.

"Good morning." Gage's gruff morning voice zinged through every cell in my body. He moved with stiffness as he came into my room and sat on the bed.

Two nights ago his back had been shredded by a demon that looked like a bear crossed with a bull. It had tried to take over Gage, but his magic protected him. All I knew was he claimed to be some kind of monster. Something very much like Max, but Gage's power uses the full moon.

Was Max a wereperson? A wolfwere? A therewolf? I didn't know what Max was—precisely. He was like a werewolf, but instead of being a man who shape-shifted into a wolf on the full moon, he was a man living as a wolf who returned to human form on the new moon. I didn't know how all of it happened, and I only believed them because yesterday Max was a tall, gorgeous man, complete with hard muscles, gloriously shaggy long hair, and a smile that could melt chocolate.

I watched him shift two days before that. And then he and Gage double-teamed me for the very definition of mind-blowing sex, which was beyond good, because I had fallen hard for Gage. It turns out I had fallen pretty damned hard for Max too. Last night with him had been pretty outstanding as well. Just him though. I'm not sure if that's because Gage was injured or because Max had claimed me to mate first.

I still wasn't keen on the whole claiming thing. When Gage tried to explain it the first time, I turned around and claimed him. Honestly, I still didn't know what anything meant. Hell, it could all be a delusion brought on by pain medications, or I could be dying in the woods having escaped from my suddenly violent and abusive boyfriend Gordon. I'm pretty sure that part was real.

There wasn't much I could do no matter the situation. I couldn't walk on my feet, so I was on strict bed rest, and I was hooked up to an IV with some seriously heavy grade antibiotics. I also recently had the pinky toe on my left foot removed because of frostbite.

"You okay?" he asked. I figured he was asking if I was handling the fact that my new lover turned into a furry beast.

I wrapped my arms around his waist and leaned against his lower back. "It's all kinds of weird, Gage. How much is real? How much is a dream?"

He twisted, so I pressed my face into his hip. His fingers traced my jaw and then my shoulder. It was an awkward position, so he touched what he could reach. "At least you didn't say nightmare."

I rolled away and started to sit up. Even though his movements weren't as fluid as they usually were, he moved with swiftness, gathering my extra pillows and helping me into a sitting position.

"Nightmare?" I huffed. "There is no way I could ever call the other night a nightmare. Okay, maybe the whole demon thing is a bit freaky, but..." I sighed and then shivered. Yeah, the memory of the sex and of him touching me was that good, so good.

Gage laughed. He leaned in for a kiss and said, "I love you." And then his lips were on mine. I melted. Somewhere, there had to be a Bailey shaped mold I was continually re-poured into to return to my human shape because I was gooey around Gage most of the time. But I knew that wasn't the case. If it were, I'd have my toe back.

His lips were soft and warm, and he poured everything he was into that kiss. Gage was a giver when it came to kissing. He gave me his strength, his passion, his intensity. He gave, and I was a greedy, selfish bitch and took. I held his head to me and sucked his tongue into my mouth to play with mine. I didn't take simple little kisses from Gage, not when his mouth rendered me into a vibrating mass of nerves and need.

He growled low in his throat and pressed me back into all the pillows he had, five seconds ago, arranged so nicely. Pillows went flying as he drove me down to the mattress.

I loved the look on his face when he finally broke off the kiss. My heart pounded in my throat, and he had taken all of my breath. I reached up and toyed with the curl above his forehead. I could live here forever, just as we were, as long as he looked at me like that. His eyes were soft and had a happy gleam sparkling in them. The smallest smile played across his lips. And it somehow made me feel as if I were everything to him.

I instantly felt guilt over Max.

"Hey." His voice was soft. "We are pack. Everything is fine."

"You say that, but I'm not pack, and I don't know exactly how to manage these feelings," I confessed.

I knew I said the wrong thing when he left the bed and headed for the door.

I was surprised when he closed and locked the door

instead of walking through it. He pulled his shirt off while he faced away from me. The claw marks across his shoulders glowed in angry red lines.

I blinked. Those had been raw and bleeding, and in serious need of stitches less than forty-eight hours ago. Now, they were healing and shrinking. They were still huge marks, and the skin pulled, but in comparison, they looked as if they had been made weeks, maybe months, ago and not a day ago.

Damn the man had wide shoulders and a broad chest. He also had a bit more chest hair than I thought I would ever be attracted to. It was curly and slightly more auburn that the chestnut hair on his head. The sheer quantity almost obscured the rock hard definition of his chest. The hair thinned out as I scanned down his body—no sexy little happy trail disappeared into his jeans. A fine dusting of body hair covered his abs. It wasn't fair how hot he was.

I sucked in a sharp breath when I looked back into his face. His crystal green eyes now held something more aggressive in those depths than that look of love I saw moments before. He stalked back to the bed and was over me again. "Do you love me?" His voice was thick with emotion. I cringed because I thought I was hurting him over the Max situation. "Bailey, do you love me?"

I nodded my head and bit the inside of my cheek. I didn't want to cry. I was in love with Gage, and yet everyone, including Gage, knew I had slept with Max last night. How was I supposed to live with that?

"I'm so sorry, Gage," I barely whispered.

"For what?"

"Max." His name was barely a breath. The guilt forced air from my chest like a pile of stones pressing me down.

"Do you love him?"

I nodded. It was hard to say anything with Gage's eyes boring into me.

"Then what's the problem? Bailey, I love you. Max loves you. We are pack. We are yours."

"But, I wasn't loyal to you." Tears stung my eyes. I was in love with both of them. How was that going to work?

"Because of Max?" Gage rubbed his face against the side of mine. "I think we need to clear something up." His voice sounded lighter, not laced with the anger I expected. Not drenched in hurt or pain. "We are pack."

"You keep saying that and I don't know what you mean," I cried out, the need of him and the guilt over Max too much.

Gage nipped at my chin. Oh gods, what was he doing to me? I was confused, but my body didn't care. My body seemed to know I belonged to this man.

"There is no guilt or shame for being with any of us. We are honored you want to be with us."

"You are speaking in the plural, Gage. I need simpler words. I need, ahhh—"

He sucked a nipple into his mouth; my thin hospital gown offered no barrier between my skin and the warm wetness of his mouth.

"You need me." His lips tickled as he spoke against my skin.

He was right. I needed him. Him making love to me right now was the only thing that would keep my brain from shattering under the confusion, guilt, and pressure of all the weird shit that was happening in my life. But my stupid mind would *not* let this go.

I gently pushed him back and started to sit up. When had he taken his jeans off? He was more than a bit distracting, kneeling on the end of the bed, ready to spring into action with one hell of an erection. I hiked my hospital gown up onto my shoulder. I wanted whatever meager protection I could have between us for the moment.

"You and Max regularly share lovers?" I needed to know where I stood with him.

He huffed, not quite a chuckle. A sexy half grin pulled at the side of his mouth. "That was a first."

Excuse me? "No way. You definitely knew what you were doing, that could not have... no."

"Bailey, you inspired us. That's all I can say. I have never shared a lover before."

"What, not even a three-way with two girls?" I couldn't help but ask. Those were supposed to be fun. I wouldn't know though, having never been invited to play before.

Gage shook his head.

"And never again?" Which would be a shame. I'd happily be the cheese in their sandwich again.

"I wouldn't say that. Bailey, we are pack now, and I take care of the pack. So, if that means I find myself in bed with you and Max, or you and one of the others, I won't complain."

"Wait up. You said others. What?" Why was he complicating things?

"We are pack. We are yours." He said that like some creepy cult mantra.

I covered my face. I wasn't getting the message. The words he spoke and the meanings in my head didn't mesh.

"Gage, are you telling me you want an open relationship?" I didn't do open relationships. Either I was in a relationship, with no outside dating, or there was no relationship. He said he loved me; he claimed me. That sounded like a relationship to me.

"Not at all. I'm saying there is no guilt, no anger if you

decide to take the pack to your bed. That is what I mean by we are yours. It is always *your* choice." His voice was substantially calmer than I expected. He was giving me the go-ahead to bang other men, and it wasn't bothering him.

"You're telling me I can take another lover and you won't get pissed off? I can screw Travis or Oz, and you'd be fine?"

He breathed heavily through his nose. The reality of me having someone else finally touched something off in him. Good. I was feeling a little used since he wasn't getting possessive.

"Not Oz. You can have Travis or Zeke, or both, probably not Mark—I think he has succumbed to the lure of your witch. Oz is not pack. Brooks is not pack. Besides, he's married."

"Oh, come on. We are pack. They aren't pack. Which is it? You can't have it both ways." My voice got louder, shrill even.

"Oz isn't my pack. He is New Moon, not Full Moon. I am Alpha of the Full Moon pack. Me, Travis, Zeke, and Mark. Oz and Brooks belong to Max. They are New Moon pack. We're two packs. You only claimed me and by extension, my pack. You didn't claim Max."

I spoke slowly, "But Max claimed me. And he let you claim me. Oh..." Realization dawned on me. That's why it was a big deal that Max allowed Gage to claim me. "Max is Alpha."

Gage nodded.

Two alphas were sharing *one* me.

"But Max isn't your pack, but somehow I'm in both packs?"

Gage shook his head. "I'm not one hundred percent clear on that one. Max claimed you and didn't challenge me when I also claimed you. Your counterclaim brought my pack into it somehow."

"So, if I were to sleep with someone, not in the Full Moon pack?" I was asking for clarity.

"Only pack. Any other man and you will either have to release your claim on me or expect there to be blood." He sounded pissed. Finally. Not that I wanted him to be angry. I wanted to know I was important to him.

"Whose? Mine or his?" I snapped right back at Gage.

"His and mine. I'd never hurt you. I love you." He reached out to stroke my fingers. "And I will continue to love you even if you were to release your claim."

I twisted my hand so that I was holding his. I focused on our fingers lacing and twisting together. Touching, not resting.

I sucked in a shaky breath. I didn't know if I wanted the answer to this next question. "And how many women am I supposed to be okay with you sleeping with?"

He lunged forward. I had pushed him too far. How dare I demand he not sleep around when he was telling me I could?

He hovered over me, and the sheer look of adoration on his face seriously brought tears to my eyes. He was big, and he could be dangerous and aggressive. But I hadn't angered him as I thought. I finally said something that made him sad. I reached up and cupped the side of his face. He leaned into my hand, closing his eyes.

"Only you. From now on, only you. You claimed me out of love, and there is some serious magic in love."

My heart melted. I lifted my head to kiss him, and he dissolved me back to goo.

"And you're okay with me sleeping with Max? It won't

make you crazy mad at me, or your friend?" I asked him, not entirely sure I was comprehending all of it.

"It will drive me crazy, but I will never stop you from doing it. I will, however, be in your bed the second he leaves to remind you of who I am to you, just as I came in here this morning to do. We are pack, and we are yours. I cannot control that or be angry about that." His voice had an edge to it. I couldn't tell if he was annoyed or having a hard time explaining something that wasn't easily explainable.

"Is this how Max sees all of this too?" Was he going to be open and welcoming if I slept with other men?

"You have to ask him. He tends to be very possessive. Or you could have sex with Travis and see if Max kills him."

The smile he gave me made me forget everything I worried about. The kiss that followed chased all thoughts from my brain. I held him close, and my hospital gown found its way off. He felt magical, all of his warmth and strong muscles. I loved his hair and skin.

His mouth was on me, my neck, my collar bone, and my breasts. He wasn't fancy. He took me simply, wonderfully, and downright orgasmically.

"I love you," I whispered to him when he curled up next to me.

"I love you. Have the pack if you desire. I will always be here."

I snuggled into his chest and didn't worry about anything.

"Eh hem," Tracey announced her arrival into my room hours later.

I was groggy—sex drunk. I pulled a blanket up higher on my shoulders. It's not like it hid anything from her. Gage was asleep and wrapped all around me. His clothes were scattered everywhere.

"Good morning," I said with a froggy voice.

"Hardly. It's afternoon," she chuckled. She fussed with another bag of antibiotics.

She reached up and hooked my IV up to the new drugs.

"I need to change your dressings later. You should probably take a shower first. Get this one to help with that." She stopped talking and focused on his back. She nodded. "These are healing nicely. They were nasty, weren't they? He should have full range of motion back in his shoulders today if he doesn't already."

She headed to the door and stopped. "I'll be back in an hour. That should be enough time to get cleaned up. I'll find you a fresh gown."

2

I was so tired of this room, especially when Gage wasn't around. It was fine to hang out and watch movies with Yuki and Jade, but dinner with my parents was awkward. I had a bed tray, and they balanced plates on their laps.

I know hauling me, and my IV line, downstairs wasn't the answer, but there had to be a better solution. I wasn't in a position to do anything about it, and I never remembered to ask Gage the next time I saw him.

Let's face it; my short term memory was muzzy because of the drugs. And when Gage was around, I wasn't thinking about my parents. If he was kissing me, I wasn't thinking anything at all.

Tracey came in while we were eating. "Why don't you ask one of the guys to bring up some of those little TV tray folding tables?" she asked as she eyed my dad struggling with where to put his plate.

"We don't want to be a bother," Mom said.

Tracey huffed and left the room.

"Mom, it's not a bother to ask."

"Of course it is. You saw how annoyed she was just now." Mom pointed out the door, indicating Tracey.

"Mom," I said the word in three syllables. "She left in a huff because you won't take care of it yourself, and she feels obligated to have to do it for you."

"Well, she didn't have to." Mom pouted.

"No, I didn't," Tracey said announcing her return. "But I couldn't bear to watch one of you spill your dinner all over your laps."

She unfolded one simple pine wood table in front of Mom and another one in front of Dad. "Better?" she asked.

"Much," Dad replied as he settled his plate and fork down.

Tracey fussed with my antibiotics, another bag.

"Am I ever getting off this stuff?" I whined.

"Soon," she promised.

Tracey passed Gage on her way out, as he stepped into my room. My brain stopped working. He was ridiculously handsome in his dull khaki and olive uniform. I wasn't a uniform groupie, so that wasn't it. I was a Gage groupie, and he'd be sexy in one of my ridiculous pink tutus.

He gave my mom a light hug and kissed her on the cheek. What the hell had been going on while I was trapped in my room?

"Good to see you, son," my dad said as he shook Gage's hand.

What? Dad called Gage son?

Gage sat next to me on my bed and patted me on the leg before leaning in to kiss me on the forehead.

I tried to talk into his head. I focused hard on his ear.

Nothing.

I tensed my whole face and focused harder.

Gage turned his face to mine and smiled. I slumped back, giving up.

"Glad you were able to stop by tonight. I wasn't sure if we would get a chance to see you before we left in the morning," Mom cooed.

My mother was cooing at Gage. Dad had called him son, and they were...

"What? You're leaving?" I hadn't expected that.

"Of course, sweetie." Mom smiled at me like I was some kind of idiot.

Okay, I pretty much was an idiot these days, but I swear I would've been able to remember if my parents had told me they were leaving.

"Your father has to get back to work. And we don't want to get stuck here in the snow. The lodge is lovely and big enough, but you don't need your parents nosing around."

I tried to smile. I have no idea what my face looked like. I nodded and pretended I knew what the fuck they were talking about. Gage squeezed my knee reassuringly. I interpreted it to mean he knew what was happening, even if I didn't.

"I wanted to make sure I got a chance to see you before you left. I've got a long shift tonight."

Everyone nodded as Gage explained why he wouldn't be around in the morning.

He stood up and leaned over me, giving me a soft kiss. "I'll check in on you when I get home."

I reached up and grabbed hold onto the front of his shirt. "I'll be asleep," I whispered.

"But I won't be." The low rumble of his voice gave me goosebumps.

He shook Dad's hand again and told him to drive safe.

"Now, you take good care of my baby. And make sure she comes home for a visit when she is back on her feet."

"Yes, Ma'am. I will."

Gage let my mom fuss over him a few more minutes, and then he left.

Dad picked up the tray tables and folded them against the wall.

Mom hugged me. "You've got a good one there, Bails. I don't think I could've asked for a nicer son-in-law."

I stopped breathing. I left the insipid I-know-what's-going-on grin on my face as Dad bustled Mom out to get her to go pack up since they were leaving early.

And just like that, I was alone and super confused.

Max?

Gage?

I tried to call out mentally but got nothing in response.

"Aaarg," I growled and thrashed about in frustration. I couldn't jump out of bed and chase someone down who might know what the hell was going on. I knew better than to ask Mom what she meant, but I was pretty sure that Jade or maybe Travis would be able to clue me in.

I grabbed the remote and aggressively hit play for the movie in the DVD player. I grumbled at the screen for all the inequities of wanting to find romance during the Regency, and for being stuck in bed with a movie as my only option.

I woke up with Travis sliding out of bed and whispering something. I don't think it was to me. I rolled over.

"Huh?"

Gage slid into the empty space and wrapped his arms around me. "Changing of the guard, go back to sleep.

I hadn't remembered Travis cuddling up with me. Mighty Bast, was it possible I didn't remember getting married? Things were happening around me that I wasn't involved in, but were directly about me. Was it possible I didn't remember everything clearly?

I wanted to ask Gage about it, but he was already breathing the deep, rumbly even breaths of sleep. I snuggled back against him and let myself be content to be in his arms.

I blearily remember hugging my parents' goodbye, and Gage, fully dressed and up, tucking blankets around me, telling me to go back to sleep.

"Wakey, wakey, eggs and bakey!" Yuki rhymed as she bounced on my bed.

I opened my eyes and pushed up into a sitting position.

"Yuki, what's going on around here?" Maybe she would give me a straight answer.

"It's lunchtime. You need to get up. Gage isn't around so I can finally talk to you. When Doc MacGee said to stay off your feet, I don't think he meant to get on your back."

"Hey!" That was judgey and embarrassing.

Yuki cackled that magical laugh and I smacked her with a pillow. Good thing she was my best friend, or I would have to get Max to bite her or something.

"Seriously, how many days has it been since the new moon? I can't seem to focus. Everything is all muzzy and fluff." I pointed to my head.

She sat back on her heels and shook her head. "That doesn't sound right. You have been really sleepy the past few days. Have you said anything to Nurse Tracey?"

"I haven't seen her." That wasn't exactly true. I had seen her, but it was always while I was mostly asleep, and she was always so sweet not to wake me up any more than she needed too.

"Did Mom and Dad leave?"

Yuki nodded. "Dad had to get back to work." Yuki was

that extended family member type of bestie who called my parents Mom and Dad.

"But why did they... I mean how..." I sighed heavily. I didn't have a clue how to ask this without sounding like I hadn't been actively participating in my own life. "Why did my parents leave thinking Gage and I were married?"

Yuki giggled. "Oh, that. Jade has magic. I guess she and Gage decided your parents would be safer back home. The FBI guys said Gordon wouldn't be interested in them. He never goes back and interacts with the family or anything. So..." She shrugged.

"But, how?"

"Magic. Jade and I know that Mom would never leave you here alone, even if we were with you. And considering how she thought you and Gordon were going off on a little pre-marital honeymoon, we figured if you were married..."

"Holy Hecate, you got Gage to marry me while I was asleep?" Damn, that's not something I wanted to miss.

"No silly. Magic, remember. Jade did her thing and made your parents think you had gotten married. They won't remember Gordon."

My eyes felt like they were bugging out of my head. "Um, what will they remember?"

"You went on a vacay with us, and eloped with Gage." Jade strolled through the door carrying a tray with food.

"I thought your magic didn't work that way," I said

My stomach grumbled. I hadn't realized I was hungry. Actually, I couldn't remember the last time I ate.

"It doesn't, but his does, and together we were able to get your parents to think a certain way that made them happy, their brains took the suggestion and ran with it."

Yuki adjusted some pillows for me, and Jade set the tray over my lap. Mac and cheese. But not boxed noodles and sauce, this was fancy spiral noodles with thick oozing cheese and flecks of bacon and peppers. Yum.

"I'm surprised there was any of this left over from the other night," I said as I eyed the bowl in front of me greedily.

Gage had made the fancy mac and cheese to accompany the grilled meaty deliciousness of the big feast the guys had put together the night of the new moon. As a consummate mac and cheese expert, I declared his cooking to be fantastic.

"These aren't leftovers. Gage made a big mess of this stuff just for you," Jade explained.

I sighed. Things inside of me melted like the cheese.

"And that right there is why it was freaking easy to convince your parents that you had fallen head over heels in love with this big burly sheriff and run off and married him," Yuki explained.

"Playing dodge 'em with the FBI and your parents took some juggling, but I think Smith and Jones appreciated not having to deal with your mom. She was a pit viper there for a couple of days," Jade added.

I looked up at her, a fork full of gooey goodness halfway to my mouth. "If Mom no longer remembers Gordon, she won't remember what happened to me."

I let the fork drop. I wasn't sure how I felt about that. Not that I thought anyone should have to remember the violations Gordon did to me, but now, I didn't have my mommy to curl up against and protect me if it all came crashing back.

Doggo padded into the room and lay his big muzzle next to me on the bed with a soft whine. I reached over and scratched behind his ears.

"Hey, big guy."

He licked my fingers. Right, Mom might not remember,

and that was probably best for her sanity, but this guy did. Gage did. And they would protect me. But could they protect me from myself? From the demons born in my brain? I picked up my ponytail and pulled my hair around so I could see it.

I sighed. Orange as a pumpkin, left out in the rain and rusted, carrot top, orange. At least that part of my ordeal was wearing away. My eyebrows were fading quickly, and by the end of the month, my pubes would most likely be fiery again.

The hardest violation for me, because it was the one that tried to erase the muchness of me, was when Gordon dyed my natural warning-label red hair brown. All of it. Lured to sleep by love and a hot bath, and probably some drugs, he had colored all the hair on my body, cut my fingernails, and tried to convince me that I was losing my mind.

I still had my fingers and focus on my hair before I realized Zeke hovered by the door, and Travis was sliding into the bed to curl around my side.

"Is your brain being stupid?" Yuki asked.

When I blinked to look up at her and nod, that's when I realized I was crying.

Jade took the tray of food away, and Yuki curled up against me on the opposite side from Travis. Doggo jumped onto the bed and lay across my upper legs. Soon Jade and Zeke were also cuddled in around me.

"It's okay to be sad," Travis whispered. "We will always catch you when you stumble."

"And if I crash down?" My voice sounded so stupid and tiny and beat.

"One of us will pick you up and carry you until you're ready to fly again." I think that was Jade.

"I understand why you did what you had to for my

parents. And you're right; they probably are safer at home. Back where the monsters are still a secret, back where I still had shine. But it's not fair you know. Mom gets to forget, and I get to pretend it's in my past when it can slam into me at any second. When do I get to be safe?"

There was a low growl from both Travis and Zeke. Yuki and Jade each held on a little tighter.

Max was too quiet; there were no words in my head from him and no growls either.

Quiet Max scared me.

3

I had a good cry surrounded by my friends and support structure. I was warm and safe. With friends like these who needed blankets?

I still had a small hole they couldn't fill. I'd never have my mommy hold me and tell me it was going to be alright. Okay, to be fair, she hadn't done that for years. Maybe Gage's arms could fill that hole, or Max's. Right now, I had neither.

Doggo was big and warm, and scary protective, but Doggo wasn't the same as Max. I guess having different names reminded me of that.

My tummy rumbled. Loudly. "I'm hungry," I whimpered.

Jade shifted first. "You haven't really eaten for a while. Let me go heat your lunch back up for you."

Zeke followed her off the bed. Yuki sat up. Travis still held on, and Doggo didn't budge.

"Okay, fellas," Jade announced when she returned. "You need to let Bails up so she can eat."

Travis helped me sit up and adjusted my cadre of pillows.

"Max, that means you. She needs to eat."

Doggo gave Jade a wolfy glare.

"Hey, Doggo, wanna go out into the woods with me?" Yuki asked, and Doggo growled at her.

"Just the back yard. Maybe Oz will come with. Come on, let's go outside. Snow is fun," she coaxed.

Doggo gave her a resigned sigh and followed her out of the room.

"I see Yuki has regained her pied piper skills. Brooks took off with her and Max." Tracey swept into the room. "Oh, good, you're eating."

"Hey, Tracey," I said between bites.

She shook a baggie of medication at me. "Last one," she announced as she proceeded to hook up my IV.

"Promises, promises," I muttered. I had heard that all before, and then the wounds on my intact foot decided to get infected.

I had always thought that a month in bed with a bevy of hot guys would be more entertaining than this.

Oh, right, when I had Max and Gage, it certainly was.

"You okay?" Tracey asked. She reached out and felt my cheek with the back of her hand. "You're flush. You shouldn't be getting anything with all these antibiotics."

I rolled my eyes from side to side. I had a mouth full of noodles and really couldn't figure out how to talk around them. I gulped the food down. "Blushing," I muttered.

Tracey did her thing, and I ate. It felt weird to be left alone and return to the professionalism of being a patient after the mini meltdown I just had. I was going to be okay. I knew it, even if I didn't feel like it at the moment.

"You done?" Tracey took the tray. It was that time again. I nodded. Feet cleaning and bandage change.

I lay back, and Tracey started to cut the bandages from my feet.

"Bailey, your feet look fantastic." She pulled out her phone and started taking pictures. "Doc MacGee is going to love this progress."

She changed gloves and went back to caring for my feet.

Her phone pinged...and pinged again. "It's going to have to wait," she grumbled as she finished bandaging my feet, and wrapping my legs back in the self-inflating compressors. I loved those things; they were like mini leg massages.

I settled back, and she pulled out her phone. "Good news, doc wants you to start walking."

"What?" I sat back up. I hadn't been on my feet more than a few minutes in the past three weeks. "How?"

"We have those walking booties for you. Next time you have to go pee, let's give 'em a try."

Suddenly, I was very nervous. Would I remember how to walk? Did my legs work?

I knew I was a mess, but today seemed like the day for an emotional roller coaster ride.

For the record, I immediately had a love-hate relationship with those walking booties. They were hard and hurt my feet. But, and this was massive, I was able to go pee all by myself. And that meant I could finally put clothes on. I was so tired of having my ass hanging out.

When Gage got home from his shift and came to sit with me, I dissolved into a blubbery mess.

I hadn't had any emotional support buddies since lunch. When he came in, I latched on to his waist and collapsed across his lap.

The smooth, even strokes he pet down my back as I cried on him somehow calmed me. I couldn't talk for a while, couldn't tell him how unfair it all was that Mom didn't have to remember, but I did, and that my middle was covered in bruises from the heparin shots. I was starting to look like a leopard, but couldn't appreciate my spots.

I could go pee by myself but didn't have any clothes to put on. That of everyone here, why did it seem like he was the only one who ever went to work? And he was always at work. None of it was fair.

"Bailey, sweetheart." The smooth sound of his voice was like a comforting blanket. Warm and soft, and I wanted to curl up in it forever. "When you're ready, I'll listen."

I sat up to face him. There was so much fighting for dominance in my head. I wanted to start with the big rocks, maybe blast them into pebbles I could manage. I opened my mouth, and the most important thing came out first. "I don't have any underwear."

"I thought you gave up on undies until you can balance on your own?"

"That's just it. I can."

His eyes opened wider, and he smiled. He saw good where I saw obstacles.

"I've gone to the bathroom by myself twice now. I have these stupid ugly booties, and I'm allowed to walk. But, I don't have any clothes, and it's cold out, and my ass is hanging out of my hospital gown. I can't even hold it closed," I wailed.

Gage laughed at me. I didn't find the humor in any of it and glared as he chuckled. "It's a very nice ass. I don't mind watching it hang out."

"I don't have any clothes, Gage! My good stuff is lost at some bed and breakfast, and I don't think Mom is planning on shipping me any."

"You want me to see if Travis has any sweats that might fit you?"

I understood why he picked Travis. The man was pretty

and cut, but not a big tall guy. His clothes would work on my body. If Gage offered me clothes, they would swallow me whole.

I shook my head. Travis would have gray sweats and faded T-shirts. I just couldn't put on anything faded and drab. Especially not now, not ever again.

"I need color, and sparkles, and laser cats on unicorns. I'm never putting another a pair of gray sweats on, you can't make me. Besides, I need panties. I can't go out shopping in a hospital gown."

Gage started to make a rumble of noise.

"And my friends aren't allowed to run out to the store to find me anything," I kept whining. It was whine or cry.

I wasn't having a good day. I could walk on my own; it should have been a fantastic day.

"Can I get some cheese?"

"Cheese? I thought you wanted underwear?"

I nodded. "Cheese will go better with all this whine."

"Wine?" He looked at me like I was a freak before he started to truly laugh. He gathered me to his chest and stroked my hair.

"I'll get some fruit and bread, and we'll make a picnic of it. Complain all you need to, Love, it helps. Maybe we can send your witch out with Mark. In the meantime, why don't you order some clothes online?"

I returned his smile with a little one. "On what? With what? I don't have a phone or a computer, and Gordon has my credit card. The FBI said not to cancel it."

After a short debate on whether or not I'd allow Gage to pay for my clothes, he won.

I was still going to be confined to rest, but, and this was the cool part, it didn't have to be in my bed. Well, I was still on an IV, so my bed was the easiest. And until I had panties to cover my rump, I wasn't too keen on hanging out in the big lounge anytime soon. Panties were a game changer.

~

Yuki was evil and had a mean streak. She was, I swear. Her sweet demeanor fooled everyone. After all, she was *Delight*. But delightful or not, she was wicked, and I'm never letting her help me buy panties. I may be majestic as fuck but one of the reasons that can happen, was because I believed in comfort.

And comfort meant cotton panties that covered my ass.

Gage decided he would let Travis take Yuki shopping for me. Since neither the Sheriff's Department nor the FBI had seen anyone remotely looking like Gordon around, he figured a quick run to the local big box store would be fine. As my bestie, I assumed I could trust her with my undergarment selection.

Travis sat on one side of my bed with a fetching half grin, half seductive smirk on his face. I wondered what the two of them had gotten up to. It couldn't be too much. I had been pretty specific with Yuki on what I liked and what my needs for panties would be. I could trust her not to bring back anything gray for me to wear.

Yuki bounced on the other side of the bed with excitement. I practically bounced too; I was one shower and a clean pair of panties away from a little freedom. I was getting pretty tired of being in this room.

Yuki acted like it was Christmas morning and I was opening presents. I had four plastic bags of assorted clothing on my lap. The first thing I pulled out was a perfect unicorn T-shirt, complete with a rearing unicorn and dolphins doing flips in the air, above a rainbow. Two more shirts of equal majesticness followed. One pair of fleece lounge pants and two pairs in flannel came out of another bag.

Yuki was spot on with my fashion needs. These pants were not plaid but covered in taco-cats, more unicorns, and narwhals. I think the narwhals were my favorite, mint green and oh-so-soft. The next bag revealed super soft socks and a mint green hoodie.

"So, these socks aren't exciting, but they're specially made for people who get swollen feet. It's what Tracey told us to get you."

Travis snickered when I made it to the last bag. He had been shopping with Yuki; he should know my undies weren't anything to get excited about. I don't do sexy undies. I want to put on underwear and forget I have it on. I don't want to fuss with scratchy fabric or strings up my crack. I expected to unveil at least one three-pack of cotton briefs with a soft elastic band to sit just below my natural waistline, and full ass coverage, in assorted colors. What I pulled out was a shoestring with a bow on it.

"You willing to model?" Travis's voice was husky and sexy.

I shoved him back with a hand to his face. "What the hell are these?"

I dumped the bag. Not a single pair of cotton briefs and no comfy pull-on sports bras either. As a member of the itty bitty titty committee, I didn't fully trust Yuki to get the right underwire full girl support I needed. The girls aren't huge, but they are big enough to require support.

Yuki had the world's cutest bras. I had skin toned comfort and scaffolding. The cost of a perfect bra was like a car down payment. I needed those things to be serviceable. As much as I would've loved a beautiful bright pink and zebra striped bra, I couldn't afford one. I didn't wear enough black or fishnet: black to hide the show through, fishnet to show that shit off.

Yuki had bought me the kind of undies she liked to wear. Yuki wears teeny tiny scraps of lace, that if she were into sex would be considered sexy, but it's lace, and it's Yuki. She wears them because "they are pretty."

She picked up a pink string, "Look at this one, don't you love the color? It's so pink."

"It is a fabulous pink." It was. "But Yuki, I can't wear this. It'll give me a wedgie."

I turned to Travis, "I'm sorry, but you're going to have to take all of this back."

He looked dejected. "What, not even one pair of lacy underthings? I promise you won't have to wear them long. Just long enough to model them and let me pull them off with my teeth." He waggled his eyebrows at me.

I know Gage said we were pack, and if I wanted some rumpus play time with Travis that would be fine. I gave him a once over with my eyes. "Maybe one pair. But the rest goes back."

4

My feet ached. They were sore and throbbing, but in a completely different way than they had been. Before, the injuries and the surgery pain stabbed and was sharp. Now, my feet had a dull ache because the stupid walking booties were hard and flat, and didn't have any support like athletic shoes or good working shoes did.

I whimpered and tried to get comfortable. The stupid IV prevented me from rolling over. There were stupid, extra bodies in my bed that got in my way. I pushed hard on the nearest chest, forgetting in my sleep rage that it belonged to a person.

Travis caught my hand against him when I tried to push again. "You okay?"

His voice was groggy and full of sleep.

I snatched my hand away from his. "No, I'm not. I can't get comfortable, my feet hurt. This stupid hospital gown is strangling me."

"I'll get you an Advil. That should help." Zeke slid from the bed and padded across the room.

I pulled at the gown that was twisted up around my

waist, trying to go back to front, and choking me in the process.

Travis sat up and quietly situated my IV. He then reached over and attempted to fix the hospital gown. In the low light of my room, I could see he was perplexed.

"Bailey, how did you manage this?"

I grumbled.

He reached up and slowly untied the neck. I assumed he was going to readjust it for me.

A hand with a pill and a glass of water appeared before me. I took the pain meds and swallowed all the water. The entire time I held Zeke's gaze as Travis continued to remove the offending hospital gown. There was something in those eyes. I was mesmerized.

"Shall we take your pain away?" Zeke took the glass, and then caressed the side of my face.

"Yes." I barely breathed. He wasn't talking about more pills.

He smelled nice. His lips were soft and warm as they pressed against mine. I moaned because Travis had sucked one of my nipples into his mouth.

I guess his plans changed, or his plan had never been to fix the offending garment—just take it off. That was one downside to when I'd finally get some panties—wiggling out of clothes. This insta-naked thing wasn't half bad when my bed partners were naked, hot, and hard.

Zeke's tongue took that as an invitation to tango with mine. It was an exquisite, slow and sexy dance our tongues played with each other. Ever so slowly, I was lowered back down to the bed.

I'm not sure whose mouth was whose, and there were so many hands. I couldn't touch all the warm skin available to me. Flat firm pecs and pointed nipples tickled my palms as I caressed the bodies on either side of me.

Mouths changed, and one pair of lips kissed a trail down my belly as another pair kept my mouth occupied. I forgot what we had been doing before. Had we been doing anything? Right, my feet hurt. I couldn't have said if I had feet anymore.

My hand skimmed down a taut set of muscular abs. And I clenched my fingers into a thatch of hair. A hand, presumably belonging to that body, pushed my hand down further and I grasped onto a firm, thick dick. It pulsed in response to my grip. I always thought that was an erection's way of saying, *"Hi, nice to be had, have more."*

I moaned. It was loud since there wasn't a mouth on mine to stifle any sounds. That mouth had moved down my neck and was licking, yes, licking its way toward my breasts.

"Oh, damn." I was never going to have sex with an individual guy again. Who was I fooling? I'd bang the hell out of Gage one-on-one any day. But, Holy Hecate, this two on one thing was amazeballs.

I thought I heard the latch on the door snick, but a second later someone's tongue found my clit, and I was too worried about levitating off the bed to be concerned with the door. Jeez, the magic that tongue delivered. I could probably open my eyes, and in the low light see who was doing what. If I paid attention to the hair under my fingers as I cupped that head to me, I could figure it out too, but I was too distracted.

I tugged the penis in my other hand toward me and turned my mouth. Damn if he didn't taste divine. Warm, salty male. Before I knew what was happening, I had another cock in my hand. We must have looked like a super sexy game of twister—mouth on dick, tongue on clit, dick in hand, mouth on nipple.

We writhed and moaned, and soon all the bodies were no longer separate, we were all connected. I lost the cock in my mouth and found another pair of lips.

I knew this mouth. I loved the way this mouth tasted and made me feel. "Gage." I smiled against his lips.

I froze. All action stopped, and I tried to push back and look at him. "Gage!"

He chuckled that warm rolling sound of his and pulled me back to his mouth. "We are pack."

Oh, gods yes, they were pack, and they worked like a fine-tuned engine. All my parts were thrumming from their ministrations.

For a brief flash of a moment, I was worried that my lack of acrobatics wasn't providing enough stimulation to all involved, but then somehow I ended up on my hands and knees, and I had a cock at both ends. Well, not *that* end. I'm not big into butt stuff. But the lady garden was getting a ramming, and the mouth had a suck fest, and the boobs were worshipped.

I got flipped around and was on my knees, sitting on someone's face while I got a face full of another set of cock and balls. I had another dick in my hand, and I was doing my best to make sure it was a happy one. My hand ensured it was delivering pleasure with confirming pulses and throbs.

I probably should have kept track, but with three of them, and in the dark, it was difficult to a certain extent. Gage's chest was unmistakable with his carpeting of chest hair, but both Travis and Zeke were smooth, silky skin over muscles of forged steel. I had never kissed Zeke before, and Travis only once or twice and those had been pecks, so I didn't know their mouths. After a while, lips were lips and tongues were tongues, and I could no longer distinguish Gage's flavor from the others.

Their glorious cocks were all so amazing and perfect. One was more substantial than the others; I could only tell when it filled my mouth. And while I thought that might be Gage because he was proportionally larger all around, I couldn't be sure. At one point or another, I had each one of them in my mouth and at another point in time, thrusting inside my sex.

We throbbed and pulsed. I screamed into the night, into mouths, and around cocks. I came from tongues on my bits, and from being pounded into. After three orgasms, I thought for certain I was done for the night.

At one point, I was left with only two lovers while the third disappeared. He returned with slippery, tingly lube, and my lady bits were revived and ready for more. I had zero complaints. The three of them made sure every nerve ending in my body sparkled and exploded like stars lighting up the sky.

There was a massive difference from when Gage and Max and I had been together. The three of us had made love as a group, to each other. Gage and Max had pleasured each other, stroking and kissing each other, and I had been the cheese in their sandwich of love. Tonight, I was the center of attention. From what I could tell, the men played solo, working in parallel to make me come and scream and come again.

"I don't know how much more of this I can take." I was exhausted. My muscles could barely function. I was ready to tap out. "I can't be the only one having orgasms around here."

"But it's so much more fun to watch you scream." Travis's purr placed him as the cock nearest my mouth.

"You aren't the only one who has come tonight." I couldn't tell where Zeke was from the sound of his voice.

"But you're all still going. I thought most men pop, and they're done."

The face between my thighs started laughing. Oh, that motion by my clit nearly sent me over the edge again. I thrust up seeking out more magical tongue. That was Gage. I was going to have to remind him how fantastic laughter while going down on me was. He obliged, and I mewed as he sucked my clit back into his mouth and swirled his tongue around me.

Holy Hecate, this was more than I could handle. I could no longer hold my thoughts together as another orgasm shot through my body. Fireworks exploded behind my eyes, and my internal muscles clamped down on the fingers that continued to thrust into me.

I cried out and pulled the closest cock I could find into my mouth and sucked hard.

"Okay, Bailey, you want me to come?" Travis—I now knew it was him from sound location—stroked the side of my face as I pulled hard.

I could barely nod; my need was all consuming. I held onto what I could grab that meant mouth, hands, sex.

Fingers weaved into my hair, not for the first time tonight, but this hold was harder. He thrust into my mouth as I sucked. I couldn't take him all the way into my throat, too much gag reflex, but I had hands and a needy mouth. I fucked him with my mouth as Gage was fucking me with his. Zeke had his mouth and hands occupied with my nipples.

Travis whimpered more than moaned, a sound I had yet to hear tonight, and hot liquid salt poured into me and down my throat. I continued to suck him down like he was a frothy refreshing milkshake.

I was still crashing around Gage's fingers when Travis pulled back. His mouth descended on mine. "And now I'm spent too."

I moaned and gave one of those whimper moans as Gage disengaged from me.

Travis's mouth was replaced by Zeke's.

"Your turn?" I asked.

"I finished a while ago. You're too hot to hold back with," Zeke answered.

"But you stayed." I pointed out.

"We're here for as long as you need us to be." Gage's voice was thick and full of lust. He crawled up my body, and I was forced back again.

"I think I'm done," I said with a heavy sigh. "Are you?"

"Last man standing," he chuckled as he hovered above me. I wrapped my hands around the thick arm muscles that bulged as he held himself up.

"We'll let you finish without us." I felt a parting tweak to one of my nipples, and I arched up.

Gage took that as his cue and crushed me against him.

Okay, I admit, all those hands, and all those mouths, and all the cocks were fantasy level personal porn come true. And from a sheer sexual pleasure standpoint, I don't think anything can top it. But one-on-one, crushed to Gage, this was love made physical, and I knew I couldn't live without him.

He thrust into me, and muscle memory told me I hadn't had him deep inside tonight. Yes, he was larger than the other two. My body held on and welcomed him home. As if none of the orgasms I had earlier mattered, my clenching muscles sprang back to life, pulling him deep inside with each, and every, stroke.

"You aren't mad that I was fooling around with them?" I asked. It was hard to think, and his actions said he wasn't mad at me, but, of course, that nagging little part of my brain picked now to make sure Gage still loved me. As if I couldn't tell by his forceful strokes and hot breath on my neck.

He pushed in deep and held me hard in place.

"Bailey," he whispered against my collar bones. "We are pack, and you can take all of us."

I ran my fingers through his curly hair, wishing for a split second that it was a bit longer.

"You still love me?"

"God woman, what do you think? I'd rather share you than lose you. Yes, I love you." His strokes started up again, slow, steady, rhythmic.

I held back a cry. The reaction my body had to his was so much more intense than anything else tonight.

Gage braced against the bed and thrust into me deep, hard, and powerful. He repeated the harder action and growled my name. He was close to coming. I already was; with each one of his thrusts, I spasmed around him. I felt him throughout my entire being.

"I." He pounded against me. "Am." *Slide back, thrust home.* "Alpha." Each word emphasized by another thrust. "And only I come inside you." With that, he released hot and hard. I could feel it, not just warmth and wet, but a gush of liquid against my insides. Everything was soaked and slippery.

Gage thrust faster, and I continued to come until I couldn't move and was crying.

Finally, Gage stopped. He froze in place. I think all of his muscles seized at once. His entire body was hard as granite, and then with a shudder, he relaxed.

I cradled his head against my chest, stroked his sweaty brow, and played with his hair.

"Would you grow your hair longer if I asked?" I know stupid post-coital discussion topic. I should've been mewing and telling him how much I loved him.

He rumbled with a laugh. "How long? It gets bushy and wild if I let it get too long."

I wouldn't mind seeing him a bit wild. "Not that long, maybe another inch or two. I want more loopy curls to play with."

"You got it, no more haircuts until you tell me."

"You'd really do that?" I couldn't believe it had been that easy.

"I'll do anything for you."

I sighed and twitched as my body zapped with residual electricity. "I noticed. That whole we are pack thing is pretty spectacular."

"We are yours. But remember, you can only do that with pack. Or Max. And I will always be the last one to come for you and the very next man who loves your body."

"If I didn't love you, I'd think that sounds a bit stalkery and possessive." I coiled the long curl at his forehead around my finger.

Gage shifted and rolled. I lost his hair but found myself surrounded by arms and the wall of his muscular chest.

"I am possessive, Bailey. I can't help it. But you claimed me, remember?"

"I remember. I claimed you out of love. I kind of like it

when you get possessive. It means you love me. And I want you to be the very next man I make love to every single time. Even when you are the one who just loved me until I have no bones," I purred.

"No bones, huh?"

"Nope, none."

5

————————

My underwear needs baffled Travis. He was tasked with returning the strings of butt floss Yuki had him buy. He managed that part of his task without any problems. Buying a pack of cotton briefs, size eight was apparently beyond him.

I made him return the nylon monstrosities he came back with.

"Cotton, my crotch needs cotton."

Tracey laughed as I threw the offending package of panties at Travis. He caught my throw and ducked out of the room.

"You need some help getting clothes?" she asked.

"They did fine on the clothes, it's the panties they can't seem to get right," I moaned at her.

She approached me with a handful of test tubes.

"What's all that for?" I asked.

"Blood draw. Make sure all the infection is cleared up, and then Doc MacGee will let you get off the meds, and then no IV."

"Freedom?" I asked. I was able to do some very light

walking, to the bathroom and back. I had made it out as far as the hall, but since my butt was still exposed from lack of proper panties, I hadn't gone exploring. My IV was on wheels, so between that and my naked ass, I was still pretty restricted to my room.

"You'll be on partial bed rest, and of course there is your FBI issue. So, I guess freedom is a relative term."

She finished siphoning my blood. "Maybe I can help with your undies situation. What do you need?"

I explained I preferred cotton briefs, nothing fancy, but color was always welcome. Gave her my size, and asked if she could get me one or two of those pull on comfort bras.

The girls were missing their extra support. My boobs do pretty well for an hour or two without anything, and I wanted to keep them that way. So far they hadn't had any lift support for weeks and coupled with the weight loss, I was afraid they were getting droopy.

She promised me she could handle cotton panties and asked if I had any secondary preferences.

"Hip huggers, but not those high leg things. They give me wedgies."

She laughed. "Anything else?"

I played with my blanket. "Yeah, could the medicine have caused me to lose a few days?"

She gave me one of those you-have-five-green-heads looks.

"After Max and Brooks and Oz all turned back, I swear I lost a few days. All of a sudden the FBI isn't asking me to repeat myself, my parents up and leave as if they had been here for weeks and weeks, and I didn't see Doggo for days."

The bed gave a slight bounce as she sat. "It's always hard these first few days. You said you feel like you've missed them? I'll switch with you in a heartbeat. For me, it's been an eternity."

"Brooks?" I asked.

She nodded.

"But Gage had huge gashes along his back, and now he doesn't even have scars. I mean, wasn't there a demon?" I laughed, sounding like a lunatic. No wonder she thought I had five green heads.

"It's been four very long days. Usually, Brooks is by my side for a week after. But with that demon out there, and the FBI here, he has been going out searching the woods."

"So, they're looking for this thing?"

She nodded. "Definitely. You know they think it's your boyfriend."

"Not my boyfriend," I growled.

"Maybe whatever your friend did to your parents to get them to leave affected you. I heard she got your parent to believe you and Gage are married. Some honeymoon you got stuck with." She patted my knee and stood up. "I'll get you some underwear when I go shopping tonight."

She looked sad. It must be the reminder that Brooks wouldn't be around for another month.

"Did you know Brooks before? You know, before whatever changed him?"

"Sure did. We had just started dating, but I knew I was going to marry him, even back then. I wasn't going to let him changing into a wolf let him get away from me so easily."

She laughed, and the sadness left her face. She waved as she left the room.

I was going to have undies by tomorrow.

Maybe.

When Tracey presented me with the much-anticipated

three-pack of panties, I was ready to shoot off the bed and put some on.

She snatched the package from my grasp, understanding my intentions. "Not until they have been washed. You don't want to go putting all those fabric treatment chemicals on your pubic region."

She did hand me something to keep my mind off the fact that I had to wait at least two more hours for a laundry cycle. Shoes. But not just any shoes, pink, fur-lined Crocs.

"You were complaining that the walking booties were too hard against the bottoms of your feet. Doc said Crocs would be good. They're big inside, so there is room for your feet to swell."

They were pink and squishy. I was so excited. Today was going to be a good day.

I was wrong.

Agents Smith and Jones came for a visit. They wanted me to tell them everything I could about Gordon.

"Like how he turned out to be a serial killer?" I sneered.

Everything I thought I knew about my boyfriend had been a lie. Why did they need to know how big of a patsy I had been? I had been taken in by his web of deceit. I convinced myself that I had fallen in love with him and that he was in love with me. He was nice to my friends and kind to my parents.

Yes, they had permission to retrieve my clothes from the bed and breakfast to see if they could find any traces of him in my clothes. I was so mad at Gordon. The Sugar Plum Bed and Breakfast should have been the most wonderful of memories for me. It was a fairy hideaway, and I belonged there. But I never wanted to see that place again. I'd never be able to forget that's where he hit me for the first time, and

I was stupid enough to convince myself it had been an accident.

"We are the closest we have ever been to catching this man. Do we have your full cooperation?" Jones asked as they stood to leave.

"Of course. I want him caught; I want to know that I can tuck these memories away for good. It's one of the reasons I'm sticking around." They didn't need to know the other reasons were the men. While I might be able to leave Travis and Zeke, and I might be able to convince myself that Max was merely a fever dream, I could never give up Gage. I hope he realized that.

Jade brought up my new clean undies, still warm from the drier. It was such a wonderful, warm, comforting feeling to have on clean undies. My skin finally felt like it could relax, no more surprise licks of cold air in places it wasn't welcome.

Never underestimate the power of having a warm butt to make you feel better. I pulled on the taco-cat pants and played tiger-tiger in picking out my shirt. Mistake.

I was so used to the IV, that it didn't occur to me that I couldn't put a T-shirt on until I got tied up in a knot with the IV lead and my bra.

"Help," I called out.

"Are you all right?" Travis asked as soon as he stepped into the room. He didn't make it any more than a step or two before he started laughing. Loudly.

"What happened? Is Bailey okay?" Jade asked as she hurried in next.

Travis leaned against the wall howling with laughter, and I sat on the edge of the bed, boobs hanging out, with my arms stuck over my head twisted up in the bra and the IV.

"Help," I said again.

Jade laughed, but she wasn't overcome with it. She pushed Travis out of the room and called him good for nothing. I had to agree.

"I guess we forgot about this didn't we?" she asked as she untwisted me.

I was glad she included herself in that, after all, she and Yuki had suggested the sloth shirt with the cat pants for my first fashion statement, post-hospital gown.

She did up the snaps on the hospital gown and made sure the back was tied up.

"How soon before you're off this thing?" She wheeled the IV back into place.

I huffed. "I have no clue. Tracey took some blood earlier. As soon as those test clean, I guess I have to wait."

I wanted to wear my new clothes. Honestly, I simply wanted to wear clothes. I flopped back on the bed and thrashed a bit in a toddler fit.

"Better now?" Jade asked.

I nodded.

Yuki bounced into the room, a pair of scissors in one hand, and a jar full of safety pins in the other.

She made the scissors go snick-snick as she gleamed wickedly. "Crafty time!"

I love crafty time. We collectively decided that the pink stripes would be the victim since cutting it up the middle would not destroy a unicorn or a sloth. Yuki cut open the sleeve to the neck and did the same opening the front.

I wasn't going to cut apart a bra. That would undo the elastic benefits. I was going to have to go bra-less. Jade and Yuki scrambled over each other to pin me in. The fabric overlapped and was quite snug across my middle. I truly had lost some weight. My bit of extra middle padding was practically gone. The boobs would have strained the limits of the shirt before we cut it apart. There was no way the fabric was willing the meet in the middle now. The pins created a ladder and cleavage effect. It was a bit sexier than I had intended.

"Yuki, this shirt is entirely too small," I complained.

"I got an extra-large," she said.

Jade grabbed my other shirts. "Yuki, are these kids shirts?"

"She wanted unicorns and cute things like she normally wears. That was the only section that had fun shirts," she told Jade. "Those pants are actually men's. I don't know why they think guys want to wear narwhals, but I figured you wouldn't care," she explained.

I laughed. "Yeah, that explains why the shirt is so tight. Yuki my boobs don't fit into kid's clothes. Hell, I'm surprised it fits at all."

"I wear kid's clothes all the time."

"Yuki! I'm like twice your size. Didn't Travis say anything when you were shopping?" I flopped my one free hand around. The sleeve was skin tight. I had to keep the other one still as Jade pinned me in, and left an opening for the IV.

If I had been feeling better, I might have appreciated the aesthetic of the tight pink on pink stripes and the gold tone of the safety pins. I might have wanted to work that exposed cleavage to my advantage. But right now, I wanted to be comfortable and not in a hospital gown.

"Travis thought I should have gotten you a T-rex shirt instead of the sloth," Yuki answered.

"You're both hopeless when it comes to shopping!"

"But you look pretty, and look Bailey, color!" Yuki waved her hands at me as if she were presenting a consolation prize on a game show.

She was right. I had on clothes! And I had my colors back, and if I had better balance, I would have spun in a circle and maybe danced a bit.

"Okay, you think you want to try to go downstairs?" Jade asked.

"If I go really slowly and one of you carries the IV pole, it should be good." I wanted out of that room so much.

I gently put my feet into my fluffy lined Crocs and grabbed the IV pole. "Let's roll!"

6

P art of the way down the stairs I realized it was a mistake. Walking put one kind of pressure on my feet. Stairs were a different beast altogether. I made it down to the first landing. I sat on a step and held onto the railing. Zeus's testicles this was hard. But, I was out of my room, and I didn't want to go back.

Jade and Yuki hovered. I felt so stupid and incapable. My feet were pissed off. My missing toe was *really* pissed off. I didn't have proper balance for stairs, and I held on to the rail like a toddler learning how to walk. Damn, I was such a loser.

I didn't want to cry, but I could feel it starting in the back of my throat.

I hadn't seen Mark in days, pretty much since the night of the big 'everyone's human' dinner. He slid an arm around Jade's waist and kissed her. That was good. I'm glad she found someone. Mark was a good guy. Of course, he was— he was pack, and I was biased.

"Need some help?" he asked.

I blinked up at him and nodded. I couldn't say it out

loud, couldn't ask anyone to pick my ass up and haul me back to my room.

He hunkered in close and told me to put my arms around his neck. "Ready?"

I nodded, and he scooped me up. I couldn't help but notice he smelled good.

"Um, I thought you were going to take me back up?" I asked as he started going down the stairs.

"You were coming down for a reason. Might as well come on down for a bit. I'm sure you are getting stir crazy in that room." He had a lovely voice. I wasn't checking him out, he was Jade's, and I had more than enough. I was merely observing, having never been this close to him before.

He deposited me on the couch in the lounge area with the big TV.

"Thanks," I said first to Mark, and then to Jade, who set the IV pole next to me.

Now what? I was out of my room and in the big room downstairs. That had been my goal—my *only* goal. Now, I wasn't certain what to do with it.

"Can I bring you anything?" Mark asked.

I looked around and shrugged. "I think, after a bit, I'll go exploring on this level if that's okay?"

Mark nodded and left. Jade followed him.

"Oh, that will be great. I can show you where everything is." Yuki was now my self-appointed tour guide.

"Everything?" I asked. "Like, what's everything?" I didn't know what was available around here. I had been in through the front door, and of course, downstairs for the big dinner party, and that was it.

"Let's see," Yuki dropped on the couch next to me. This level is shaped like a big X."

"This level?" How big was the lodge?

She nodded. Pointing slightly to the right she said, "That way is the kitchen and a service elevator downstairs." She rotated and pointed behind us, to what was the middle of the X shape where a heavy oak-beamed long counter and huge front doors were. "So, that used to be the check-in desk. I guess it still is when they have retreats here. Over there behind those double doors are some conference rooms."

The areas she didn't point out were obvious; open seating on the opposite arm of the X from us with a large stone fireplace and an even larger oil painting of what could only be a landscape of Yellow Stone; and a small restaurant-style dining room directly behind us, with another colossal fireplace and painting. Another landscape, this painting featured a beautiful mountain waterfall in the middle of the forest. That must be the waterfalls that gave this town its name.

"There aren't any antlers in here." There were no hunting trophies at all.

"I noticed that too. I'm glad because the wild boar down-stairs creeps me out."

"What's downstairs?" I knew there were stairs going down, the grand staircase kept on going with flights wrapping around and down.

"Downstairs has a bar with pool tables and the stuffed boar. The laundry and equipment storage are down there. Travis showed me this huge pantry in case they get snowed in for months. There's also a patio like thing, but that's mostly for getting the camping stuff in and out. If you want to sit outside, the front porch here is huge, and there is a fire pit on the back deck."

I blinked, it sounded like this place was bigger than I expected. Of course, I really hadn't put too much thought into it. It was a big building; I remember that much from when we first arrived. And I knew my parents had a suite, not just a room. But I was in what was essentially a generic hotel-like room, with extra medical equipment brought in. It was large, bedroom sized, nothing special. I had no idea how many rooms there were.

Feeling curious, my feet weren't throbbing so I stood up.

"You want to go look around?" Yuki asked.

Brooks and Oz pushed through the kitchen doors. Brooks went straight to Yuki's side. Oz let out an audible sound of disappointment and found a spot to lie down. Brooks was so big she didn't have to reach down to scratch behind his ears in greeting. "Oh, your fur is so cold, you must have been playing out in the snow."

Brooks took that opportunity to shake as if he had wet fur. Fortunately, he wasn't wet, but fur took flight.

I wafted the air in front of my face, not wanting to breathe in wolf fur. It couldn't be good for the lungs.

Yuki giggled and headed for the kitchen. I guess that's where my tour was going to start. I grabbed the IV pole and slowly, carefully took a few steps.

Travis burst through the service doors and gaped at me. It was the first time he had seen me in clothes. He gave me a wolf whistle and slid up next to me. "Don't you look sexy?" He tried to wiggle a finger into my exposed cleavage between pins.

His fingertip tickled my breast, and I giggled at his touch and flirting. He cupped a breast and ran a thumb over my nipple. It stuck out a bit without a bra to contain its enthusiasm.

The noise was more like a roar than a growl. And then Doggo was on top of us, having bowled both Travis and me over. It sounded like a truck came crashing through the service doors from the kitchen.

Max's growls and snarls gave me chills, and that was before I saw his jaws wrapped around Travis's arm. Max was trying to get to the other man's neck.

I picked up the IV pole and hit Max as hard as I could several times. Someone was screaming. I didn't know if it was me or Travis or Yuki. Mark appeared out of nowhere and grabbed Travis out from under Max's jaws. I slammed a fist into the wolf's snout.

MINE, YOU ARE MINE.

Loud and fucking clear in my head for the first time in days, Max snarled at me. Blood covered his muzzle.

"How dare you! I may be yours, but he is *mine*. And if you ever want me to be yours again, you had better learn to respect that!" I don't know where I found the courage to yell at him. He was terrifying, but I was pissed off.

The wolf lunged at me but stopped before he attacked. I fell back screaming, terrified. After all, a wolf I had trusted for safety and security, and let in my bed, was now attacking one of my lovers and me. I couldn't fight him. I didn't have any strength or weapons.

"I thought you loved me." My voice was small and scared. I didn't want Max to hurt me. I didn't think I'd have the wherewithal to survive it if he did.

Doggo...Max, whoever he was right now, stared at me for what felt like an eternity. And then he ran. Like a shot, he tore through the lounge and crashed out the front doors. Faster than I realized I was capable of moving, I was on my feet and dragging my IV after him.

"Max!" I shouted. "Max." This time I was crying. He was gone.

"Who are you?" a woman with flowing golden hair asked me.

About halfway up the front steps, a beautiful woman with perfect hair and perfect makeup, in a designer winter coat stared at me.

The cold hadn't yet hit me, but I was very much under-dressed for the weather. Looking at her designer coat, I realized I should be cold. I probably didn't look like I belonged at some exclusive executive retreat lodge. She did. The large wolf running past her didn't seem to bother her in the least.

"I'm Bailey. Look my friend is hurt. I need to get back inside." I pointed with my right arm over my shoulder.

She nodded and followed me in.

Travis was on the lounge couch. Mark and Jade were washing him off and bandaging his arm. He cussed—a lot.

Yuki sat in the corner crying with Brooks pressed into her. He looked like he was ready to take on anyone who said anything threatening against her. Oz looked bored. He was still pouting from the other night.

The woman dropped her purse, also designer, onto a chair and rushed over to the scene. "Where's Gage? Someone should call Tracey." She took her coat off, and to no surprise, she was dressed in professional designer clothes.

I hobbled over, completely useless. I didn't have a phone, didn't know Tracey's number. Didn't have a way of contacting Gage. Didn't know where any first aid supplies were. Completely useless.

I sat in the closest chair I could find, staying out of the way.

"Bails, come here." Travis winced.

I hobbled over to him and sat on the arm of the couch.

He reached up, and I held his hand. He squeezed hard as a wave of pain hit him.

Ms. Professional and Perfect stood up and pulled her cell phone out. She spoke with abrupt, authoritative tones. I noticed she hadn't gotten any blood on her. I had blood splattered across my front, and there was a lot of it on the floor.

It looked like a lot of blood. My vision went blotchy, and Travis was squeezing my hand extremely hard again.

I rolled back to consciousness with Travis's face close to mine. "I'm the injured one here, no trying to steal my well-earned attention." He gave me a dazzling smile that I could tell held pain.

"Sorry, but the blood," I managed to squeak.

"Bailey will be fine. You need to keep pressure on that bite. What the hell got into Max?" Jade asked.

"Tracey is on the way," the woman announced.

"Gage said Max didn't share well. I guess he didn't like the tickle Travis gave me. That or he's lost it, gone wolf completely," I answered Jade as I pushed back up into a sitting position on the arm of the couch so I could be next to Travis and continued to hold his non-injured hand.

I looked over at the woman as she watched us curiously. For a second, I panicked, but Mark and Travis seemed to know who she was. We shouldn't have talked so openly like that around a stranger.

"I'm sorry but who are you?" she asked me again.

"I'm Bailey," I said as if that answered everything. "Who are you?" I had to ask since no one was forthcoming with introductions.

"I'm Gage's fiancée, Kathleen." She blinked at me as if I was the one asking dumb questions.

I gaped at her. Unable to fully fathom the words she was saying.

"Holy shit, what happened here?"

Suddenly, my attention was grabbed by agents Smith and Jones running from the front door to Travis. Jones had his hand on his holster at his back and was eyeing a crying Yuki crowded by a large wolf. "Are you okay miss? Miss?"

Yuki finally wiped her eyes and nodded. "Just a little scared."

"Did one of these animals do this?" The agents became more official than usual. "Whose blood is all over the place? Should you be cleaning that?"

Jade had come back in from the service doors and was beginning to clean up all the blood. I felt woozy again. I wasn't sure if it was the blood, or the fiancée, or being up for so long.

Tracey ran in and pushed Agent Smith away from Travis. She worked efficiently and smoothly. Gloves on, syringe prepped and, "This is going to poke a bit." She began injecting Travis in several places around his arm.

I should have stayed in bed. I started crying.

"Look, I don't know who you are, but right now, this isn't about you, so pull yourself together," Kathleen ordered.

I was too emotional, too overwhelmed, and also too freaking nice to say what I wanted to say. I cried more instead of telling her that this was, in fact, all about me. Me, me, me, me, and me.

"Someone get some towels," Tracey said to the room in general.

Kathleen walked off with purpose; clearly, she knew where the towels would be located. I didn't have a clue.

"Yuki, why don't you and Brooks go outside for a bit? And take Oz," Tracey directed. I guess the wolves were distracting. And Yuki still crying wasn't helping. I was crying, and I know I wasn't helping the situation.

"Should we be concerned with what's going on here?" one of the Feds asked.

"What is going on here?" Gage asked as he took off his gloves, having come in from the cold. He watched a sad Yuki walk passed him and gave me a confused smile, before giving the agents a nod of greeting.

"Bailey, you're up and dressed." Gage blinked at me. Seeing me in all my colors must have caught him unexpectedly. Maybe he hadn't believed me when I said I lived in color. His eyes lingered on the cleavage treatment of the tight T-shirt. He swallowed, hard. "You look amazing."

Gage sidled up next to me and ran a proprietary hand down my back. I leaned away. I wasn't really happy right now on so many levels—so many. One of them being Gage having a fiancée. I don't date men in relationships—ever. So, I had another fantastic entry for my memoir on how completely a little romantic vacation could and did go wrong. Great, let's add adulterer to the list.

Travis bit out a sound of pain. I squeezed his hand, and he gripped back harder.

"What happened to him?" Gage asked.

"Looks like one of your dogs went after him," Smith said.

"When you find the animal, you'll have to put him down," Jones said.

"No," Travis groaned. "He was provoked. Protecting Bailey. My fault. Triggered him."

"Travis, that's no—"

"That's exactly what happened." Mark cut me off. He shot me a glare that I would've had to be super clueless to miss. *'Shut up, Bailey, FBI in the room, don't be dumb,'* was my rough translation of that look. I kept my mouth closed.

Gage nodded. "I'll sort the dog bite out, gentlemen. How can I help you this evening?" he asked the agents.

"More questions?" I whined. "Didn't I answer everything again earlier?"

"Yes, you were very helpful. Just... Can we go somewhere private to have this conversation?"

"Go ahead, I'm not leaving Travis," I said.

"Miss Hastings, we—"

"Everyone here knows what's going on already. Well, almost everyone." I glanced over at the service doors where Kathleen disappeared to get Tracey some towels. Screw her, and the 'this isn't about you,' bullshit. For once in my life, it was about me—and not about her.

I knew her type—perfect, have-it-all women that hired little me to pull off the perfect Pinterest picture party for their little spoiled brat children. Looked great, borrowed great ideas, couldn't actually do the work, but told the rest of us how to do it. I'd bet money that Kathleen's expensive wardrobe was limited to the colors taupe, silver/gray, black, and winter white. Her underwear would be nude with black lace panels. Or all lace and always silk. Her idea of a sexy dress would be red, and of course, she would wear matching red lingerie.

Damn. I wonder if I still had a job. Double damn. I definitely had some jealousy issues.

Kathleen came back into the room holding an armful of towels. "Here you go, Tracey." She set them in a tidy pile next to the nurse. She stood up, brushed nonexistent wrinkles from her perfect Chanel skirt and turned to Gage.

His hand on my back stopped moving. "Kathleen, what are you doing here?"

His face was completely devoid of expression. Perfectly

blank. How was I supposed to know what he thought if he didn't react?

"I came to see you, and found myself in the middle of chaos and a room full of bleeding strangers." She smirked.

Oh, I didn't like her even more.

"I'm hardly a stranger, Kathleen, even if you don't like me," Travis managed between teeth clenching bouts of pain.

"I wasn't referring to you, Travis. I believe you would fall under chaos."

That made Travis laugh, which was good because he was able to lessen his bone-crushing hold on my hand for a minute.

"Gentlemen, who are you and why are you here exactly?" She directed her attention to the FBI agents.

Gage patted me three times, squeezed my shoulder in what I can only imagine was supposed to be a reassuring gesture, and stepped between Kathleen and the FBI. He scooped his hand under her elbow and led her away from everyone.

"Who the hell does she think she is?" Was all I heard as they pushed through into the kitchen.

7

"I gnore her," Travis said.

"Gage is engaged?" I gulped.

"Was. Kathleen still thinks she's going to be the Grande Dame of this place someday and comes around and lords over us until he comes back and kicks her out," Mark said.

"Okay, Travis. You're all cleaned up." Tracey sat back on her haunches. "I'm going to want to see that again in the morning."

Travis let go of my hand and sat up. His forearm was wrapped in bandages from wrist to elbow. "I get to skin his ass next time I see that wolf," he grumbled.

"Miss Hastings." Agent Jones caught my attention again.

Loud screeches coming from the kitchen caused everyone to pause and turn to look at the doors. Whatever Gage and Kathleen were discussing, she wasn't happy about at all.

We all looked around at each other, super uncomfortable with the situation in the other room.

Kathleen shoved her way back into the lounge. She

stopped in front of me and glared at me. "So, you're Bailey, huh?"

All I could do was nod. I had no idea what the hell had been going on in the kitchen, and I had told her twice who I was.

Gage followed her from the kitchen. His expression was grim. He had four fresh scratches across his cheek where it looked like she had clawed him pretty hard.

Kathleen turned on him. "Married?" She shuddered with rage. She turned back at me and shook while making a squealing kind of ragey sound.

She turned and stormed off, picking up her coat and purse on her way out the front door.

Everyone turned their attention back to Gage. He looked like he was sucking on his teeth. "You met Kathleen then."

"Miss Hastings." The FBI agent sounded exasperated.

"Yes, Agent Jones?" I was finally able to focus on the agents. I was going to ignore Gage, and pretend the whole Kathleen thing had not happened. I couldn't deal with it. I just couldn't.

I hobbled over to one of the seating areas away from the lounge. It provided a semblance of privacy, without having to walk too far. My feet were not happy at the moment.

Put me in regular clothes and shoes, and I think I can take on the world. Foolish me, I could barely conquer the lobby and lounge area.

I sighed as I sank into the overstuffed chair. I closed my eyes to let the adrenaline calm down. I tried to ignore Gage as he perched on the arm of the chair. Typically, I would have leaned against his hip. I leaned away from him.

Fiancée? I needed to know what the hell was going on with this Kathleen woman. And frankly, he wasn't one of my most favorite people at the moment. I swear him and Max, what the fuck was happening with them?

I opened my eyes again and stared back at Agents Smith and Jones. I giggled to myself. Really, they needed to come up with better fake names. At least Smith and Smith ran with it.

"Okay, fellas, what do you want?" I wasn't going to go over anything again right now.

"Miss Hastings, we believe our perp, Gordon Dryer, aka Hanson aka Jamal, is still in the area. However, we haven't spotted him. And we believe it's because he is lying in wait for you. By keeping you in hiding, we are also keeping him in hiding."

My forehead scrunched up. I didn't want Gordon to know where I was. I felt safe here, despite what had happened with Max, I felt safe. Or not. My heart started to pound in my throat, and it was hard to swallow.

Gage placed a hand on my shoulder. I shrugged him off. I didn't need his bullshit in the middle of my panic attack.

"No." I couldn't shake my head much. Everything had started trembling. I did my best impression of a small ball by pulling my legs up and wrapping my arms around my knees and hiding my face in my knees. "No," I whispered again and again.

Gage stroked my back, and that's when the tears fell. I wasn't safe. I didn't have anyone to protect me. Gage had betrayed me, Max turned vicious and ran away, and my mom had her memory changed. She didn't know I was in trouble—so much trouble.

"Go away," I said it everyone, all of them. I wanted them all gone. If I was going to be on my own in this, I wanted to be alone. They should've left me in the woods to die. Gordon should've killed me sooner. I wasn't strong enough for this. My clothes were pinned together and covered in blood. I never should have gotten out of bed.

I heard Travis's voice. Holy Hecate and poor Travis had gotten attacked by one of his friends because of me. This whole situation was spiraling out of control. Tracey's voice joined the conversation. I didn't listen; I didn't care anymore. Let them deal with the FBI. Let them figure it all out. I was done. I wanted my life back. I wanted clothes that fit, and to not be tethered to this stupid IV pole anymore. I wanted my toe back.

When I woke up, I was warm and surrounded by strong arms. I relaxed back into Gage's embrace before I remembered I was mad at him. I struggled to escape his hold.

He rolled onto his back. "You feeling better?"

"No. I'm stilled pissed at you." I sat up on the side of the bed. I still had on my blood splattered clothes. I wanted to get out of this stupid shirt and get back into a hospital gown. I felt ridiculous with my boobs on display like I was advertising at a nightclub.

"Go away. I need to change." I looked down at my shirt and tried to figure the easiest way to get out of it. I started with the safety pins along the left arm.

Gage walked around to my side and took over removing the pins. "Why are you pissed at me? What did I do?"

I pursed my lips and shook my head. He was too stupid to even know he had done something wrong. How had I been so in love with him? I'm an idiot. I fall for the worst men, serial cheater, serial killer, vicious werewolf. Oh, Bast, I was batting a thousand.

"When were you going to tell me about Kathleen?"

He had the nerve to chuckle. He chuckled! "When are you going to tell me about the boy you broke up with three years ago?"

"What?" I looked at him then. "What does someone I dated when I was twenty-one have to do with this?"

"That's when Kathleen and I broke up. She returned my ring three years ago."

"Then why did she tell me she was your fiancée?"

"She likes the prestige of being the Sheriff's fiancée. She drags it out at her convenience when she thinks it will get her preferential treatment. It's one of the reasons we broke it off."

He had finished my arm and was removing pins from my shoulder.

She wasn't in his life. I felt the ice in my spine melt. I leaned toward his warmth.

"Did you honestly think I'd start something with you if I had a promised commitment with her? What kind of man do you think I am?" He sounded tense, restrained.

I sucked in a shaky breath. Things were not going the way I thought they were, and my brain was being stupid, as Yuki would say.

"I don't know, Gage. Everything is a mess. Max tried to rip a hole in Travis, and then this posh, polished woman shows up and starts bossing everyone around like it was her right and place. So, it made perfect sense that she would be the kind of woman you would be with. Smart, in control, beautiful, stylish."

"Control freak and a little bossy when it isn't her place to be." His knuckles stroked down my cheek.

I looked up at him.

"Why are you with me? And don't say because I claimed you. I'm a mess, and I have a serial killer after me."

"Remember our whole monsters and magic talk? I don't know why but I fell in love with you the second I saw you, all blue lips, cold, shivering and cussing at Max. Trust me that should not have been my initial reaction to you. The magic in you called to the magic in me, in all of us." He sat on the bed, holding my gaze.

"Look, Kathleen and I dated for a few years. We were dating when the accident happened."

"Accident?" I asked.

Gage held up his hand with a nod. Okay, that was a story for another time. "She stayed with me, even though I didn't know what was happening that first month. At the time, we lived together in a small house, and then I inherited the lodge. She always thought this was going to be hers too. Our relationship didn't survive the process."

"But you were good for a booty call, weren't you?"

His expression told me everything. He wasn't saying no to her when she came around to take care of urges.

"You've been stringing her along?"

"Not at all. I wasn't sleeping with only her. She knew that. It was merely physical at that point."

"And that point lasted until when?" The judgment in my voice was thick and angry.

Gage stood up. He played with the handful of safety pins he held. "Bailey, I really want the pleasure of removing the rest of these pins. But I think that maybe you need some time to cool off. Today was the first time I've seen or even spoken to Kathleen in over a month. And the last time I saw her, it wasn't for a fuck either." He crossed the room and picked up my hospital gown. He tossed it onto the bed. "Neither of us comes from pristine pasts. I haven't grilled you about your past lovers."

I opened my mouth to protest. I had been grilled plenty over Gordon.

"Gordon doesn't count, that's a unique and fucked up situation. I have never once placed the fact your last lover turned into a serial killer at your feet. So, I think a little consideration of my previous situation might be in order."

He walked out the door and closed it behind him.

He walked out.

He closed the door.

The door was closed.

I stared at a closed door.

This day was back to being fucked up ten ways to Sunday.

I began removing the rest of the safety pins. My boobs strained against the shirt. Yeah, it would have been much more fun if he had been there to run his fingers over my skin.

I threw the shirt across the room, and the handful of pins scattered as I threw them too. I pulled the hospital gown on and slowly, methodically snapped the sleeve up my arm and over my shoulder. Reaching behind me to secure the ties was a bit of a stretch. I got up, went pee, left my pants on the floor and crawled back into the bed. I left the Crocs on my feet, pulled the blanket over my head, and wished I could disappear in a puff of smoke.

Tracey came in and unhooked my IV. "Doc says you should be good. But, we're going to leave the port in your arm for a day or two to be certain."

Watching her move through the room picking up my mess was like watching a movie, underwater. I felt so disconnected from the world around me.

"Travis is healing nicely. By next week, you won't even know anything happened," Tracey said.

I don't know why she bothered talking to me. I don't know why anybody bothered.

At some point, a tray with food was brought up. It was cold by the time I ate it. I deserved only to eat cold soup and stale bread. When a meal with mac and cheese was delivered, I couldn't eat. I didn't merit anything so wonderful.

No one came to visit. No one snuggled up against me in my sleep. I was a pariah they were obligated to care for.

I was staring at dust motes when there was a knock on my door.

"Miss Hastings?" Agent Jones entered my room, followed by Agent Smith

I pushed up so I could see them.

"What do you want now?" I didn't care anymore. I was numb.

"Well yesterday, we tried to ask you..."

I stopped hearing what they said. Yesterday? I had been left alone for at least a week, what were they talking about yesterday. Yesterday, I barely got out of bed to go pee. I was unclean and gross. I hadn't even put on clean panties in days. I had to stink to high heaven. There was no yesterday with these guys.

I blinked a few times, trying to figure out how to hear them again. Mouths were moving, but noise wasn't making it into my head.

"What?"

"We tried to explain this yesterday, but clearly the timing and events you were dealing with right then, it didn't work out."

I shook my head. "I didn't see you yesterday. Did you talk to Sheriff Masterson about my case? He hasn't spoken to me for a few days, so nothing got passed along."

"Miss, Bailey, no, yesterday, your friend had just been bitten by one of the dogs."

I shook my head again. "That wasn't yesterday. That was a million years ago, last week."

Tracey came in then. "Hi, guys. Bailey, are you feeling better, hun?"

"We don't think she is feeling well. She's having some memory issues," Jones told Tracey.

"I remember just fine. But what they were calling yesterday happened at least a week ago." I wasn't crazy. I know what being left alone for days at a time felt like, I experienced it.

Tracey sighed and began to shoo the FBI from my room. "She isn't up for this right now, guys. Can you wait down-stairs? Let me have a chat, and then I'll be down, okay?"

They seemed to listen to her and left.

Tracey sat on the bed. She picked up my hand. "You aren't feeling okay, are you? And I don't mean your body; I mean your heart."

I blinked back tears.

"Everyone has abandoned me. I've been alone in here for days and days. Gage walked out, and he must be keeping everyone away. And Max, why did he do that? Why bother bringing me food and sending you to check on my feet and the IV when no one cares? They should've left me in the woods." I cried against her shoulder for what felt like hours.

"Hey." After a long time, she stroked the hair away from my face and pointed to the bedroom door.

Gage leaned against the door. He was in his uniform, looked like he had been in it for a long shift. But, he still looked super sexy. I missed him so much.

He cleared his throat, but he didn't move.

I pushed up and sat on my own. "I'm sorry. I was a total bitch about Kathleen. Do you still like me, maybe a little?"

Tracey got up and patted Gage on his shoulder as she passed him. She said something I couldn't hear.

Gage moved the rest of the way into to room and wrapped himself around me.

"It's been days since you've held me. Why did you leave me alone for so long?"

He kissed the top of my head. "Darling, I had to go to work. Tracey said you felt abandoned. It's been one hell of a long double shift, but it hasn't been days. It's been hours, a lot of hours."

"No, I've been abandoned, left alone by everyone for days and days."

He rumbled deep in his chest, not quite a chuckle, but with humor. "I know how you feel. But honestly, do you think I could leave you alone for that long?"

"You did. You've never worked a double before."

"I know, Love. There was a bad accident out by the free-way. People didn't make it. It made me realize I can't *not* have you in my life."

"Was that a double negative? Use smaller words."

He shifted and pulled something out of his pocket. "Look, I got you this."

He slipped a bright pink silicon ring on my finger. A little diamond shaped icon was engraved into the band.

I stared at it. It was perfect. Okay, maybe I dreamed of something with sparkle, but this had a little diamond on it, and it was pink.

"I told Kathleen we were already married for a reason. I don't want her to think she can find the tiniest of openings to work her way in through. When you're feeling better, we can go into Jackson and find you a proper ring. The only reason your parent's believed we were married was there was some truth there."

It was tough to swallow the dust in my mouth. "You want to marry me?" I squeaked more than talked.

8

Gage shook his head and placed my hand over his heart. "I'm already married to you. We need to have some paperwork drawn up to make it official."

He still loved me. I hadn't fucked things up on a colossal level when I had been a bitch about Kathleen.

"Do I get a say in this?"

"You claimed me, remember?" He kissed me then.

I melted against him.

I remembered. I claimed him, and with that, I got a bevy of male beauties. I hadn't expected to get a legal claim on him too. "Max is going to be pissed off."

"When he gets his head out of his ass, then he can marry you too."

"Yeah, he can. But you're the first husband. How soon can we get paperwork?"

He shook his head and lowered his lips to mine. "I have no idea, and right now, I'd rather think of other things."

"Like what?" I asked against his mouth. I loved the tickling feeling of moving my lips across his without actually kissing.

His kiss was his answer. The rest of his actions provided supporting statements and a most satisfactory conclusion.

I was loved, and after a shower I was clean, and I had happiness to banish the gloom that threatened to pull me so far under I didn't want to escape. The port in my arm was taped down and sealed. It pulled a little bit, but Tracey was right, it was better to leave it in than have to go through the ordeal of being stabbed a million times again to get another one inserted. Apparently, my veins liked to play hide-and-seek and were champions at dodge-needle games. Some of the bruises on my arms were from the hospital trying to get me hooked up. Of course, that first time, I was dangerously dehydrated. But why risk it?

I pulled the tight bra down over my breasts.

Gage let out a loud dejected sign.

"What?" I asked as I pulled on one of the T-shirts.

"I hate to see those get put away."

"Zeus's testicles!" Really? I was trapped with a kid's shirt halfway on over my head.

"What happened?" Gage laughed as he extracted me from my clothing.

"Yuki bought me really cute shirts. She went for style rather than size, and I forgot they all came from the kids' section." Damn, I had panties, I had pants, I had a bra, but now I didn't have a shirt.

"Be right back." Gage left, not bothering to put his shirt back on. And his pants weren't fastened. He left his boots on the floor. He needed to hurry back. I was very tempted to take the rest of my clothes back off and let him do to me what he had just finished doing to me.

When he came back and tossed a bright teal shirt at me, I seriously had to think about putting it on.

"Get dressed, Bailey. The FBI is probably still hovering

around downstairs. They have been itching to talk to you for hours."

I pulled the shirt on. It was a local ski resort shirt, no unicorns or sloths. But, it was a bright, happy color. Gage understood me already, even though he had only seen me in clothes once before. I pulled the hoodie on, oh, it was comfy. I had been cold yesterday in that cut up shirt, but I had been determined to get out of here. Funny, now Gage was home I really didn't want to leave this room.

Dressed in clean undies, narwhal pants, a teal ski shirt, and my mint hoodie I felt as if I could face the FBI.

I ran my hands through my damp hair, trying to give it a bit of fluff and body. I could use a cat-eared headband. Maybe Tracey could find me one next time she went shopping.

"Come with me." Gage scooped me into his arms.

I gasped in surprise. "You know I can walk now."

"Uh huh." He smiled. "I like having you in my arms."

A girl could get used to this. I giggled when he dropped me on his bed.

"Oh, are we gonna do it in here?" I started to pull my hoodie off.

Gage sighed, "I can't believe I'm saying this, but keep your shirt on. I have to get dressed, and we still need to talk."

We. Need. To. Talk. Never a good combination of words.

"Kathleen?" I asked.

"Not unless you need to talk about her more. Not Kathleen. I'm sorry I didn't tell you about her earlier. It's about the FBI, you know what they want?"

He dropped his pants, and I forgot what he was saying. He had a magnificent ass. Watching him get dressed was easily as sexy as watching him take clothes off.

He should be an underwear model. They wouldn't have

to pad the package area. Okay, maybe he was packing too much there.

"Bailey."

I looked up into his eyes.

"Did you hear a word I said?"

"I was distracted." I looked back at his crotch—all that magic skin hid behind a layer of boxer briefs.

"You're distracting yourself. Pay attention." He pulled a long sleeve T-shirt on, the kind with three buttons at the neck. He had one hell of a sexy neck.

The bed dipped as he sat and pulled on socks, and then a pair of jeans. His boots followed.

"FBI?" I asked.

"Do you remember what they were asking you yesterday?"

I shook my head. I vaguely remember they were talking to me when I curled up and went into mental hiding.

"Well whatever they say, whatever you choose, I fully support you."

"Gage?" What was he hinting at?

"They want to use you as a lure. I'm not a fan of this plan. But on the other hand, if it means we can get this guy and ensure he is out of your life forever, I'm all for it."

Gage held out his hand and led me out to the stairs. I had to hold onto the railing, but this time I made it to the big landing before I had to stop for a rest. Gage waited patiently until I either caved and asked for help or was able to finish on my own.

I was determined not to let these stairs defeat me. I may not be able to do anything else for the rest of the evening, but I was going to make it down the stairs.

Slowly, and with a long pause halfway down, I made it

the rest of the way on my own. When I got to the ground floor, I was seriously wobbly.

"Gage, I need you." I held out my hand to him. I couldn't quite balance on my own. I didn't realize I had relied so heavily on that IV pole.

We walked at my pace, which meant very slow. Yuki waved to me from her spot curled up in a chair with a wolf across her lap and a book in her hand. Another wolf was playing carpet well away from her.

Oz, he really was taking this too far. He'd rather not be friends with her in wolf form since she wasn't mildly interested in him sexually as a human, and yet he had completely missed out on Jade who had been interested in him as a human. His loss.

There was no sign of the rest of anyone; then again, this was a big place.

Gage directed me down the hallway with the conference rooms. Turned out, there was also a workout room in this direction. He held open the door to the first conference room with one hand and kept my arm in a stabilizing grip with the other.

The FBI agents sat working on their laptops at a large conference table. Gage put me in the closest chair and then sat next to me.

"Oh, good, Miss Hastings." I wanted to correct him. I was Mrs. Masterson now, well at least in my head I was.

Jones closed his laptop and Smith pulled out a note pad for notes.

"As we started to discuss yesterday, we believe the perp is still in the region. We cannot find him because he is lurking, waiting to spot you. You are well hidden away here. This lodge is very remote; it's not the kind of location he'd stumble upon. He'd have to know you are here and seek this place out."

I held out a hand stopping him.

"Whatever I agree to do, I don't want him to even know about the lodge. This is my home now, and I need to feel safe here."

Gage squeezed my knee, and I smiled at him.

Jones continued to lay out their plans, ways, and places that Gordon might see me. If I agreed, then starting tomorrow, I'd make forays out into town. Also, since Gordon was familiar with Jade and Yuki as my best friends, the FBI felt they would be useful in helping to lure Gordon out as well. Yuki was a very distinct individual, and if Gordon couldn't remember her and her connection to me, then he was blind.

I couldn't agree for Yuki and Jade. I had a suspicion Jade would not like the plan seeing how she was Yuki's guardian.

"I guess we should run this by everyone. We'll need the guy's help, but Jade and Yuki need to agree first. Will you go find them?" I asked Gage.

He excused himself.

I turned to face Jones. "I want him caught. I'm not repeating my ordeal a million times to every other FBI agent, lawyer, or judge. I want this over with so I can get on with my life."

"That's all we want for you."

The conference room seemed smaller once everyone and Brooks walked in. It wasn't so bad after they all sat down. Gage and Travis sat on either side of me. Zeke was next to Travis, with Yuki, Jade, and Mark, in order, on his other side. Brooks lay down across the end of the room behind Smith and Jones. Smith shifted uncomfortably, but Jones seemed to take it in stride.

Oz was not participating.

I let the FBI explain their plan.

"No!" Travis and Jade spoke at the same time.

"It will be fun," Yuki said. She had a twisted sense of fun.

"I don't want to expose Yuki to that man," Jade explained.

"What happens if something goes wrong and he gets away with Bailey again?" Zeke asked.

"That won't happen," Gage growled.

"We wouldn't let that happen," Jones said at the same time. "Miss Hastings will be under constant surveillance and in the company of one or more of you at any time."

"What about you?" Travis asked.

"I don't like this," Mark said.

"Nobody likes this. It is an effective sting plan to get Gordon to expose himself, and for us to sweep in and nab him. We won't be visible. If he is aware the FBI is surrounding the area we risk him running before we get a sighting," Smith said as he closed his computer.

"So, what's the plan exactly?" Jade asked. She wrung her hands together. She didn't like this idea, but she seemed resolved to let Yuki participate.

"I think the best approach is for you and Yuki to be seen someplace rather public. Downtown shopping would be a good start or going in and out of a few convenience stores up by the freeway. You can have any number of undercover agents with you that you want." Smith tapped the table lightly as he spoke.

"Also, the Sheriff's Department will be involved so you can have some of them as well," Gage added.

"I'm going with Jade and Yuki," Mark said. The way he said it made Yuki sound like an afterthought, but at least he realized if he was trailing along with Jade, that meant Yuki was a package deal.

"What do I do?" I asked.

"While they are calling attention to themselves, we want you to start getting out and about," Jones continued the plan.

"I can't walk a whole lot." I grimaced. Out and about sounded exhausting.

"You can go to the grocery store or the big box out by the freeway. They have those motorized shopping carts. You will definitely be noticed in one of those. The goal right now is to get you to places so you can be seen."

"I'll be with you where ever you go," Gage added.

"Me too," Travis chimed in.

I shrugged. "I can go shopping, and the FBI will pay for it?"

Gage gave me one of his more dazzling smiles. "Yes, you can go shopping. What the FBI doesn't fund, I'll pay."

I shook my head. "No, the FBI is paying for this. Right, Agent Jones?"

I made him laugh. Finally, he broke that frozen stoic look on his face. "I can authorize the FBI to reimburse you up to…" he looked over at Agent Smith.

"Two-fifty?" Smith suggested.

Nodding, Jones said, "Two hundred and fifty dollars. Go wild."

A buzzer sounded somewhere in the room. Travis pulled his phone from his pocket and looked up. "Dinner should be ready," he announced as he stood up. "Will you be joining us?" he asked the FBI.

The next morning, I woke up in the middle of a pile of men. We hadn't had a marathon of sex, simply cuddles and sleep.

I was too much nerves and anxiety for sex. Today, not only did I get to go out in public for the first time in almost a month, I might see Gordon, and my stomach didn't like that prospect at all.

Dressed in unicorn lounge pants and a pink ski resort shirt—apparently, Travis had a collection of shirts from all the various places he worked, and he only wore them while working at those places. The ski resorts provided him new brightly colored shirts every season, so he had shirts I'd wear, even if they didn't have unicorns on them—my mint zippered hoodie, and another jacket, also from Travis's closet and I was ready for my first excursion.

Jade and Yuki with Mark and an undercover FBI agent whose name I did not catch, but I bet was Smith, had gone into town to be seen.

"Are you ready for this?" Gage asked as I stood outside the front door on the big porch.

"I'm as ready as I'll ever be."

9

Travis jogged up to us, holding up a slip of yellow paper. "Can we do this at the grocery store? We need a few things."

"Like ice cream," I confirmed.

Gage chuckled and jogged down the stairs. I stayed where I was. There were no railings nearby, and I was still unstable.

"Hey, man," Travis called out.

Gage stopped and turned around. He looked chagrinned when his eyes met mine. He jogged back up to me.

"I'm sorry, Love." He scooped me into his arms and carried me down the stairs.

Once off the porch, it was much colder than I expected. Travis had fooled me. He was dressed similarly in a hoodie under a denim jacket and no hat. Gage was in his uniform, so he had on a down jacket. I needed a down jacket, a sleeping bag, about ten hats, and an entire pack of wolves gathered around me for heat.

"Oh, shit it's cold." I shivered so hard my teeth clattered.

Travis shrugged, "It's not that bad."

Gage placed me in the car and directed Travis to get the heat cranked. "I'll be right back." He kissed me and then returned to the lodge.

When he climbed back in the SUV, he had arms full of warm knit things for me. "The colors aren't going to make you happy, but these will keep you warm until we can get you properly outfitted for life in a Wyoming winter."

I nodded. I should've asked the FBI for more money. Two-fifty would barely get me a proper winter coat.

Gage was right, the colors weren't my favorites, browns and olive drab, at least there was no camo anything. He was also right in that this stuff would keep me warm. He provided mittens because those were warmer than gloves. The knit hat was dull but warm. And instead of a scarf, he brought out a blanket for me to wear as a shawl over the meager coats I had layered on.

Finally all bundled up and with an escort of FBI agents trailing behind us, we went to the grocery store.

Gage carried me from the parked car into the lobby area and placed me on one of those motorized scooters. It took a few minutes rife with giggles and feeling silly, but I figured it out and zoomed away from Travis's side.

"Hey now, no running away." Gage laughed as he caught up with me in an easy stride. The scooter's top speed was crazy slow. I probably could hobble faster, but my feet and wobbly legs would not thank me at all if I did.

Travis stuck fairly close to his list as he shopped. We started in the veggie department and worked our way through the aisles. I didn't behave. Freedom! And in a store with food. Anything and everything that caught my eye was tossed into the basket on the front of my scooter.

"You cannot have doughnuts and cupcakes." Gage sighed as he removed the goodies from my cart.

"Why not? It's your fault for bringing me to the store hungry."

"You should have said something," Travis said. "Keep the cupcakes, put those stale ass doughnuts away. If you want doughnuts, we'll take you to Keiko's."

"Keiko's, definitely," Gage agreed.

"What's Keiko's?" I asked.

"Who is Keiko," Travis corrected. "She makes magic." He swooned.

"The best damn doughnuts you have ever had. And you should listen to me about doughnuts. I'm a cop."

"You're a sheriff." It was my turn to correct.

"And a sheriff is still a cop in a different department. Yeah, let's go to Shaefer's Doughnuts after this."

We met a chill in the freezer department. Kathleen stood in the middle, blocking the aisle with her basket artfully hanging from her crooked forearm.

The scooter made a "beep beep beep," as I started to back up. I crashed into Travis's cart.

"What the fuck, Bailey? Oh, that the fuck," he said as he saw her.

I didn't want to be here.

Kathleen stood perfectly poised as if waiting for us to approach her. That wasn't happening. I tried to back up again, and Travis pushed back with his cart.

"You have every right to shop here, don't let her intimidate you," Travis hissed. He swerved around me and progressed into the challenged territory in front of the ice cream.

I'd rather never eat ice cream again.

Gage put his hand on my shoulder. Where had he been? "Come on." He squeezed me and then entered the fray.

I took in a deep breath, letting it out slowly. Okay, I could do this. I pushed the little lever, and the cart whirred forward.

Gage stood facing Kathleen. Travis crowded her with his shopping cart.

"I see you're doing much better, Travis." Icicles dripped from her tongue. I didn't think it had anything to do with where in the grocery store we were.

"You know me, resilient."

"I wouldn't make such presumptions." She sniffed.

"No, you only make proclamations." He continued down the aisle, leaving Kathleen with Gage, and me with my insecurities.

Insecurities be damned, I needed to make it through this obstacle. After all, I was out here to be seen. I had a killer to lure out into the light. And damn it if I wasn't the fucking light right now.

"Hi, Kathleen, right? Gage didn't really have much of a chance to introduce us before. It's fair to say everyone was a bit distracted at that moment."

She rotated slightly to look down her nose at me. Okay, she was pissed. She had been having her cake and letting him eat her out too. And now, no more sugar. She was going to need to find her own hunk in a uniform. This one was mine.

"You actually married her?" Kathleen asked Gage. I didn't miss her complete and total disregard for my friendly greeting. I didn't need her to like me, but I didn't need her to see me as an enemy. I didn't know what kind of pull she had in this community. She could be the difference between me liking my new home, or being miserable. After all, I was giving up life in a city for a tiny town on the side of a mountain.

Wow, was I really doing this? This was home. I was going

to be married to Gage as soon as he got a judge to sign off on some papers. I was moving—I had moved, I guess. At some point, I'd have to go back and get a few things from home. At least my landlord knew I was off—benefits of living with my parents. I was going to have to call Brian about work. He probably thought I was dead.

I felt the weight of everything I faced push down on me. I no longer had it in me to be fake nice to this woman. I wasn't going to go out of my way to be mean; I no longer had the energy to deal with her bullshit.

I held up my ring finger. I kept all other fingers balled up into a fist, so it looked like I was flipping her off while I showed off my pink silicone wedding band.

"Excuse me." I stifled the need to say please. I advanced the scooter, forcing her to move.

"A cheap plastic ring means nothing. I see you're not wearing one."

Gage sounded exasperated.

Kathleen continued, "She is a bit young for you. Is she even legal?"

My hackles should have been on full alert. But, I was too tired for her shit. Let her be petty. I knew how to let her type think she was winning when in fact everyone around her would see that she was a certified mean girl.

We made it through the rest of the store and the checkout without incident. I insisted on walking and pushing the cart to the car. I was stable enough if I had something to hold onto. Note to self—ask Tracey about rehab. I needed to learn how to balance sans digit. This was harder than it should've been.

"Shaefer's and doughnuts next. You'll like Keiko," Travis announced.

"No." I curled in under my pile of wraps. "I just want to go home."

"Okay, back to the lodge," Travis said as he steered us out of the parking lot.

"No, home. I want to go home. I can't live here." I felt like crying. One minor snub in a grocery store and I couldn't handle anything anymore.

"Okay. Can you give us a few days to work out the details?" Gage asked. His tone was flat.

"Gage, no!" Travis growled.

Gage's tone didn't change. "You think you can stay with your parents while I wrap things up here? I should be able to get a job in the St. Louis Police Department without any problem. I'm not familiar with Missouri. Will we be able to get a house a bit out of town so that I can run on the full moon?"

It was obvious he was thinking out loud. "I could leave the lodge for Travis and Mark to run, they already do. We could take out a loan so they could make the ADA upgrades and that would give them more business. I don't think Max would be able to leave. I guess we could make arrangements to have you visit here once a month."

"Gage, man, what are you talking about? You can't move."

"I have to be with Bailey. If she can't be here then neither can I. I don't know what that will do to the pack. Maybe it means we split up and everyone goes lone wolf. I don't know how Max will take it, with her being his mate and all."

"I'm not Max's mate. If I were, he wouldn't have gone away like he did." My voice sounded so small and defeated.

The car stopped, and a loud series of horns blasted, I assumed at us.

Travis turned and looked at me over his seat. "Bailey,

Max left so he didn't hurt anyone else. He can be a grade-A asshole, but he wouldn't hurt you. He'll be back after he's cooled down enough to listen."

"He ripped a hole in your arm. How can you defend him like that?" I didn't understand.

"Because I love you too, and I know how he feels."

With that, Travis turned around and started driving again.

I sat slumped in a chair watching TV in the lounge. I had a big bowl of ice cream, and I pouted. The rom-com on the screen didn't entertain or distract me from my worries.

Yuki came crashing into the room as she does. She held a bag out to me.

"Travis called Mark and said you needed one of these. Oh, Bailey, he is so right, you need this. I couldn't pick out one, so I got you three."

I took the bag. It was brown paper with Shaefer's and a doughnut in black ink on the front. I looked inside.

The scent of cinnamon and sugar teased my nose. Maybe I had been rash earlier when I said I didn't want a doughnut.

I picked one up. My fingers were instantly covered in a sugary glaze. My teeth sunk into a cloud of carby bliss. Oh, wow. I understood now.

"Did you meet Keiko? Travis said that's the woman who makes these."

Yuki gave me a big smile. The kind of smile she makes friends with instantly. Everything felt a million times better with that smile.

"She has magic."

"This doughnut is magic," I said around a mouth full.

"Well, yes. But she has real magic. Jade said so. She told Jade about a hair salon that has an open chair before Jade had even mentioned she's a stylist. Have you seen downtown yet? It's so adorable like it's out of a TV show or a movie— picture perfect little town. Oh, Bailey, we're totally moving here. Jade has an appointment tomorrow to talk to the salon owner, and Keiko said I have a job at the bakery. I can start whenever I want, and she knows a caterer who needs a party coordinator. It's like they were waiting for us to move here."

I felt deflated. "I'm going home."

"No, you can't. This is your home. Gage and Max and Travis and Zeke are all here. And Jade and I are going to be here. This is your home now. Don't let your brain do stupid things, Bailey."

My brain had been doing some seriously stupid things since Gordon broke me. And that really was it. I was broken.

"You are hardly broken," Jade announced as she walked up.

I started to ask how she knew what I was thinking.

"Eat the magic doughnut," she told me. "We need a different movie. This one is depressing. No wonder your brain is doing stupid things."

She picked up the remote and found an actual rom-com, heavy on the com.

"Better." Jade sat by my feet and leaned against my knee. "Bailey, shit right now is really heavy, but we need you, we love you. And Yuki is right; there are jobs ready for us to walk into. There is magic in this place, and it's good."

"I thought you said there were demons?" I asked.

"There are, but there is more good here. Besides, the magic in St. Louis is spread out so thin I can barely taste it. I feel like I can breathe here."

"That's all good for you. I'm glad you can breathe, but I can't do anything."

"Bullshit," Gage said as he pushed in through the service doors from the kitchen. "I don't know what you're talking about, but I heard you say you can't do anything, that's bullshit, Bailey."

"Oh yeah, what can I do, Gage?"

"You really want me to tell you in front of your friends?"

I threw my hands up in a whatever shrug.

"Woman, you turn me inside out every time you make love to me. You make me forget there is a world out there beyond these walls. You make all the blood in my brain leave for my di—"

"Okay, you can stop." I cut him off. "That's sexy and all, but that's not what I meant."

"Bailey, you are recovering from a very serious trauma. And you are doing that very well." He changed tracks.

"No, I'm not. My brain is being stupid like Yuki says."

"I don't know about it being stupid, but what it's doing is natural. Your brain is trying to protect you from more hurt. Right now, I'm guessing it thinks Kathleen is a major danger to your wellbeing. How can you know for certain that she isn't a rival challenge?"

"Yeah, how can I know? How do I tell my brain that she's not a threat, when I," I thumbed myself in the chest, "can't tell she's not?"

"That's easy," Yuki chirped. "Gage doesn't love her. He doesn't go all derpy looking at her."

"Oh, and he goes all derpy looking at me?"

My eyebrows were up by my hairline when I looked from her to him.

"Derp," he said.

I laughed. "Okay, so I shouldn't make any rash decisions about moving yet?"

"Please, Love, stay. But, if you do go, I am coming with you. You aren't getting rid of me."

"Or me, so make sure your mom is ready for the whole pack to move back in with you." I hadn't noticed Travis joining us.

~

A small front rolled in and dumped four inches of snow overnight. I thought I had stability issues before; the snow was going to make it worse. Tracey found a crutch for me. That helped more than I realized with my balance.

I was getting stronger every day. I could make it to the bottom of the stairs all by myself. I needed help carrying my crutch down, and I felt like I needed a nap after I made it down the stairs, but I did it.

Today's fishing for Gordon included Jade and Yuki returning downtown to make arrangements for their potential new jobs, and Gage and Travis taking me shopping again. Gage said the little run-in with Kathleen reminded him that he needed a wedding band and they had some at the store.

There was something magical about being carried through the snow by Gage.

"I could get used to this you know." I smiled up at him. I think his face got more and more beautiful the longer I looked at him. His jaw was so strong and square, and those cheekbones. "I bet you have a beautiful skull."

"That's not creepy or anything." He smiled, and his lips did their thing, exposing perfect teeth. Our kids wouldn't need orthodontia.

"You never had braces did you?"

"Why are you asking me that? No, I didn't. My crooked teeth bothering you?"

"Crooked? I was thinking you have perfect teeth. And since you have such perfect bone structure, it makes sense that you also have perfect teeth."

He jutted out his jaw and ran his tongue around his lower teeth. "These aren't straight. But they aren't so bad that I needed to have them fixed. Why are you looking at my teeth?"

"What else am I going to do with your face right there? Besides looking at you makes my brain not be so stupid."

He placed me in the back seat and kissed me before climbing into the front next to Travis.

"I'd tell you two to get a room, but then we would never get to the store."

"Travis, why don't you carry me around?" I knew he had to be strong enough to pick me up. He was almost completely healed from Max's attack, so I knew he possessed magic. I assumed that also meant superhuman strength.

"What and deny Gage of his brute manly man image?"

"He'd have to fight me for you, and he knows that he wouldn't win." Gage laughed.

We arrived at the big box mart past the edge of town by the freeway. I insisted on being allowed to hobble across the parking lot with my crutch. Travis and Gage stayed on either side of me in case I slipped or fumbled. The snow made a satisfying crunch sound under my crutch and shoes. However, I was more than happy to settle onto one those little motorized carts.

Gage wouldn't let me use the crutch like a jousting lance, party pooper.

First stop was to find some T-shirts in my size with appropriate fabulousness emblazoned across the chest. The selection was meager. I was going to have to rely on online shopping. I did get a few long sleeved shirts in some good colors and patterns. The men's section had some sassy shirt designs, and even though the shirts were black, the rainbow kittens were not. Jeans with big flower patches were still in style at this store, and so several pairs made it into the cart. Travis suggested I try them on before I committed to buying anything. I think he didn't want to be seen returning any more of my clothes.

Even though I had lost some weight, it hadn't come off my butt, so the jeans fit as I expected them too. They were a little less snug across the belly than they usually were, but that's because the weight I lost came off my middle. I was always a little more jiggly in the tummy, no matter what I did. I was never bothered by it, and it never seemed to be the repulsion magnet my mother tried to make me think it would be. Now it was gone, replaced by amazing technicolored bruises from the heparin shots Tracey had finally stopped giving me.

I was looking forward to being her friend and not her patient. I still had the port in my arm. She had taken three more vials of blood this morning, and according to her, if Doc MacGee said this batch was clear, she could take the port out.

Jeans, shirts, I already had the right kind of panties; now that I was getting me back, I wanted a proper bra. I zoomed the scooter into the underwear section.

Zoom is a relative term. The scooter didn't move any faster than Gage walked. Travis kept holding up wildly inappropriate bras for me. They were pretty and sexy, and I'd love to wear them, but the girls didn't fit in those. And the selection this store carried that did fit the girls was even more boring than what I typically wore.

I sighed; bras-by-mail was also in my future. Well, when I went back to St. Louis to gather the things I wanted to move out here, I'd go bra shopping and find something appropriately sized and maybe even sexy.

We left the store with no bras, much to Travis's disappointment. But, I did have a slew of more lounge pants, some actual jeans, loads more socks, and a bunch of T-shirts.

Not a sign of Gordon.

10

Part two of today's fishing for Gordon trip involved meeting Yuki and Jade downtown after their appointments.

Gage had us meet at a family owned barbecue place. Everything in downtown Wet Waterfalls was family owned, even if the family that owned it was not the name above the door.

"I expected a diner and not a barbecue joint as one of the mainstays of the downtown restaurant businesses."

"The diner is on the other side of Main Street." Travis pointed up the street.

"Oh, okay. So there is a diner, a barbecue place, what else you got around here?"

Yuki had been right; this town was adorable. The sidewalk was wide, and the shops had planters—full of snow—by their front doors. Awnings protected the doors, and big picture windows had the shop names painted in fancy letters across them.

I had a bit of a struggle climbing into the picnic table the restaurant used for its seating. The entire atmosphere was like sitting on a back porch, instead of inside. I was glad it wasn't a real porch and that we weren't really outside. I still didn't have a proper Wyoming-Winter coat.

Lunch was fabulous, but I was more than ready for a nap by the time we made it home, and Gage carried me in.

Brooks met us on the steps of the Lodge. He had a bounce in his step and a serious wag to his tail.

Yuki ran up and greeted him with a big ruffle to his neck fur. "You want to play?"

She seemed to be fine with the warm clothes she had. She handed the box of doughnuts Keiko sent her home with to Jade and ran off to play in the snow.

Gage set me down on one of the chairs and began taking off his coat. I made a pile in the chair next to me of my hat, gloves and mittens, and the wrappings that comprised my "coat."

I picked up my bad foot and held it carefully.

"I need a pair or four of those new socks. These are wet."

I'm not sure what I said, but instantly the guys were in front of me kneeling. Warm hands cupped my feet. Travis had socks in his hands; Gage had my feet in his.

"Can you feel your toes, Bails?" Travis asked as Gage blew warm air onto my foot.

"Mark, we need some warm, dry towels stat," Travis directed.

"Get her out of these pants; the cuffs are wet." Gage was up and rooting through the shopping bags. He whipped out a pair of my new pants. They weren't fun ones, but they were a pair of warmer ones. Gage said until we could order something that fit my style better, I'd have to suck it up and wear plaid. I could handle plaid, as long as camo wasn't involved.

Travis had my pants off before I could protest. Mark

tossed a bundled up towel to Travis. It was warm—I don't know how he did that so fast. Microwave maybe? Anyway, I had fresh pants on and a warm towel wrapped around my feet.

My pink Crocks, wet socks, and taco-cats—they were cleaned after the incident with Max—lay in a pile.

"How do your feet feel, Bailey?" Gage looked worried.

"They're fine. I think."

"Toes?" Travis asked again.

I wiggled the nine I had. "I can't wiggle—"

"Call Tracey!" I was in Gage's arms, and he was running up the stairs.

My heart sped up in response to his obvious concern. "What's the matter, Gage?"

"You can't feel your toes. Frostbite is a very real concern, and you've already lost one toe."

"Right, that's why I can't wiggle it."

He stopped and turned me around in the hallway at the top of the stairs.

"Jesus, Bailey. You can't feel or wiggle all of your toes because you don't have all of them?"

"Right." I nodded. "I'm trying to wiggle that little fucker, but it won't respond, but my brain thinks it should."

Travis was by our side with an electric blanket in his arms. "Why are you waiting, get her in bed."

Gage started laughing. "She can't feel all of her toes, because she doesn't have all of her toes."

"And she's in danger of losing more if—"

"No, Travis, listen. I can feel nine toes just fine. My brain thinks I should feel a tenth toe and it's a little annoyed that it can't make that toe wiggle. My toes are all good."

He visibly relaxed.

"So, you can take me back downstairs, where I can get a pair of those new socks, right?"

Gage carried me back down, Travis followed in our wake.

"Are you okay?" Jade asked. "What was all that about?"

"Hand me my shoes." I reached out for my pink Crocs.

"Those are wet. You need dry shoes."

I rolled my eyes at Travis.

"Look, Bails, this time it was a misunderstanding. Your wet socks were nothing more than temporarily wet socks. Had we been out hiking that could have been a very dangerous situation. You already lost a toe to frostbite. No one wants you to lose another one." Travis hadn't ever been so serious and stern. I could understand why he was a good trail guide. He knew when to have fun and when to be serious.

"Seriously, frostbite?" Jade asked.

"It's no joke, Jade. You can easily die of exposure around here in the winter. I want you listening to Travis and the others when they give you suggestions on how to dress and prepare for going outside." Mark tucked her in against him.

"You just want me to listen to you." She shoved against him.

"Well, yes, actually, I do. Frostbite can happen fast, less than thirty minutes. And the cold can be deceptive, especially when the wind is still."

They really liked each other. Okay, today my brain wasn't stupid, and it knew moving here was going to be the best decision we ever made.

I had my feet in fluffy new socks, all nice and dry. Instead of putting the stupid blue Crocs on, I challenged Travis to carry me over to the TV.

My choices of Crocs had been blue or camo. Never

camo. The only reason I had a second pair of shoes was Travis insisted that I needed a second pair just-in-case.

He had been more than right.

Up for the challenge, Travis lifted me with ease. He shifted me a bit, showing off that he could carry me without any problems. "You feel nice. I see why Gage insists on being the one to carry you everywhere."

Yuki screamed—piercing and terrifying.

Travis half dropped me. My feet landed with a painful thud on the floor. Everyone else ran for the door. I hobbled to my crutch and followed them out.

Outside, everyone stood frozen in place. Something that wasn't quite a bear stood on its hind legs at the base of the stairs. Yuki lay on her back pushing up the stairs and away from the creature. It was fuzzy but not from its mangy fur. It glitched in-and-out of focus like an old television set.

Its head was a grotesque cross between a bear and a bull. Twisted horns erupted from oozing wounds on its forehead. Claw, talons, I don't know what those should be called, but at the end of each paw, the creature had what looked like fists full of mini scimitars. Whatever the thing was, it was very, very male. Very erect male. Its legs ended in hooves, not the repeat of paws I expected.

"Demon," Jade whispered. She surged forward. She punched her arms out to the sides, and I swear blue flames surrounded her hands.

Holy Hecate, Demeter, and Isis. Jade seriously had magic.

Gage lunged and reached out for Yuki.

That's when I noticed Brooks on his side in the snow, a pool of blood growing around him.

Travis and Mark both crouched and growled.

The demon roared and took slow, heavy steps toward

Yuki. Everyone moved in slow motion. I felt like even I, with my instability, could dart in and grab Yuki and get her back out before the beast could take another step. Zeus's testicles it had a tail, tipped with flames.

Gage moved like he was in some kind of frame-by-frame slow-motion animation. Yuki wasn't moving. Jade looked like she was about to clap her hands together, but she barely moved. Travis and Mark were frozen, posed in crouches, snarls on their faces.

The demon took another lumbering step. He was moving, but no one else was.

I screamed. There was no sound.

Suddenly, out of nowhere, like a bolt of furry lightning, Oz struck the monster. With a whoosh of air, we were all moving. My scream filled the air. Gage pulled Yuki up the stairs and was running her inside like a quarterback with the last touchdown of the Super Bowl. Jade's hands smashed together, and a bolt of blue plasma burst forth and hit the demon in the chest. Travis launched into the air, and Mark circled the beast.

Oz landed on the monster and worried at the back of the demon's neck. It couldn't dislodge the wolf, and he hung on with his fangs and his claws. Mark and Travis kept the demon occupied by attacking it from the front.

An orb of glowing blue light formed around the demon. The orb had knocked the wolf and the men away from the beast. The blue bubble seemed to shimmer and... solidify wasn't the right term, but it became more cohesive, more real, for lack of a better description. It contracted and shrank around the beast, imprisoning him.

Travis stayed down. He was hurt and struggled to get back up. I hobbled over to him and helped him up.

"Bailey, what the fuck? Get inside. I'm good."

"No, you're not! You're hurt, leave it, come on."

I screamed in frustration when I was lifted from my feet.

"Damn it, woman, and you're out here in your socks," Gage growled as he carried me inside. He placed me next to Yuki. "Get dry socks on, now!" he ordered, and then he was out the door.

I tried to scramble up after him.

"No!" Yuki cried and pulled me down with her. "Gage said you need dry socks," she said between hiccups.

"Okay, okay," I said.

Yuki held onto my arm as we made our way across the room to where my shopping was still scattered from earlier.

I pulled on a pair of new socks, and then I put on my new blue Crocs.

Gage burst through the front doors with Brooks in his arms. The wolf whimpered as Gage lay him on the floor. "Hold on, buddy. Tracey is already on her way."

Mark carried a limping Travis in. Travis had one arm wrapped around his rib cage. I knew he had been hurt. Jade followed them in slowly.

"Where's Oz?" Yuki asked.

"He went after the demon. It got away from us," Mark answered.

Yuki let go of my arm and went to the front door. Tears streamed down her cheeks. I thought she collapsed when she went to her knees, but seconds later Oz was all up in her face with happy doggy kisses.

I was very glad he got over himself and came to her rescue.

I was keenly aware that Max was still missing. If he had been here, that demon wouldn't have been able to get away.

Tracey came running in, followed by Zeke. I had never

seen him in scrubs before. He always dressed so dapperly, I assumed he worked in a haberdashery.

She ran to me. "What's going on? How are your toes?"

She was still reacting to the call they placed when Gage and Travis thought I couldn't feel my feet.

I turned her and pushed her toward Brooks. "I'm good. Brooks is hurt."

She slid to her knees next to him. "You bastard, what have you done?"

Gage sat by silently, handing her the tools she asked for. Getting her whatever she needed.

"Oh, no you don't, you asshole, you told me you were going to get me pregnant, you can't leave me before you get me knocked me up." She was yelling and crying.

Yuki hugged onto Oz. Mark wrapped a bandage around Travis. The energy coming from Tracey wasn't good. When she stopped and cried, I think we all cried with her.

Jade slid next to her. "Can I have a go?"

It seemed like an odd thing for Jade to say. She didn't know medical stuff. She rubbed her hands together, and that blue glow from earlier appeared. Right, she knew magic stuff.

She spread her fingers wide above the still figure of the wolf. Blue arced away from her fingers and surrounded Brooks in a glowing orb.

All air was sucked out of the room when the magic struck. The orb looked like it had been pulled into the wolf's body. The sound was deafening, but utterly silent at the same time. Brooks took on that fuzzy glitchy appearance like he wasn't fully there. Instead of glitching with nothing, his human form flickered in and out with his wolf form.

The switching back and forth went faster and faster,

until it was impossible to see anything except a blur of light. Wind swirled in front of where Jade and Tracey knelt.

Another loud, soundless boom shook the lodge, and Jade fell back on to her butt. Tracey collapsed forward around Brooks. Her sobs were silent, but they racked her body.

Brooks whined. We were all already frozen in place watching Jade's magic. But now, all of our attention was on Brooks. He whined again. Tracey moved away from Brooks, and we all gasped as one.

The wolf twitched, wiggled, and rolled up into a sphinx position. He made happy whining sounds and buried his muzzle into Tracey's neck. She was crying again, only this time laughter and happiness drove those tears.

I sat down in the nearest chair and finally exhaled. I think I'd held my breath since I first saw the demon outside.

Mark had picked up Jade when she fell back. He cradled her to his chest.

"Is Jade okay?" I asked.

She nodded. "That was a lot of work." She laid a hand on his chest. "I need to rest."

He lifted her and carried her upstairs.

Gage ruffled Brooks' ears. He went to Travis and checked the other man's wrapped ribs. "Go on to bed and get some rest."

Zeke was by Travis's side and helping him up the stairs.

Yuki stood quietly behind Gage, with Oz pressed to her hip. "Thank you." Her voice was as tiny as she was.

"Can you tell me what happened?"

Her head bobbled around. "I don't know what happened. Brooks and I were playing snowball catch, and then suddenly the monster was there. I ran for the lodge and Brooks attacked. The only thing I think I can say is it's not Gordon. I know some of you were thinking that earlier, that maybe he was the demon. I would've noticed earlier if Gordon had that evil in him. I think a witch sent this one. You'd have to ask Jade. She would know."

Gage nodded. "Thanks, I'll do that."

He crossed the room to me. "You okay?" He lifted my chin with a finger, so I had to face him.

"Does that kind of thing happen a lot around here?" I asked. "I can't say I've ever seen a demon like that running around in St. Louis."

I tried to laugh. If I didn't, I'd cry.

Gage shook his head and lifted me to my feet. He pulled me into his embrace. "I can't say no. I didn't exactly believe in werewolves until I became one."

11

———————

"You said it! You admit it. You are a werewolf."

He laughed. "Yes, I admit it. It's not like I could've come right out and said what I was when I first met you. I was still trying to figure out how to let you know I'd fallen for you."

"Fair enough. But I had a crush on you right away. You're the one who carried me out of the woods." I sighed and leaned into him.

"Only after we tried to get you to move on your own."

"All of that wasn't a dream? Max was trying to lead me to you. Right?"

"Yeah, when you wouldn't follow, we had to come to you. He would've led you to the lodge if you had been capable. Instead, we did our best to keep you warm until we could be more helpful."

"All of you saved my life."

"We knew then that you were special. Look, I can't promise we will ever find out what that demon is about, and I can't promise that other weird shit won't happen, but I do promise that I will do everything in my power to protect you. Please stay and marry me?"

I placed my hands on either side of that perfect face of his. His eyes glowed with an unearthly green; they were that intense with his own magic.

"You asked." I blinked back tears. "I can't help it if my brain gets stupid, but I don't ever want to think of living without you." I kissed him. His mouth was warm and soft on mine.

"Good. I'm sorry I didn't ask earlier, I should have asked and not just assumed." Gage lifted me and carried me into the kitchen and set me on the counter.

"Hey, I thought you were going to carry me upstairs and make love to me. That was the perfect moment."

"It was, but we need to feed people. Everyone is hurt and recovering. Lots of food is needed. You can help."

I had finally gotten to see the kitchen. It was huge. I don't know what I was expecting, but what I got was a large stainless steel hotel kitchen.

Gage pulled up a stool and placed it in front of the counter, shifting my ass to the seat. He handed me a big knife and began pulling veggies from a large double door refrigerator.

I chopped onions, mushrooms, and peppers while Gage browned ground beef and started a large pot of noodles.

In relatively quick time, we had a large pot of spaghetti ready to feed everyone. Gage opened two more large packs of ground beef and placed the raw meat into large stainless steel bowls for the wolves.

Gage left me perched on my stool for a moment. When he returned, Tracey and Brooks followed him into the kitchen. Brooks went straight to the stainless bowls on the floor. Tracey dished up several bowls of spaghetti and put them onto trays. Gage followed her from the kitchen carrying two of the trays while she carried one. I guess they were delivering food to the rest of our recovering party.

A few minutes later, Oz came through the swinging doors and went straight to the food bowls. I hobbled out to the lounge and let Yuki know we had food. She told me to sit, and she went into the kitchen and came back with a bowl for each of us. We curled up on either side of the couch, eating in silence.

It had been an emotionally exhausting afternoon. We didn't need to talk to fill the silence, but I think we needed to be together. I don't think anyone wanted to be alone tonight.

We were all so tired. Beat, literally and emotionally. After a big bowl of noodles and sauce, Yuki and I, with Oz, piled together and watched a movie. Gage took care of business. He made sure he knew what everyone knew.

I figured he spent a good long time talking to Jade. If what Yuki said was true, a witch was behind the demon. Then Gage had to track down a witch, find out which one of the guys pissed her off and rectify the situation. Assuming that's even what was going on.

By the time he carried me to bed, he was exhausted. I knew he wasn't thinking clearly because he took me to his room, not mine. We stripped down in silence, and I slid in underneath his sheets. His bed smelled like him. This was his domain, and I was now in it, not the other way around.

I realized this would always be Gage's, and only Gage's bed. I was welcome, but if I were to have the pack as lovers, that would have to be in my bed.

I curled up into Gage and knew that I was okay with that. Sometimes, I'd need to be just for him. Just as there were times, I needed only him.

Tonight was one of those nights. Tonight was only us holding each other.

At some point, I woke up comfortable and warm. I reached out for Gage. His side of the bed was empty. The sheet was cold. I sat up, my gaze scanning the room. He leaned against the window, looking out on the snow.

Light licked down his muscular form, across his broad shoulders and around his ass. He looked carved from marble in the blue light of the moon.

"It will be full next week," I said as if he wasn't already keenly aware of the moon phases.

He turned his gaze to meet me.

"I like you in my bed." The light picked up a slight grin playing across his mouth.

I titled my head to the side and shrugged. I liked his bed too, but I'd like it better if he were in it with me. He turned to continue gazing out the window.

I scooted out and hobbled over to him. His skin was warm and smooth as I ran my hand over his back and arm. I pressed against his side and followed his gaze with my own.

Snow and more snow.

Close to the lodge, the ground was a clean blanket of white, and then the trees started. Those woods continued for miles and miles up the side of the mountains. Not a steady slope, the terrain swelled and lowered, and continued up. At some point, the trees were interrupted by a scar of freeway cutting into the side of the mountain range.

And once upon a time, a terrified woman ran across that freeway and jumped down the side of that mountain not wearing any shoes, because the monster driving the car she was in was more frightening than the prospect of freezing to death.

I buried my face against Gage's ribs. He would say I

traded one monster for another. I'd never trade this one for anything.

"Can you tell me what happened?" I asked. I needed to hear someone else's story. I was sick to death of mine. I was tired of having to repeat it over and over again for the FBI. And I was tired of reliving it in my head.

Gage moved his arm, so he held me tight to his body. I was warm snuggled next to him, even though I could feel the cold coming from the glass. I wasn't cold though I was naked.

Gage started quietly. "My uncle was a wizard or a male witch, whatever they call themselves. I think. He owned this lodge. It's been in the family since it was built in the nineteen-twenties. Change that. My mother's family has owned this land forever. There has been a hunting lodge here since before Wyoming was a state.

"My great-great-great, whatever, grandfather had vast tracts of land for cattle and wanted a mountain getaway. I think he was looking for mineral deposits he could mine. This building was built in the twenties after oil was discovered on family lands, and the falls became a tourist destination. Over the years, the oil dried up, and tracts of land were sold off, and the falls were no longer a popular vacation spot, so the lodge stopped being the grand thing it was.

"My uncle took over the keep of this place when I was a kid. I remember Mom bringing me one summer. I grew up in Casper. Mom's family never forgot they once were oil kings of Wyoming, even though they no longer had any money. I grew up with this expectation of wealth and fallen greatness. It was pretty weird considering my father wasn't a wealthy man, but my mom expected him to treat her as if. It was messed up." He shook his head and looked down at me. "You're shivering. Come on, back in bed."

He lifted me with ease, even though I could have taken the few steps back to the bed. He slid in behind me. I lay back against his chest, and he pulled the blankets up, tucking me in against him.

"So, your mom is embarrassed fallen oil royalty?"

He huffed, "Yeah, that's it exactly."

"Your uncle, he gets this property, and your mom?"

"They both inherited it. Vague memories of conversations I wasn't part of made me think that Mom wasn't happy to receive partial ownership of this place. It was a big dump that first summer she brought me out here. Uncle Dan was excited. He saw great things for this place. The ski resort at White Pine was doing well, and he expected overflow business from that.

"Mom wasn't nearly as enthusiastic. I think she brought a real estate agent up to look at it. The news couldn't have been good. She let Dan buy her out at the appraised rate. She was pissed about that one for years. The next summer, she had started working and didn't know what to do with me, so she shipped me up here to work for Dan.

"She kept my sister in Casper, but not me. I grew up those summers helping Dan restore this place to its former glory and camping out in those woods. He worked on it for four years straight before it was fit to open for business. That first year, only half of the lobby was complete, and half the rooms were still being refitted. The basement was a mess. But he hit the mark by offering executive retreats.

"After high school, I was up here full time. After a year, Mom leveraged a few threats, and I had to go to college or else."

"Oh, yeah? What did you study?"

"I was a dual major. Hospitality and criminal studies. I

wanted to know how to run this place, but I also knew I'd be allowed to follow in dad's footsteps without any problems."

"Your dad was a cop?"

Gage moved his head against my hair. "Yeah. Killed while on duty. Drunk driver hit him while he was helping to change a tire."

"I'm so sorry, Gage."

"Hmm." He kissed my hair. "I never intended on actually being in law enforcement. It was acceptable to Mom while running a resort was not. Funny thing though, I excel in law enforcement. I was even accepted into the program at Langley."

I twisted to look up at him. "No way? You were gonna be a Fed?"

He chuckled. "No, I was going to complete the program and then come back here. Or so I thought. To be honest, Langley was Kathleen's idea."

"What did you want to do when you grew up? It almost sounds like you did what everyone else wanted you to do, not what you wanted."

"I knew from the very moment I stepped into this building that this was my future. I polished that staircase back into its glory. Becoming a sheriff was for Mom and Dad. It gave me a paycheck, and a means to be here. My plan still is, I think, to get an MBA so I can better understand the business aspect. Dan hired on Travis to be a guide for the executive groups, take them out camping. My combination of training and working some of those excursions put me in a prime spot for running search and rescue training.

"That's how the guys all met. Search and rescue teams. That's when the accident happened."

"Accident?"

"I'm not sure what else to call it. It was a sneak attack—

three wolves against seven men in the middle of the night. When I came to, I was pretty torn up. I had claw marks down my face, my chest, my gut. The campsite was demolished. The guys were scattered around. They looked like broken dolls. The wolves that attacked us were dead. They looked they had been taken out by a bunch of bears.

"I checked the guys, they roused slowly, but everyone was whole. We cut the trip short and hiked back here. The nightmares started shortly after that."

"Nightmares? You mean you didn't turn in to a wolf right away?"

He shook his head. "No, we weren't attacked on a full moon."

"And Max and Brooks and Oz were still human?"

"Yeah. It was weird."

I stroked my fingers across the arm that held me. "Tell me about the nightmares."

12

Gage's voice was a soothing low rumble. I could listen to him for hours.

"The night before the full moon, at sunset, I started shifting. Kathleen was screaming, and I didn't know what was happening. And then I was a wolf. Stayed that way for three nights, woke up in the woods, human. Met the guys at a bar and we laughed our way through it. 'So how was your weekend?' 'A little hairy.' And that's how we knew. Went to check on Brooks first. And found Tracey staring at this huge ass wolf. He was waggin' his tail, happy to see her, and she was plastered against the wall, having let herself into his place. Brooks, then Max. Took a while to track down Oz since he wasn't originally from around here, he had come in for the training. Got the three of them up to the lodge with Dan. He seemed to know what was going on without ever asking any questions.

"After that first full moon, things started changing."

"What kind of things?" I asked.

"I got stronger. I've always been fit. Doing construction

on this place made me strong, but somehow I was stronger, had more endurance."

"Your endurance is exceptional," I teased. It was. He wasn't a bang-bang you're done in the sack kind of guy.

"That kind of endurance too." He laughed. "We did our best to get things straightened out for the guys who stayed as wolves, not knowing they would shift back for three nights opposite of when we shifted into wolves. Tracey married Brooks right away when he did shift back. Kathleen stuck with me, said she was willing to get married. Life wasn't too upended. You can plan for the full moon, and we kept our minds. We didn't turn into raging monsters. Or so I thought.

"It was a few months before we figured out we were each missing a chunk of time on the night of the actual full moon. Again, something that can be planned for, and the other pack turned into our guardians on that night. Max keeps us from scattering, so we don't wake up alone and in dangerous places. And he keeps us away from populations of people, in case something goes wrong."

"Is that why Max is Alpha over you?"

Gage made a low grumble in his throat. "I'm Alpha of my pack. He is Alpha of his. We work together."

"You do work very well together," I purred. "But Gage, I'm not trying to diminish your alpha status, you do defer to him."

"He keeps my pack safe, but he does not lead my pack. I respect him."

As the light beyond the window turned from blue to dusky pink, I realized I had been listening to him all night long.

"What happened to your uncle?"

"Cancer. He left this place to me. I kept Travis on, and we

officially moved everyone in. We still run search and rescue training, and it's still an executive retreat with hiking and skiing and camping. But it's also home now. I guess it always has been home, just took a while for it to be official."

"And your mom?"

He huffed a half laugh. "Mom thinks Dan saddled me with this place. She wants me to sell it so I can get on with my life."

"She still an embarrassed ex-oil royalty?"

"Every day, but her current husband does pretty well for himself."

"You said Dan was a wizard?"

"He didn't blink an eye when I confessed what had happened. Muttered something about 'not in his woods,' and he took off for a few days. We found more dead wolves; they hadn't died by natural causes. I think he went out into the woods and took out whatever it was that turned me and guys into wolves."

"Are there a lot of normal wolves out there?"

"Wyoming has a healthy population, and we are close to those population centers. So yeah, we get a few coming through."

I think he could have gone on to a fish and game report for the state and I'd have happily listened to him. I could no longer hold my eyes open. I snuggled against his warmth.

He had been attacked, that had to have been traumatic. I sat bolt upright.

"You can't turn me into a werewolf, can you? What if Max had bitten me and not Travis, would I be like you?"

Gage sat up and wrapped his arms around me. He began rocking back and forth slightly, enough to soothe. "I don't know. It's never happened. We make sure, for those hours we don't have control, that we're away from humans."

"But you said you were there for me in the woods for two nights, wasn't that during your rager blackout period?"

"Shh, it was, but that time we had to protect you above all else. You aren't going to change into a wolf. And if you do, I'll be right there with you. Bailey, that's not something you have to worry about."

He lay back down. "Come on, you were almost asleep. I've kept you up entirely too long."

"You've kept me up longer." I couldn't help but tease a little.

He laughed. "That I have. Sleep. I have an early shift today."

When I woke up, Gage was gone. My best guess was he had been gone for a few hours. I slipped my clothes back on and hobbled my way across to my room.

Tracey looked up.

"Oh good, you're awake." She didn't say anything about my morning hobble of shame across the hallway. "I see the crutch is helping."

"Yeah, it helps a lot. So, what did Doc say about my blood work?" I asked as I sat on my bed. It was freshly made. I had no idea who did housekeeping around here. My bed was always clean and made for me.

"Doc said we could lose the port. Ready?" She snapped on purple nitrile gloves and stepped over.

After peeling away all the tape, and there was a lot of it, she pressed a cotton ball to my arm and slid the little catheter tube out of my arm. I sighed. This symbolized that it was really over. Now, I needed to work on my balance.

Tracey packed up everything she had needed for my care. This was no longer a makeshift hospital room.

"How do I go about getting some rehab? I really need to learn to walk again."

"I put a call in for you the other day. I'll follow up on that. I gave them my phone number since you don't have a phone. Do you know when that's going to get taken care of?"

I shrugged. "The FBI was trying to track it. Maybe it's still in the back of Gordon's car. If he's in town, maybe I can get it back when they catch him."

I hadn't thought about being able to get my phone back. When I did think about it, I mostly hoped I had backed it up recently so I could get my photos off of it. I hated losing pictures every time I changed phones. I needed to get better about that.

Tracey left, and I took a shower and put on fresh clothes. I put on my new jeans with the embroidered flowers up the leg, cats in space shirt, and a pair of thick fluffy socks. I put an extra pair of socks in my hoodie pocket in case the pair I had got wet. I didn't need or want a repeat of yesterday's miscommunication over my toes, and I wanted to keep the nine toes I currently had.

I grabbed my crutch and hobbled down the hallway as if somehow removing the IV port from my arm magically cured me.

I sat at the top of the stairs and cried for at least thirty minutes before Travis found me and carried me back to bed. I had no way to easily get down while holding the crutch. I was stymied beyond reasonable thought.

Travis was warm and comforting, and he smelled like fresh laundry.

"Did you make my bed?" I sniffed against his chest as he held me.

"Of course, it's my job."

"I thought you did trails and skiing, and shit like that."

"I'm also maintenance and household. I'm a bit of a Travis of all trades around here."

I smiled, not up for laughing after my failure to make it down the stairs solo. I didn't realize how tired I had been until I woke up again. Clearly, I needed a nap.

This time, the stairs did not defeat me. Cuddles and more rest helped greatly. I slid the crutch down to the landing and held on to the railing to hobble on down. I took a rest at the first landing before sending the crutch sliding to the big landing. I repeated the process all the way down to the main floor.

I crutched my way into the kitchen to see if I could find food.

The double refrigerator was huge. At first, I thought it might be super refrigerator-freezer set, but when I didn't see any ice cream, I deducted that there had to be a freezer unit around somewhere.

"What are you getting into?" Travis's voice scared me, and I jumped, dropping the crutch.

"I'm hungry."

"Why don't we go into town and find something. You do need to be seen, remember?"

"Can we get doughnuts?"

He smiled, and his blue eyes gleamed.

Keiko's doughnuts were definitely magical. They were like eating cinnamon clouds. I could see how and why Keiko would hire Yuki. She would fit in the shop perfectly. I bet as soon as Yuki started, sales would double, if not triple.

"You're Yuki's friend?" Keiko asked. She had come from behind the counter to sit at the small round table with me and Travis. "She is delightful. She told me about you."

"I hope it was good." I gulped down the bite in my

mouth and brushed the sugar from my cheek. If this woman had an in with the caterer, I probably should try to make a better effort at being presentable than glomming down on her doughnuts and letting myself be covered in sugar.

"Did she tell you about the job?" Keiko asked.

"The one you are giving her? I think that's wonderful." I didn't want to presume she meant the one for me, even though my insides were dancing around with nerves. I'd be aces at party planning for a catering company. I was always requested to work for the more elaborate parties at the shop. And I ensured repeat customers. But that was what we could do at a party store; imagine what level of party planning and coordination I could get into with a catering and event place.

"Yes, I can keep an eye out on her while Jade is at the salon. This town needs a little enlivening wake-up. I think you three are just the shot in the arm we need."

Her choice of words made me think that she realized Yuki needed to be watched over, protected.

"Wow, thank you. It's exciting moving to a new town and starting a new life." Which reminded me again, I needed to call Brian about work. I guess I needed to officially quit now.

"Yuki told me you do party planning."

I nodded. I couldn't speak; I didn't know what to say. If I said 'yeah,' I was being too informal. I didn't want to insult her by saying 'yes ma'am' when she clearly wasn't very old. Nod and smile.

She slid a folded up piece of paper across the table to me; inside there was a phone number. "You give this number a call and don't wait until you are situated. She'll understand that you need time to get settled, but isn't it better to have a job already lined up before you are ready to get back to work again?" She patted my hand, the one holding the note, and went back behind the counter.

She held out a bag full of deliciousness to Travis as we were leaving.

"Can I borrow your phone when we get back?" I asked as I followed him up the street to where the SUV was parked.

"Sure, why?"

I held up the piece of paper. "I have a job lead."

"A job? Sounds like you're seriously moving here."

I swatted him on his shoulder, and he danced ahead of me on the sidewalk, mocking me and my slow, precise movements.

It was a good thing I was moving slowly. I swear Gage would've hit me had I been able to walk at a normal pace. Then again, if I had been able to walk at a normal pace, he probably wouldn't have driven up on the sidewalk in front of me with all of his lights blazing away.

He unrolled the window to the Sheriff's Department's SUV. He turned to face me as he slid on a pair of reflective aviator sunglasses.

If this were a movie, that would've been hot. But this was real life, and I'm pretty sure that got me pregnant. He eased out of the vehicle and rested his hands on his belt and sauntered to stand in front of me.

"You got a license for that, ma'am?" He looked at my ass.

"Don't need one, I've got an in with a local sheriff."

"ID?"

I shook my head. "Don't have one. Shit, I don't have an ID. Gage, we're going to need to fix that so I can get a job."

I broke our game. He smiled and laughed.

"There goes my tough guy act to get one of those doughnuts."

Travis was on the opposite side of the SUV from us. "Doughnuts are over here, you jackwagon," he called out.

Gage glanced over his shoulder to where Travis shook the bag of doughnuts.

He laughed, and then returned his attention to me. He pulled me in tight and kissed me hard. "I've got to get back to being official. I'll see you tonight."

His embrace curled my toes, all ten of them. There was enough curl there for extra toes.

I twinkled my fingers at him and watched as he pulled out. I was going to marry that man. It made my insides all kinds of happy.

Gage's vanishing vehicle held my attention as Travis pulled the SUV up and stopped it along the curb. Only it wasn't Travis. I was tackled like a football player and pushed into a car. The door was slammed behind me, and the car was moving before I had my orientation back. This wasn't the SUV. I frantically looked around, and then it took everything I had not to throw up.

13

_____

I was in the back of Gordon's car, and he was driving fast. The back doors wouldn't open. Stupid child safety locks. I began kicking at the door. The vehicle swerved, and Gordon reached back hitting me and pulling on my hair.

"You never should have run away from me. I've been worried sick about you." His voice was eerily calm. "Now look what you've made me do."

I was screaming to stop the car and let me out. I discovered if I lay on the seat, he couldn't reach me. I continued to kick at the door and window. The Crocs weren't very hard shoes; they weren't a helpful battering ram like a pair of steel-toed boots would have been.

It was hard to stay on the seat as the car swerved and bounced around. We kept getting bumped, hard. I sat up and looked out the back window. It was fogged up and dingy, but I could tell there were cars back there chasing us.

I hit Gordon again, pummeling him with my fists. He reached behind the seat at me and batted at my hands. Finally, he grabbed a handful of hair. The car was hit from behind, and I jerked. Gordon yanked at the same time, and a chunk of hair with skin ripped from my head.

Oh damn, that really hurt. I had difficulty breathing. My head stung but with the force of a nuclear explosion. Shocked, I sat back and put my hand to my head. Holy Hecate, blood, a lot of blood.

My vision went swimmy, and gray blotches filled my view. I very much did not like this new reaction I had to blood. It's not like I didn't see it on a monthly basis. I used to be able to handle blood. I felt myself slip under. I had to have rolled off the car seat and onto the floor. I think that's what shook me back to consciousness. I crawled back up onto the seat and then slid across the bench seat and hit the door pretty hard.

The car slid side to side in a wild fishtail motion.

There was a loud bang, and I crashed into the opposite door. My head hurt, and I was getting bashed around. I wanted to cry, but I was too terrified.

Gordon was in the front, cursing. He swerved, and we missed being hit again.

The cars chasing us were trying to stop Gordon by ramming the car. I found a seat belt and tried to strap myself in. Stupid thing was stuck. I wrapped it around my arm the best I could and held on. I was directly behind Gordon, but since I was holding on, I couldn't reach him. I kicked the back of his seat. I wasn't going with him willingly or quietly this time.

I reached up to my throbbing head. My fingers came back with blood. Right, I was still bleeding. I looked around for something I could use to maybe stop the bleeding, and then I remembered I had extra socks in my pockets.

I unballed the pair of socks and folded one of them and

pressed it against my scalp. I don't know how big of a chunk he got, but it was bleeding like crazy.

If he didn't like my hair so much why had he ever said he did?

We were slammed from behind. The sound was deafening, metal on metal. I hit the back of Gordon's seat with bone-crunching force. Before I had time to recover, the car was spinning. It was like a nightmare version of a ride at the county fair. Only this time, I wasn't giggling and laughing. This time, I prayed the roads were level and not on the side of a gully. This time I held on for dear life.

The noises were like dinosaur screeches of explosions, the motions rough and abrupt. My head hit the window before I figured out I could brace myself with my feet against the back of Gordon's seat and my arm on the ceiling.

Gordon's airbag deployed with a pop and a hiss. The car continued to spin, and then it tipped. The spinning stopped, to be replaced with a teetering rocking motion. I slammed onto the bottom door. The window made an eerie shattering noise under my leg.

I wanted to throw up. I couldn't see anything outside the windows. The front window had shattered into a thousand spider webs, and all I saw were sky and branches out the window above me.

The car kept rocking, and then it continued to roll and land on the roof.

I screamed. Gordon grunted. I thought he might actually be unconscious. His seat belt held him in upside down. I tumbled onto the ceiling—lying almost flat.

Finally, the car stopped moving.

There was a roar, the car jerked and the piercing sound of metal assaulted my ears.

"Oh, gods no." I didn't need there to be more to this wreck. "Please, oh please, oh ple—"

The car door flew off, and Gage looked in at me.

"Bailey!"

I started laughing and crying. This ride was over, and I wanted off. I scrambled forward as Gage reached in to pull me out. I was bundled in his arms.

"Ow." Everything hurt.

He looked at me, his skin was ashen with fear, and I think he was shaking as much as I was.

Men in dark blue down jackets with yellow FBI letters across the back pulled Gordon from the wreckage.

He was face down and his hands cuffed behind his back. The way he lay limp on the cold ground made me think he was still unconscious.

After several minutes of being surrounded by Gage, he lifted me up and carried me over to the familiar SUV with Travis standing by the driver's side door. He bounced on his feet with nervous energy. I noticed the front bumper was a bit smashed. I guess he participated in the ping-pong game the Sheriff's Department and the FBI played with Gordon's car.

Gage placed me in the back, buckled me in, and told Travis to get me to the hospital. He had to wait with the FBI for an ambulance, but he didn't want me there, he wanted me in treatment ASAP.

This was a very different ER experience than last time. This time, I actually remembered it. And I didn't have Doggo to brace me and keep me safe. I had Travis who spent all of his time on the phone. Every time he ended one call, another one would come in. He stepped out of my ER cubicle to take a call more than he was in with me.

Doc MacGee checked me out again.

"I would've thought you had more than enough of your fair share of hospitals, young lady."

He carefully examined my head and my wrist, that hurt like a banshee but was only sprained somehow in the crash, and he examined my foot and toe, making sure I didn't injure that any more than it already was. And then he made noises about my head.

"Bailey, lovely to see your natural coloring shine through, I hate that we are going to have to cut it all off." His tone was so easy going, no big deal, let's just shave your head.

"All of it?" I whined.

He placed his hand on his head indicating where the tear was in my skin. I was going to need stitches and another freaking round of antibiotics.

"Could you only shave half my head? I could have one of those tough hairstyles that were all the rage a year ago."

He laughed. I was serious.

Needles in the skull hurt. Okay, so the needle didn't actually pierce my skull, but holy mother of Bast that shit hurt.

I entertained the emergency room with a barrage of colorful language.

Tracey slid into my cubicle and pulled the curtain closed. "Oh, my God, Bailey, I just heard." She gave me a big hug. "Are you, you know, okay? I mean okay-okay?"

I knew what she meant: was I mentally holding it together now that my kidnapper ex-boyfriend and serial killer suspect, was in custody?

I let out a huge sigh. "I don't know. I'm still pretty shaken up from the car accident. Well, from the whole thing actually. One second I was flirting with Gage, the next I was bum-rushed into the back of a car and being kidnapped again. Tracey, this is all surreal."

I wanted Doggo back in bed with me, I wanted his solid presence reassuring me the way no one else had managed to do in the weeks previous while I had been in the hospital. I wanted Max back. I started crying. I didn't know where he was. Would he ever come back? How much did he hate me?

Tracey wrapped her arms around me, and I sobbed.

It was all too much.

Doc MacGee came back in while Tracey held on and I cried. He gave me a gentle pat on the shoulder. I blearily looked up at him.

"I'm going to go ahead and admit you for the night. Let's get you settled into a bed. No wolf?"

That set me off again, and I couldn't breathe; I cried so hard. I gulped at the air as if it wasn't working. I was given an oxygen mask, and they rolled me through the halls to an elevator, and then down another hallway.

Travis came crashing into the room as the orderlies were shifting me to the bed. "I misplaced you."

"You were on the phone," I sniffed.

"Your boyfriend wanted a blow by blow recap of what was happening."

"I kind of needed my other boyfriend to hold my hand. Travis, they put stitches in my head, and I was alone."

"I'm so sorry." He reached out for me and stepped in.

"Not now, lover boy. I need to get her changed." Tracey came in with a fresh hospital gown and all kinds of packages that could only be sanitized oxygen sensors and blood pressure cuffs.

"Tracey! You can't be the nurse for this ward. I'm not that lucky."

"Nope, but your boyfriend has some serious pull, and I'm to be your official private nurse."

She held up a pair of scissors. Let's get you changed.

I had already lost the coat, the wrap, the hoodie, the shoes, and socks. "You can wiggle out of your pants, but the only way I can see that shirt coming off is over your head, which is a no go right now."

I reached up and gingerly felt the bandage. Oh geez, I had one of those full head wound bandage things going on. She was right, I wasn't going to want to pull anything off or on over that for a good long while.

"Or we cut it off." She made the scissors go snick-snick.

Why did everyone do that evil scissor cutting action when it came to talking about cutting my clothes up?

I looked down at the shirt. I liked these crazy space cats. Travis could go to the store and get me another one. I held up the hem and cringed away from the scissors as Tracey put an almost straight seam up the center of the shirt.

Snick.

The bra had to come off too. Damn. My boobs had really enjoyed the warm hugging support of this style. It didn't do much for lift and separate or for showing the girls off to their most dominant presence. But this bra was comfort and security.

Snick, snick, snick.

"Do you want me to find something like this with a front closure?" Tracey asked.

She had a chest, she understood.

I nodded. That was a mistake. I breathed through the discomfort. "That would be nice."

She snapped me into a hospital gown. Hello, my unfashionable friend from days gone by.

I felt like I was back where this all started, but it wasn't, not really. This wasn't full circle. This was a loop-dee-loop in the middle of my life.

Tracey held up a pink butterfly needle. "I special requested pink for you."

"No," I groaned. "I just got free of my stupid IV this morning, not another one."

"I know, but think of it this way, at least this time you are well hydrated, and... done."

I looked down at my arm, she was right. This time the IV ported in one stick.

I stuck my finger out for the oxygen sensor and lifted the other arm for my blood pressure. I was used to this routine. Once she recorded my stats, I watched her hook the IV up. A big bag of saline—always a big bag of saline—and a smaller bag inside of a dark plastic sleeve.

"Oh goodie, more antibiotics."

"Yep, no messing around. Maybe if Doc hadn't taken your toe off, we would let this go with some pills, but not with what you were dealing with a few days ago."

I watched her prep a needle of something; she injected it into a branch of my IV tubing.

"Oh, that's kind of warm," I said as I felt that medication hit my system.

"It's to relax you. You'll be asleep in a few minutes."

It was less. As I started to doze off, she told Travis that I wasn't to have a rotating door of visitors. Gage could come up, and that was it.

Gage, yeah, it would be nice if he visited.

I heard a familiar rumble of a voice. I cracked my eyes open and scanned the room for Gage.

There he was— being ridiculously sexy in that boring sheriff's uniform. But damn if those pants didn't do wonderful, sexy things for his butt.

He laughed.

I heard the lighter sounds of a woman's laugh. Oh, good, Nurse Tracey.

"Gage." I managed to say before I felt the draw of sleep pull me back under. But I didn't slip in all the way.

"Damn, she is stoned. What do you have her on?"

"Same thing we put her on last time."

"Last time she wasn't so chatty, Trace Nursey."

"Oh, shut up, Mr. Sheriff-butt-pants."

"That's Mr. Sexy Sheriff-butt-pants to you. Will she remember any of this?"

"Probably not."

What were they talking about?

I came around again at least one more time.

Gage sat on the edge of my bed, playing with my fingers. He seemed to like the ring on my left ring finger. I know I did.

My throat hurt like I had been screaming.

Fucking Demeter, I had been screaming.

I groaned. Gage's gaze met my eyes. His eyes were full of worry, but his smile was life itself.

"Hi, baby," I tried to grumble out.

"Darling, how are you feeling?"

"Like I was in a car crash. That was real wasn't it?" I tried to push into a sitting position.

Gage reached across my lap and pressed the button to lift the top of the bed. Oh yeah, I forgot about how nice hospital beds were that way.

"Water?"

I nodded. I sipped from the offered bottle. My throat felt better.

"Zeus's testicles, I feel beat up. My hair hurts." I reached up and very gently touched my big head bandage with my fingertips.

"Stitches in your scalp will do that. Need a pain pill?"

I winced. "Yeah. I swear this is worse than my foot."

"You were on some heavy stuff when they took your toe." He reached across me again and hit the pager button.

"Can I help you?" the nurse over the intercom asked.

"Bailey needs a pain pill," he said.

"Someone will be right in."

He picked up my hand again. I liked it better when he was touching me.

"How long am I in for this time?" I really didn't want to be here. Being in the hospital drove home the fact that Doggo had run off and was nowhere around.

"MacGee wants you in for twenty-four hours."

"Observation?" I asked.

"No, he's convinced it's safer for you here than at home. You are strictly here to rest and take your meds."

I pouted. "That means no sexy play time?"

"Bailey, I know you got banged up pretty good, and you do have a head wound, but did you also hit your head? You are in no shape for sex." His tone was much sterner than I had anticipated, after all, I was half playing. Maybe a quarter playing.

"So, you're saying you don't think I'm sexy?"

His posture drooped and he closed his eyes against my stupidity. And that is what it was— stupid through and through. But a really horny stupid.

"I love you, but sexual activity of any kind right now would be too hard on your banged up body. You are covered in bruises and trust me, your head would not like being on the receiving end of even slow and steady making love."

"I could be on top." I reached for his belt.

"Bailey! No."

I folded my arms across my chest. "Spoilsport." I pursed my mouth shut and glared at him.

He dropped his head to his chest.

"Love, what's the matter?" His voice was quiet.

"Gordon almost got me, and I want to. No, I need to scrub him from my memory. When I'm with-you-with-you, I don't think about anything except your skin on mine, your hands, your mouth. When you're in me, everything is right in the world, and I don't ever have to worry about or think about the bad stuff ever again. And that euphoria lasts for hours and hours and hours. You are like a dose of sexy amnesia, and I can forget the ugly things that happened to me."

"Damn, woman." His voice was husky, and his breathing was almost labored. "You are sexy."

"Even with half of my head shaved?"

He laughed then. "Remember, I fell in love with you when you were shivering and had blue lips. I think the shaved head only enhances your appeal."

I kicked at him with my knee. "Tease."

"Do you know how hard you are going to be to resist the next few days?"

"What? Are you serious? You think this is sexy? Gage, do you have a kink I need to be aware of? You aren't planning on keeping me injured, or anything pervy like that are you?"

A genuine smile crossed his face.

"I want you healthy and strong, so I can take you out on hikes and show you what real camping is like. No, you're coming into your fertility. So unless you want to get pregnant right away, it's hands off."

"Oh Gage, who failed you in sex ed? It's not hands that

make a woman pregnant." I held up a finger to continue, but then I stopped. "How exactly do you know that?"

14

My mouth opened and closed a few times like a goldfish.

"If you're counting days from my period; Holy Hecate, I can't believe I'm saying this. Not all women ovulate fourteen days later. I don't even know when I do ovulate. It's not exactly something I can feel. Not like my ovaries go pop and launch an egg into uterus space."

I stared at him hard before collapsing behind my hands. "Oh. My. God."

I took a deep breath, put on a seriously fake smile, pretended to be a fully functional adult, not freaked out about talking about fertility cycles, and dropped my hands so I could face Gage.

His face was hidden behind his own hand. He quaked with laughter.

Who was the adult now? Hmm? I swear his laughter lashed a steel rod to my spine. "And while we are on the subject of fertility, how do I know you haven't already gotten me pregnant? We haven't exactly been using protection, and even if I were still on the pill, which I'd like to be, I am also on serious pill negating levels of antibiotics. Besides, I'm pretty sure you got me pregnant the first time you held my hand, and again this afternoon with those damned sunglasses."

Gage continued to laugh.

I nudged him with my knee.

"Sunglasses? My sunglasses got you pregnant? Damn, you're easy. Excuse me, freakishly fertile." He shook his head. "If I've already gotten you pregnant at least twice, then protection is a non-issue, don't you think. I can't get you pregnant again. Can I?"

"Gage!"

"Darling, your body chemistry changes as your hormones change, and it changes the way you smell."

"I stink. I have antibiotic sweat and IV pee. How can you smell anything beyond that?" I took a quick whiff at my pits. "Oh, yuck. If you can smell all of that, how can you stand to be near me?"

"How do I smell to you when I'm hot and sweaty?" he asked.

That was a stupid question, he smelled good, all man and Gage and sexy.

"You always smell sexy," I said. "But I don't have a wolfy nose."

"My wolfy nose thinks you smell like mine."

My stomach knotted up with the smolder he gave me right then. A little bit of dangerous leer and all kinds of hot sexy man came rolling off of him.

I gulped, and my pulse quickened.

"Okay." I tried to scooch back a little bit. "So, I take it you can smell ovulation like you smelled my period?"

"Exactly. And you smell amazing. So, it's a good thing you're in the hospital."

"Why?"

"Or I wouldn't be telling you no. I'd seriously be trying to find a way to get inside of you without causing you any pain. You smell like mine, and there is a serious drive inside of me to mate with you and impregnate you."

"What? You don't want to have kids someday?"

"Yes, someday. But this urge is not for someday; it's for right fucking now. This is going to be interesting," he scoffed.

"What's interesting? You have a primal urge to get me knocked up, and it's funny? How exactly is that funny?"

"Bailey, you said yourself that you wanted sex. I want sex, but not because I am obsessed with touching you, but because I want to make you pregnant with my child. Interesting in that we're either going to have kids right away or we are going to have to be religiously good about protection and birth control—especially if we both experience an increase in sexual needs when you're fertile."

"How come Travis didn't act all super horny around me earlier? If you can smell it, can't he?"

Gage shrugged. "I don't know how much his senses were impacted. Does being alpha come into the equation? You know only mated alpha pairs breed in the wild. Maybe he doesn't have the urge to impregnate you. You could ask if you're curious. Same with Zeke, he is the least dominant of the pack."

My mouth opened as I thought of something. I closed it again—stupid Doggo.

"Max?" I asked.

"What about Max? Will he smell you? Probably, but we can't exactly ask him right now can we? Look, when he cools off, and he will, there will be plenty of time to ask him."

I twisted my hands together. This was going to be weird.

"I'm only fertile for a window of time, right? That's how the female body works. I could still get pregnant from the last time we had sex."

Gage nodded. "True."

"So, we are going to have to do better about protection. But, that's not where I was headed. Max is where I was headed." I closed my eyes; how to put this?

I left my eyes closed. It was easier not to look at Gage. "Max isn't going to try to hump me or something like that if my smell becomes more enticing and he's a wolf? I'd have to sync up with a new moon for that to work with him right?"

"Right. I don't think Max will try anything while he's in wolf form. But, I'm pretty damned sure next new moon he'll be humping you." Gage laughed.

"Stop it; I'm serious. I don't want some wolf trying to get freaky with me. That's nasty."

"You do nasty." His voice was sexy and low and all kinds of yum. I had to pause and check myself. He was right; I did nasty with him and thought of doing more of it.

I took a deep breath. I know I was flushed. "I don't do that kind of nasty."

I was flirting with disaster as I flirted with him.

I think the promise that a nurse could walk in on us at any time, and my stupid head wound were the only deterrents keeping him from flipping me over, dropping trou, and doing the deed doggy style right then and there.

Gage stood up and crossed the room. He rubbed the back of his neck. "We'll handle some form of birth control when you get out of here. I'll make sure you have plenty of condoms in your room for playtime."

He paced a little bit. This room wasn't very big, not as big as the last room I had. He stopped and faced me. His expression—fierce. His voice—possessive.

"I don't want the other guys coming inside of you. Not even with condoms."

I started to nod, but a throb pulsed through my scalp—bad move. "You said as much before. Only you get to come inside, and you are always the last one. Always. I love you, Gage. And I know we are making this all up as we go. I've never heard of a poly relationship like this one. Usually, it's a couple with a third or a pair of couples. But we are pack, and you are mine. And I am Max's, and the three of us are pack too."

My thumb played with my little pink silicone ring. I huffed out a sort of laugh. "First husband. We'll see how things work out, maybe even first daddy too?"

He stared at me for the longest time.

He stepped over the bed and fell to his knees clasping my hand hard in his.

"You are my one and only, Bailey. Maybe we'll let Max be first father?"

Tears burned my eyes. How could he be so wonderful, and sexy, and everything, and love me, and still consider pack above himself?

"Everything okay in here?" a nurse, not Tracey, asked as she entered the room. "I brought ibuprofen for Bailey. Is that right? All you want is an Advil?"

I stopped myself from nodding. That was hard, but nodding hurt so no nodding for me. "Yeah, that's all that works without putting me under."

Gage stood up and crossed to the far side of the room.

I took the pill and swallowed it down with the water she gave me.

"I'll be back in a few for your vitals. Don't get her too riled up okay?" She directed the last bit to Gage.

He gave her a nod. "Yeah, no. I'll be sure not to be too exciting."

Did he not realize simply standing there was exciting?

She left, and we were alone.

"I should probably go—"

"No!" I cut him off in a panic. "Don't leave."

"I'll come right back. I want to get out of this uniform. It's not comfortable to sleep in."

"I thought you were going to leave-leave, and I was going to have to be all alone tonight."

"Love, I'm not going to leave your side but for a few moments."

"Call Travis and make him bring you clothes."

Gage looked at me long and hard. "You're a smart woman, Bailey Hastings." He pulled out his phone and sat in the chair that was going to be his perch and bed for the next eighteen hours or so.

My nurse returned and took my vitals, and told me my meal would be delivered soon.

Travis came in, and he looked like a whipped puppy. His blue eyes were big and round and terrified. He put a duffle bag down next to the chair and handed Gage paper to-go bags smelling of fast food. He looked at me only momentarily and then he started to leave.

"Hey, don't I get a hug or anything?"

Travis looked at me, at Gage, and then back at me. "I thought you were mad at me."

"Because I got pissy about the stitches?"

He nodded. Everyone around me kept nodding. I swear they were doing it to show off that they could. I knew they weren't, but my brain was being momentarily stupid.

"And for not being there when Gordon nabbed you."

"Oh, Travis, no. I'm not mad at you about that. You were getting the car, so I didn't have to hobble so far. No one is to blame for that except Gordon. And he's in custody. Come here."

Travis half slid toward the bed.

"I love you. I know you didn't do anything. And it's Gage's fault you were on the phone with him when I needed stitches."

He picked up my hand. "You're going to blame him?" He titled his head toward his alpha.

"Yep. So do I get my kiss?" I lifted my face toward him.

He cut a quick glance over at Gage and then kissed me on the cheek. "Big man is a tad bit possessive tonight. Best not to push my luck," he whispered, kissing me again before squeezing my hand and then he left.

Gage fended off the Feds while I rested. Doc MacGee was a smart man. It was safer for me in the hospital, because Gage got them to ban the FBI unless they were rolled into the ER for any reason.

I didn't sleep as well as I'd have liked. I had no snuggle buddies. I got why Gage didn't join me in bed, because he would have joined with me and we both agreed, not good timing.

By the time morning came around, and the nurses, not Tracey, woke me up and took my vitals, and replaced my antibiotic drip with another bag, I was done.

"I want to go home," I whined.

Gage sat up from reading one of the smut books Travis had tossed into the duffle bag for me. He looked sad.

"Well, I guess now that Gordon is in custody, once you identify him, nothing is keeping you in Wet Waterfalls. I'll put in for a leave of absence to get you back to St. Louis, and to see about getting a job there."

I started to shake my head, right, not a good idea. "Not St. Louis, Gage, home. The lodge."

I think I saw moisture rim those green eyes of his when he looked at me.

"Yes," he smiled, and I melted just like I did the first time he grinned at me like that. "Let's see if Doc MacGee will let me take you *home*."

Agents Jones and Smith were waiting for me when I got home.

Home.

The lodge.

Wow, a lot had changed in such a short period of time, but I knew this was the right choice to make. It gave me chills to know that Gage would upend everything about his life and follow me to St. Louis if I decided I needed to go back. The thing was I was totally willing to do the same. Okay maybe it took me a little longer to realize it, but there it was. And this was home because this was where Gage was, where *my* pack lived.

I insisted on hobbling up the front stairs on my own two feet. Not that I didn't enjoy being carried like a bride by Gage, but I needed to take ownership of my body. And frankly, I'd tell him to keep on carrying me up to his bedroom; head wound be damned.

"We need you to identify the perpetrator."

"Really? You pulled me out of his car, and you still need me to go down to the station, stand behind a two-way mirror, and identify him out of a lineup?"

Gage cleared his throat.

I turned to face him. "What?"

"We don't have any two-way mirrors. They want you in the same room with him."

I felt really wobbly.

Gage was by my side with an arm around me, holding me up. He eased me into a chair.

"Don't make me." I could barely get the words out.

"You will be perfectly safe. You will be surrounded by guards the entire time," Smith explained

I had heard that line before, and I still ended up in the back of Gordon's car. "Sorry if I find that hard to believe," I sneered.

"We can understand your reluctance," the other agent said.

"Reluctance?" I shrieked. "I have eighteen stitches in my scalp, a sprained wrist, and countless nicks and bruises because you guys said you would be watching my back. I spent the night in the hospital, and am back on industrial grade antibiotics. Excuse me for having some trust issues when you want me to walk into a room with that man voluntarily."

Gage stepped over to the FBI agents, and they had a little confab without me. I sat with my arms crossed over my chest, back in a hospital gown because they had cut my shirt off. At least I had jeans and clean undies. But no bra, no shirt. I felt suddenly very exposed and vulnerable.

Gage knelt in front of me.

"Bailey, darling, I will be by your side the entire time. And he will be handcuffed. Once you identify him, the FBI can take him away. And this will be over."

I wouldn't look at him. I pouted. "It won't be over Gage. It will never be over. I'm not talking to any more agents if I go."

He rubbed my knee. "You won't have to talk to anyone for anything other than identifying Gordon."

"I'm not repeating my whole freaking story again." I pierced him with a hard stare. I needed him to understand I couldn't do that again, not after I had come so close to being kidnapped by that man again.

"No one is going to ask you to tell them what happened to you." He did his best to reassure me.

"I'm not doing this in a hospital gown. I need clothes."

Gage nodded at my demands.

"And I'm not doing it today. I want a shower and some food, and then I'm going to bed. My head hurts."

Gage leaned in. I thought he was going to kiss my cheek. He whispered, "And afterward, I will personally make sure to erase him from your mind for hours." And then he kissed me before standing up.

I placed my hand over his kiss and smiled to myself. Okay, I could do it. Gage was one hell of a consolation prize.

"You heard the lady. Not today. She's hurt. She's tired. She's hungry." With the grace of a party host, he managed to get the FBI to leave and stop pestering me.

I was warm and safe in my lover's arms as he carried me upstairs. He settled me into my bed, removed my shoes, and helped me out of my jeans. He tucked me in and promised to return with my favorite mac and cheese.

15

Yuki held my hand with crushing force; which was surprising since she wasn't particularly big.

Gage was on my other side as promised. Jade was to the side and behind me. Her hand rested on my back. Mark stood behind her. Friends and safety surrounded me. They promised I wouldn't be in the witness room alone.

I still wanted to throw up. The last time I had to see the man he hurt me, again. I didn't want to count the stitches, didn't want to count the toes. I did far too often.

"I never got the sense that he was evil before," Jade said as Gordon entered the room.

"Not evil, but he's like Bailey, he's infected," Yuki said.

I looked at her. We were whispering in hushed tones as they brought a line of suspects in. At least the room was long and narrow, and the side we were in was in the dark. I'd have felt better with a mirror, or bars, or any kind of barrier other than this phalanx of friends.

"Are you saying I'm infected?" I asked.

"Yes, but you're infected with positivity and happiness.

His infection is like a dark abscess that is feasting away at his humanity."

"Sounds pretty evil to me," Gage's voice rumbled through my arm, where I was pressed against him.

"Did you ever notice this infection in him before?" I asked Yuki.

"No. He was probably masking it. You know like how you can get sad or angry? That masks your joy. Maybe he was actually happy there for a while. Maybe the torment in him leaves him at peace for a time, and then it comes back and pushes him to torment others."

"Back against the wall, face forward," the sheriff that brought the line of men in barked. He had ex-drill sergeant all over him.

There were six of them. They lined up against a wall that actually had lines painted on it indicating height. The lights were shown on the men, so they were all squinting. If they were anything like stage lights, those men wouldn't be able to see anything past a few feet.

I was as good as invisible to them.

"Who are the other guys?" I asked Gage.

"Other people we have in custody, office staff. We try to always present five or six, so the perp doesn't feel singled out. Sense of justice served and all that crap."

"You actually have that many line ups going on around here?"

"Two or three a year. It's not very common."

Agent Smith, a completely different Agent Smith, cleared his throat. "Are we ready to proceed?"

I nodded and winced against the throb the motion started. "Let's get this done."

"Bailey?" Gordon asked. He lifted his handcuffed together hands to shield his eyes and tried to look past the glare of the lights. "Bailey, hun, is that you? Will you please tell these people they're mistaken, they have the wrong guy."

"No talking," the sheriff barked.

"That's him, the chatty one," I said.

"Will number four, please take a step forward," Smith directed.

The man next to Gordon stepped forward.

I let out an angry sigh. I identified Gordon Dryer-Hansen-Jamal-Whatever-he-called-himself. Why were they playing games?

"No." It was hard not to bark like the drill sergeant officer.

"You may step back. Number three step forward," Smith said.

"Yes, him."

"Is this the man who held you captive and tried to abduct you on Tuesday?" Smith asked.

Had that been a Tuesday? I wasn't clear on dates or days, they all blended together, but I was clear on one thing. I pointed. "That man, number three, is the man I knew as Gordon Dryer. Him." I thrust my hand, pointing hard, so Smith, and anyone else who could see me, saw who I indicated.

"I identified him, may I leave now?" I was getting pissy. I had been in this room with Gordon for far too long. I thought I was going to have to look at him, say 'yes that's him,' and then be allowed to leave.

"Bailey!" Gordon yelled. "Don't listen to that lying bitch. I never laid a hand on her."

I pressed back against Gage and Jade. Yuki stepped in closer to me.

The drill sergeant sheriff was waving the other line up guys back out the door they had come in through. Gordon stepped around guy number two. He was hovering in the room. And he kept yelling at me and yelling at the FBI, telling them that I caused the accident, that I ran away from him, and he'd been looking for me for days.

Smith of the previous Smith and Jones stood in front of me, his hand tucked in his jacket, behind his back, hand on the gun he holstered there. Even with an armed FBI agent in front of me, it didn't feel like enough protection.

Smith must have read something in Gordon's body language to step up like that because that's when Gordon tried to lunge. He rushed in my direction. He actually made it halfway across the room before he was tackled.

"I should have killed you when I had the chance. You never would've made me a good wife, not like the others. You piece of shit whore."

And suddenly I was whisked from the room. It felt as if our unit of me, Gage, Yuki, Jade, and Mark were all moved as one.

I could hear Gordon still yelling, but I couldn't make out his exact words.

"He is not a complete person inside. His brain is broken," Yuki said the strangest, yet most insightful things. Gordon was definitely broken.

I found myself, with my support system of friends, in a dated lobby waiting room. The chairs were tubed-steel and green vinyl, the walls some generic color halfway between yellow and cream. Someone pressed a water bottle into my hands. I was shaking like a junkie.

Gage unscrewed the cap for me, and I drank.

He spoke with another sheriff and two FBI agents.

"We can go. You did well, Bailey."

I felt like I needed to throw up. My head throbbed, my

toe hurt—the missing one—I wanted to find a nice dark hole and crawl in and not come out until it was over.

"But it is over," Jade spoke so quietly.

I blinked at her. I had never really wondered how she could do that—answer me when I hadn't spoken. Now, I knew she was a witch.

She gave me the sweetest, most reassuring smile, and then I was buried under an avalanche of Jade and Yuki hugs. This was much better than a dark hole.

"Let's go home," Gage said.

"Can we stop for doughnuts?" Yuki asked.

I had cinnamon and sugar smeared up the side of my cheek and a smile on my face. I felt like I was getting me back on the inside. It would take a while to get me back on the outside, especially now that I was missing half a head of hair.

From what Jade told me, after looking at what the doctors had cut away and shaved off, she would be able to give me a decent style that I might want to keep for a while before growing it out.

I didn't know. As soon as the stitches on my head were out and that wound healed, I pretty much never wanted to see it again. Too bad I didn't have hairy feet to hide the fact that I was missing a toe.

"We should celebrate," Yuki announced.

"Celebrate what?" Gage asked.

"Gordon is in custody and Bailey is getting her light back. Can't you feel it?"

She was right. I could feel it. Knowing Gordon was locked up made all the difference in my world.

"Doughnuts weren't enough of a celebration?" He laughed. Her happiness was infectious; she really was *Delight*.

"We need ice cream, and balloons, and cake." She lifted the doughnut in her hand in salute.

Gage parked the SUV in front of the lodge, and we all clamored out. "Sounds like you want a birthday party," he said as he closed his door. "We need to go to the store and get organized."

I leaned on a new crutch next to the SUV—my last crutch was lost during the abduction and car chase. I was suddenly exhausted. This morning had taken so much effort. From struggling to get into a proper bra for the first time in weeks—Tracey had not been able to find a front closure, but she had found a decent, normal underwire for me—to undergoing the ordeal at the Sheriff's Department. I had done plenty.

"You need to plan a party if you want to do it right."

Holy Hecate, party planning. I had completely forgotten to call that caterer or to call Brian.

"Hey Yuki, can I borrow your phone to call Brian?" I asked as I hobbled up the stairs after everyone else.

"Sure. I told him you weren't dead when I quit the other day."

"You've already quit?" I felt bad. I hadn't called to even check in to let him know everything was actually okay with me.

I followed her inside and flopped into the first chair I encountered. She handed me her phone, and I called.

"Hi, Yuki." Brian's voice was flat. I could tell he was mad at her for having quit.

"Hey Brian, it's Bailey."

"Bailey! Oh my God girl, you're alive! What the hell did

Yuki even mean when she told me you were alive? Why wouldn't you be alive? Oh, and you're fired, you know that right?"

"Brian..."

"You don't get to turn a long weekend away into a month and expect to have a job when you decide to call. That's not how jobs work. I thought you knew that."

I held the phone away from my ear as he continued to rant away.

"Brian..." I tried to break into his tirade.

He continued telling me how the owner insisted he fire me, but he would hire me back. I'd have to take a pay cut, but I wouldn't need to start at the very bottom again. "I'm going out on a limb doing this. You realize that, don't you?"

"Brian, I quit!" I finally had to yell over him.

"You can't."

"Look, the owners already fired me for not showing up. And while I could actually get my job back cause I have proof of being in the hospital and then in protective custody, I don't need to do that."

"What do you mean protective custody?"

I was telling him much more than I had intended. I was going to quit, tell him I enjoyed working with him and ask for a reference. Instead, I told him that my boyfriend tried to kill me, but the FBI had him now.

"You aren't moving to that little town with Yuki, are you? The one in Wyoming?"

"The very same." I nodded as I spoke and immediately my head told me that was a bad idea.

"You and Yuki both can't abandon me."

"Sorry about that. Does this mean you won't give me a reference?" I winced.

"I'm going to have to come see what's so special about

this little town." Brian was so adamant in his tone, I more than half believed him.

"You have a couch? Prepare it for a visit from me."

"I have more than a couch, Brian. You let Yuki know when you're coming, and I'll get you all set up." I wanted to laugh. I didn't know if the little town of Wet Waterfalls would be able to handle a full-blown me, a Yuki, and a flamboyant Brian. But it would sure be fun. "Come in the spring, after the snow has melted."

"I'll come when I please. Snow means skiing and ski instructors in tight pants."

I laughed. He wasn't wrong.

I eventually ended the call with Brian making plans to visit when he felt like it, a job reference anytime I needed one, and a job if I decided that Wyoming was too much wilderness for me.

I fished the number Keiko had given me out from my pocket. Considering everything that happened, I was lucky to have this number still.

I dialed. The phone rang. I felt my nerves clench and the breath caught in my throat. I did not do the whole cold calling about a job very well.

The phone on the other end was fumbled, and there was a muffled "umph," followed by some not-quite cuss words.

"I'm so sorry about that. Dropped the phone."

I couldn't talk. That voice was familiar and not in a friendly way.

"I'm sorry, I must have dialed the wrong number," I blurted out.

"This is Kathleen's Catering, not who you meant to call?"

I would never have called Kathleen intentionally. Never. "Mistake, my bad, sorry."

I should have just shut up and hung up.

"Is this that Bailey woman?" I heard as I finally did hang up the phone.

I held the phone and stared at it. Great, Kathleen was the caterer who needed a party planner. Hades's tits.

The phone rang. The display listed the number I called. There was no way I was going to answer that. I clicked the side button to end the incoming call. I hoped it didn't send to voice mail. Then again, it would go to Yuki, and she wouldn't know it was me. Or would she?

Gage walked up to me and sat on the arm of my chair. He was on his phone.

He ended the call and looked at me. "So, why exactly were you calling Kathleen?"

I held up the piece of paper from Keiko. "Job lead. I didn't know she was the town caterer. I was actually calling her for a job."

I wanted to curl up and die of embarrassment. I can't believe it, the one person who was never going to give me a job in this town had the job I was perfect for.

Gage reached down and brushed the sugar and cinnamon I still had on my cheek off.

"I'll find something else, I guess. I did like the idea that there was a perfect job waiting for me here. Like how Jade and Yuki walked into their new jobs."

"Other than that, how are you feeling?"

I looked up at him. I loved that man, so strong and yet so caring and gentle. "I'm tired. I need to go lay down."

I started to shift so I could get out of the chair and Gage's arms were around me, lifting me. I rested my head against his strong chest.

"Take me to bed or lose me forever," I said jokingly. Really, I just wanted a nap.

"That's the plan." His lowered voice all sexy like that sent a shiver down my spine that made my tenth toe twitch.

"I promised I'd help you forget this morning. I don't see why we can't get started on that now."

I didn't know how he managed to carry me. I was nothing but goo. Completely melted by him.

"I don't have any protection. Don't we still have to worry about fertility and all that?" I asked as he mounted the stairs.

"I have an entire box of condoms in my room, and I plan on using every single one of them this afternoon." Holy Hecate, he was sexy.

I gulped.

"The whole box just today?" I squeaked.

He cocked his head to the side. "Today and tonight. I'll have to get more for tomorrow."

"At that rate, you might as well buy them by the case. How long do you think we will need them for?"

"Now until the wedding," he answered.

"And when is that?" As far as I knew, Gage was getting some papers signed, and that was it, he hadn't mentioned a wedding.

"Next week, right before the full moon. You, me, and Judge Neeley. It's all arranged."

He lowered me into his bed and then kissed me on the forehead. "You get some sleep; I'll erase your memory later."

I grabbed him by the collar and pulled his mouth to mine. I kissed him with a hungry need.

"Or I could do that now." He fell into bed with me, and I forgot about the world.

PART III

ENDING TORMENT

1

Life wasn't exactly going as planned. After all, no one plans for the man they're in love with to abuse them with plans of killing them. At least, I didn't; and now, even my dreams betrayed me.

My fingers barely grazed along the top of the heavy pine beam railing, my lime green fingernails a bright contrast to the warm golden tones of the highly polished wood. I didn't hold on for balance. I didn't need to as I skipped down the stairs. My feet, with matching green toenail polish, landed firmly, yet gracefully, on the treads. The only reason I paused on the main landing, where the stairs merged into a single wide grand staircase, was to admire my beautiful, handsome husband.

His presence commanded any space he filled. At six-two with shoulders as broad and thickly muscled as his, he filled space. His stunning perfection caught me off guard at times. His dazzling white smile would flash, and his green eyes would catch the light just so. It was as if I was seeing him for the first time, and I would need to catch my breath.

He was why I loved trailing my fingers down the smooth

beams of the railing. I loved touching what he loved. The summer he turned nineteen he spent hours upon hours restoring and hand polishing this centerpiece of the lodge's lobby. His uncle owned the lodge back then, now it was Gage's.

Today, he stood in a shaft of filtering sunlight, the beam singling him out like a spotlight. He lifted his eyes to mine—wowza, what a man.

I reached up to brush my orange and teal hair back from my face.

"Ow, fuck, Hecate, Demeter, and Isis!"

I rolled over, alone in bed—something I wasn't used too. Ever since Doggo saved me, and led the pack to me, I haven't been alone in bed. Doggo, who turned out to be some kind of reverse werewolf, had been with me since he found me. He even stayed with me in the hospital.

He stayed with me during his new moon shift into a human, and, oh boy, did he stay with me. But after his return to wolf form, he attacked one of my new lovers in a fit of jealous rage. I hadn't seen him since.

Gage, my betrothed, wasn't around. I knew he had a double shift tonight so he wouldn't be back until much later. Even so, Travis, the lover Doggo bit, typically slipped into bed for sleep cuddles. He was nowhere to be seen, and if not him, then Zeke, the quietest, and probably best dressed, of the pack. I punched my pillow and flopped over on my side.

Wrong side. My stitches throbbed with a sharp spike of pain the second I slammed into the pillow. Stupid move. Stupid, stupid, stupid.

With more care of the side of my head, I rolled over to my other side and eased down onto the pillow. I didn't need to be as gentle, no stitches, but I was still cautious. The stitches still throbbed in protest.

In the morning, there was no sign of Gage having slipped in while I slept.

My descent of the grand staircase wasn't nearly as graceful or as quick as I dreamed about. I still loved running my hand over the smooth pine Gage spent time on in his youth. To me, this glowing polished wood told me he had dedication, perseverance, patience, and knew how to bring the best out of something he cared for.

Feeling particularly wobbly, I boot scooted down the stairs like a toddler who couldn't do stairs even with a death grip on the railing. I pushed my new crutch ahead of me. The old one was a casualty of an incident I'd rather forget, but the eighteen stitches on my head reminded me constantly.

Unlike my dream, where I gazed lovingly down on Gage, and he smiled back, now I gazed lovingly, but he scowled at Sheriff Kelley. They both wore their uniforms. While Sheriff Kelley looked fresh in her uniform, Gage looked like he had been dragged under a truck. No wonder he didn't come to bed last night—he hadn't come home.

Home. That gave me a happy, tingling feeling up my spine.

That happy feeling dissipated fast when Gage turned his glower on me. Officer Kelley had a serious sour-puss expression on her face. Somehow, whatever happened, I could tell they weren't mad at the situation—they were mad at me.

I decided to stop at the top step leading down from the main landing. It looked like a pool full of khaki-clad sharks down there, and I wasn't much of a swimmer these days.

"Good morning, Officer Kelley. I haven't seen you for a while." A while? Maybe a week, but it seemed like forever since everything had happened.

She narrowed her eyes and returned her focus to Gage.

She shook a piece of paper out to him, expecting him to take it from her. He didn't. He crossed his arms and shook his head.

I scooted about halfway down the stairs so I could hear them. They both knew I was there. I knew they knew because they both, at one point or another, shot me with glares and laser eyeball rays. Officer Kelley was pissed at me about something.

I bit the inside of my cheek and tried to think. What could I have done to piss this woman off? Had I stolen her man? And if so, which one was hers? That wasn't it. If I had stolen her guy, she would have given me that death stare days ago.

The exasperated look Gage gave me made me feel guilty, but I hadn't done anything.

"Will you tell Sharon here all of your interactions with Kathleen?" He tossed his hands up in frustration.

Oh, her name was Sharon, yeah, that fit her. And I took her friend's man. Yep, okay, I could see what was happening here. A line in the sand over Gage had been drawn, and Sharon was on Kathleen's side of it. Gage said Kathleen tried to use her connection to the Sheriff's Department as a form of leverage in town, and that was one of the reasons their engagement ended. Looked like Kathleen was attempting to leverage her friendship with Sharon in a similar fashion, and that would be why Officer Sharon Kelley was over here first thing in the morning, all nice and crisply dressed trying to catch Gage out after he had a long night's double shift.

"All of them?" I sighed heavily as if this was going to be exhausting.

I pointed with one pointer finger to the other one, starting my count.

"I met Kathleen the night—" I paused. I wasn't about to

let Sharon know anything about Travis and Max's altercation. Besides, I didn't even know if she was aware of the dual aspects of the guys. "The night the FBI said they wanted us to go fishing for Gordon." I closed my eyes and paused again.

He was in custody. He. Was. In. Custody. I was safe. *Breathe, damn it.*

"So, last week some time." I ticked over to my next finger, counting my second encounter with the woman. "Then again two or three days later, we ran into her at the grocery store. I tried to be friendly, she sneered at me, so, I flipped her off and bought more ice cream than intended."

With exaggerated movement, I lifted my right hand as if I was going to continue to count, but instead, I flipped my wrists. "And that's it. That's all I have interacted with Kathleen."

"You've been harassing her on the phone," Officer Kelley bit out.

"I called her once following up on a job someone told me about. As soon as I recognized her voice, I said wrong number and hung up. That's not harassing her. That was a wrong number."

"You just said you were looking for a job. You had her number," Officer Kelley corrected me.

"If I had known it was Kathleen's business, I wouldn't have called, so that makes it a wrong number for me. Look, I don't even have a phone. Did she say what number all these harassing calls were coming from?"

"Sharon, that restraining order is not legit, not over some phone calls."

She shook the papers at Gage's face. "Keep her one hundred yards away from Kathleen, she's dangerous."

Kelley threw the papers at Gage's chest and stormed off.

"One hundred yards? Fine, I don't have any intention of getting near her. Kathleen's really pissed that it's over between you two, isn't she?" I asked Gage as I watched the other sheriff leave.

"It's been over for a long time, Bailey." He walked over to the stairs. I scooted down a few more steps, so we were eye level.

"No Gage, as long as you were banging her, in her head, you'd come around." I shook my head.

"And you know this how? Suddenly you have great insight into Kathleen's mind?" he asked.

"She's a woman. And you're one hell of a catch in a town like this. Anywhere actually. You're a sheriff, so steady job, a pillar of the community; you own this lodge, so you have equity. You probably have a savings account and a retirement plan, and you are crazy good looking."

He leaned in, and his green eyes sparkled at me. "Is that what you think of me?"

I shook my head again. "That's what a woman like Kathleen would think of you—stable, husband material."

Gage laughed.

"I think you're sexy as hell and not a loser, and that's all it took for me."

"Aren't those the same things?" he asked.

He was getting perilously close. I leaned back on my elbow, teasing him to lean in more. It worked, he placed a knee on one of the stairs, and I could feel his breath on my skin.

"Hardly, Kathleen probably had you checked out and confirmed you were going to inherit this place before she ever got into your pants. Am I right?"

He nodded, and his rough, unshaven cheek grazed against mine. "You didn't care about my portfolio, did you?"

"What's a portfolio? I just want what's in your pants."

Gage started nibbling on my ear, and I lay back against the stairs. The treads probably should've been uncomfortable against my back. With Gage against my front, I couldn't bring myself to care. His lips grazed along my jaw before pressing to mine. His tongue found mine, and they danced together as our mouths attempted to merge us into a single being.

"Ew, get a room," Yuki said as she skipped past us on her way down the stairs.

Gage rolled off and sat next to me. I sat up and scratched my eyebrow.

"Mood killer," I called out as she disappeared behind the service doors to the kitchen. "So, a restraining order, huh?"

Gage pulled the papers from his back pocket. He flattened them out and flipped to the last page of the stapled document. "This isn't real. This isn't even Neeley's signature." He held up the paper for me to see.

"Couldn't another judge have signed it?"

"There are no other judges in Wet Waterfalls. I'll get Neeley to look at this later. And get the correct information to Kelley and the rest of the department."

"One hundred yards isn't such a big deal, is it. I'll just stay away from where ever she lives."

"The catering company is located in the middle of town."

I shrugged. "So what? I can avoid her block."

"Bailey, the entire town isn't even one hundred yards long. She is trying to keep you out of Wet Waterfalls all together by doing this."

I slumped forward, burying my face in my hands. "The whole freaking town? That's not fair," I groaned loudly.

"What's not fair, young lady?"

I looked up to see a rather well dressed—seriously, the men in this town knew how to dress—older gentleman. He strolled in like he owned the place, twirling a walking stick. A gods-be-damned walking stick! I wasn't thrilled that people could waltz in here any time they wanted. I get it was a hotel on one level, but it was an exclusive hotel, and more importantly, it was now my home. I'd have to talk to Gage about some kind of key code system.

"Judge Neeley." Gage stood.

I wasn't about to stand up. I couldn't, not after that little blow Gage delivered about Kathleen trying to ban me from the entire town.

"I came to meet your bride and turns out, I have walked in on some drama?" He cocked his head to the side and began removing his gloves.

"Hi." I gave the man a shy smile. I really wasn't up for too much else. "Pardon me for not getting up. I'm still a bit wobbly on my feet, and today it seems a bit worse."

"Everything about you looks a bit worse for wear. I've heard your story. How are you feeling?" He shook Gage's hand, and then sat down next to me and patted my knee.

I was having a hard time wrapping my brain around this guy being a judge. Judges were stodgy and didn't have a sense of humor. Not that I ever actually met a real judge before. This guy was too much like one on a TV sitcom, and less like the ones on all those cop shows.

"I feel a lot like I look; like I've been dancing the tackle cha-cha. I just took another hit."

Judge Neeley looked up at Gage for translation.

Gage held out the document Sheriff Kelley had thrown at him.

The judge flipped to the last page. He scoffed. "That's what Kathleen Addams was in my office about yesterday?

This isn't my signature. Sloppy forgery." He handed the papers back to Gage.

"Don't worry about Kathleen. She's entered a pissing contest she can't win."

I choked on my spit. I liked this guy.

"I probably should do due diligence since I am here, and find out if there is any substantiation to her claims." Judge Neeley looked from me to Gage, and back at me.

I sighed and started to do my finger count down again.

"None." Gage cut me off. "Bailey has only ever seen Kathleen twice, and the only time she called was because she was following up on a job lead that Keiko Shaefer had shared. Bailey didn't know the number was Kathleen's, and she tried to treat it like a wrong number and end the call as soon as she realized she had called Kathleen."

When the judge looked over at me, I nodded.

"All right then, I will give Ms. Addams a call into my office this afternoon. Don't worry about this nonsense. Let's talk nuptials." He clapped his hands together. I think he was more excited than I was.

"I thought it was just going to be us signing the paperwork?" I asked.

"Oh, please tell me you'll at least have a little social gathering and celebration?" He looked up at Gage who stood in front of us.

Gage shrugged. "Yes, Yuki is planning something, and I believe balloons and cake are involved."

"Good, good. Now, about the additional husbands."

I was very much surprised my eyes didn't pop out of my head and roll down the rest of the stairs. How much did this guy know?

I looked at Judge Neeley with nothing but panic.

Gage kicked at the bottom step. "Nothing is going to happen until Max agrees. Bailey said he's husband two."

I had? I didn't exactly remember that. It was true, I just didn't remember. My throat felt like sandpaper. Bigamy was technically illegal, and polyamory confused people—and this guy was a judge.

"Don't worry, dear, it's all good. Gage will legally be your only husband. The rest will be ceremonial husbands. I just needed to be clear on my timelines. So, only the one celebration this time. Should I go ahead and lock in a date in two weeks?"

He knew? How many people knew, and how much did they know?

"I haven't seen Max for over a week," I said.

"Don't worry, dear, he'll come around." And with that, Judge Neeley stood up. "I will see you in two days." He extended his hand to shake mine, then shook Gage's and left.

I don't think I could take any more surprises this morning.

2

————————

It didn't matter what I thought. Surprises happened.

The next one was a good one. A package delivery guy strolled through the door while I still sat perched on the stairs.

He tried to be professional and courteous while Gage signed for the delivery. He couldn't take his eyes from me. I admit I looked pretty rough.

"Car accident," I said.

Delivery guy made an 'O' with his mouth, and his eyes went wide in a matching shape. "I hope you feel better soon," he said as he left.

I opened my mouth to say something about that front door when Gage handed me the box, and I forgot what I was about to say.

I ripped into it with as much enthusiasm as I could muster, which wasn't much. I ended up having to hand it back so Gage could pull a tool off his sheriff-issued utility belt and cut the box open.

"A phone!" I squealed.

"You'll need to contact your provider and get everything transferred over."

I could handle that. But I had a phone!

"Who did this?" I asked. I needed to thank someone since I hadn't made arrangements. And it was the latest model, so I really needed to thank them. I couldn't afford to drop that kind of change on a new phone.

Gage shrugged. "Don't know. Is there a note?" He started up the stairs and kissed me on the temple. "I need to take a shower."

"You going to bed?" I looked up at him. I wouldn't blame him if he did.

"Not now. I'll take a long nap later. Can you get yourself where you're going?"

I nodded and returned to looking for a note when he headed upstairs.

No note. This was the kind of thing Yuki would do, but I know she didn't make that kind of money, same with Jade.

I finished butt bumping my way down the stairs, hauled myself up with the help of the railing, and then slowly limped my way into the kitchen.

Coffee and laughter hit my senses as I pushed through the doors.

"Hey Jade, you're up kind of early," I said as if I was always up this early, and knew everyone's habits.

"I'm going into the salon today for a brief orientation, and to cover any walk-ins during lunch."

"Wow, already?"

She nodded. It was great how easy her decision to move here was going. In less than a day of proclaiming she and Yuki were moving, they both found jobs downtown. As a hair stylist, Jade lucked out that a chair was available at a local salon. And Yuki was offered a job on the spot at Shaefer's Doughnuts, where Keiko made the most heavenly, cloud-like doughnuts. Maybe it was Yuki's personality that Keiko responded too; perhaps it was a being half-Japanese bonding thing. Either way, it was great my two best friends had jobs in Wet Waterfalls.

I wasn't quite so lucky, seeing how the one job lead I had, thanks to Keiko, was at Kathleen's catering business. That wasn't going to happen. I could find something else, even if event coordinating for a growing caterer were ideal, working for Kathleen was the opposite of ideal.

"You want to come in and get your hair washed?" Jade asked.

I gasped. I had been exiled to half-bathing bird baths with washcloths since I got the stitches in my head. I loved having Jade work her fingers through my hair. She was the magician, well; witch, now that I knew she was *actually* a witch, who kept my naturally red hair enhanced with streaks of purples and pinks. She had worked her magic with some vitamin C tablets and stripped the traumatizing brown dye from my hair while I was on strict bed rest after the surgery that left me with nine toes.

I wasn't allowed to wash my hair because of the gash and stitches that held my scalp together.

"I'd love to have my hair washed. You can..." I waved at the bandage covering my head.

"Let's call Tracey, and see if she can meet us at the salon. I can get your head clean, and then she can re-bandage you."

This was the best idea since the invention of ideas. Okay maybe not, but my scalp was itchy, and I could use some cleaning.

Mark, one of the men in Gage's pack, and Jade's current boy-toy slipped a plate of bacon between us. "Eat up."

The surprises were getting better and better.

~

I sat in the front seat of the SUV and watched the trees and snow pass by my window. It was pretty here. Really scenic, and this was the first time I could truly pause the noise in my head long enough to admire everything.

I hadn't been allowed out enough to recognize where we were. I didn't know any of the landmarks. I thought we were headed into town to run a few errands, but we could've been heading out to the highway where convenience shopping had sprung up a few years prior.

The lodge was pretty remote, but I thought town was closer than this. "Where are we going?"

"I have a little surprise," Gage smirked.

With the quality of today's surprises, I wasn't going to complain.

I was confused when he parked in an area that looked like a glorified road pull-off.

He gave me a dazzling smile and then got out of the car. I continued to look out at the snow covered everything. It was picture perfect pretty—basically wilderness on the side of the road in cold snow—pretty, but cold, too cold for me to want to be out in it for any length of time.

I still didn't have a proper winter coat, and I sure as hell didn't have shoes or boots. I still hobbled around in fur-lined Crocs because my foot had swelling issues when it was tired.

Gage walked to the back of the car, opened the tailgate, and shuffled stuff around in the trunk. When he got to my door, he had a huge grin on his face. He was pleased with himself whatever he had cooked up. I opened the door.

"What are you up to?" I asked. This had better be a good surprise. I admit, my stomach started to twist up a little with apprehension. I had survived some pretty fucked up shit this past month. I wanted to continue to survive.

From behind his back, Gage presented me with a lurid pink parka. I gasped.

"It's safety pink, for search and rescue. I figured this was perfect for you."

He laughed as I struggled to get out of my seat belt and take off the layered blankets and jackets I currently wore. I slipped my arm into the thickly quilted sleeve and sighed. I felt warm immediately, and I could tell there were no hidden holes for the wind to sneak in and bite me.

"Gage, it's perfect!" I snuggled into my new coat and pulled the hood up. The white fur lining of the hood kept catching my peripheral vision and distracting me. I thought I saw Max, but when I turned my head, I realized it was just the coat.

"Good, now, let's go for a hike."

Suddenly, my beautiful man had three heads, and they were all a rather odd shade of green. "What do you mean hike? I can't walk."

"But you can ride." He turned around and presented his back to me. "Come on, piggyback."

"Gage, I'm..." I was going to say too big, but this man was built like a bodybuilder, and he carried me around the lodge like I weighed no more than a down pillow.

"Won't you get tired carrying me on a hike?" I asked as I wrapped my arms around his neck and then my legs around his waist.

He grabbed onto the underside of my thighs and hefted me into place. "It's not that far."

"I thought you were tired?" I cajoled.

"I am, but this is important." He kicked the car door closed and started up a trail partially hidden behind branches covered with snow.

Gage was right, this was worth trekking into. In no time at all, our trail followed next to a small river. The water looked almost still in its peaceful journey. Of course, that changed as soon as I said anything.

"That's the Wet River." Gage's breath made puffs of mist as he spoke.

"Aren't all rivers wet?" I asked stupidly. And in this case, it was a stupid question.

"Yes, Bailey, they are. But they aren't all named Wet now are they?" His tone would've been perfect coming from any kindergarten teacher, ever.

"Sorry," I said, chagrinned. "Why is it called the Wet River?"

"The Wet is a tributary of the Wind River. This is the Wind River Range, you know that right?"

I laughed. I barely had an inkling of where I was, beyond some postage stamp sized town in Wyoming.

"Gage, I haven't had a real clue as to where I am for a while now. It's all hospital, woods, lodge—safe or in danger. As long as I'm with you, I'm safe. That's all that matters."

He stopped and turned his head over his shoulder to look at me. "You are safe with me. If I wasn't an officer of the law—"

"I know," I cut him off. "You don't have to say anything that would compromise your professional integrity." I had the feeling he was going to say he'd personally kill Gordon given half a chance. And I loved him for it, but I wouldn't let him actually say it out loud. That way, if it ever happened, I couldn't testify to meditative anything.

"Bailey, I..."

I kissed him on the cheek. "It's cold out here, where are you taking me?"

The river next to us grew more active, and I swear it steamed. Gage rounded a bend, and we came to the end of the trail. There were benches and railings, and it looked like stairs leading into the water.

Gage backed up against one of the benches and let go of my legs. I stood as he turned around, and wrapped his arms around me. "Welcome to Wet Waterfalls."

I scanned the area. It was beautiful. Snow blanketed the trees in a thin gleaming layer of white. The river bounced but didn't rage, and it definitely steamed. A small fall of water defined one edge of a large natural pool that the stairs lead into.

"Where are the falls?" I asked, expecting something huge and grand and noisy, like in the painting in the dining room of the lodge.

He pointed at the pile of rocks with water running down their face.

I laughed. "That's more like a water drop. I thought you said the falls were once a tourist draw?"

"They were. There's a natural hot spring feeding into the river right here. See all that steam? It was said it had magical restorative healing properties. Turns out, it's just sulfur."

"We aren't going swimming, are we? Cause you're nuts if you think I'm taking off my clothes out here." It was too cold, and cold and wet from everything the guys told me was a dangerous combination.

I sat down with the back edge of the bench sharp against my butt, gazing out at the waterfall. Even if it wasn't what my mind's eye thought of as a waterfall, it was pretty, and I'd want to come back when the weather was warmer. Gage played with my fingers. I looked back at him when he took my mitten off and began working my ring off.

"What are you doing? That's mine, no take backs."

"I didn't do this right the first time," he said, holding my hands in his.

"I said yes. Doesn't that make it right?" I really didn't understand why he was doing this, he had already asked twice in the last week.

"I always thought I'd bring the love of my life out here to propose," he said as he gazed into my eyes.

"You actually thought about how you'd pop the question? Did you bring Kathleen out here? Am I getting an often repeated routine?"

"Bailey, will you let me do this? No, I didn't bring Kathleen out here. That should've been a clue that she wasn't the right one for me."

"Sorry." I couldn't help but grin like an idiot as he knelt in the snow and held that pink silicone band out to me again.

"Will you marry me?"

I felt giddy like it was the first time he asked. Butterflies swarmed in my stomach, and my heart skipped beats.

"Yes, Gage, I will marry you." He was up with his arms wrapped around me. I watched as he slipped the ring back on my finger. I know it was only a temporary ring in his mind, and the diamond was a shape etched into the silicone, but it was pink, and it was perfect.

I kissed him then. His lips were amazing every time. I was surprised that steam didn't rise off our bodies. He certainly cranked my personal temperature up.

"Let's get you back to the car. We have more stops to make." Gage turned his back to me, indicating it was time to piggy-back ride part two.

"No fucking way," he muttered before stepping away from me.

"Hey!" I called out as my balance wobbled without him. I sat heavily on the back of the bench and grabbed a nearby branch to keep from falling. The tree dusted me with snow. Spikes of cold where snow made it past my hood and touched skin were not welcome.

"Are you just going to stare at us, or are you coming over here?"

I couldn't see who Gage was yelling at. All I saw was a cluster of trees and more snow. And then the snow moved. Another surprise. I closed my eyes and hoped it was a good one.

"Holy Hecate. Max?"

He looked at me but otherwise didn't move. I couldn't tell from his body language if he was still pissed off at me. I couldn't tell from my dry throat if I was still pissed at him or not.

"Doggo?" I sniffed and swiped at tears.

That must've been the magic word because everything about him changed. He bowed and opened his mouth in a doggy grin, tongue hanging out. He pranced a bit and then ran straight for us.

He was on the bench and in my face. I grabbed his scruff and tried to hug him, but his whole body wiggled, and he licked at me. He jumped off the bench and back up to head butt and paw at me a few times.

"Glad to see you got your head out of your ass," Gage said. "Look, we need to tell you a few things."

Doggo sat, or rather, squirmed in place. But his ears were up, and his attention forward.

I love you, Max. I tried to think into his head.

His return thoughts were less clear, but I heard them. *Love. Sorry. Missed. Love.*

"Bailey and I are getting hitched."

Doggo growled. It wasn't menacing, but it was a complaint.

"And then if you behave, I'm going to marry you, so get over it," I chided him. "And I'm also going to marry the rest of the guys at some point, so stop trying to kill Travis."

"We are pack, and we are hers," Gage brought out that mantra. I was beginning to understand what it meant. They were mine, but I was also theirs.

"Max, please understand." I needed him to be on board with this. "I love you all, but you can't do that again. You scared me."

He licked me. I took that as an apology.

Gage carried me back to the SUV. I was so happy. Max was back, Gage wanted to marry me so much he asked me for the third time, and today was just going really well, despite its rocky start.

I thought I saw a familiar person hiking away from where we had left the SUV. "Isn't that Mark?" I asked as we got to the car.

Doggo tore off and ran in the direction I swear there had been a person. If he managed to head in the same direction, I had to have seen someone.

Nothing.

3

We climbed into the SUV, and Doggo leaped into the back. I forgot he could practically fly.

This was right. This is what home felt like. I snuggled down into my new coat, the color made me happy. Being warm made me happy. Everything made me happy, and after the past few weeks I'd had, I deserved this.

Gage was right, downtown was barely one hundred yards long. I closed my eyes and pushed that thought away. I didn't need thoughts of Kathleen ruining my moment of happiness. Why should my own brain help out when she was capable of doing that all on her own?

Our first stop was the baker—an actual baker with a case of pastries and decorated cakes.

The scent of warm sugary carbs made my mouth water. I selected a cherry turn over from the case, a difficult decision since there were so many attractive options. I ate while Gage and the baker discussed wedding cakes.

Every bite I took was an explosion of pastry flakes. I dusted powdered sugar and crumbs of the puff pastry from my front.

"What's your favorite flavor?" Gage turned and asked me. I sat in a cafe seat near the door. Max sat guard on the other side of the picture window. No dogs allowed.

Doggo and I played a little game through the window. I would point to a spot on the glass, and he would nose the same spot on the other side. The window was going to be a nose printed mess by the time we were done.

"I like carrot cake, but I also like regular white cake when the frosting is really fancy, and the cake is there to show off the decorations. But the frosting has to be really good. Too much dye and it tastes bitter."

I knew he was ordering our wedding cake, but part of me almost didn't think this was real.

He returned to discussing something with the woman behind the counter. She had been friendly enough when we first walked in, but the longer they talked, the more her expression looked like she smelled something foul.

"What's your favorite color?"

"I can't believe you are even asking me that," I answered.

He laughed. He looked as happy as I felt. "Right, dumb question." I heard him say "pink," after he returned to his conversation.

I returned to my game with Doggo.

The doorbells tinkled as someone walked in. I didn't bother to look up. I was having too much fun flirting with Doggo.

"You can't be serious?" Oh, I already knew that voice entirely too well.

I looked up to see Kathleen sneering at me.

I'm never serious, that's boring. What I really said was, "Oh, hi. Gage?"

I wasn't mentally prepared for a showdown with this woman.

"Kathleen, I'm so glad you stopped in. I have those cookies you order. Give me a second, and I'll grab them from the back." The woman helping Gage was entirely too happy to see Kathleen. I thought it was really rude of her to abandon Gage mid-order, but then again, if it got Kathleen away from me faster...

"You know you can't be here right?" she asked me.

I shook my head. "No, what do you mean?"

"You can't come into my town and harass me this way. You were served notice this morning, you're in violation—"

"Of nothing, Kathleen. Bailey is in violation of nothing," Gage said. But she seemed to ignore him.

The baker came around her counter with an arm full of pink baker's boxes that I can only assume were full of cookies. "Here you go. Eight dozen sugar decorated fall motif. Are you going to be needing more as we get closer to Thanksgiving?" She set the boxes on one of the other tables, and Kathleen opened each box to inspect the cookies.

"These looked fantastic as always." Oh, Kathleen could be nice, just not to me. "I have three dinners lined up. I need to confirm guest numbers before I can let you know the exact amount, but right now, it looks like four dozen. I'll let you know."

She smiled sweetly at the other woman and picked up her boxes. The baker opened the front door for her. Kathleen paused to sneer at me. "Why are you still here? I'm calling the Sheriff's Department."

"That's not necessary, Kathleen." Gages voice rumbled through me and reminded me that I wasn't alone.

She took one look at him and flipped her hair in a dramatic I-am-not-talking-to-you move, and started out the door again.

"Say hi to Judge Neeley when you see him this afternoon." I twinkled my fingers at her.

She stopped, and her spine went stiff. Good, I got a hit in.

I cut my gaze to Gage. He leaned on the counter smirking. It looked like I score points with him too.

"I don't know who you think you are, but you can't talk to my customers like that. You have to leave."

The baker hadn't acknowledged my presence even once since we had come in. Even when I had picked out a treat from her counter, Gage had to repeat my order for her. Now, I really didn't like her.

"Excuse me?" I blinked in shock at the woman.

"You heard me, get out. And take your mutt. I should charge you for messing up my window like that."

I stared at her completely confused. We were customers, and I was pretty sure the cake Gage was trying to order was going to be more money than some stupid cookies.

"Okay, fine. I'll leave." I seriously thought about licking the inside of the window, opposite some of Doggo's licks on the outside, to really mess up her window. I slowly stood up and started putting my coat on. "Gage, I'll be right outside."

I grabbed my crutch and before I took a step she had turned to Gage and was telling him it turned out she couldn't make the cake he wanted.

"We can do something smaller," he suggested.

No, it turned out she couldn't do anything for him at all.

"Come on, Bailey, let's get out of here." Gage strode to me and took my crutch. I clutched on to his arm as we left. As much as I wanted to run away, I just didn't move that fast.

"We can get a cake at the grocery store. It'll probably taste better, that pastry was really dry." I couldn't help myself, I had to get a jab in somehow.

Doggo was by my side as soon as we were out of the door. His presence provided a bit of stability. I hated that I didn't have my balance back. It felt like it was getting worse at a time when I should've been getting better.

We walked past a boutique, and a flash of yellow caught my eye.

"Can we go in there?" I asked.

Doggo took guard position by the front door, and Gage led me inside.

I pointed over to the display of scarves I saw through the window. They were semi-sheer, and they felt like silk. The colors were amazing, with artisan quality dye work that looked like everything from a garish pink sunset, to ocean waves.

I hadn't planned for our wedding to be anything more than us signing papers and being done with it, but the sense I got from Gage and Judge Neeley, we were having a little celebration. I should dress up a little bit. I didn't have a clue what I was going to wear, but I knew what kind of veil I wanted.

I found a watercolor silk that looked like a wash of sunshine and flowers.

"Gage, can I borrow some money?" I asked eagerly as I rubbed the soft, smooth silk between my fingers. I didn't have a clue how or when I'd pay him back, but I didn't have my credit card, and I no longer had a job.

"What do you want, Bailey?"

I showed him the scarf. He raised his eyebrows and looked at the price tag. He nodded slowly. It wasn't cheap. He reached up and removed it from the display.

"Anything else?"

I shook my head. "Not from here." There was much more, so much more. I was going to have to get Jade and

Yuki to help me. I now had a veil, and I was going to need a dress.

My euphoria of finding a beautiful yellow veil was quickly grounded.

"Hey, Gage. I saw Kathleen the other day," the shop keeper said as she took the purchase from Gage.

Oh, for pity's sake. I stopped listening. Another one of Kathleen's fan club. I limped over to a large table display of vintage broaches. Not being as stable as I should be, I pumped into the table, and it shook.

"Hey, you need to watch your step." I was blown away by the rude attitude of Kathleen's friend. Then again, if she really was Kathleen's friend, she wasn't mine.

Another line had been drawn in the snow; so far the baker and this shop keeper were on Kathleen's side of the line. But I had Gage.

"I'll tell Kathleen you said 'hi,'" she called out after Gage as we left.

"You do that, she'll know you're lying," I called out in reply. My passive aggressive meter broke. My comments were only going to get more aggressive and direct as today went on if I had to keep listening to women coo about Kathleen to Gage.

"Is it going to be like this in every shop?" I asked him.

He shook his head, "No, darling, it won't be."

I leaned into him and buried my fingers into Doggo's thick fur. So what if Kathleen had friends. I had friends too, and I had these two.

We walked passed a hardware shop and walked into another shop, a florist. Great, this was going to be another friend of Kathleen's. Of course, the caterer would be friends with the florist and the baker, and... I sighed and hoped this one wouldn't kick us out because I wanted some flowers for my wedding.

I expected Doggo to take up watch by the front door, but he followed us inside.

"Max!" A young woman, okay, she had to be a teenager, nineteen tops, came out of nowhere and wrapped around Doggo.

His tail thudded against the floor.

She ruffled his ears, "Haven't seen you around for a while." She looked up at Gage and launched into his arms for a monster-sized hug. "Is it true? Rumor has it you're getting married, and it's not Kathleen."

"Damn, news in this town travels fast." From the look on her face, I had said that out loud.

She gave me a bright smile, and her dark eyes sparkled with mischief. I liked her already.

"Channie, this is Bailey," Gage introduced us.

Channie stuck her hand out to me.

"Channie's mother owns the flower shop."

"Yeah, but she's gone and abandoned me. Leaving me to run this place all by myself. How am I supposed to be open for business and make deliveries?" she asked Gage. I was pretty sure it was a rhetorical question.

"Abandoned you?" I asked.

"Yeah, the woman went and took a vacation to Florida, and stayed. She met some man down there and came back long enough to get her things, hand me the keys, and so long. I have nightmares realizing my mom moved to Florida for dick. It had better be good dick, that's all I'm saying."

I laughed. I knew that one a bit too well. I was moving to Wyoming for some damned fine dick. I sympathized with her mother.

Channie gave me a once over with her eyes, glanced at Gage, and then scanned me again.

"So, what kind of flowers are you looking for?" I guess I passed her test, whatever it was.

"Can you do a flower crown?" I asked.

Her face lit up with excitement, "Can I do a flower crown? What colors do you want? What are you thinking?"

I pulled out my yellow veil. "Something to go over this. I think pinks and oranges would look good."

"A yellow veil? Seriously? Like Ancient Roman, or is yellow your favorite?" She fingered the fine silk.

"Like Ancient Roman. I wanted something that would cover all of this up, and still look pretty." I circled a finger at the bandage around my head.

Channie and I talked flowers.

Gage wandered off at some point.

He and Max came back as we were assembling the collection of flowers for a small bouquet. I set aside a bright pink lily for Gage's boutonniere.

"Everything settled?" he asked.

Channie nodded. "It's all picked out and will be ready. I can deliver it the morning of the wedding."

"Add it to my bill," Gage said it like he ordered flowers all the time.

I gave him a big toothy grin. My stomach tried to do a flip. We were getting married.

"You don't have Babs doing the cake do you?"

"Is that the baker?" I asked.

"No, she decided she wasn't able to help us out," Gage said.

"I figure we can get one from the grocery store. Those are usually pretty good anyway." I wasn't going to let Kathleen and her cranky friends ruin this for me.

"Sounds like a good plan. Babs does really good cookies, but her cakes are really dry," Channie said.

"So are the turnovers." There's flakey, and then there is dry like sawdust.

"I'll go get the car, you wait inside. Max will stay with you."

I sighed. I was glad Gage wasn't going to make me walk back. I wasn't feeling any more stable. And I was doubly glad Doggo was with me. Gordon couldn't nab me again. Of course, Gordon was in custody, so that wasn't an issue.

"So, Bailey, what are you going to do now that you're moving here for a man?" The tone in her voice had a definite edge of judgment to it. Considering her mother up and abandoned her for a man, I didn't blame her.

I shrugged. "No idea. I need to find a job. And hopefully, one that doesn't mind that I need to sit down until I completely regain my strength. Or that I will have a rather punk-rock hairdo for a while as this mess grows back out and I can do something with it. I thought I had a hot job lead, but it turned out to be working for Kathleen, and..."

"You don't need to explain anymore. She has a nasty attitude, and a good chunk of this town thinks her shit don't stink. And she believes them. Trust me, she stinky."

I couldn't help myself but laugh. "Not a member of her fan club?"

"Hardly. Unfortunately, we work a lot of the same jobs. Hazards of being in parallel industries. You know, you have a really good sense of color," she said.

"Thank you. Not everyone appreciates my color aesthetic."

"They wouldn't, people get very hung up on what they think flowers should look like. Have you considered working at a florist?"

4

———

I blinked a few times. "I don't know anything about flowers."

"I can teach you about flowers, what I can't teach you is how to put colors together the way you have. Most people want to toss in a single color flower, maybe an accent of white and then some green. But you have a real flair."

"Wow, thank you. I'd love to. I don't know how soon I'll be allowed to go back to work. Do you need someone right away? I mean, if you have to get someone in right away, I understand if you can't wait."

She looked at me. I could tell she *was* thinking, I just couldn't tell *what* she was thinking.

"What I need is someone who can mind the shop while I make deliveries. You wouldn't have to do anything, just sit at the counter in case someone comes in. And then when you get stronger and can give me more hours, you can help put orders together. We can start you off slow, so when your doc says you can do something for a few hours a day, you could maybe do this?"

I could do that. I could sit at a counter for an hour or two until I was stronger.

"Could Max come with me?" I asked. I was going to need some kind of guardian for a while until I started to know in my bones that Gordon was in jail.

"Of course, he can. Max is a good dog, aren't you?" She made baby talk sounds at him and ruffled his ears.

Gage had to carry me out of the flower shop. I was too tired after my morning activities. I whined that Jade said she would wash my hair, but Gage insisted I return to the lodge for some rest, and possibly a nap.

I slept warm and safe with Doggo next to me for the first time in over a week.

I woke up with a warm fur blanket. I forgot how comfortable it was to sleep next to him. I'd never need an electric blanket again.

I cracked open my eyes and to Tracey fussing on the side of my room. My skin chilled as a split second of panic spread over me. I didn't want to be hooked up to an IV again.

"Bailey, I need you to wake up."

I pushed up into a sitting position. Doggo shifted but continued to play blanket.

"What's up?" I asked

"It's time for your meds." Tracey handed me a horse pill and a cup of water.

I glared at her, but I swallowed my pill. "I almost miss the IV."

"Liar," she laughed at me.

She was right. I hated having to live in a hospital gown and drag that pole around. I was much happier with my butt in underwear.

My head itched. I stopped mid-reach before I actually scratched.

"What time is it?" I asked. I probably missed Jade at the salon already.

She gave her watch a glance. "Two-fifteen. Why? I'm tracking your meds."

I shifted and pushed on Doggo. He wouldn't budge. Stupid big wolf. I leaned over and kissed the top of his head, so happy to have the big brute back where he belonged.

"Jade said if I came down to the salon, she would wash my hair."

Tracey turned and leaned back against the counter. "Oh, Bailey, I don't know. We really need to keep the wound dry."

"She'd be really good on only washing the hair side of my head. I itch. You could come with and make sure everything is cool," I whined.

Tracey sighed. She didn't say anything for a while—a long while.

I watched her anxiously and gave her my best puppy dog pleading eyes. It always worked on my mom.

"Okay, we can go get your hair cleaned."

"Yippee!" I may have been disproportionally happy. But my scalp was bugging me almost as much as it did when I needed to rinse the dye out.

I swung my legs around to the other side of the bed and hobbled around to find my Crocs.

"Can you drive?"

"Why don't we find out if she's even available first?" Tracey was definitely more logical than I was being.

By the time I managed to get myself downstairs, Jade wasn't even at the salon.

She lounged across the couch with her feet up watching TV.

"Hey, Bails." Jade sounded really tired.

"I missed you at work, huh? How was it?" If I were at one-hundred percent, I would've returned her greeting with enthusiasm. I tripped a little because I wanted to move faster. I wanted to bounce. I fucking wanted my balance back.

Closing my eyes, I paused and took a deep breath. Right foot, crutch, left foot, step. I was back to talking myself through the walking process. Slow, methodic, purposeful action is what I needed to focus on the get across the lobby.

Doggo had already cut his way across the vast room and was through the double doors into the kitchen, so, no support from him.

With a whoosh of air, I collapsed next to her feet on the far edge of the couch.

"It was good, but I'm exhausted."

"You aren't used to working. In a couple of days, your body will adjust to your new routine," Mark commented as he entered through the double doors.

Did he have exceptional hearing? Or was he eavesdropping? Of course, Jade was tired after two weeks off work. My eyes rolled of their own accord. I really needed to learn to control my reactions and lack of poker face better.

"I see Max came back," Mark continued. He handed Jade a tall glass of water.

She took the glass and stared up at him with her eyebrows screwed up. "I really need a beer, Mark."

"You need to hydrate, that's why you're sore," he explained. "Beer is going to dehydrate you further."

"I want to relax," she countered.

"Your muscles will naturally relax after you rest and have had some water."

She drained the glass. With a harrumph, she set the glass on a side table.

I reached over and slid my hand over Jade's feet. She sighed with relief. I wasn't in a position to get up and grab her a beer. I wasn't coordinated enough to walk and carry something, but I could rub her feet.

She was tired because she'd been on her feet with her personality turned all the way to ten. Jade as a stylist was different from Jade as a person. She didn't need Mark mansplaining what she was experiencing. She needed the man to bring her a beer.

"How was it?" I asked.

Jade closed her eyes as I twisted my hands around her feet. I didn't rub feet often, but I knew what I liked. I assumed Jade's tired feet would appreciate the same thing my feet liked.

"Today was great. But I swear everyone waited until lunch to come it, so I had to juggle three walk-ins right away. I thought you were going to come in?"

"Gage made me come home and take a nap. Tracey said she'd bring me down tomorrow to make sure everything was okay. That way she can re-bandage me after you get me cleaned up."

She nodded. "I can do that."

She slid her feet out from under my hands and stood up. "I need a fucking beer. Can I get you something?"

"Yeah, sure. I could use a snack."

I relaxed back into the couch. I curled my feet up underneath me. Big mistake. My four-toed foot still hurt. Instead, I swung my feet up to take over the space Jade abandoned. Picking up the remote, I flipped through channels.

Doggo jumped up onto my legs. I ruffled his fur and sighed. Happy.

Jade returned and gave Doggo the stink eye. The glare was well earned, we stole her spot. I had a bowl of popcorn, a puppy warm lap, one of my best friends, and a rom-com. Life really was pretty good.

"What's Yuki up to?"

"She's spending the day with Keiko."

"She started already?" I asked.

Jade and Yuki were already plugging themselves into the Wet Waterfalls community. I was a little envious, but I was marrying in, not that I was being well received.

Doggo whined in response to my unintentional grumble as I thought about Kathleen.

"What are we doing with your hair for the wedding?" The question came from out of the blue— at least, it felt like it.

"I got a yellow veil, and I'm having a flower crown made. This is turning into a much bigger deal than I thought it was going to be."

"And it's not nearly as big as you deserve. Yuki wants a huge party. Gage wants you to be happy. He's off trying to get a cake now."

"Hades' tits, Jade, I need a dress."

"You want to head into town?"

My stomach sank. "I don't think I can. Half the shop keepers in town already hate me simply because Gage is marrying me and not Kathleen. I get the feeling they were some kind of perfect power couple, and even though they aren't together anymore, I think everyone has been expecting them to get married—especially Kathleen."

I felt defeated. I didn't even know where else we could go shopping. I didn't feel mentally strong enough to face downtown again.

After Yuki came back from work, she and Jade took off

to run around and check out what they could find out about the town, and maybe do some shopping. I wasn't up for an adventure, neither mentally or physically. They did promise to see if they could find something for me to wear for this wedding party everyone was planning around me. I was the professional party planner, but apparently, I wasn't allowed to plan my own wedding. Everyone was off doing something. Mark had taken off, Zeke went to work, Travis was buying supplies, and Gage was upstairs sleeping.

I threw popcorn at the TV. Fortunately, with Doggo back in my life, he ate everything that fell to the floor. My fabulous morning dissolved into an afternoon of boredom. The movie I was left in front of wasn't one of my favorites.

The movie ended, finally.

"Let's go find something else to eat," I said to Doggo. He finished eating my popcorn mess off the floor and followed me as I slowly hobbled through the double doors.

By the time Gage found us in the kitchen, we had finished off two half gallons of ice cream—they were mostly eaten before I got to them—leftover mac and cheese, a bag of potato chips, and some corn chips and salsa. I slathered a piece of bread with peanut butter and handed it to Doggo. I felt slightly guilty giggling at the way he pushed his tongue against the roof of his mouth, trying to eat the sticky stuff.

"What are you two doing?" Gage smiled at me.

I turned into a blob as gooey as the peanut butter. That man just had that effect on me.

"Hi there. We were bored." Doggo made a slurping sound as he worked on the peanut butter. "And hungry."

Gage slid onto one of the stools. "Can I get one of those?" He nodded at the sandwiches I slapped together.

I pushed one over to him. It was a sloppy mess. I wasn't

going for picture perfect sandwiches. I was going for make it and eat it.

"Is it always this quiet around here?" I really wasn't complaining. After all the excitement of the past few days, I didn't mind.

"It's a small town, Bailey. There's no nightlife." He chewed at me. "That's when we curl up by the fire..."

"And tell ghost stories?"

He laughed. I loved his laugh.

"Hard to tell stories when you work nights," I complained.

"We'll have mornings together."

"Not if I get the job at the florist," I said.

"Channie offered you a job? Bailey, that's terrific. What did you say?"

"I said I didn't know a thing about flowers, and I didn't know when Doc MacGee would release me for being ready to work." I continued to make another sandwich.

"And?" he prodded.

"And Channie said the job would be waiting for when I could start. She wants me for my sense of color."

I melted a little more at his renewed smile. "You do color very well."

"How do you know? I haven't had a chance to really go shopping, or order anything." I swept a hand in front of this evening's outfit—mint colored narwhal jammie pants, a black t-shirt with laser-eyed kittens, and my mint hoodie. I was positively subdued in my choices.

He leaned over and caught my hair, letting its length slide through his fingers. "Color comes naturally to you."

Holy Hecate, this man did things to my insides. Too bad he was already in uniform and headed out to work.

I swatted at his hand. "Stop." I was a sucker for men who

liked redheads. That was one of the first flirty things Gage ever said to me, and it was etched on my memory forever. I guess it's a good thing my hair was red.

"Do you have a double tonight?" Those shifts always felt so much longer than they really were.

He shook his head. "No, but I'll still be in late."

I looked at him from the side of my eyes and blinked slowly. "You can wake me up when you get home."

He slid from his stool, and wrapped an arm across my back, pulling me into him. He kissed my temple. "It will be my pleasure to wake you up when I get home."

Doggo let out a grumbly woof of a complaint.

This was my life now—a quiet mountain lodge in a quaint small town, a handsome man, and a cranky wolf. It felt so simple, so easy. Truth of the matter was, nothing about the situation was simple. My wolf was cranky because Gage was capable of making love to me, while it would be another two weeks before Max would be human again. And it only seemed quiet because the rest of the pack was out occupying themselves.

Nothing had been easy since before I met them, maybe it would settle down soon. After all, the reason I was here was now in jail. With Gordon out of the way, the danger to me was erased. Maybe easy would happen.

5

My quiet evening ended when everyone who had abandoned me returned home. Yuki and Jade returned first. They had success shopping, discovering that this tiny town had several church sponsored thrift shops. They bought a variety of pieces for my wedding consideration. I had options!

Travis returned and complained about the state I left the kitchen in.

"I'm sorry. It's easier to pull things out than it is to put them away." I shrugged and emphasized how difficult everything was with the crutch.

"Cheap excuse, Bailey, you got it out, you can put it away." I didn't realize how possessive about the kitchen Travis was, especially since he claimed to not be a cook.

He shoved my mess to the side so that he could use the counter to put down the bags and boxes full of supplies he had purchased.

Slowly, I managed to get my dirty dishes into the sink, and the bags of chips put away. The jar of peanut butter, now empty, soaked in the sink, waiting to be recycled. After my mess was mostly contained, I helped to unpack Travis's shopping.

"These go in the pantry." He showed me what items would be stored in the downstairs pantry. He reloaded boxes that I had so carefully unpacked.

"You have to lug all that stuff downstairs now?" I asked.

He cocked a half smile at me, and his eye twinkled with mischief. "The boxes get to take the service elevator."

"Yuki mentioned that. How come there's an elevator going down, but not one going up?"

"It goes up," Travis said.

"Wait. I've been struggling up and down the big staircase out there, and all this time there's been an elevator?"

Travis handed me the crutch and nodded his head to the side. "Come on." He stacked the boxes with supplies, one on top of the other, before picking them up. "I'll show you the elevator."

Travis led the way down the hallway next to the kitchen, into a utility service area of the lodge. He stopped next to the laundry facilities. A small roll-up door, like a mini garage door, was set into the wall. He set his boxes down and pulled on the chain, exposing a cabinet-sized space.

He slid the boxes in. "We have a dumb waiter. Yuki called it a mini elevator for stuff when I first showed it to her. We use it to run supplies, or laundry up and down. It's not for people."

"So, you've been in it?" I asked.

"Of course," he laughed.

"Do you think I could get Gage to put a real elevator in?" I was getting really tired of those stairs. As beautiful as they were, it was exhausting hobbling up them.

After helping clean up, Travis offered to teach Yuki, Jade, and me how to play poker.

"You haven't seen Mark have you?" he asked as he shuffled.

Jade shrugged. "He had stuff to do today. Haven't seen him since breakfast."

"Too bad he's missing this."

"You guys play a lot of poker?" Jade asked.

"Mark thinks he's some kind of card shark," Travis said.

"You're saying he would over explain what we were doing?" Jade scoffed.

Oh good, Mark's 'know everything' attitude hadn't been lost on Jade.

"I'm saying, it'd be fun to watch him lose," Travis smirked. He proceeded to explain how to play basic five-card draw.

Jade yawned and looked bored. If I didn't know her, I would've said she was bored because the game sounded a little too complicated. Yuki stared at him with intense focus.

He ran us through a demonstration of how the game worked.

Excitedly, Yuki spread out her hand of three twos, a three, and a four. It was a terrible hand, but she was proud of it.

"I should fold a hand like this, right?" I asked as I spread my hand out. My cards were all over the place and in all four suits.

"Should we make the stakes interesting?" Travis waggled his eyebrows at me.

"Oh, yeah. Let's play for chocolate," Yuki offered.

I had to suppress a laugh. His disappointment was palatable. Travis wanted to play strip poker. It was so painfully obvious. Yuki's chocolate suggestion had been a glass of cold water on his plans. He had forgotten, she wouldn't have been interested in strip anything.

Travis won another hand.

"Don't worry, you'll get the hang of it." I'm pretty sure those were the wrong words to say.

"We could play for shots," Yuki suggested.

"Sounds like fun." Travis pushed away from the table, and returned a few minutes later with four shot glasses and a bottle of golden whiskey

I shot her a glare, was she trying to get Travis drunk?

We played another hand. Travis won again.

Zeke stopped by to watch us stare at our cards. "Don't let him talk you into strip poker. I swear that's his fantasy, strip poker with a table of beautiful women."

Yuki and Jade made knowing eye contact. Jade shrugged. "Why not?"

"Okay, Travis, you want to play strip poker?" Yuki asked. That delightfully evil lilt was in her voice.

He answered her with a bright toothy grin and a gleam in his eye.

Jade stretched and yawned after we declared the game over. She and Yuki were still fully clothed. I lost my hoodie.

"Travis is never going to play poker with us again," I declared.

"He's never going to underestimate women again," Jade smirked.

"That was fun. He kind of does have a cute butt. Still not interested in touching it," Yuki said.

Travis had gathered his clothes in front of his naked body and went into the kitchen to get dressed.

"You cheated," he said as he rejoined us, once again fully dressed.

"No cheating, just used your own ego against you." Jade stood up and stretched again. "I've got work in the morning. Goodnight."

Yuki followed her upstairs. The wolves in residence followed Yuki, just like they had when she first arrived.

"Did you know they were going to do that?"

"What? Play strip poker, or hand you your ass?"

Travis screwed up his face. "Both?"

I laughed. "Totally. Next time, stick with playing for chocolate." I yawned and felt like my jaw was going to open so far there would be nothing left of me, just a big yawn.

"You think you could put me in that dumb waiter and winch me upstairs?" I didn't feel like I'd survive the trip up on my own.

"How about I carry you instead?" he asked.

"You're always wanting to show off. Sure."

Travis wasn't as physically big as Gage, and I didn't feel as delicate in his arms, but he had no difficulties carrying me up to my room.

My fingers trailed along the top of the heavy pine beam railing. This dream again. I liked this dream. Gage was in it. My fingernails were back, long and pointed like claws, and painted bright red. The color complimented the warm golden tones of the highly polished wood. I didn't need to hold on as I skipped down the stairs, and my bare feet had ten toes.

I paused on the main landing to admire my beautiful, handsome husband. I knew this was a dream, and we weren't married yet, but I also knew he was my husband. The man standing next to him was also my husband, but I didn't know who he was. I guess maybe he was pack, and either I hadn't met him yet, or I had simply forgotten. After all, dreams twist memories up to suit their purposes.

Gage stood at the bottom of the stairs gazing up at me. I went weak in the knees and lost my balance. My toes were literally melting off. I looked down, and my left pinkie toe was gone. If I didn't sit down, I'd start losing other toes.

Carefully, I brushed my blonde hair back from my face. Whoa, my hair was really long, down my back all the way to my butt, and white blonde. I flipped my hair over my shoulder a few times, enjoying the feel of its silky fall. I ran my nails across my scalp...

"Ow, fuck, Zeus's left nut!"

"Bailey, what's the matter?" Travis's groggy voice, the dark room, the pain in my head all drove home the reality that my dream was a far cry from my physical reality.

Okay, so Gage had restored the grand staircase, polishing the natural oak beams back to their current state of glowing beauty, that part of my dream was true. My beautiful husband—also true in a matter of hours. Me tripping delightfully down the stairs without having a death grip on the railing, so much dream. Same with the long swinging hair.

I was tired of waking myself up this way. My head itched. While I was awake, I could stop myself from trying to touch the wounded side of my head. Asleep, I was constantly hitting the bandage. I couldn't wait until I could get my hair washed tomorrow.

I curled into Travis's chest and cried. I had hit the stitches in my head, and they hurt so bad. Not only physically, but mentally.

I cried all of the memories from the first and second kidnapping into Travis's embrace. All of Gordon dying my hair and trying to convince me I was someone different, all of the car accident and the stitches on the side of my scalp. And then I cried some more because even while I loved Travis, he wasn't Max, who had saved me the first time by trying to lead me to safety. Max, who had gathered the packs to keep me warm in the forest after I had escaped. Max, who ran away after attacking Travis in a jealous rage, and who had stayed by my side in my hospital bed for two weeks before that, making sure I was safe.

And he wasn't Gage, who always made things right, because he was alpha, and that's what he did. To say our relationship was complicated was an understatement. Not only was it complicated, but we were also making it up as we went. So far, everyone was happy. Well, everyone except for Max, and he was going to need to get over it.

Travis hooked a finger under my chin and tipped my face up to his.

"Bad dream?" he asked.

"Yeah." I wanted to nod, but nodding moved my head entirely too much. "I went to scratch my head in the dream, and I hit my stitches."

He tipped his head and gave my bandage a soft kiss. He slipped his face alongside mine and kissed each of my eyelids, and then my cheeks. Travis worked his soft lips across my face until he found my mouth.

I sighed into his kiss.

He rolled me onto my back and had the hospital gown I slept in shoved up and to the side. One hand tugged at my panties, while the other supported him above me.

I was delightfully distracted from my stupid dream.

"Get a condom," I whispered.

"Why? I won't tell if you don't," he said between kisses. "I'll pull out. I promise."

"Condom or no sex." I froze up and stopped responding to him. I put my legs together and lay still like a board.

He slid out of bed and rummaged for a condom from the drawer where they now lived in my room.

Gage had some magic powers in him. One of which was he could smell biological changes in me, and that meant while I was potentially fertile, everyone wore a condom. Even with the rule that only Gage or Max could come inside of me, everyone wore a condom.

In a pack, only alphas mated to breed. I wasn't ready for that, and neither was Gage. And we hadn't had a chance to discuss the situation with Max since he came back. And in his current state, he wasn't exactly in a position to have a family planning discussion.

With Max being human only three days a month, it complicated the whole communication issue.

Once I decided I might be ready to have kids, Gage already conceded first father to Max, and Max didn't even know it.

Travis placed the condom pack in my hand, and while I unwrapped that, he unwrapped me. My panties slid right off as soon as he used two hands to pull them down. And the hospital gown was only held on with a tie in the back.

He straddled my waist, and I slid the condom down his length. He hissed and tilted his hips toward my hands.

"Did you—" Before I even finished my thought he was drizzling cool, thick lotion into my hands.

I wrapped my fist around him and began stroking him as he rocked above me.

"Hot damn, Bails." He fell forward onto his hands, caging me in under his body.

I ran my still lube slippery hands over my breasts. Travis pressed his groin down and began stroking between my breasts. This was hot, and this was definitely something I was going to need him to repeat when the others were playing along too. I hadn't expected him to make love to my breasts this way, maybe I wouldn't have insisted on a condom if all the action was going to take place on the upper half of my body.

Apparently, Travis had been turned on much higher and for longer than I thought. He finished his need with a groan of release and satisfaction.

He pushed himself back to a sitting position, still straddling above my middle.

"I need to take care of this, I'll be right back." He carefully swung over and off the bed.

I propped up on my elbows. I wasn't anywhere near being done. Hades, I was barely getting started. Travis made noises in the bathroom, and I found my hospital gown and pulled it back on. I rolled over on my side and pretended to fall asleep. I was too tired and too raw to hash it out with him right now. Travis was a great team player, but his solo skills left me underwhelmed.

He snuggled back into bed, and I think I'd finally fallen asleep when I heard a rumbling whisper. The bed shifted, and the body wrapped around me changed. Travis slid out, and Gage rolled in. The arms were longer and thicker. The body took up more of my bed.

I rolled over and into Gage's arms.

"Long shift?" I asked.

He grunted low in his throat. I was learning that meant bad night.

"You smell like sex," he grumbled.

"I smell like Travis had sex. I assisted. I did *not* have sex." I don't think I even attempted at masking the bitterness in my voice. "You wouldn't be up for fixing that would you?"

I nuzzled into him and ran my head around against his chest, and along his jaw like I was some big cat rubbing all over him.

"I am always the next man you make love to."

"Even if I didn't actually do anything?"

"Even if. I thought you were asleep." He rubbed his chin against the unhurt side of my head.

I yawned. "I was. I figured it was worth asking."

"I've had a long night, darling. I'll still be the next man in the morning unless you need me now." He bundled me closer and made tired huffing sounds.

"I always need you. But I think you need sleep more."

His even breathing told me he was already asleep. My poor tired guy, he must have had a very rough night.

At some point, in the dark still hours of the early morning, Gage woke up. And then he woke me up with his lips on my skin.

I moaned as my brain realized what was happening. "Yes, please, and thank you." The sound was groggy and rough coming from my half-asleep throat.

"Shh. Hmm." Was all the noise Gage made.

Unlike Travis, I didn't have to remind Gage to get a condom. He was already prepared. He had taken care of everything, including removing my hospital gown, before waking me up. And he woke me up beautifully. With his mouth on my breast, he slid two fingers into my sex.

I levitated. I was so ready for him. Travis had left me half frustrated—only half because I was pretty damned tired. Gage was here to finish the job the other man had started. And he did. He finished me well.

I was whining out an orgasm from Gage's fingers before his cock got anywhere near me. And once it was in me, my whines turned to cries. Always a gentleman, Gage made sure I came first before he let loose and let his body rage with lust.

I curled up on my side when Gage left to clean up. He wrapped around me when he returned to bed. In moments we were both asleep, and our joining had passed like a sexy dream.

6

I was all nerves when I woke up. It wasn't like today was the day. No, it was the day before *the* day. There was shit to get done. My internal party planner was on high alert; the only problem was I didn't have the master list to check off. This wasn't my party to plan and organize. Not that I'd ever coordinated a wedding, but a party was a party.

Sigh. I actually had career plans of evolving into a wedding planner once I discovered how well I did at planning over the top birthday parties for the elite rich in St. Louis. I guess all of that's changed. No more party planning for me. Especially not since Gage's ex, Kathleen, was the only caterer in town. It was almost too bad. I would've rocked that job.

Distracted by my lack of prospects—working for a florist was a complete left turn, then again, Gordon turning into some kind of serial killer was also a complete left turn. My life had taken so many twists and turns lately, I had no clue where I was headed other than down the aisle with Gage.

I paused at the base of the stairs, crutch slung over my

shoulder like a purse. I looked around the lobby. How had I gotten down here? I turned and looked back up the stairs. The last time I made it all the way down on my own, I had to sit on my ass half way down and boot scoot the rest of the way.

I was still on my feet. Hmm, I guess being distracted helped. Unfortunately, I was no longer distracted, and walking without the crutch to help me limp along wasn't an option.

I cursed my way into the kitchen. *Right foot, crutch, left foot, step.*

Gage sat on a stool, eating a bowl of cereal. He was in his uniform. It felt like he was always at work. Logically, I knew he wasn't, after all, starting tomorrow, he didn't work for three days. But he had put in a few doubles to cover for the time off. I needed to sit down with him and a calendar so I could learn his routine.

I scooted onto the stool next to him.

"Work?" I asked. I reached over and took a sip from his coffee cup. It was straight up black, and strong. I felt the caffeine hit me within seconds. No wonder he could do double shifts if that's how he took his coffee.

He smiled around a mouthful of food and nodded.

"Are they going to give you any time off for this wedding thing?"

"I get time off for the wedding." He reached out and picked up my hand, and played with my fingers.

I loved his touch. Of course, I loved what he did when he touched all of me, but simple, little things like this made my heart skip a beat.

"Have you heard anything about that stupid restraining order? Can I go into town without a police escort?"

"Kathleen isn't—"

"Yes, she is." I cut him off. "She already has. If she has Officer Kelley convinced that it's a legit order, then maybe she's gotten other people to think so. Tracey is taking me into town so Jade can wash my hair. I'd like to know I'm not going to get arrested."

He gave me a half grin and returned to his cereal. He nodded as he ate. I took that to mean he was thinking.

Not as patiently as I would've liked, I watched him chew and swallow. He took a drink of his coffee.

"I'll check in with Neeley, first thing."

I continued to stare at him.

"And I will be sure that Kelley knows it's not a legal restraining order."

"Thank you." I eyed his coffee. I wanted a sip, but not of that heated up motor oil.

He glanced at the coffee and then up at me. "You want one?"

I nodded. "Do we have any cream?"

He crossed the kitchen and opened the refrigerator. "No, how about milk?"

I agreed, and let Gage fix my coffee with plenty of milk and sugar. He took a sip before handing it to me. "Are you sure there is coffee in there?"

I took the mug from him and tasted the drink. "I like a little coffee in my morning sugar. But this might be a little too sweet."

He kissed my temple.

I leaned into him. "Is this what you do when you abandon me in the mornings? Get up and do normal things like eat breakfast and go to work?"

He chuckled. "It's exactly what I do, Bailey. What did you expect?"

I shrugged. "Dunno. Power lifting shipping containers, run a full marathon?"

He laughed again, and this time planted a kiss on my lips. "Be good, I love you."

He handed me a small stack of cash, "for shopping," and then left.

After I had my breakfast, Tracey arrived to take me out for my day of errands and getting ready.

Yuki started early at Shaefer's Doughnuts. Jade left to go to the salon before we made it out of the lodge.

"Do you have everything you need?" Tracey asked as she led me to her car.

The New Moon pack swarmed around us as we walked out of the lodge. They acted like they wanted to go run, but felt required to be near us. I guess that made sense since, in another form, these wolves were men we loved.

"Gage gave me some money, so I should be okay." I ruffled Max's thick fur.

"No, I meant for the wedding tomorrow." She started ticking items off her fingers. "You have a bouquet? A garter? All that other stuff, you know, something old, something new, something borrowed, something blue?" Tracey walked patiently beside me, letting me determine our pace.

"No, I don't. Um, I guess the mini dress Jade and Yuki found yesterday will work for something new. New to me counts, right? Flowers are all set. I need the rest of it."

"We have goals for today all set then. What time is your appointment with Jade?"

"She said to show up around eleven thirty, and she would fit me in. You have a new bandage for me?" I asked.

"Everything's in the car," she said as she opened the passenger door.

Brooks slithered past and climbed into the car. For as large as the wolves were, they moved with grace and fluidity.

"Get out!" she barked at the animal. "You aren't coming with. Go run with your pack."

I looked down at Max. "What are you looking at me like that for? You heard her. Go have fun."

They didn't need to be told a third time, and the three wolves ran across the parking lot, disappearing into the woods.

"Where to first?" Tracey asked as the car rolled out of the parking lot.

Our choices for the day were to head out to the shopping by the freeway, where there was a single strip mall of chain stores and a big box store, plus a truck stop, and a selection pack of gas stations. Shopping grew up there more for the traffic headed up to Jackson than for the citizens of Wet Waterfalls. Our other choice was to head into the quaint town of Wet Waterfalls. Downtown was barely a few blocks long and only a couple of blocks wide.

"Doughnuts."

We headed into town.

Armed with half a dozen cinnamon and sugar-coated doughnuts, Tracey and I headed up the street. There were a few shops she thought I wouldn't encounter members of Kathleen's rabid fan club.

Fortified with one magical doughnut and I meant that literally, not figuratively. Yuki was certain that Keiko, the shop owner, was a witch like Jade. She was a guardian, and our mutual best friend Yuki was *Delight*. Not just delightful, but the human equivalent of delight. It made sense to me, people and animals flocked to Yuki's side where ever we went.

I've seen Jade's power, it emitted from her hands like a

glowing blue flame. So, if she could do that, why couldn't there be a witch who made the best doughnut I'd ever tasted?

I didn't have magic, but I was infused, or infected, with Joy. Apparently, that's why Gordon had targeted me. But he was in jail, and I never had to think about him again. I crammed another doughnut into my mouth and focused on happy sugary thoughts.

We walked past the shop where I bought my veil, and Tracey led me into another boutique that I'd blindly missed the previous day.

"Hi, Sandra," Tracey said to the shopkeeper.

"What brings you in today ladies?" Sandra greeted us.

"Bailey here needs something blue, and a garter. But not a blue garter, that's always such a cop-out."

"Getting married? How nice. Destination wedding? I don't think I've ever met you before."

Tracey cut a side glance to me before nudging Sandra with her shoulder. "This one landed Gage Masterson."

"Sheriff Masterson?" Sandra fanned herself.

I laughed. I fully understood—Gage was freaking hot.

"So, you're saving him from Kathleen?" she asked.

I felt my shoulders relax now that I knew her stance in regards to Kathleen. I hadn't realized how tense I'd been since we arrived in town. I knew the restraining order that blocked me from being here at all at the same time as Kathleen was bogus. It didn't mean that everyone else knew it.

"You aren't the woman they found in the woods, are you? Did you really run across the freeway to escape a murderer?"

The smile on my face fell as my jaw dropped. How did she know? I get this was a small town, but I thought all of that information was between me and the FBI. Did that mean that everyone knew about the guys?

Tracey rubbed my back between my shoulder blades. The pressure was a comfort.

"Yeah," I said slowly. "That's me. I didn't realize that had gotten out."

"Oh, honey, you were so brave. When he snatched you off the sidewalk the other day, and all those cars went tearing through here like they were running from the devil, I was so worried."

She knew about that too. I felt really wobbly. "I need to sit down."

Tucked into the corner, behind racks of essential oils, Sandra had an upholstered seat with a matching footstool. I sat and watched as she and Tracey continued to talk about some other person's expected twins. I got it, this town thrived on gossip. It was the pre-technology version of social media.

Eventually, I felt more together. I let them talk, and I nosed around the store. Sandra was a witch. She had to be. The shop was filled with essential oils, crystals, herbs, incense, candles, and more. I could go on listing her inventory, but it was all metaphysical and spiritually oriented. Even the jewelry seemed to have a talisman-sense about it.

My eye was drawn to a bright blue strand of chunky turquoise. The color was too perfect, maybe the stones were dyed. I didn't care. The cerulean tones would coordinate beautifully with the colors in my dress, and contrast nicely with the yellow veil.

I was so certain it was the right necklace—I stopped looking, and ran the big beads through my hands. Not only was the color right, it felt right.

"Did you find something?" Sandra asked from the other

side of the shop where she and Tracey continued their conversation.

Oh yeah, she was totally a witch. She couldn't see me, and she hadn't checked on me earlier. It couldn't have been a coincidence.

"I did," I said as I hobbled back to where they stood.

I held the necklace out the Tracey. "What do you think? Something blue?"

"It's beautiful. Let's get that wrapped up for you, shall we?" Sandra led me back across the store to her register. On the wall, behind the counter, was a locked display of large glowing marbles on stands. It was an interesting collection. I had a hard time taking my eyes from it.

Sandra looked over her shoulder to see what had mesmerized me.

"Pay that no attention. That's where I keep the troubles of the world locked up. "

"Too bad I can't get Gordon locked up in there," I muttered.

"Was that the man?" She didn't need to say 'who hurt you,' or 'who tried to kill you.' I knew who she meant.

I nodded with a sigh. It was over, he was in jail. It didn't matter how many times I repeated that. I needed to hear it over and over again.

"I should stop in and say hi to Channie," I said as we left the shop. I wanted to do more than say hi, I wanted to let her know that I was enthusiastic about the job unless she had changed her mind.

"Sure. We'll pass it on the way to the salon." Tracey closed the door behind me.

I pulled my hood in closer to my face. It felt colder coming out of the shop than it had been when we went in. I saw Mark across the street and turned to shout to him, but there wasn't anyone there. I wasn't used to the movement of the fur on my hood. My brain kept thinking it saw something in my peripheral vision other than what was really there.

The warm air of the florist was a welcome reprieve to the biting cold of the outside.

The doors chimed, and a man called, "I'll be right with you," from the back.

"Is Channie around?" I asked. I didn't mean to interrupt whatever he was doing—I just wanted to say hi.

Mr. Tall, Dark, and Holy-Cow-the-Men-in-This-Town-Were-Hot stepped through a curtain of plastic strips. His long black hair hung loosely over his shoulders. His cheekbones could cut glass they were so finely chiseled.

"Channie is out running deliveries. Is there something I can help you with?" If he'd asked me a month ago, I would've said, 'yes, help me off with my clothes.' Now, I was well spoken for, but I could admire the finery.

"She's putting some arrangements together for me for tomorrow. I just wanted to pop in and see how things were going. I'll just see her tomorrow." I waved my hand around like an idiot.

"You want to leave a message?" he asked.

"Tell her Bailey said hi." I waved and pushed on Tracey to leave.

I got dumb around good looking men. It didn't matter that Gage was hotter by far, and I seemed to be able to talk to him

"Who was that?" I asked once we were back on the sidewalk.

"What Dylan? He's Channie's brother."

"She has a brother? She didn't tell me she had a brother. I can't work for her if her brother looks like that."

"I thought you were in love with Gage?" Tracey laughed at the awkwardness of my situation.

"I am!" I yelled a little too loudly.

"You're funny, Bailey. You have an entire pack of fine men at your disposal, and you get all flustered around a pretty package."

"How do you do it? How do you keep your cool when you deal with good looking men? And don't you dare say it's because you're so very married to Brooks."

"Have you seen my husband? He is supa-fine. It takes a lot to distract me away from that."

I didn't believe her. I stopped in the middle of the side-walk and stared at her.

She shrugged. "Okay, fine. I've known guys like Dylan, and Max, and even Gage entirely too long to be distracted by them. It's part of keeping cool as a nurse. If you start working for Channie, in no time, you won't blink twice at Dylan. Trust me."

I sighed. The gravity of my situation weighed me down. "How am I supposed to do this?"

"What get married? It's surprisingly easy. You say 'I do,' you sign your name, and then you love the hell out of each other."

I lifted my free hand out to her. "But I've got..."

I've got four men I'm supposed to be marrying. I wanted each of them. I thought the whole 'we are pack' thing was going to make it easier. Gage turned me into goo, but one good looking guy with long black hair and I got all tongue-tied.

"Bailey, you're getting married. All that means is you're committing to Gage. It doesn't mean the rest of you magically changes. You aren't going to suddenly start wearing dresses and cleaning the house in pumps and pearls unless that's the way you were before you got married. You're still going to hate broccoli even if your husband thinks it's the only vegetable in the world."

"You hate broccoli?" I asked. I got her point. I'd always be insta-stupid around good looking men, even if my husband were the best looking man on the planet, which he was.

She rolled her eyes. "I can't stand it. It smells like farts."

She made me laugh. I'd survive getting married just fine.

7

Tracey pulled open the door to the salon. A woman in a dark coat stepped through to exit at the same time I tried to enter. I hobbled to the side and mumbled an apology as I looked up into her face.

Zeus's testicles, sideways.

Kathleen tossed her perfect shiny gold hair over her shoulder and finally focused on me.

"That's it. I'm calling the Sheriff's Department. You can't keep harassing me like this. You're stalking me. I have a restraining order against you. You need to leave." She rained a tirade down on my shoulders.

Dylan may have twisted my tongue into knots, but Kathleen sharpened it and turned it into a cat-o-nine tails. I lashed out with all the pent up venom over being mistreated by her, and by everything I endured from Gordon. She received the anger I had over missing a toe and having stitches in the site of my head.

I advanced on her and growled.

"Bullshit. You forged Judge Neeley's signature on that restraining order. It's not legal. So back the fuck off. Get over it. Gage is marrying me. You don't have to like it. Hell, you don't have to like me. But you do need to stop verbally attacking me in public every time you see me. Do it again, and I'll be the one getting a legal restraining order against you. How you like them apples?" I stared at her with everything I had.

She backed up and grabbed her phone.

I turned and limped into the salon as if it was mine and not hers. The door closed behind me, and I started shaking.

"Bailey, what was that?" Jade sauntered up to me. "Are you okay?"

I wasn't okay. I didn't chew people out. In my head, I have a wicked, sharp tongue, but those words never made it out of my mouth. I couldn't stop shaking.

Jade grabbed my elbow, and guided me through the salon, past the stylist chairs, and the dome driers. She parked my butt in one of the sink chairs.

"You want some coffee? Or water?" she offered.

"Water," Tracey answered for me. "Are you going to be all right?" Tracey brushed my hood back and looked into my face. "That was impressive. Did she really forge Neeley's signature? That's classic Kathleen."

Jade handed me a cup of water. I stared at it as my hand quaked and sloshed the water around.

"You need to drink that, not spill it all over."

Jade was right. I took a sip. I felt like I could breathe again.

"I'm sorry, that was bad."

"That was beautiful, Bailey. You always look like you want to say those things and never do. Good for you for sticking up for yourself. Yuki is going to love it," Jade said.

The doorbells chimed.

"Get your coat off. I'll be right back." She left to go see who had come in.

Tracey helped me off with my coat and began working on the bandage on my head when Jade returned. She wasn't alone. I was holding still for Tracey, so all I saw were a pair of black tactical boots. I knew those shoes.

Lifting my eyes, I peered up at Gage. He stood with his arms crossed, those sexy as hell aviator sunglasses still on his face.

"We got a call that a woman was being attacked in front of this place, and I get down here to find that my fiancée just had some kind of smackdown with Kathleen."

"You should've seen her Gage. It was epic." Jade started.

"Epic? Kathleen is calling it assault."

"You know what a liar that woman is. Bailey didn't touch her. As a medical professional, I'll testify to that," Tracey defended me.

I didn't like the cold stare Gage gave me from behind those glasses, so I returned my gaze back to the floor as Tracey gently worked on my head.

"She threatened to call the Sheriff on me. I guess it wasn't a threat."

"What happened?" He squatted down, so he was at my eye level. He swiped those glasses off, and I was a goner. I couldn't believe I'd gone giddy talking to Dylan. He didn't have green eyes like the ones looking at me right now. Even though I was probably in real trouble right now, it didn't matter, Gage still loved me. I could see it.

"She pushed all the wrong buttons, and I yelled at her. Tracey and I were laughing at something stupid, so I wasn't looking when I tried to walk inside. Kathleen was leaving, and we were both trying to go through the door at the same time. I tried to get out of her way. When she bothered to see who was in her way, she threatened me with the restraining order." I shifted my gaze back to the floor. It was hard to keep going with Gage's intense gaze locked on me.

"I lost it, Gage. I yelled back." I was ashamed of my behavior. I wasn't some bad-ass that chewed people out, as much as I liked to pretend I was.

"Tracey?"

"That's all that happened. Kathleen was all snooty, she started it. Bailey yelled, and ended it," Tracey said.

Another officer came into the back of the salon where we were gathered.

Gage stood up, and the two of them spoke in hushed tones. I strained to hear what they were saying.

"Miss Addams is saying she feared for her well being. She wants to press charges," the other officer said.

"Damn it," Gage bit out.

She was going to win. I was going to have a very real restraining order against me, and I wouldn't be allowed in town ever again. Gage would have to call off the wedding. He couldn't be married to someone like me. I ruined everything.

Gage squatted down in front of me again. This time he rested a hand on my knee.

"You think you can swing by the station after you're done here?" he asked.

I nodded. I wanted to say no, I couldn't. I wanted to scream. But look what happened the last time I yelled. I got in trouble.

"You're not arresting me?" My voice was tiny.

"No one is getting arrested, Bailey. We just need you to go in and make a statement. If Kathleen pursues this, we want due diligence on your behalf, okay?"

I sniffed. "Okay."

Eventually, they left. Apparently, Kathleen had been in the front half of the shop the entire time, blaming me for everything from ruining her mood to global warming.

"Forget all of that for a minute. Let's get your hair washed." Jade eased me back in the chair.

"No soap," Tracey said.

I closed my eyes and enjoyed Jade's fingers on my scalp.

"Lordy, Bailey, did they cut your hair with a butter knife?"

"Butchered?" I squeaked.

"Completely. In a couple of weeks, it'll be long enough for me to even it out." Jade ran warm water over my hair.

"How does it look, Tracey?" I was afraid to look at my own wounds. I trusted Tracey to tell me the truth.

"It's healing nicely. But I have to agree with Jade, they did a number on your hair. At least that grows back.

I was tired of having numbers done on my hair. First Gordon dying it brown and then having to have half of it mowed off because he tried to literally scalp me.

I relaxed back under the steady water pressure and Jade's magic fingers. I had no idea if she actually used magic when she washed my hair, it just felt that way.

She pushed the back of my seat up and wrapped a towel around my head. She gently pressed the towel into my hair, never rubbing or doing anything too vigorous.

I followed her to one of the salon chairs.

"I had thought about putting you under a drier, but I figured that would get uncomfortable really fast. The shaved side of your head will dry quickly, but I want to blow out the long side okay? No going outside with wet hair around here."

I agreed. When Jade finished my hair, Tracey wrapped my head up like a mummy. There wasn't an easy way to bandage a head wound. So the whole head went under wraps.

I felt almost a million times better. I still had to deal with the Sheriff's Department and the mess with Kathleen. My stomach rolled into knots.

"Let's get this over with and then go get some lunch," Tracey said.

I nodded. I'd need food, even if I didn't feel like eating right now.

We waited in the lobby of the Sheriff's Department. I hated this place with its dated paint job and old vinyl seating. It didn't help to know that somewhere in this building, Gordon sat in a cell. Fortunately, I didn't have to wait for long before I was called back to give my statement.

I sat next to an old desk, while the officer on the other side of a computer monitor asked me questions. I repeated exactly how we tried to go through the door at the same time. No, we didn't bump or touch at that time. I wish I could've directly quoted what Kathleen said, instead I gave them a generalization of she said, I said.

"I may have actually said 'how do you like them apples.'" I looked up at the officer and grimaced.

"At what point did you strike or threaten to strike Miss Addams?"

"What? I never touched her. I told her to get over it." I was dead, that was it. I had survived all the crap from Gordon, and Kathleen was going to be my downfall.

"What did she need to get over?"

I swear, I told him all of this.

"That she and Gage Masterson were no longer a couple, and never going to be a couple again," I told him again.

He smirked. "How exactly can you be sure of that?"

"Because we're getting married tomorrow."

He slid over and looked out from behind his monitor. "You're marrying Gage? You're the serial killer girl?"

I rolled my eyes and looked up at the ceiling. Why did he think I was bandaged and bruised? Did he think all of this came from a beat down with Kathleen? "Yeah, that's me. I was going to the salon the get my hair washed because it hadn't been cleaned since before the second time Gordon nabbed me and the FBI finally caught him."

I was never going to be allowed to repress those memories. At least Gordon was in jail.

"I'm sorry we had to take time out of your afternoon."

"What's going to happen? I'm not getting arrested am I?" I was sick to my stomach with the thought.

He shook his head. "I doubt it. Kathleen Addams has a habit of making trouble for Gage. I understand they were engaged once. If you're really marrying him, then she's just trying to get us to stir the pot for her. Don't worry about it. We know all about you, and trust me, you have more friends in the department than she does. You're one brave lady."

After that, he let me go. I didn't exactly feel better, but I did feel assured that everyone knew Kathleen was being overly dramatic.

I forgot to zip my coat up before I stepped outside—stupid move. It was crazy cold. I pulled my hood up and blew at the fur by my eye. I thought I saw Mark again. I turned my head to see nothing. The stupid fur was messing with my vision.

"Do you think Gage will get mad if I cut this stuff off?" I loved the fur, it was cute, but it was making me nuts.

"You know you can just snap it off," Tracey said.

"Shut up." I reached up and pulled at the fur. Well, mighty Bast, if the fur lining didn't pull away from the hood with a series of pops as the snaps let go.

Tracey and I headed out to the freeway where one of the chain restaurants had delicious hamburgers and fries.

When he got home tonight, I was going to need Gage to remind me why I agreed to move someplace this cold. I needed warm cuddles by a roaring fire with a hot man—with all of them actually. The bone cold chill I felt after having dealt with Kathleen was going to require several hot men. Good thing I had a few.

8

I didn't get cozy fire cuddles. After dinner, I fell asleep in front of the TV. Gage carried me upstairs and headed into his bedroom.

I leaned into him. He smelled exceptionally nice tonight. "Gage, I know we are getting married tomorrow, but..."

"You want to sleep apart, in your own room?" His voice was so soft and low. There was no way I didn't want him my bed. But it needed to be my bed, not his.

"After the ceremony, it's just you for a while," I started.

"I'm not asking you to do that. We are pack."

"I know, but I want to. I want to be just with you for a bit after we sign those papers. So tonight," I swallowed hard. "Tonight, I want pack. Can you do that for me?" I didn't want him to feel that I was pushing him away.

"We are pack." Was all he said before he turned around and carried me into my room.

Part of me was still a little pissed at Travis's lackluster solo run from the night before, but I wanted to share with pack, and that meant he was invited back into my bed.

Gage kicked into my room. I hadn't had him carry me

bed-to-bed before. He had carried me to bed many times, only he never stayed. He always laid me down gently, adjusted my blankets, tucked me in, and kissed my temple before leaving. This time, he was laying me out on the bed for his pleasure, for my pleasure—for pack.

I wanted to start with Gage and end with Gage. The emotional energy was different when Max was around, but with Gage, he was my alpha—my first husband.

My toes curled—all ten of them. Ghost limbs were very real, and a whole lot of weird, but I wasn't going to think about that right now. My stomach danced.

His mouth was on mine, and I stopped thinking about the logistics of how we were going to let Travis and Zeke know they were invited to join us.

I fumbled with his tucked in shirt. I wanted skin. I wanted chest hairs under my fingers, grazing my nipples, tickling my lips. I wanted his warm body, and my need was jacked up from the consistent happy-buzz I seemed to carry around with me since I first met him, turned into something that soared higher than the clouds.

He seemed to need my skin as much as I needed his. The buttons on my shirt flew in every direction as he pulled the front apart, never mind that someone would have to sew all those buttons back on.

"Hey, I don't have enough clothes that actually work right now. You can't go around destroying everything. I'll end up back in that stupid hospital gown," I complained.

Demeter and Isis if I didn't love the way smiles played across his lips. "I actually quite liked that hospital gown." He caressed the tops of my breasts. The skin of his fingers felt rough from the cold, dry weather.

"These are so tantalizing when you were in it, knowing you weren't wearing a bra. And talk about easy access.

Have I told you how much I enjoyed watching your ass before?"

"I was in a hospital gown, it wasn't sexy."

I pulled on his belt buckle. We had entirely too many clothes on. I did miss the easy access of the hospital gown, a tie, and a few snaps and nothing. Right now, I wasn't a fan of my panties, they were in the way. The rest of the time, panties were my friend.

Gage had my jeans around my ankles and slowed to navigate the fabric over the bandage on my foot.

"Damn woman, you wear sexy underwear."

I looked down at my body. I had on grannie-panties in a pale blue, and a skin-toned bra. Nothing said sexy about my functional choices.

With a few kicks, he was down to his boxer briefs. Intrinsically, there was nothing sexy about our garment choices. "I could say the same about you."

He stood next to the bed and looked at himself. "I'm not as hot as you seem to think I am."

"Does it matter? I love you, and for some crazy reason, you seem to think that cotton panties are sexy. I'm not gonna say no."

"Good, cause I'm all about the yes tonight."

His lips were 'yes' all over my chest. At least, that's what I kept saying when my bra came off, and he sucked my nipples, one at a time, into his mouth. I held his head to me and wrapped my legs around his. Every part of him felt wonderful against my skin.

His kisses trailed between my breasts, down to my stomach. And then, his kisses became more tender, more loving and random. It took a minute to realize he was kissing my heparin shot bruises. If I hadn't already been in love with him, that would've tripped me over into full-blown undying love. As it was, his kisses cemented me to him for life. I wasn't going to need those signed papers to keep me with him forever and ever.

His tongue plunged into and swept around the rim of my bellybutton.

"Oh." I hadn't expected the pull of his tongue on my sex, while I still had panties on.

Gage fixed that, and my panties were tugged off. He sat on the edge of the bed, divested himself of his drawers before he was up and rummaging in the dresser for the condoms.

He could have gotten me pregnant right then, and I wouldn't have cared. He leaned over and slid his hand under the pillow my head rested on. "Should be easy enough to grab those as needed."

I mewed a positive sound. The more I needed his body, the less I could talk.

"I'll be good, I promise, but I need to feel you." He positioned himself between my knees and lowered into me. I thrust up to greet him with my hips—welcoming him home, where he belonged.

He slid back and thrust hard, and then didn't move.

I traced my fingertips over his cheekbones. His dark lashes spread across his cheeks. His closed lids hiding the intense green gaze I didn't think I could live without.

He shuddered, and I was afraid he'd forget his own rule of condoms until after the shift with the full moon. "Gage, baby, time to get dressed. You feel really good inside."

He growled and opened his eyes. There was a flash of a green more intense than anything I'd seen coming from his eyes before. His eyes didn't look human.

I flinched back and pushed him off.

He crouched between my legs. I felt more like prey he

was poised to launch after. A few tense moments passed as we stared at each other. My heart sped up and pounded into my throat. He never looked sexier, I never felt more desired than in those few seconds when I should've been afraid of the beast in him.

He surged forward and buried his face into my neck, and thrust an arm under the pillow retrieving a condom. He shoved the foil pack into my hand and growled something as he sucked on the skin along my collar bone.

I fumbled, opening the condom. "Here."

I tried to give it back, but he rose up in front of me and guided my hand to his length. We both sighed as my hand covered him. His cock throbbed with need. And I needed him in me right now. My own sex was already pulsing with want.

He eased the head against my delicate flesh, and I exploded. I had no control as I orgasmed around him. He thrust, I moaned, and the world was stars and colors and light.

I know I said tonight I wanted the pack, but right this second, I only wanted Gage.

I continued to crash as he plunged into me. He roared and pressed into me. I had serious doubts the condom would survive.

Gage rolled and held me to him. He situated me so that I straddled his hips. I hadn't noticed when Travis and Zeke had entered the room, but they were crouched on either side of the bed, nude, with full erections saluting me in the middle.

I reached out to pull them to me. Each one descended on a breast. Gage began rolling his hips under mine. I had a dick in each hand, Gage buried deep inside, and two beautiful men teasing and toying with my nipples. This was a bridal send off. This was pack.

We twisted as a unit. I ended up on my hands and knees, a cock in my mouth, a mouth on my sex. We writhed and moaned, and tongues and fingers replaced cocks. We rolled again, and I was on my back. Travis straddled my ribs again and began stroking my breasts, rubbing the head of his shaft over my erect nipples. With pack, this worked, this worked amazingly.

Gage's tongue circled my clit, Travis stroked my breasts, and Zeke stood over me while Travis sucked on his cock.

I hadn't noticed if those two had played together before, but I was pleased to see it now—more than pleased. Watching Travis's mouth move over Zeke's dark skin heightened my own arousal as Gage sucked on my sex, and Travis thrust against me.

My pitifully short nails bit into Zeke's calf as Gage brought me to another orgasm. Zeke lost his balance momentarily and cried out. I don't think it was me causing him pain. The kind of suffering that caused that noise had nothing to do with fingernails in skin. Everything combined and Travis pulled harder, and I saw his jaw work and suck Zeke further down his throat.

The three of us came simultaneously. Zeke into Travis, Travis across my chest, and me around Gage's tongue and fingers.

Gage sat back and let out a hearty laugh, and the rest of us sank into a puddle. They were done, I was limp and as near boneless as I could possibly be. But Gage was still capable, still ready, still the last man standing, and the last man I'd make love to tonight.

Travis got a damp towel and wiped me off. Gage took the towel from him and proceeded to continue to wipe me off, even though there was no more sticky mess to clean up. I think he just wanted to drag the rough terry cloth across my sensitized skin.

Travis pulled Zeke into his arms, and they curled up next to me, while Gage poised back between my legs. At one point, I know I'd thought making love to Gage alone with the other two in the bed would be awkward, but it wasn't. I squeezed someone's hand as I came around Gage's pounding shaft again.

I fell asleep surrounded by the men I loved, and who loved me, well satiated, safe, and protected.

At some point in the middle of the night, I woke up to mouths on my body.

Fresh condoms were put on, and it was my turn to suck on Zeke.

I was so ready for Gage when he slid into me from behind. I screamed my orgasm around Zeke's cock in my mouth. He let loose down my throat. Travis released into Zeke's hands, and Gage roared as he exploded.

The four of us slept and banged, dozed, and screwed and screamed, and had more sex than we had sleep. Travis and Zeke slipped out of the room predawn. I think Gage may have kicked them to the curb. We welcomed the dawn together with another series of orgasms as he made love to me.

9

Today was the day. Nerves I didn't know I had were somersaulting through my tummy. For as casual as we'd been about the whole thing—just getting married, just signing papers, just following up on what my parents already believed—I wasn't feeling particularly casual.

I got dressed and made my slow pathetic way downstairs. I ran my hand over the polished railing of the stairs. It was nothing like the reoccurring dream with Gage waiting for me below. My fingernails were still pretty short and devoid of color. But I did like touching the smooth, shiny wood. It almost felt soft.

I held on and one step at a time eventually made it to the lobby. The New Moon wolves looked like lumpy fur rugs as the lazy beasts lying in pools of weak sunlight. The TV was on in the lounge, but no one was watching it. I pushed into the kitchen.

"What are you doing here?" Yuki asked.

"Hello to you too. Where am I supposed to be?" I asked in reply.

Yuki and Travis were making a mess of some kind of prep work. I assumed it was food for the party later.

"Where is everyone?" I yawned and began limping toward the refrigerator.

Travis cut me off. "What do you think you're doing?"

"Getting some breakfast. Did Jade go to the salon?" She said she would be able to take me to the florist and pick everything up from Channie today. If she had gone into work... I hoped she remembered to get the flowers.

"You sit." Travis pointed to a stool. "I'll make you something. We expected you to sleep in."

I followed orders and took a seat. "I've been getting up early all week. I think my body knows if it wants sunlight, I have to get up for it. It gets dark so early now."

Gordon and I had left for our little weekend getaway in October. The pack found me during a full moon, and tomorrow night the moon was full again. That meant it was November. No wonder it was so cold outside, and it got dark so early. Zeus's testicles, that meant I missed Halloween.

What did mom expect me to do for Thanksgiving? I hadn't started my Christmas shopping yet.

"Bails, what's the matter? You look like you're panicking. Is your brain being stupid?"

I gave Yuki a manic smile. My brain was totally being stupid. "I just realized it's November and I'm not ready for Christmas."

Travis laughed. "Christmas is a long time off. You really don't need to be worrying about that right now. Are you the type to find something to freak out about so that you don't stress over the imminent disaster?"

I scrunched up my face and pursed my lips at him. He was so right about me. "I'm getting married. I'd hardly call it a disaster."

"I would. I'm not the groom." He laughed, but I sensed there were some sadness and truth in his words.

The microwave pinged, and he pulled a plate out and slid it in front of me. "When did you have pizza?" I should've been more concerned with why I was being served pizza for breakfast, or how there was even pizza left over; I've seen how the guys eat, they consume everything.

"Yesterday, you were out. Why? Is there something wrong? Are you judging my breakfast?" Travis teased.

"Not at all. Pizza is the perfect food. It contains all the food groups—grain, vegetables, and dairy." I shook my head. There wasn't anything else to say. I wasn't judging his breakfast.

"Is there anything I can do to help out?" I asked as I took a bite.

"You can make sure you're ready by four," Yuki told me.

"Okay, so I'll start getting ready at two."

"Good, go take a nap or something."

I got the distinct impression she was trying to get rid of me.

"Man, you'd think I could at least finish my breakfast before you kick me out." I pouted. "Have either of you seen Gage this morning?"

Travis shook his head. Yuki shrugged. I guess that meant no. I finished my pizza, and with a dramatic flourish made my exit. They both ignored me. Fine. Actually, it was fine. They were busy getting my wedding put together.

I flopped on the couch and tried to distract myself with a cop show on TV. With the satellite feed, I had access to hundreds of channels. Absolutely none of them had anything that interested me. I wandered back into the kitchen.

"Get out, Bailey," Yuki yelled at me.

After about an hour, Jade returned. Dylan followed her in carrying a box full of flowers.

Tracey had been right. Eventually, I wouldn't see him as being really hot. Today was that day. He was cute, and his long hair really was appealing. But his dark eyes didn't sparkle, and he was thinner through the shoulders, and his lips were thin.

"Channie told me you're going to come to work for us," Dylan said. He stopped and balanced the delivery box on the back of the couch. "You should've said something yesterday."

"I didn't want to interrupt you. How do the flowers look? Do you have my crown?" I lifted up onto my knees so I could look into the box.

He handed me a square one.

I bit the inside of my cheek, flopped back down onto my butt, and lifted the lid.

"Oh, this is gorgeous," I cooed as I lifted out the wreath of pink and orange lilies. Channie had blended in some of the dark pink flowers that I liked but didn't know the names of. "This is going to look amazing."

I held the crown over my head and tried to look up at it, picturing what it looked like without a mirror.

Dylan made a non-committal noise and carried the flowers in through the service doors.

I put my floral crown back in its box and felt the nerves of getting married replace my boredom. I realized I was going to need help carrying the box upstairs, and stood, intending to ask the party in the kitchen for help.

As I situated myself with my crutch, thought through the initial process of how to walk— *right foot, crutch, left foot, step*—something I had to do to get started every time—Gage came in through the front doors. He was in his uniform. He looked really good in his uniform. He made khaki and a gun belt look hot. But he wasn't supposed to be in uniform right now.

"Why are you in your uniform?"

"I had to go in." He wiped the knit hat off his head and pulled his gloves off. The pink around his nose and cheeks told me it had gotten colder outside.

"You don't have to go back, do you? They aren't making you work a full shift today?" I know I was whining. It was panic induced. We were supposed to be getting married this afternoon.

He leaned down and kissed me. I felt the cold from his jacket and smelled snow on his skin. "I'm not going back in. I had some paperwork to finish up. What have you been up to?"

"Nothing, they won't let me do a thing." I gestured at the service doors indicating everyone on the other side.

"As it should be." He headed for the kitchen.

"Don't give me that. I'm bored. You at least had something to do." I followed him through the doors.

Dylan passed us carrying a ladder.

"I'd gladly trade finishing up reports with being bored and watching TV." He winked at me, and my insides did new and unusual things involving flips and panic and excitement.

"Get her out of here. She keeps pestering us," Travis groused at Gage. "Go watch TV or something."

I stared at the man with open jaws. I had hardly been pestering them.

"Has anyone seen Mark?" Jade asked.

I shook my head. It wasn't worth telling everyone that the fur on my hood kept making me think I saw him in my peripheral vision.

"No why?" Gage asked.

"Now that you mention it, I haven't seen him for a couple of days," Travis said.

"He was supposed to help out, and he's not answering his phone. Dylan is sticking around to help with the heavy lifting to pick up the slack."

Oh, phone! My new phone was probably charged by now. I had something I could do. "Gage, will you help me set up my new phone?"

I was already all nerves, and the phone was an exercise in frustration. By the time my service provider figured out what needed to happen—I needed a specific chip so the phone would work with their services—it was time for me to get ready. I still had no phone, and now it was panic time.

Gage carried me upstairs to my room so I could get ready. He left me with a kiss that would melt the ice caps and told me he would see me later. *Eep.*

10

"How do I look?"

"You look amazing. I still think you should've put on that pink thong. Gage could take it off and..."

"Yuki!" The warmth of blush spread over my face.

"Just because I don't do the sex, doesn't mean that I don't know that you do. I know Travis thinks the thongs are sexy, he said so. Don't all men think that way? Won't Gage want you dressed all sexy for tonight?"

I bit the inside of my cheek. Tonight there would be no sexy time, tonight, there wouldn't exactly be a Gage—at least not a Gage that needed to see me in sexy underwear.

I didn't feel amazing. I was about to get married, and I didn't exactly have on what I considered bridal quality clothes. I was stuck in a small town with minimal shopping opportunities and no time to order anything online or make a trip to a bigger town.

I had to remind myself that at least this wasn't a hospital gown, and no one expected to see me in a wedding dress. And I did look cute, just not particularly bridal. My hair was covered with my fancy dyed silk veil. I chose the bright yellow because when I was a kid, I once read that Roman women wore yellow for protection, and to look like a flame. With my red hair, I knew that a yellow veil would be amazing. It was the only part of this wedding that matched my childhood wedding expectations. A crown of brightly colored flowers topped the veil.

Jade and Yuki scoured the shops the other day and found a mini dress that looked floral but was really covered in fairies and unicorns. I wore the chunky turquoise necklace for, something blue. I slipped the garter over the purple leggings I borrowed from Tracey this morning because it was too cold to go bare legged. Jade found an old penny in the bottom of her purse, and she slid it into my right shoe. I was covered, something old, something new, something borrowed, something blue. I had my colors. I had a hint of my personal flair. I just didn't quite feel like I had me back yet.

I hobbled down the hall and stopped at the top of the stairs.

"Are they ready for us?" I asked.

Yuki looked over the railing and waved at someone. I couldn't look.

"See you at the bottom, Bailey." Yuki took my crutch and left me at the top of the stairs.

I was on my own. I wasn't capable of making a grand entrance on my feet, I was too nervous to be stable. I made my way down, boot scooting down the grand staircase on my butt. Gage waited for me at the bottom of the stairs.

He was sexier than he had been in my dreams these past few nights.

I wanted to cry as soon as I saw him. The smile on his face made me nothing but jittery nerves. He had that sexy curl in his hair right above his forehead.

He mouthed, "I love you," and I stopped where I sat on the top stair at the main landing.

I couldn't have moved even if I wanted to. He was gorgeous, and I was stunned into place. I'd only ever seen him in jeans or his uniform, or naked. Naked was probably my favorite. Gage had a way of making a khaki uniform look sexy as hell. What he did for that brown suit should've been illegal.

It must've been the only suit he had in his closet, the one he wore to weddings and funerals. It fit as if he paid the big bucks to have it custom made. With his mile-wide shoulders, any other suit would've strained, or completely burst out the shoulder seams. With it, he wore a dark blue shirt and a silver tie. The colors were dark, somber, formal. Gorgeous.

My breath caught in my throat as he strode up and stopped a few steps below me.

"Allow me to carry you down."

In his arms, I felt like a princess, a true bride.

He was my prince, my alpha, and I was the luckiest women that ever existed in time and space. I couldn't take my eyes from his face.

"I like your suit," I whispered.

"I love your colors. You make the world fade away to nothing but black and white."

A smattering of applause and cheers met us as he turned into the dining area.

I scanned the room full of smiling faces. The pack was here. Zeke must've dressed Travis because instead of his sloppy casual style, he was as dapper as Zeke. Tracey was there with Brooks leaning against her. Jade and Yuki smiled at me.

Doggo stood next Judge Neeley as the group gathered

next to a decorated table. The table was festooned with the brightly colored flowers I had selected. Balloons floated among the rafters. A tall round cake in bright pink frosting served as a centerpiece. Several documents and a fancy pen were on display, waiting for Gage and me to sign.

Judge Neeley wore a snazzy forest green and dark purple outfit. The suit was plaid in greens, his vest was dark purple. The shirt he wore was pale lavender, and his bow tie was green. I liked this guy and his sense of color. The little hankie in his breast pocket was a bright yellow to match my veil.

Gage set me on my feet in front of the judge.

Doggo pressed against my hip. I threaded my fingers into his fur and held on for support. With my other hand, I held on to Gage's arm.

My face hurt because I smiled so hard.

Neeley said a few words and handed Gage the pen with a flourish. Gage let go of me long enough to lean over and sign the marriage papers. He handed me the pen, and even with my hands shaking I managed to sign on the line under Gage's name.

Judge Neeley clapped his hands together. "I now proclaim you husband and wife. You may now kiss your bride."

Kissing Gage was hard. Max had moved in between us, and I was smiling like a complete idiot. I leaned over the wolf in front of me and kissed my husband. Gage wrapped his arms around me and pulled me closer.

Doggo complained with a growly whine.

Gage broke off the kiss and pushed Doggo out of the way. "You'll get your chance later."

Everyone cheered and Yuki declared it was time to cut the cake.

Gage and I posed for a cake cutting picture and then served up pieces of pink and white cake. It wasn't until I served cake out that I noticed Mark wasn't there.

I looked at Jade, she hadn't seemed any less happy, so I figured it had nothing to do with their relationship, or maybe it did.

"Where's Mark?" I asked.

She shrugged. "No telling. He never showed this afternoon. He's been a little weird the past few days."

"You think it has to do with tonight?" Not that the other guys were acting oddly, but there was a sense of impending occurrence. That feeling that something is about to happen. Maybe it was just my personal anxiety over officially getting married. Maybe it was that I'd finally understand what Gage had been hinting at for the past month with all of his talk of monsters and magic, and demons and beasts.

I knew his story. Something had happened to him and the guys out there in the woods. Something had made Max, Brooks, and Oz all turn into wolves and stay that way except for three days a month on the new moon. The same magical accident had turned Gage, Travis, Zeke, and Mark into werewolves that turned on the full moon. Max had shifted to human before my eyes, and three mornings later, I woke up with Doggo, his wolf form, in my bed.

Now, I was going to finally see Gage shift. The first three nights of my honeymoon would be spent with my new husband out in the woods running with a wolf pack.

The FBI agents, Smith and Jones, who had been responsible to the operation that caught my abusive serial killer ex, an operation that resulted with my head full of stitches, rushed in through the front door.

I really needed to talk to Gage about better security.

"Agent Smith, Agent Jones, would you like some

wedding cake?" Yuki asked with a jubilant bounce as she pranced over to them, plates in hand.

The agents slowed as they headed into the dining area. Jones waved off the cake. Smith did not.

"We have a problem," Jones announced.

I sat crying in one of the overstuffed leather chairs that compromised one of the seating and conversational arrangements in the lobby. They weren't the joyful tears of a new bride.

Gage paced. Doggo pressed against my knees. The rumble of his low growl vibrated through my legs.

This wasn't the news I wanted these two men to bring to me today of all days.

"Why didn't you contact us earlier?" Gage's anger was barely contained.

My entire wedding party had gone from happy to somber with six words. Six words that put a shiver down my spine, and a knot of fear in my stomach.

"Gordon Jamal has escaped our custody." That's what Jones said. Now he was telling us the details. And I did mean us. Everyone sat around, taking up all of the chairs, sitting on the backs of other chairs as the FBI had our attention.

In the dark hours of the morning, US Marshals picked Gordon up to transport him to Boise where the multiple murder cases could begin the prosecution process.

"Apparently, they stopped to gas up their vehicle before leaving town, and that's when he got away," Jones told us.

"No," I whined. I wanted to curl into a ball and disappear. I didn't want to go through this again. I couldn't. I couldn't put myself out there as a lure. They hadn't even asked, but I already knew I couldn't do that again.

I lifted my hands to cup my head carefully. Under my veil and flowers, I had half of my hair shaved off, and a ragged tear full of stitches holding my scalp together—all because of Gordon—all because I managed to get away from him. I couldn't handle this. I couldn't.

No one noticed Gordon had gotten a hold of a bobby pin, or had any idea of how he would've gotten a hold of one. It had been left behind along with the cuffs he had gotten out of. He tricked one of the Marshals into opening the backdoor. No one knew exactly what happened, the man was dead. His partner had been using the restroom.

"What did the surveillance cameras show?" Gage asked.

Travis rubbed my arm, offering soothing comfort.

Smith scoffed. "What do you think? Nothing. The view was partially blocked by an old hornet's nest."

"We didn't mention anything because they were hoping for a quick retrieval," Jones added.

Smith pulled a piece of paper from his jacket. He unfolded it to reveal a blurry black and white print out.

"Do any of you recognize this man?"

Jade gasped.

Gage snatched the paper from the agent. He threw it at Travis.

Travis and Zeke stared at it open jawed.

"Who is it?" I asked. The print was divided into four blocks, each one a slightly different photo of a gas station.

"What is that asshole think he's doing?" Zeke asked.

"Who is it?" I had to ask again.

"Mark," Jade whispered. "It's Mark. And it looks like he's running with Gordon."

She looked sick, green around the edges.

Gage looked like he wanted to punch something. I'd never seen him so angry, betrayed.

"You waited almost twelve hours to inform us of this. We could've been out there helping you. Now—" Gage threw his hands up in frustration. "Sunset is in less than thirty minutes, and I need to protect my wife," he growled at the FBI agents. "You need to leave."

Judge Neeley was out of his chair and bustling the FBI agents to the front. He knew, he had to know. "Tracey dear, will you fetch my parka?"

When she handed him the coat, he thanked her before telling her, "Keep Brooks and Max in tonight. Also, this front door, make sure it gets locked." He pointed down to the floor. I had never noticed the front doors had sliding bolts that locked into the floor.

Good, we had locks. That only temporarily settled the riotous butterflies in my stomach.

Gage didn't give the FBI a second look, and lifted me into his arms and caressed the side of my cheek. "Come on."

He carried me up the grand staircase, and this time I really was a bride. Only the nerves in my stomach weren't dancing with the anticipation that I was going to make love to my husband, this time, the nerves were heavy with dread. I closed my eyes and leaned into Gage, breathing in his warmth, his strength.

He kicked open the door to his bedroom and set me on his bed. He turned to face the window. His jacket came off, and he laid it over the top of a side chair. I should've been distracted by my husband undressing. Instead, I was distracted by the knowledge that Gordon escaped custody. He was out there, and he wanted me. But he didn't want me the way Gage wanted me. Gordon wanted me dead.

Gage turned to face me. I was up and reaching for him. I

ran my hands across the smooth fabric of his dress shirt. He felt so strong and solid under my fingers. He looped a finger under his necktie and worried it side to side.

"Let me," I barely whispered.

I carefully pulled the silk fabric through the knot he had formed earlier.

His hands slid to my hips, and he began swaying. Warm breath caressed my cheek. I focused on loosening the knot, and he rested his cheek against my forehead. Even after the tie was completely free, we gently moved to music in our hearts.

He smelled good— clean cotton shirt, the pomade he used in his hair to keep the curl in place, aftershave— husband. I wanted to kiss him, to finish taking his clothes off. I reached up and began unbuttoning his shirt. Gage captured my hands in his, stopping my progress. He held me to him and rocked with me.

"This isn't fair." I don't know if I was complaining that we didn't have time to consummate the marriage, or if it was because Gordon was at large, or both.

"I know. I know. I need you to stay inside. Once we shift, we'll head out and hunt this asshole down. But Bailey, you stay inside; you stay safe. There is plenty of food. No one needs to leave until we come back."

"Do all the doors actually lock?" I asked. I had made Gage aware of my security concerns, and he had brushed them off like a gnat.

"All the doors have locks. All but the doors that we use on a regular basis stay unlocked. This is a town where people never lock their front doors and barely lock their cars. But we do have locks in place here. We just don't typically use them."

"Tonight?"

"Right now, the guys are making sure you will be secure. All doors locked."

I sucked in a shaky breath. I didn't like this. Gage was leaving me for three days, and Gordon was out there.

Gage stopped moving. He squeezed his eyes shut, and his shoulder rose into his neck. He looked like pain had seized him.

I stepped back and pressed my hand to his chest. "Gage? Sweetheart? Are you okay?"

The hand wrapped around mine tightened and turned fever hot before his muscles relaxed under my fingers.

"Sunset is closer than I realized." His voice was grave, and thicker than usual.

11

Gage ripped his shirt open, scattering buttons across the room. The man had no respect for button-down shirts.

He grimaced and stretched his neck to the side. He rolled his shoulders, and there was a loud cracking down his spine.

"Do I need to leave?" I was scared. I knew what was happening, but I didn't know if this was going to be dangerous or not. I tried to back away from him.

He tightened his hand on my wrist. "Stay. See me. I don't want you to be afraid of me."

I didn't want to be afraid of him either. "Okay." My voice was tiny.

He released my hand, and I backed up to the bed again.

Gage's shift was different from Max's. The shift rolled over Max in a stretch. It had been graceful, beautiful. Gage struggled. Bones creaked, and joints popped. This shift sounded painful, looked painful. Gage groaned and growled.

He looked up at me, sweat turned his hair darker. His face was red with effort.

He groaned out words. I didn't understand him at first.

"What?"

"Don't trust Mark." He groaned with pain. "Gotta catch Jamal."

He fell to the floor, breathing heavily. He spasmed and threw his head back before curling into himself.

When he spoke again, it was more muffled, like his mouth was the wrong shape. But the words were clear. "Kill them both."

A cold sweat broke out on the back of my neck. Panic lodged in my throat, a rock of fear. What in the name of Demeter was I doing closed in a room with a werewolf? He was turning into a dangerous, deadly beast. Gage was a deadly man. Why hadn't I clued in before this? At any time, the man could have hurt me; he was big, roped solid with muscle. He trained at Langley, he was a sheriff, and he knew how to cause harm.

I was an idiot. He twisted and growled on the floor between me and the door. I couldn't watch this anymore. I scrambled back onto the bed, pressing against the wall as far from him as I could. As if it really would protect me, I curled up with my head tucked down, hands clasped over the back of my neck in classic tornado drill style.

The bed dipped under his weight. I whimpered. I had no way to defend myself. I was so stupid.

A cool long nose nudged at me. The beast on the bed gave out the most pitiful doggy whine. He continued to nudge at me. I turned my tear-streaked face to him. If he was going to bite me, he could've done so by now. I was terrified, not knowing what to expect.

Doggy kisses licked at my face before I had focused on what he looked like.

"Gage, stop." I pushed him back.

He lay in front of me, sphinx style, with his tail slapping the mattress.

I really was an idiot. There was no need to be afraid of this wolf. My husband was still behind those eyes.

"I freaked out." I swiped at my tears with the heel of my palm. "I panicked, I'm sorry."

Gage started to stand but lay back down. His ears were pricked forward, his eyes open wide, and a big doggy grin with lolling tongue told me this was a happy animal. He was a beautiful animal. He and Doggo made a pair—black and white, wild and tame. Gage was large and black with no markings on him. If Max was a ghost in white, Gage was the shadow in the dark. But his eyes were his, unnatural green in that black canine face.

"You are pretty." I breathed out and reached out to stroke his fur.

Gage twisted and rolled over onto his back, exposing his belly to me. I laughed as I ruffled the fur on his chest. He was almost this hairy in human form. Not really, but the thought was there before I could stop it.

"We are pack?" I asked.

He whined and twisted upright again. His face was in mine with more licking kisses. I pushed him back. "We discussed this. I don't play that way."

The wolf that was my husband jumped off the bed. He was huge. Using him as a support, I made it to the door and opened it so he could exit the room.

I was swarmed with wolves. They flowed in and around me before I had a chance to leave the room. Gage let out a low growl, and they swarmed out, pulling me with them in their furry tidal pull. I couldn't identify everyone yet. Doggo, Max, was as big as a bear, and snowy white. I was actually surprised to see that Gage's wolf was taller through the shoulders. There were three new wolves, Gage was easy—he was the biggest and all black.

Brooks I knew, he was also dark, but brindled with golds and browns in his coat. Oz, Zeke, and Travis all took on the form and coloring of timber wolves. Pale legs and faces with grays and browns along their backs. I couldn't distinguish them by sight—at least not yet.

I teetered at the top of the steps. "Hey, I can't do this with all of you pushing on me."

I grabbed onto the railing, as they flowed past me and down the stairs. Gage stayed by my side. He patiently made his way down, as I sat from step to step, never leaving my side.

When I made it all the way down, I stopped and stayed where I was. I couldn't move around and make sure all the doors were locked. I didn't even know where all the doors were.

"Okay boys, say your goodbyes and then get out!" Tracey said with good humor.

The combined pack swarmed around her. Brooks stayed around her the longest. Yuki giggled as she was swarmed next. She knelt down to get the full impact of doggy kisses and head butts.

They circled Jade, acknowledging that she was important too. She reached out and scratched a few ears. "Get the bastards, okay?"

She was answered with a series of yips and growls. They were much louder than I realized.

I was swarmed one last time. Gage pressed into me and

licked my face. "Go do your thing. And then come back to me."

Tracey held the front door open, and the combined super pack flowed through it, out into the snow. She closed the door with a thunk and pushed the floor lock into place.

I hobbled to one of the front windows and looked out. The pack ran around in the snow, playing, happy to be in wolf shape. Gage posed at the end of the parking lot, a dark silhouette against the blue light of the evening. He lifted his head and howled. The sound was intimidating, and loud. It was a warning to his enemies that he was on the hunt. It was a call to the others to stop messing around and follow him. The rest of the pack returned his howl. Every hair on my body stood on end. I shivered against the goosebumps.

That pack of feral apex predators had just been running around in this lobby like a bunch of oversized puppies. They followed Gage into the woods. Doggo took up the rear. He paused and looked back at me. They were going to protect me. All of us.

I watched until I couldn't see them anymore.

"Now what?" I asked the room.

I turned around to find I was alone. A shiver teased down my spine. I didn't like being alone, not after being surrounded by the pack.

I hobbled to the closest chair. I scanned around for my crutch. Yuki had to have put it somewhere. Hobbling from one chair to the next, I made my way over to the lounge. I was done. I collapsed on the couch.

"There you are!" Yuki pushed through the service doors, a pitcher of bright green margaritas and a stack of glasses in her hands.

"What's that?"

"Margaritas and," Yuki turned to look at the doors.

"Nachos are coming. We figured we needed a 'girls only' weekend."

"Even if it's the middle of the week," Tracey said as she entered the lounge area. She and Jade each carried a tray covered in food.

Yuki dragged the low coffee table closer to the couch. The trays had plates of basic nachos, chips covered in melted cheese, and bowls with all the fixings so we could each customize our food.

Tracey flopped back into one of the chairs. "It's going to be nice to hang out with friends during this. Usually, I'm totally alone. I mean," she sighed. "It's not like Brooks is around the rest of the time, he is and isn't. But even three days without the furry beast around gets lonely fast."

"Think of it as doing your bridal party in reverse order. I mean, you certainly got laid all night before the wedding."

Tracey choked on her drink. Jade laughed. I died a little bit of pure mortification.

"Yuki!" Sometimes that woman had no filter.

"I'm not wrong." She defended herself.

"You aren't." I managed to squeak. She wasn't, we certainly had consummated all night long. I had to be bright pink.

I reached up and patted at my floral crown. "Hey Jade, can you help me get this off?"

I spent my first night as a married woman bonding with my friends. We ate nachos, invented a rom-com drinking game, and ate too much cake. Yuki was right—it was more like doing the whole bachelorette party-married-honeymoon in reverse order.

I managed to completely ignore the nagging in the back of my head that out there was a man who wanted me dead, and that one of the men I'd trusted for the past month may be working with him. It tried to get my attention more than once, but I drowned it with more margaritas.

We all slept that first night under throw blankets in the lounge, too buzzed to safely make sure I made it upstairs.

Yeah, I was going to have a serious chat with Gage about a security system, and an elevator. Of course, by the time he got an elevator in, I'd be completely healed and wouldn't need it. He should still get one put it.

In the morning, I staggered up to his room and went back to sleep. I wanted to somehow be closer to him, and his bed smelled like him, only him. I would've called it a nap, except I think I slept longer during the day than I had the previous two nights combined. When I woke up I realized I'd survived the first night. I missed Gage, but I wasn't a depressed blob of insufferable lovesick bride like I feared.

I hobbled to my room where I changed before hobbling my way back downstairs. I was determined not to be some kind of slacker. We'd had a party, and no one had bothered to clean up. I eyed my surroundings, plotting what I'd conquer first. I wasn't walking well enough to be able to carry a loaded tray, but I could collect plates and glasses unto the tray for someone else to carry into the kitchen. The flowers needed fresh water, and the balloons that decorated the ceiling, now hovered against the floor, all lifting oomph gone.

There was work to be done, so I lobbed off a chunk of almost stale cake and began eating. This time, I could appreciate the flavors on my tongue. If the cake was this good after sitting out all night, I must've really been a bundle of nerves yesterday to have missed the taste. I savored another bite and wondered where Gage had finally gotten this made. I doubted he went back to the bakery, that woman had been such a shrew. I couldn't imagine her cake would've been any tastier.

At first, I thought I had imagined the sound, but then the banging on the front door got louder.

I grabbed my crutch and limped my way over to the window next to the doors. Agents Smith and Jones looked at me rather impatiently through the window.

I lifted the lock and let the door swing open.

"Where is Sheriff Masterson?"

"Hello to you too," I answered. "Come on in." I pushed the big door closed and locked it behind the FBI agents.

I hobbled over to the closest conversation cluster of chairs.

"How can I help you today?" I asked as I sank down into the comfortable depths of the overstuffed chair.

"We came to discuss something with Masterson. We've had a situation."

"Another one? Gage isn't here. He and the guys went out into the woods for a few days."

"Didn't you just get married?" Smith asked. His brows screwed up together, and his expression told me he thought the timing was concerning.

I smiled. "Yeah, we did. This had been planned for a while, so we decided to do things a little back to front. I'm having my all-girls retreat at the same time. The honeymoon will wait for a few days. Besides, it's not like we're able to get away for a while." As a half-assed excuse, it didn't sound bad.

"Camping? In the snow? Aren't they worried about bears, or wolves?"

I shook my head slowly. I still couldn't just toss it around, willy-nilly shaking and nodding away. "They train people in this. You know he runs search and rescue in the area, right?"

Jones cut a glare to the other man, and rested a hand on his shoulder, getting him to stop. This line of questions clearly was distracting from the direction they needed to head in.

"Do you have a way of getting word to him? We would like to bring him in," Jones said.

"Why, what's going on? And before you tell me it's not something I need to worry about, let's get clear on this— Gordon tried to kill me, not once but twice. I think I deserve to be kept in the loop when we're discussing my safety. After all, you're the ones who lost him after I risked everything to help you catch him."

"And yet your husband went out into the wilds knowing Gordon is at large?"

Jones clearly thought we were playing fast and loose with the concept of my safety.

"If Gordon is in the area," I gestured indicating the woods, "and out there, my husband will find him before your people ever will. Remember, he is the search and rescue guy. Besides, I think this is now personal."

"It wasn't before?"

"I mean, even more so. If the guy in those photos you showed us was Mark, that means he betrayed everyone, not just me, but all the guys on the..." I paused, I couldn't call them pack, "team."

I looked from Smith to Jones and back again. "They have to be able to rely on each other. Trust that the other guy has their back. How would you feel if one of your oldest friends suddenly was in league with your wife's murderous ex? Gage may have claimed it to be personal before, because of the relationship that we developed, but that never really was more than him being angry on my behalf. Now, with Mark's involvement, now, it's personal."

"Are you telling us that Masterson would be willing to take on this Mark, and Gordon on his own?"

I made a noncommittal face. "He's not out there on his own. Look, Gage is nothing if not excruciatingly honorable. If he can bring in Gordon alive, he will. Now, what brings you here this afternoon? You want some cake?" I hitched a thumb over my shoulder indicating the mess in the other half of the lobby.

Jones let out an exasperated sigh. "We were hoping to get more insight into his friend Mark Sanderson. We haven't been able to find out too much. The only Mark Sanderson we were able to identify any details on died about six years ago. We think your friend may have actually taken over the deceased's identity, or he faked his death and moved here."

"Did he have any connections to Gordon? The dead guy?" I asked.

"He was originally from Boise also, that's the only connection we've found so far."

My blood ran cold. Lots of people were from Boise.

I covered my mouth, I wasn't feeling so good. I tried to swallow down the bile in the back of my throat. "What if they knew each other? It's my fault then."

"What is?" Jones asked.

"Mark came with us when I identified Gordon. I mean, he had been around during several of our conversations when you named Gordon as Gordon Jamal. Maybe Mark didn't know him as Dryer, or maybe he did. Maybe he knew Gordon used a bunch of different names, and knew all of them, so he heard you use them in conversation. He insisted on backing Jade up that day."

Jade walked down the stairs and was about to pass us on her way into the kitchen.

"Jade." I stopped her. "You need to come be a part of this conversation."

"Why me?" she asked as she flopped into another chair.

"You know more about Mark than any of us," I said.

She held her hands up and shook her head. "Whoa, no. I slept with him, that doesn't make me an expert on him."

"But you still talked with him more than I ever did."

"What can you tell us about him?" Smith asked.

"I can give you some basic details, height, eye color. Look, I wasn't even with him enough to be able to tell you if he has any position preferences."

Jones's ears turned pink. Smith adjusted his tie uncomfortably.

"Mark was a nice guy at first. He kind of turned into Mr. Know-it-all-mansplainer, and was a bit of a dick about it." She looked at me. "I know you thought I was sad he hadn't been around the past few days, but honestly, it isn't a big deal. I was trying to figure out how to end it with him. This turning into a traitorous douche thing he has managed to pull has made it a lot easier for me."

"Was his personality change sudden or gradual?" Smith asked.

Jade rolled her eyes side to side. "He was always a know-it-all, but now that you mention it, the super douche thing seemed to really happen when you guys said we would go outside in an attempt to let Gordon know were in the area."

"Did he know Gordon's name before that?"

I shrugged. I had no idea how many times Mark had been in the background during my many, many meetings with the various agents the FBI sent to talk to me.

"Not a clue."

"Are you guys serious? You think Mark may have known Gordon before?"

I had to think. How long had Gage said he known Mark?

"What is it?" Smith asked.

I held up my finger. I needed a minute. Gage said their accident happened during a training exercise. Travis was the only one who worked for his uncle before that. But I got the impression the guys knew each other.

I slumped, defeated. It was Oz who lived out of the area. But that didn't mean Mark hadn't been new to the area. I couldn't tell the FBI about the accident, but I could tell them about the camping trip when it happened.

"I don't think this is anything. Gage said they met a few of the current team during a search and rescue training expedition. He wasn't specific on who. I know Travis worked for his uncle. But I don't know about the rest of the guys."

"Maybe I can help?" Tracey approached us.

"Max grew up around here, so he's known Gage for years. Zeke was here on a training rotation at the hospital, that's how I met him. I introduced him to Brooks who was on Gage's S-and-R team at the time. He decided to stay in the area after that—joined the team."

"You know everyone?" Jones asked.

"It's a small town, hard to not know everyone in emergency services. There aren't that many of us. I don't think Mark was around more than five or so years ago. He transferred into the fire department. You can't be serious? He knew the man who abused Bailey?"

"We're looking for connections. We'll check in with the fire department." Smith stood up.

"If Masterson checks in with you, let him know we'd like to speak with him."

Jade followed them to the door and let them out before locking the door again.

"What are the odds that Mark actually knew Gordon from before?" I asked.

She shrugged.

This was all very odd. I wanted Gage and Max back.

"Have you seen Yuki?" Jade asked.

I shook my head.

Suddenly, we were all on our feet. Jade ran back upstairs.

"I'll look downstairs," Tracey announced.

I hobbled to the lounge and pushed my way into the service area and the kitchen.

"Fuckin' A." The back door was open. I hobbled onto the back deck. There were too many footprints, I couldn't follow a trail.

"Yuki!" I yelled.

She bounced up the deck stairs. "What?"

"Where have you been?"

"I've been cleaning the kitchen. I took the garbage out. It was stinky. Why?"

"We really need to stay inside. The FBI was just here. They think Mark may have known Gordon back in Boise years ago."

A loud snorting noise came from the woods. We stopped and stared, waiting for the sound to happen again. It sounded like a huff from a large horse or a cow. We looked at each other and ran inside. Okay, Yuki ran, and I hobbled really fast.

We leaned on the closed door once inside. Yuki drove home the bolt to lock us in before we collapsed in a fit of nervous laughter.

"I can't find her," Jade cried as she crashed into the kitchen. "Yuki! Oh, gods."

Jade pulled Yuki into a firm hug. We were all shaken by the FBI's news

"Where was she?" Tracey asked as she followed Jade into the kitchen.

"She was cleaning while we talked," I answered.

Tracey propped her hands on her hips. "I guess we should all kick in and finish taking care of this mess."

My second night as a married woman was spent with more margaritas, and chick-flicks. We decided the size of the hero's biceps was in direct proportion to how much of a chick-flick we rated the movie. Cars were only part of the plot as a way to make sure men paid to see the movies we watched. Lots of big biceps.

12

I survived two nights without Gage, Max, or any of the other guys. I honestly thought I was going to be a mess, all weepy and missing them. But I was having fun with the girls. We ate too much of the wrong things, vegetables could happen later. We drank a little too much. No one was driving, so we were okay. We giggled, something there is never enough of, and we watched movies starring really hot guys. I appreciated the transition from rom-com to hulked-up action hero flick. It turned out that most adventures have a romance deeply seated in the storyline.

In the dark hours of the night, we talked philosophically about relationships and goals.

The conversation grew and morphed, and we ended up discussing what a man really wanted and needed in a relationship. Beyond food and companionship, Yuki didn't understand the desire for a sexual relationship, but she fully understood the need for a connection that would last a lifetime.

"You have that with us," I said.

"No, I don't. You're married, and where do I fit in?" she asked.

"You have me, Yuki. And you will always be with me, even if I do get married. I mean, did Mark make a difference between us?"

"Of course not. But I don't think he understood me."

"Men don't understand a lot," Tracey chimed in. "And you confuse them."

"Do I confuse you?" Yuki checked.

"Not at all. But I'm capable of telling the difference in a person being friendly, and a person acting sexually interested in me."

"That's because you're not a man," I said.

"That's the truth."

We all headed off to bed after an exhausting day of lazing about.

Out of habit, I went to my own room this time. In just my panties and socks, I limped over to my undies drawer and pulled out the thong Yuki and Travis had purchased on their ill-fated underwear shopping trip. I held it up. Our earlier conversation about what men wanted had me questioning my underwear choices when it came to sexual desires.

Would I really be more desirable if I wore this scrap of pink lace? Would I feel sexy? I felt sexy when Gage looked at me. It didn't matter if I wore clothes, or had stitches in my scalp. What mattered was what I saw reflected in his eyes. What would I see if I wore these?

I slid my briefs off and slid the thong on. I had to adjust it a bit. The string up the butt crack wasn't particularly comfortable. In order to pull the back up, I had to slide my hand between me and the lace and shimmy the front down.

There wasn't much front. I'd have to make a time investment on personal grooming if I really were to wear this style. Not that I'm overly hairy. It's just that the hair I had poked through in places.

I limped my way into the bathroom so I could look in the mirror. My view was from thighs up. I didn't find it to be a particularly alluring scene with my pubes trying to escape. The bruises on my middle had turned from leopard spots to lurid splotches of green and yellow as they faded. The bruises on my arms were also finally starting to turn green.

Touching my head, I was grateful for the bandage. Here I was, trying to see if I looked sexy, and I looked abused and broken. Nothing about my reflection said sexy. I wondered what Gage really saw when he looked at me?

I could guess what Travis saw. It wasn't flattering; I was a giant vagina in his eyes. Of course, my reaction was all based on his rather unsatisfying solo flight in bed. I was going to have to get over that. He was a wonderful team player. From now on, we'd work with his strengths.

There I stood, in the bathroom, a giant vagina in a bright pink thong. I laughed. Travis would deny it. What did Zeke see? He was so quiet and meek. Did he know he was allowed to have opinions? Gage was right—Zeke was the least dominant of the pack, of both packs.

I decided that Max would hate the thong. Why not be naked instead? Either have clothes on or don't, but stop messing around with a tease somewhere in the middle.

I decided I'd have to model the thing and ask. I limped back into the bedroom. Picking up the hospital gown I wore as a nighty. I heard a scream. High pitched, piercing, loud, terrified. It sounded like Yuki, and it sounded like it was coming from the parking lot out front.

I hobbled over to my window and looked out.

"Hades' tits!" It was Yuki, and she was screaming in the parking lot.

Why she'd gone outside, I couldn't begin to guess, but that didn't matter. She wasn't moving, just standing there and screaming as the bull-bear demon lumbered up to her.

"Run!" I yelled from my closed window. She couldn't hear me.

I shoved my arms into the hospital gown and pulled the loop over my head. I had stopped tying it a while ago and started slipping it on over my head. Something I could do now that I was no longer hooked up to an IV. I shoved my feet with a little too much force into my fur-lined Crocs and hobbled as fast as I could with my crutch down the hall. Jade was already tearing down the stairs in front of me.

I threw the crutch and slid on my ass, bumping down quickly. I didn't even notice the wood on my butt. Tracey sprawled across the floor. I crawled over to her and checked for a pulse. Her breathing and pulse were strong and steady. "Tracey? Tracey?" Nothing.

Yuki screamed again, and I left the unconscious woman. I crawled over to my crutch and rushed out the door as fast as I could, which was pretty fast considering.

The demon had Yuki under one arm and was disappearing fast into the woods. Jade ran after them. The demon had a companion—a tall, thin wolf, all gray with a dark patch over the base of his tail. I didn't remember seeing that spot of color before. Was that Mark?

"Jade! Jade! Mark is in league with the demon!" I yelled as I ran.

Cold air temporarily assaulted my ass. "Zeus's testicles." I cursed, I had run out of the lodge without anything on except the hospital gown and the stupid thong.

I caught up with Jade. She bent over her knees huffing billows of steaming air. "I lost them. They went this way, but who knows after that."

I hobbled in the direction she pointed. She'd catch up and overtake me in no time. I kept moving.

The night was still and dark. Snow crunched under my crutch and my feet. I turned to Jade jogging up when the snow crunched under her boots. At least she was fully dressed.

Snow glistened an eerie, pale blue as the light of the waning full moon broke through the bare branches above us.

"Wait." Jade threw out an arm. "Look snow." She pointed at the ground.

Yes, snow, I saw it, but I no longer felt it. My ass should've been freezing, but it wasn't. "So what?"

"Look at the snow! They made tracks."

Holy Hecate, they had. There were two sets of tracks. Wolf prints zigzagged around and over the other set. Those prints looked like hooves made by a much heavier animal.

"You think Mark had something to do with the demon all along?" I asked.

Jade shrugged and took off running. I limped behind. They had Yuki, and she was *Delight*. I couldn't let that thing hurt her.

I followed until I reached a clearing. The snow was a mess here. Wolf prints covered everything, at least where I could make out prints. I saw human-sized footprints. Were those Yuki's or Jade's?

The demon prints exited the clearing in two different directions. Had he circled back? The human prints went one way, and then I found a place where there were two sets of human prints. Same person running back and forth? Or two humans?

I followed the human trail. Maybe they'd managed to lose the monster.

The woods grew denser, more pines, more tall branches full of needles blocking the light of the moon. I could barely make out the tracks. I followed the broken snow.

I reached a small clearing and realized I'd made a mistake. Broken snow didn't mean my friends had come this way. I had no idea when I had lost their trail, but it was gone. I was alone in the forest.

I closed my eyes and tried to listen past the yelling in my head. If I focused, maybe I could hear something over the "*stupid, stupid, stupid,*" chanting that I yelled at myself.

Something screeched, and I spun to face the noise. Snow packed into my shoe. My toes felt the wet before they felt the cold. I was fucked, and I'd done it to myself.

I turned back the way I came, or so I thought. I realized my mistake when there was no longer snow on the ground. The trees above me were too dense to let the light snow through. Now, I was thoroughly screwed. I had no trail to follow, it was dark, and I was so underdressed it wasn't funny.

"Jade? Yuki?" I barely whispered their names. I didn't want the beast-demon-thing to find me first.

Oh, gods, Gordon was out here too.

What had I done? A breeze licked up my back. Suddenly, I felt the cold like a knife, sharp against my skin. I began screaming.

I collapsed onto my knees and kept screaming. I couldn't stop. I was dead, and I didn't want to die. Not now, not after surviving. I had a husband I wanted to see, and a second husband to marry. I had children I wanted to make and give birth too. All of that was going to freeze up with me, lost in the woods.

Laughter replaced the screaming. Eventually, crying racked my body. I'd come full circle—running away from a

monster to die in the woods to a month later—running into
the woods after a monster, and I was going to die.

A cold nose nudged my face and licked my tears. I
blinked and dug my fingers into the thick fur at Doggo's
neck. I held on and cried even more. He had found me.
More warmth and fur surrounded me. The pack had
found me.

My breathing evened out, and I came up for air. I
grabbed Doggo's face.

"You found me again, oh thank, Demeter." I turned and
wrapped an arm around Gage. I pulled the two of them
close.

"I'm sorry I came out here. The demon, he took Yuki."

My wolves growled and backed away from me.

Where?

I laughed, they were in my head! I had almost thought
that had been a dream, but they were there, and I could
hear them.

"I don't know. Jade ran after them. I couldn't keep up.
That's how I got lost. I think... I think Jade and Yuki got
away. I'm not sure."

Doggo started away from me. The rest of the pack
flowed around me and down a path.

Come.

I followed as fast as I could.

"There was another wolf with them. Tall, skinny, dark
spot on his butt. Could that have been Mark?"

I was answered with a howl. The sound sent shivers
down my spine.

Mark.

The hunt was on.

They ran. I hobbled until I could no longer see any of
them.

"Gage? Max? Guys don't leave me alone." I took in a deep breath, trying not to panic. Instead, I got a lung full of frigid air. I began coughing.

Dark fur pressed against me. I laced my fingers into his ruff and kept coughing. "Doc MacGee won't let me out of the hospital again after this."

Gage stayed with me until we reached the pack and the demon.

The pack spread out to gang up against the bull demon. The wolf I saw earlier stood behind the demon, his head lowered, his teeth exposed.

Mark.

He faced off against his own pack.

I backed up into the protection on the trees. I didn't want to be in the middle of this fight.

The demon pushed at the ground with his hooves and bellowed. Mark shot out from behind him and tackled Gage. Max went straight for the demon. After a pregnant pause, the rest of the pack entered the fight. Snarls and growls filled the air. Occasionally, one of the wolves would whimper in pain, but mostly they fought in near silence.

I leaned my back against the rough bark of a tree as if one meager trunk could protect me from the battle. I couldn't watch, there was too much blood. Blood belonged to those I loved.

I heard the bellow, and pounding footfalls of the demon running away before I peeked out and saw him fleeing the scene. Two wolves lay motionless in the snow.

Max nosed into the closest timber wolf. I didn't know who he was, but he matched the coloring that belonged to either Travis, Zeke, or Oz.

"Please don't be Travis," I whispered as I tiptoed out from behind my tree.

The wolf roused and staggered to his feet.

I let out a whoosh of air. Relieved he was okay, even though I still didn't know who he was. All the wolves ignored the other downed wolf—the one with the dark spot at the base of his tail—Mark.

"Get me out of here, and then find Yuki," I pleaded.

I followed where they led, trusting they would get me home. I hoped it'd be soon. I'm not sure how long we walked. My whole body was numb from the cold. I couldn't feel my skin. I knew that was problematic.

A scream cut through the woods to my left. I spun and stumbled.

Gage pressed against me. I held on.

The scream sounded again. "Go!" I yelled at the wolves. "He can't get Yuki. Save her."

The pack tore off, and I stumbled after them.

Someone jumped into the path in front of me—a wolf by their side.

13

For a split second, I couldn't register what was going on. My eyes and brain wouldn't synchronize. I expected to see Jade or Yuki with my pack. Instead, I was looking at Gordon. I couldn't wrap my mind around the unexpected appearance. Hadn't that wolf been dead last time I saw him?

"You stupid slut," Gordon spit out.

"Deadman," I replied.

I took a step back and faltered. An involuntary scream escaped my lips, breaking my façade of bravado.

"Stay away from me, Gordon. My husband is going to kill you." The corners of my mouth tilted up. I liked saying 'my husband.' I had the worst timing when it came to finding pleasure in something. Now wasn't the time to admire my ability to claim a husband, and know he would rip Gordon's throat out.

Gordon barked out a laugh. "Not if he doesn't find me. And he's never going to find your body."

Had I really been in love with this man only a month ago?

Mark lowered his head and snarled.

"So, I take it you two do know each other. Where's your demon?"

"Demon? You have quite the imagination there, Bailey. I had hoped to enjoy knocking that out of your system, but now, I think I'll just kill you and be done with it."

"And then what?" I asked. I took another step back. There was no way I could outrun this man, but I still wanted distance between us.

"How do you know Mark?"

The wolf's ears twitched as I said his name.

"I think I should be asking the questions. How do you know him, and what happened to my brother?"

Brother? Now that I thought about it, they did sort of resemble each other, but their coloring was off. Gordon was overall darker. Then again, the FBI had hinted that he had been dying his hair. Their names were completely different. Sanderson, Dryer, Hanson, Jamal. Who knew which was real. Did he even?

I shrugged. "He was like that when I first met him." I huffed a half laugh. "I wonder if he would've helped to save me if he'd known I was running away from you?"

Mark moved behind Gordon, and my gaze followed the wolf's movement. My pack had returned and circled around behind Gordon. He didn't even know it. I felt a surge of pride knowing they were here to protect me. Mark faced off against his previous pack again, this time guarding Gordon's back.

My smile spread wide and victorious across my face. My nose twitched.

The wolves were low and honed in on Gordon like fur missiles ready to launch.

The scent of cinnamon and sugar filled the air. I ignored the warm huff of breath on my neck.

Gordon's eyes bugged out at my resistance to him. I had won. He may have tried to break me, wanted to kill me even, but he hadn't. I won.

I took a step forward, picked up my crutch, and swung it like a major league ballplayer going for a home run.

He held up his hands to block the blow from his face. The crutch kept moving, his arm got tangled in the middle of it. Bone cracked before I even finished my swing.

I connected with the side of his shoulder. The impact twirled us around like a macabre dance. Suddenly, I was face to face with the demon, with only Gordon between us. Oh, that's what he had been afraid of, not me.

"Fuckin' A." I breathed out.

I fell back on my butt, and the demon grabbed Gordon. The demon tossed my crutch away and then bit into the man. Its teeth sunk into Gordon's flesh with no resistance. With a face shaped so much like a bull's, I hadn't expected it to have long pointed teeth.

Gordon screamed before he stopped thrashing. The demon worried at the bite he'd made in Gordon's shoulder. His arm made a squelching wet ripping sound. Despite the amount of blood and gore this time, I didn't pass out.

Gordon made a gurgling sound and fell limp. His arm lay on the churned up snow, the rest of his body, hung mangled from the snouty jaws of the beast.

My wolves shot into action, and the demon disappeared under a blanket of snarling, rending fur.

"Get up!" Jade scooped under my armpits and pulled me back. She grabbed the crutch and came back to me. We ran as best we could. I almost didn't hobble.

We made it to a small clearing where Yuki waited, hugging herself.

She looked no worse for wear, considering the beast had run off with her tucked under his arm like a football.

Jade used my crutch like a giant pen and started drawing sigils in the snow.

"What are you doing?" I panted. "I thought your magic was limited?"

"Yeah, but I can breathe here. I'm stronger here. Look, I have an idea. Can you get the pack to bring the demon this way?"

"I can try."

I limped back in the direction we escaped from.

Max? Gage? Bring the beast this way.

I rolled my eyes around waiting for a reply.

A howl filled the air, followed by more howls. I shivered at the sound.

Guys?

Mark is dead.

I can't say I was saddened to hear that, not after his betrayal. Jade, on the other hand, might not be quite so joyous, after all, she'd slept with the man. I decided not to say anything, the timing wasn't appropriate.

Mark was dead. Gordon was dead. Now, we just needed to take care of this demon, no telling where he had come from. From the way he bit into Gordon, I think it was safe to assume the two of them hadn't been in league. But somehow, Mark had been connected to both?

I felt the ground thump.

"It's coming this way!" I yelled. I scampered out of the path that we had taken. The path the demon would follow into the clearing.

The monster rushed in. A few wolves herded him with bites and snarls. He stopped when he saw Yuki. Jade stood with her arms around the other woman. The two of them stepped back, and the beast took a step forward.

Jade dropped Yuki, and her arms lit up with blue magic flames. I rushed to Yuki's side, and we clung to each other.

The rest of the wolves flowed into the clearing. "Back!" Jade yelled as she pushed her hands high into the air above her head.

The sigils in the snow glowed with the same eerie blue that emanated from Jade, and lifted into the air, surrounding the beast.

The pack paced in a circle around the glowing symbols that encased the demon.

He grunted and bellowed. Air steamed from his nostrils. He thrashed, but couldn't break free of the spell Jade cast around him.

She said words that had no meaning to my ears and crashed her hands together. Blue plasma shot from her hands and crashed against the invisible barrier formed by her glowing magic. An orb of glowing blue flame surrounded the demon.

Jade continued to chant, casting her spell. The orb rose from the ground, carrying the monster inside. Jade moved her hands in a slow defined shape, like some form of mystical dance. Her lips moved, but I could no longer hear what she said.

The orb rotated. The beast thrashed, and the orb shook. I was afraid it would crash to the ground, and the enraged monster would escape again. The blue grew in intensity, and the orb began shrinking. The movement was a throb and a pulse. Each breath Jade took seemed to push the compression smaller and smaller. The demon roared. The shaking against his containment so strong, I could feel the reverberations in the air.

I dragged Yuki back away from the clearing. We crouched just inside the tree line. If needed, I wanted to be able to hide, if that was even possible.

The orb continued to slowly shrink. When it was the size of an overlarge beach ball, Jade began quaking. I was afraid she wouldn't make it. I limped over to her and wrapped my arms around her shoulders, supporting her shaking body. I felt the energy surge through her as she pushed hard against the monster.

With a scream, she fell limp. There was an explosion of air followed by a sonic boom, and a pop. The force of the air knocked us down. I looked around to see if the beast had broken free. All I saw were wolves knocked over on their sides. Fallen trees and branches, all blasted away from the center of the clearing. Blood trickled from Jade's nose.

"Oh gods, Jade? No!" I cried as I collapsed over her still form. Yuki pulled on my shoulder to get to Jade. She rested her head on the other woman's chest and began repeating a low droning mantra. I couldn't hear words, just sounds.

I looked around the clearing. Jade's sigils still marked the snow, and in the very center of it all was a large blue marble. Gage was the first of the wolves up. He approached the marble, sniffing at it.

"Don't touch that. It might not be safe," I cried out to him.

He started. Huffed at the marble and then trotted over to me. I still had my arms around an unconscious Jade, and he nudged his way under one of my arms.

Jade roused and muttered.

I collapsed back onto her and Yuki, crushing them both in a fierce hug. Jade tried to say something from under the press of Yuki and me.

"What?"

"Get the ball, it holds the demon."

Yuki moved and was up. I watched her pick up the now shrunk blue orb of magic. She tossed it up in the air like a toy. It looked remarkably familiar. I flinched, not knowing if it would break open setting the monster free.

"We'll have to destroy it. For now, it's contained." Jade's labored breathing told me more about her state of exhaustion than anything else.

"I know where we can put it to be safe," I said. If all those glowing marbles in Sandra's shop contained demons, we could keep this one there. After all, she said the case was full of the world's troubles. "We have to get inside before we all freeze." I was keenly aware of sitting in the snow with nothing on my ass.

With Yuki's help, I lifted Jade to her feet. The wolves surrounded us and guided us through the woods and snow.

The lodge seemed miles away. Maybe it was, maybe we were all just cold and tired.

Tracey ran out and met us in the parking lot.

"What the hell happened?" she asked.

"You okay? You were knocked out, but I had to go. The demon had Yuki." I was too tired to cry, even though I felt like I needed to. "And Gordon and Mark were out there."

She scanned me up and down, taking in my outfit. "Do you have a death wish? Jesus Bailey, are you trying to die from exposure? You're gonna be lucky if your ass doesn't have frostbite."

Everyone limped inside, wolves included. In an unorganized mob, they escorted us up the stairs. I was the slowest, and at the back of the pack. Gage and Max stayed by my side.

"I want an elevator put in," I complained.

Yuki and Jade hobbled into one room. They were

followed by most of the wolves. This didn't surprise me. After all, Yuki had that draw.

Tracey with Brooks, Gage, and Doggo, followed as I limped into my room.

Tracey made the wolves stay in the hallway before she had me stripped out of the limited amount of clothes I had on. It certainly wasn't as if they hadn't seen me naked before, and if Brooks hadn't, he wasn't paying attention. But she actually said, "Sit. Stay." And she clearly meant it.

"I won't ask," she said when she saw the thong. She checked me and made me take a shower. Checking me twice while I was under the hot water. Muttering the entire time how lucky I was, and I had better not catch pneumonia after all of this.

She carefully dried my hair and made sure I had on leggings and a long sleeved t-shirt to sleep in.

"I'm burning this," she said as she wadded up the hospital gown. "Tomorrow, we're shopping for proper Wyoming pajamas."

I sighed as she tucked me in, and then let in my personal guard beasts.

I curled up and slept with wolves, Doggo on one side, Gage on the other.

When I woke up, Gage's arms were around me, and Doggo was pressed warmly against my back.

Gage made a rumbling wake up sound deep in his chest.

I snuggled in closer. "Good morning," I cooed.

"Bailey Hastings, I should..." His voice was rough with morning grogginess.

"Don't you mean Bailey Masterson?" I batted my eyelashes up at him. "We're married now."

He ran a finger over my cheek and gave me a toe melting smile.

"Hastings. I'm taking Hastings. We will all take Hastings. Now, Mrs. Hastings..."

Gage flipped me over and ran his fingers over my skin.

"Hey, that tickles," I complained. "What are you doing?"

He didn't stop. He continued to trail his fingertips over every inch of me.

"Making sure you're okay, looking for any signs of frostbite."

I squirmed, rolling over. It was a tight squeeze between him and the wolf. "Tracey gave me a complete exam last night. I'm fine."

"Don't scare me like that again. And for my sanity, and the sake of the nine toes you have left, stop running around in the woods without proper clothing."

"Yes, dear," I said with a bite of sarcasm.

Doggo made a complaining whine as we jostled the bed.

"Get out of here, Max, I'm going to make love to my wife now. *Alone.*"

EPILOGUE

Two weeks later.

I sat in Max's lap as I leaned over and signed the marriage documents. My whole body zinged with excitement. Max wore a wreath of small white flowers in his mass of wild hair. Judge Neeley clapped and pronounced us wife and husband.

Max's kiss felt magical and was all the more special because I only had two more nights to celebrate with him.

We both wore all white. Per his request, everyone wore white. Apparently, Max had always wanted an all-white wedding party. So, my handsome man got his wish. My dress dripped with vintage lace. I found an actual wedding dress after a marathon shopping morning that ended at one of the church thrift shops in town. The puffy sleeves and lack of waistline shouted nineteen-eighties, the label said Gunny Sax. It was perfect.

Behind us, a long table was spread with all the fixings of

a traditional Thanksgiving dinner. We celebrated only a few days late and combined the feast with a reason to be thankful. Our wedding cake was pumpkin spice, and delicious, and not purchased from the bakery downtown.

Jade leaned tucked in against Oz. He finally figured it out that last night of the full moon and hadn't left her side since. Last weekend, when she and Yuki returned to pack up their shared St. Louis apartment, he went with them, in wolf form.

With the ceremony concluded, I walked holding on to Max. My stability was better, and I had graduated from the crutch to a cane, but I would've held on to Max anyway. I sat between my two glorious husbands, with my two soon-to-be-husbands across from me. Travis and Zeke agreed, they wanted a spring wedding, so we'd wait until the woods were green, and wildflowers bloomed in the mountain meadows.

I had much to be thankful for this year. I was happy. I was safe, and I could move forward with my life, never having to remember certain events if I didn't want to.

I never wanted to have to think about Gordon again. The FBI did find him a few days after the moon waned past full. The official report was death from a bear attack.

Thanks for reading Ending Torment, and the entire mini-series Wolves of Wet Waterfalls.

There is more from the world of Wet Waterfalls with Witches of the Wildwood trilogy: Hard Licks , Bites Back, and Holds Tight.

Keep reading for a sneak peek.

HARD LICKS

BOOK 1 WITCHES OF THE WILDWOOD

Chapter One

Boom.

Rattle.

My stomach tried to drop out of me. My heart picked up its pace. My reflexes instinctually dropped the hair from the grip of the curling iron before I froze.

I held my breath for five pounding heart beats before letting it out in a rush, and relaxing.

"I hate those things," I muttered as I worked the hank of hair back around the flat iron.

"Hmm?" Kathleen, the woman in my chair asked.

"You didn't feel that?"

"Earthquake." I had moved to Wet Waterfalls, Wyoming not quite nine months ago. I followed my two best friends, and responsibilities, out to the small town wilds of mountain living, or so I thought. Wet Waterfalls had proven to be full of surprises. Good ones and not so good ones. But the one thing I had not expected way out here were the earthquakes.

"I didn't notice," she said casually as she took a sip of her wine. "You'll get used to them."

Boom.

Rattle.

This time the sound was louder, and the shaking felt closer. I cut a quick glance over at Oz to see if he was bothered at all. They say animals have a keen sense of earthquakes. Did that count for magical beasts too? Oz was a new moon were. He shifted for the three days around a new moon into a smoking hot human man, with all the smoking hot human man body parts; the rest of the time he looked like a large timber wolf. He was bothered— sitting up, alert, ears pricked forward— in a very focused manner. It looked like he knew exactly what the problem was.

Boom.

Rattle.

"After shocks. I felt that one." She leaned forward and placed her wine glass on my work counter.

I took a steadying breath and reached forward to return to curling her long golden hair. She had good hair, and even though she hated my bestie, Bailey, she insisted I work on her hair. 'You have magic fingers Jade, I swear my hair has never been this healthy in my life.' She had no idea.

Well, she knew who and what Oz was, so maybe she did.

Boom.

Rattle.

"Okay, those are getting stronger and closer together."

Oz was up on all fours.

Boom.

I stopped noticing the rattle and focused on the glass of wine. Concentric circle waves bounced across the surface, very much like that water cup in that dinosaur movie Jeff Goldblum made when he was younger, and buffer. I'm not going to say hotter, because I would 'yes Daddy' that man any day. Fine is fine. And those were impact tremors.

Boom.

So, not aftershocks. Footsteps. Big ones.

Oz must have realized it seconds before I did, because he was out the door. I finally got the wolf-man to stop making epic jumps through the plate glass window. I got it, he's a big badass wolf and could make the big heroic entrance or exit through the window. But he had a logical human functioning brain, and the front door pushed open. I'm pretty sure the combination of stitches and the bills from the glazier and the sign painter from his last sail through the front helped to change his mind. I made him pay for it.

Boom. Boom. Boom.

"That's not an earthquake," Kathleen announced.

I was out the door, fast on Oz's heels.

It was definitely not an earthquake.

The squeal of tires followed by the sickening thud-crunch of metal, with a hint of high pitch screaming as the metal tore from places it should not have torn away from, made my stomach completely dropped out of me. That typical eerie silence that follows an accident was filled with the labored huffs and snorts of a large bovine walking down the middle of Main Street.

A sheriff's green and tan SUV blocked one end of the street, and now an accident blocked the other. Of course where Main veered to the east was clear, and that's where the big guy was headed.

In my short time in Wet Waterfalls we had more than a few long horns make their way through the middle of town. And once even, a few strays decide to come window shopping from a nearby cattle drive. It had taken more than a few steer cutting through town to feel like tiny mild tremors without the stomach dropping feel that accompanied earthquakes for me.

This creature walked on his hind legs, and mark my words he was a bull—a really big bull— and not some poor lost farm critter. Oh no, this was one hundred percent demon kin. He had the head and horns of a buffalo, but the snout looked more like it belonged on a bear. The torso was shaped like a super roided out body builder— all shoulders and pecs, and sinew, and bulging muscle on top of bulging muscle. From mid waist down he walked on hoofed feet and cow-like legs. Like a satyr, but a buffalo satyr. And his junk, it was large and in charge, dangly bull balls for days. The last time I had seen one of his lot was when Bailey's boyfriend at the time had turned out to be a serial killer, and in her very successful and bad-assed escape rescuing herself, landed here in Wet Waterfalls. That demon had not been nearly as intimidating or large. And he had been scary as fuck and some of its cousins.

There had been a whole lot of evil going on in the woods last fall. In addition to a show down with a serial killer and his werewolf brother, they had somehow gotten mixed up with a demon cavorting around the place. We still don't know if there was an actual connection between Mark, Gordon and the demon. I subscribe to the concept it was just a very ill-timed coincidence.

That demon now lived in a very pretty display shelf, safely encased in a magical orb. And I planned to do the same with this one. I didn't pause to see who might catch the action on their cell phone. I really didn't have time to think. The Minotaur of the Labyrinth's great, great, great-grandson was tearing up my new home town, and my boyfriend Oz was barking at his heels.

"Oz, get back!" I yelled as I planted my feet.

Shoving my hands through the viscous sludge of air that separated the average person's perception of reality and the realm where I pulled power from, I felt the buzz of magic surround my arms. I wrapped my hands around invisible magic in one dimension to bring to me in this one. Yellow light crackled and moved around my limbs like dancing lightening. I pulled my hands back to my chest. Dragging the magic to me took physical strength. I grimaced at the effort. There was an audible "thwap pop" as the other place released me and the magic I had gathered.

Pulling the magic into shape was like pulling taffy. Sticky and slow, I dragged at the glowing glob of power creating a larger, and larger sphere. Once big enough— I dragged this one out to the size of a large beach ball of glowing yellow— I hurled it at the beast. If my orb wasn't large enough it could bounce right off the demon, and I would have to start all over again.

Luckily, I caught him. Now I had to keep him. I shoved my hands back through space, pulling out another handful of power. This time I shot the power in a stream of lightening and energy feeding the orb. To my right another stream of power shot out and hit the orb.

Sandra from the metaphysical gift shop was throwing her power into my orb. I caught her gaze and she gave me a quick nod. I knew she had power. After all, the shelf with the collection of demon orbs lived in her shop; like a pretty display of handmade glass marbles, all for show, and not for sale.

I took a step forward and spread my energy wide, time to change the game now that the beastie was caught and I had backup to make sure the orb would hold. Spreading my arms wide I began pressing my hands in toward each other, as if I moved air into the space in front of me, which is exactly what I was doing. I focused and pressed the orb smaller.

Minotaur man fought against the power. He did not make things easy on us. If it weren't for Sandra's help, he would have broken out. I'm sure of it.

He fought hard, but we had him. Or, we would have. My focus was all on the beast, and my peripheral was on the steady stream of power Sandra provided, so I didn't see where it came from. One second I'm pressing the orb down, collapsing the dimensions around the demon, the next, BAM!

The orb exploded out in a blaze of yellows, oranges, and reds. The sound was deafening, a combination of the big bang plus the bellows of a very pissed off minotaur.

I was knocked back on my ass. My ears sang with the high pitched screams of tinnitus. I was down, but not out. Damned if I was going to let this guy get away. I scrambled to my feet. Planted them in the road, and pushed hard into the power.

Demon boy had other plans. As much as I wanted him captured, he clearly did not. As I reached for magic, he lowered his head and charged me in a very bull-fight smack down fashion.

"Jade!"

I heard my name a fraction of a second before someone hit me in a tackle from the side. Another fraction of a second later large split hooves the size of serving platters smacked into the road next to my head. I might have screamed. I heard Oz bark and growl. The body on top of me groaned.

The hooves continued to pound the pavement. I could only assume he took the eastern fork split off and headed out of town. I know I would have if I were him.

"You okay?" I asked the weighty body on top of me.

I tried to roll onto my back, but I was effectively pinned in place. I blew a hank of hair out of my face. Not mine, mine wasn't long enough to get into my face.

"Hey."

"Gimme a sec." The dulcet complaining tones of Dylan greeted my ears. "I think beastie boy stepped on my leg."

"Shit. Is it broke?" I asked.

He finally shifted enough so that I could lay flat. Dylan pushed up on his hands, boxing me in underneath. He grimaced as he wiggled around. I think his leg really hurt, because he didn't exactly notice at first that he was grinding against me, hip to hip.

I licked my lips and tried not to grind in return. Dylan was hot. With dusky skin, fine cheek bones, and long black hair. He was someone I enjoyed the occasional flirt with. I'd enjoy more than a flirt, but he was hard to read. Plus the whole I had a werewolf boyfriend tended to scare guys off.

"I can move my foot, so I don't think anything broken. Hurts like a motherfucker though." He looked at me, his expression flat. His left eyebrow twitched up as he clued in to our predicament. His hips stopped moving about.

I must have frowned.

"Oh really?" He smirked and wiggled his hips again. Well, it was more like a thrust.

I definitely counter thrusted.

"What about Oz?"

"I don't fuck dogs." I blinked and tried to make my eyes as big and as innocent as I could. I think my expression was lost on him, because before I finished my sentence, his hands were knotted in my hair, and his mouth pressed to mine. His lips were hot and I needed them. I needed him.

My black yoga pants were thin enough that I could feel

the rough hardness of his jeans right up against me. It was tantalizing and promising as he ground into my increasingly damp sex.

I heard a low growl off to one side. I flailed an arm about until I found fur, and pushed hard.

"Back off Oz," I managed to say between kissing and sucking on Dylan's tongue.

I'm not sure how long we necked and humped right there in the street before I heard someone clear their throat right above my head.

Dylan pushed back, and I looked up.

"Oh hi, Gage."

Bailey's first husband looked down at me. He cleared his throat again.

"Sheriff Hastings."

In an incredibly feminist move, unexpected from a prime alpha male like Sheriff Gage Masterson, he took Bailey's last name when they got hitched.

"Having a little orgy in the middle of town?"

I glanced around. Oz sat with his back toward us, and most people's attention seemed to be either with a group on the side walk— probably making sure Sandra was all right — or with the accident up the street.

Dylan let out a throaty chuckle. It reverberated through his body and straight to my groin where he still rested most of his body weight. "More like a public display of affection."

"Are you offering to join us?"

Gage gave me a dazzling smile. I could see how he melted Bailey's panties so damned fast. "I don't play without the wife."

I gave him my best mock pout and sighed. "And Bailey is ridiculously monogamous."

Gage quirked his brows together.

"Wrong word, but you know what I mean. Whatever it is you are, she doesn't play outside your marriage grouping." And grouping it was. Last fall she had married Gage, and then Max. And this past spring they finalized their group marriage with Travis and Zeke, who had been part of the group from the beginning, just they had wanted an outdoor wedding in a field of wild flowers. It had been serene and romantic and lovely.

I knew Gage was a team player, Bailey was crap with secrets. But his team roster was already filled, and as a rule I didn't fuck my charges and platonic best friends. So, he knew I was joking around.

"Exactly," he responded. "Need help up?"

"But I'm comfortable, man," Dylan whined.

I knew exactly what he meant. I hadn't noticed any of the stray little rocks biting into my back until Gage decide to break up our party.

"Actually, yeah. My leg."

Gage stood and got a hand under Dylan's arm and basically lifted him completely off me and the pavement. He hopped around on his good foot, and I pushed up into a sitting position. I guess Oz forgave me for necking in the middle of the street, because he nosed up under my arm and sat next to me with my arm draped over his shoulders.

"What was that thing?" Dylan asked. He balanced with one hand on Gage's shoulder as Gage rolled up the leg of his jeans. There was a scrape that looked like nasty road rash. It was red and angry, and the beginnings of a bruise bloomed around the edges. Nothing was bleeding, and his leg didn't look deformed— no visible signs of a break.

"Come over here, I can take care of that."

With Gage's help Dylan limped over to me. As I worked

my magic on his leg, Gage spoke, "That was a nightmare. Too many people saw it. Saw what you did."

"It's not like people here don't know there are things that go bump in the night." Dylan gave Gage a knowing gaze.

Half the town probably knew what Gage and his search and rescue team were. They were the best kept secret everyone knew.

"Locals, sure, but tourists?" Gage nodded in the direction of the accident.

"Mutant buffalo. Tell them it had rabies or something. Most of them don't know better than to not pet one like they are in some kind of petting zoo."

"I'm sure you'll get a decent PR spin on it. If you're lucky our crashed tourists are a little tipsy so you can convince them they were delusional. Okay, try to put some weight on your foot."

Dylan winced, and hissed as he let his foot touch town toe first.

I grabbed his ankle and pulled down, throwing him off balance. Forcing him to put his weight on his foot.

"What the fuck?" He glared at me.

"Ya big baby. You're gonna have one hell of a bruise, but the insides are fine," I said as I stood up, and brushed pebbles from my ass.

He stepped on his foot a few times, and then began bouncing around on his toes like some kind of boxer or something.

I looked down the road to Shaefer's Doughnuts, and saw Keiko. She had just turned and was shooing Yuki inside. Yuki gave me a little wave over her shoulder. That reminded me, demon loose on the street— I should check on my charges.

"Bailey wasn't at work today was she?" I asked Dylan, who ran the floral shop with his sister.

He shook his head.

Okay, I had to assume Bailey was safe at home. I had visual confirmation that Yuki was fine, besides she was with Keiko. Keiko was not without her own powers. Even if I wasn't sure what those powers were.

"We're good here?" Gage asked.

I nodded. "And you know where I live if you have to ask more questions."

"That I do." Gage gave us each a nod and sauntered off. I did not watch his ass. For very long.

"Kathleen!" I cried out and ran back into the salon.

Oz and Dylan were on my heels.

"All taken care of? Sounded like a small herd of buffalo." Kathleen hadn't moved. Well not much. She now held an empty wine glass, but her attention was all on the magazine in her lap.

"Yeah, something like that. Driver swerved and hit a phone pole. Let me wash up real quick and I'll finish you up." I didn't fully lie, the driver had hit a phone pole, and the demonic man-bull beast was somewhat like his own herd.

She lifted the wine glass and rocked it back and forth showing off its lack of contents. I snagged the glass from her. She didn't look up.

I slid the glass on the counter in the back, and proceeded into the bathroom. I splashed water on my face, and washed my hands. According to my reflection I did not look like I had just had a run in with a large beastie. My lips were a bit swollen, but that was Dylan's fault, so was the wicked camel toe wedgie I pulled out of my crotch. I made myself tinkle, and washed my hands again. Once situated I returned to the backroom, poured another glass of cheap watered down wine— I swear no one ever noticed we did that, it's not like we charged them for it, that way we didn't need a liquor license— and returned to my station.

Kathleen smiled and tossed her golden locks around. "Perfect as usual, Jade."

"You have good hair. Makes my job easy."

I stayed put behind the register as she left before I dashed to the door and locked it. Returning to the lounge couch, I shoved Oz out of my way before collapsing. He repositioned himself across my lap. Dylan sat perched on the arm of the couch his elbows resting on his knees, hands clasped. He stared at me.

"What?" I asked.

He shrugged. "Figured you were gonna want to talk about all that." He waved a hand, indicating outside.

"Daedalus's worst nightmare? Well, I don't know if you've noticed but this town has some pretty hinky things happening."

"Hinky? Huh. Interesting term. Yeah, you could say that again. You seem to fit right in don't ya?"

"What's that supposed to mean?" I glared at him

He took a long slow breath and re-laced his fingers. "It mean's your special skills haven't escaped notice. But that's not what I'm referring to.

I dropped my gaze from his face to his hands. He had long graceful fingers, and I had liked them twined in my hair. He stopped twisting his hands, the only sign of nerves I got from him and pushed off the couch. "Oz has staked claim, so the point is mute."

He moved toward the front door. I loved watching him walk away, but I hated to see him leave.

"Dylan," I said.

He stopped and turned, that left eyebrow cocked up in question.

I pointed outside. "That's a conversation that needs to happen, but my brain is stuck on the minotaur thing right now. Come by tonight. I'd like to see what would have happened."

Oz growled and seemed to have suddenly gained a hundred pounds, pinning me in place.

I shoved at him.

Dylan cracked a grin. It changed the entire structure of his face. The way his cheeks peaked and his eyes seemed to sparkle, reminded me exactly why my panties were still not completely dry.

He unlocked the door and pushed his way out.

Oz growled some more.

"Really? You are going to have to knock this bullshit off."

I heaved and pushed him off me. "I need to go check on Sandra. Minotaur first, then you and me are gonna have a little confab about our relationship."

I left him on the floor glaring his doggy eyes at me. I should have been afraid, he was a wolf. But I also knew behind those eyes was a man who I adored, that needed to understand the confusion in my head right now.

Monsters first, love second.

I pushed into the metaphysical gift shop. I gave the collection of demon orbs behind her register a quick glance. The midnight blue one with cerulean swirls was mine. It really did look like a beautiful hand-blown marble, in a collection of equally pretty glass balls. They were deceptive. They were powerful. And each one contained evil in one form or another.

～

YOU NEED MORE LULU

ALSO BY LULU M. SYLVIAN

Legatum

Paranormal shifter romantic suspense

Shifter Vacation Stories

Reverse age-gap vacation romance

Berserker Boys

Geekdom meets Vikings meets hot shifter romance

Second Endings

Paranormal ghost romance

Rockers

Rockstar romance, some contemporary, some paranormal

Holiday Strippers

Contemporary, ridiculous, romance

ABOUT THE AUTHOR

 Bio-engineered to be the only redhead in a generation of blonds, Lulu feels that "aliens" may actually be the best answer for a life-time of being asked, "Where did you get that red hair from?"

She did not come into writing from years of scribbling words on paper. Her background is rooted in visual arts and making pictures. Encouraged to make those pictures out of words Lulu began writing just to see what would happen. What happened was two full-length manuscripts in three months.

Lulu cannot ride a horse, a motorcycle, spin a hula hoop, or play roller derby. Yes, she has attempted all of those, even if it has been decades since she's been on a horse or a motorcycle. She embraces the crazy that comes with that one little genetic mutation, and attempts to live up to the reputation that proceeds her. Lulu would like to apologize for her contribution to the hole on the ozone layer from her use of hairspray in the 1980s.

For more information, visit:
www.LuluMSylvian.com